A Father's Law

A Father's Law

Richard Wright

HARPER ● PERENNIAL

NEW YORK ● LONDON ● TORONTO ● SYDNEY

HARPER ● PERENNIAL

P.S.™ is a trademark of HarperCollins Publishers

HarperCollins books may be purchased for educational, business, or sales promotional use. For information please write: Special Markets Department, HarperCollins Publishers, 10 East 53rd Street, New York, NY 10022.

FIRST EDITION

Designed by Nancy Singer Olaguera

Library of Congress Cataloging-in-Publication Data is available upon request.

ISBN: 978-0-06-134916-4

08 09 10 11 12   OV/RRD   10 9 8 7 6 5 4 3 2 1

THE ENIGMA OF RICHARD WRIGHT'S
LAST UNFINISHED NOVEL

"I started a brand-new piece of prose, the idea of which had been simmering in my mind for a long, long time. I'm pounding on the machine morning and night. . . . Now I'm free, with white sheets of paper before me, and a head full of wild ideas, ideas that excite me. Maybe writing with me is like being psychoanalyzed. I feel all the poison being drained out."

Letter from Richard Wright to Margrit de Sablonière,
August 2, 1960

"The last pages written by our great authors on the point of death need our attention. *A Father's Law* is one of those rare instances of a thriller within a thriller in our literature. Wright writes the main core of this unfinished outpouring of a novel as a thriller, but the real thriller is that the author will no longer be around to give us the answer because he reaches his 'breaking point' through death. Leaving us with mourning and, for his readership, with 'frustration' and also a new line of reflection on why thrillers play the role of 'sedatives' in our society: you start out reading smugly reassured that the writer owes you the solution for your money and patronage."

Letter from Julia Wright to Hugh Van Dusen,
Editorial Director at HarperCollins, July 25, 2006

As he said it himself, the idea *took him by the throat.* There was the excitement of feeling slightly better, of beginning over, leaving the much-criticized manuscript of *Island of Hallucination* (the intended sequel to *The Long Dream*) on the back burner for a time.

There was the thrill of being gripped by a new powerful idea and, even though he was still feverish and weak, of sitting up at the Underwood for a go at what was to be the first and only draft of *A Father's Law,* interrupted by the end of a rainy summer, bureaucratic and political harassment, money-earning concerns, illness, and, unexpectedly, death at the age of fifty-two.

For me, months later, there was the emotion of discovering it where he had left it last. But when? Mourning warps one's sense of reality, sometimes sharpening memory, other times blurring dates out of sequence. I surely would have paid no heed to it the day after he died when denial filled the pit of panic and aloneness. I was the only member of the family in Paris when his death occurred. Over the phone, I had been gingerly told that he had died, darling, the night before and would I wish to stay where I was, with the French family where I was doing *au pair* work? "No," I said, raw instinct surging out of my refusal to believe. "I want to see him at the clinic morgue and then go keep watch over his studio."

Keep watch. . . . When I read those words later in the manuscript I knew that even the day after, ugly reality was seeping through. I spent the night of November 29 to November 30 alone in his tiny studio waiting for Ellen and Rachel to fly in from London the next morning.

I remember curling up on the green sofa, not even wanting to look at his empty bed with the fake-fur blanket. The papers and objects strewn over his long rustic table of a desk held no possible interest for me. I was like a trapped animal curled around frozen pain but tense with vigilance. No, I didn't see the manuscript then. It was later, after the funeral, when Ellen went back to London to terminate her business there that I took to returning to the studio, unable to mourn except in denial and vigil.

It was then I found it—or it found me. Did I roll the last page out of the Underwood? Or was it in one of my father's binders by his bed (he would never go out without the manuscript he was currently working on clasped in one of his favorite cardboard or leather binders)? It all rings a bell. I started to read and never stopped till those 306 pages were finished. And I wanted to protect both protagonists—the father *and* the son.

That draft—so peculiar, so unwieldy, like a patchwork quilt of psychological horror with some pieces not quite fitting—became an integral part of my mourning. It was almost like a long letter, unsubmitted except to a few loved ones, and now to me. The notes I took ended up in dusty boxes at the other end of the Atlantic but not buried since they are to see the light of day.

I was riveted by the conflict between the generations, by all that is left unsaid and that can lead to violence. All that is written and that can lead to understanding. Ruddy Tucker is not Richard Wright. I am no Tommy. But the interstices between the author and his children, my sister and me, were deeply fascinating to me.

The studio where I read had *no* doors except two in the back, one leading to his tiny kitchen and one to a miniature bathroom. The rest were archways from bedroom and office to living room. I remembered an anecdote. My mother, Ellen (his recently estranged wife), used to tell us about our living in the big apartment on rue Monsieur le Prince: "Dick used to complain about the noise you kids made in your rough and tumble games at the other end of the apartment. I used to say: 'Dick, stop complaining, just close your office door.' And Dick would answer: 'No, I can't do that because I wouldn't hear if something happened to them.'" In *A Father's Law*, the black chief of police, Ruddy Turner, feels rejected by his son Tommy's insistence on shutting himself in his room, endlessly typing. Tommy is a university student, enigmatic, invisible to the rest of the family, pounding away on his machine, aloof to his father's pride, affection, and concern. In another novel written from exile, *Savage Holiday* (1954), a brutally slammed door locked by a gust of wind becomes the deadly prop for the tragedy of guilt and murder that ensues. In *A Father's Law*—his attempt at psychological thriller—my father goes into one of his favorite fields of study since the portrayal of Bigger Thomas: the psychology of murder, i.e., the sociological, racial, political, cultural, and historical forces that, given a certain context, opportunity, and lack of communication, can lead to the act of murder in most of us. His reading had spanned Freud to Reik, Fredric Wertham to Clarence Darrow.

Reading this faulty, sketchy, sometimes repetitive draft was an opening of a door for me back then, in 1960, because he was voicing words he could not bring himself to voice outloud to us—his family: his own mourning, the recent 1959 loss of Ella, the mother who had believed in his creative gift. Tommy's sick girlfriend, his repulsion for her congenital syphilis, makes moving reading because Richard had not been able to cure Ella of her life history of seizures. Had he shut the door back then and removed himself because of his helplessness? Far from not being enough, his love for his mother had left him wounded because it highlighted that helplessness.

Now, just a year and a half before he set to work on his last draft from exile, she had died thousands of miles away, in Chicago. He had not spoken a word after wiring the money to the States for the funeral. Silence lay heavy over the studio and the split in my parents' marriage.

Is the root cause of Tommy's rage—discovering that the girl he wanted to marry had an illness with a symbolism as grim as AIDS—a screen for the writer's rage against those who had the financial and political power to give his mother the unsegregated care that would have made her well again, well enough to take a plane to Paris?

My father's preoccupation with another story—which suggests that Bessie Smith may have bled to death because the white hospital near the scene of her accident would not admit her—is a reflection of this trauma in his ability to love but not to save. In *A Father's Law*, this mingling of rage, guilt, self-disgust, and feelings of betrayal are attributed to Tommy—and the targets of the rage are symbols of the power of Law (from moral law to law enforcers), which were already being subjected to the heat of the Civil Rights protest movement. Richard Wright had met and spent hours in discussion with Martin Luther King in Paris in 1958, just after the stabbing attempt on Martin's life.

But there is more to be said about disease—or dis-ease as R. D. Laing used to spell it. My father had battled a severe amoebic infection for years, and although he had just been told he was clear of it, it is interesting to note that he experienced the infection as a poisoning (the word comes back as a leitmotiv in the draft) and that he would have had issues of confidentiality in his love life.

This manuscript caused Michel Fabre, one of Wright's earlier biographers, to ask whether *A Father's Law* might not be related to "[Wright's] attitude and questions concerning Julia's career and the understanding between them." The answer to this question is long enough to fill a book or two but an incident coincidental in time with my father's work on Ruddy and Tommy's relationship does come to mind. Tommy is eighteen in the novel. I was eighteen when my father died. Before his death, I sometimes visited friends of my parents. In one of those French homes, I came across a young black man aged twenty-seven, just out of the U.S. Army and on his way to join the Peace Corps in Africa. He was quiet, broody, handsome. In a rather inexperienced bid to be noticed by him, I invited him back to the studio to meet my father, who had accepted. The young man agreed. But as soon as I left them alone, in the doorless living room, I knew something was very, very wrong. They were not communicating. My father was sullen, the young man silent and edgy. When the former soldier left, my father, who rarely scolded me—and even then did not raise his voice—explained: "Don't you understand that we are living in times when people who dislike what I write might try to use you to get at me?" "But who would want to harm you, Daddy?"

That day I learned what the cold war was about, that History was something real, that you could breathe it, that you lived in it, that you could be bruised by it and unconsciously hurt those you love. Not quite the "History" they were teaching at the Sorbonne.

Another instance of my father's concern about me and our relationship is evidenced in his June 1960 letter to me, written two months before he started work on *A Father's Law*. In it, he let me know that he approved of my choice of attending university as long as I didn't forget or leave behind the world "your father comes from."

In *A Father's Law*, we get the sense that Tommy as a brilliant university student has surpassed his police chief of a father in terms of education—and that Ruddy feels Tommy's "superiority complex." So we are dealing here with issues of trust and distance between the generations. Furthermore, we are dealing with generations within the black bourgeoisie. E. Franklin Frazier had written in 1957 a book by the same title, *Black Bourgeoisie*, which my father had considered brilliant and illuminating enough to use as the sociological keystone of his 1958 novel, written from Paris, *The Long Dream*. In *The Long Dream*, Tyree Tucker, a character with more charisma but perhaps less depth than Ruddy Turner, becomes rich as the black undertaker of southern Clintonville's "colored" district, since whites were loath to bury the black dead. Both Turner and Tucker are black bourgeois owing their money and favor to tokenism. But Wright and Frazier were in agreement that tokenism could not solve the problem of race in America—and this was being debated at the dawn of the Civil Rights era.

Tyree Tucker, the father in *The Long Dream*, is killed by the white police when he has served his purpose. *A Father's Law* is a sort of *Training Day* in reverse, with the police chief father, a good black Republican Catholic, trying to solve his son's contradictions and attempting to come to terms with the truth about his son's criminal tendencies.

There is eeriness in my father's premonition that criminality was doomed to bloom among the elite, that the energies of the Tommies of America might better be used by a cause or a movement for justice, that syphilis would overtake us under another name, and that youth serial killing on American university campuses would eventually inspire a prize-winning film in Cannes.

Tantalizingly, we are left with what appears to be a one-and-only draft. Perhaps, with further drafts, we would have known more about Tommy.

Who, then, is Tommy? We are offered only a door ajar on his mind. He haunts us. He hovers, his mind never really outspoken. He is potentially (had we had a finished, polished novel), as fascinating as Bigger—a tennis-playing, articulate, analytical Bigger.

Just one last thought about where Tommy might have come from: he remains linked to my father's interest in the Leopold and Loeb case (1924) and Wright's admiration for Clarence Darrow's defense based on dis-eased minds. The other piece of the puzzle being Alfred Hitchcock's film based on the Leopold and Loeb affair, called *Rope*. My father would definitely have seen *Rope*, say in the early 1950s. Hitchcock's scenario portrayed two rich, white, brilliant, neo-Nazi teenager students attempting to commit the "perfect" murder by killing a young Jewish boy and hiding his body in a wooden chest in their dining room, meanwhile inviting their friends and university professor to dinner—with the body concealed right there. *It is the teacher*, who is in touch enough with the minds of the two young murderers, who becomes suspicious.

Seeing youth through the eyes of parents, teachers, governesses, etc. Yes, Wright liked tales with open-ended, multilayered meanings like *The Turn of The Screw* by Henry James.

My father never turned the screw with his children.

He was a gentle teacher in times of difficulties, harassment, and blacklisting.

He never told me about Bente because he did not want me to come to grief. But at more or less same time, he was writing *A Father's Law*, he was corresponding with a young Swedish girl who had read his books and expressed to him her despair over a world that could wound human beings so deeply. Her letters seem to have stemmed from a pervasive sadness of their own. She wanted my father to convince her not to commit suicide. He wrote back, again and again, never closing the door. She nevertheless took her life in October 1960. Richard Wright died of officially reported "natural causes" due to an "infarctus" on November 28, 1960.

Was she Tommy Turner's rage turned inward?

My father left me to discover I had had a twin-in-despair he was trying to save.

Although he had failed with Ella.

I think I know now.

I am alive and kicking.

On the eve of the centennial of his birth, Richard Wright's lesser-known paper son, Tommy, will see the light of day.

— *Julia Wright*
Paris, July 17, 2007

A Father's Law

CHAPTER 1

H e saw the dim image of the traffic cop make a right-face turn and fling out a white-gloved arm, signaling that the flow of cars from the east should stop and that those toward the south now had the right of way, and at the same instant he heard the cop's shrill whistle: *Wrrrriiiieee* . . .

Yes, that was a good rookie. He had made change-over in traffic smartly, the exact manner in which the *Metropolitan Handbook for Traffic Policemen* had directed. The footwork had been perfect and that impersonal look on his face certainly inspired confidence and respect. That's the way a policeman should work. Well done, Officer, he mumbled in his sleep as the officer now did a left-face turn, again flinging out his flashing white-gloved hand and sounding his whistle: *Whreeeeeiiiiiee* . . .

"Ruddy!"

"Hunh!"

"Ruddy! Wake up!"

Wrrrriiiiieeeeee . . .

"Hunh? Hunh?"

"Ruddy, it's the telephone, darling!"

Wreeeiiieeeeee . . .

"Oh!"

"It's the telephone, Ruddy!"

"I'll get it, I'll get it," he mumbled, blinking his sleep-drugged eyes in the dark and fumbling with the bedcovers. He sat half up and sleep rushed over him in a wave, seeking to reclaim him. "This rush-hour traffic . . ." He sighed, his voice trailing off.

"Hunh? Ruddy, are you awake?"

"Hunh?"

"Darling, the *tele*phone!"

Wreeeeeiiiiiii . . .

In one stride of consciousness, he conquered his sleep and pushed his feet to the floor, reached out to the bedside table and lifted the receiver. He cleared his throat and spoke professionally: "Captain Rudolph Turner, speaking."

A woman's sharp, crisp voice sang over the wire: "Ruddy, Mary Jane . . . Mary Jane Woodford."

"Yeah, Mary Jane. What is it? What's up?"

"Who is that, Ruddy?"

"Wait, Agnes. I'm trying to talk. Switch on the light."

"What was that?"

"I was talking to my wife, Mary Jane. Spill it. What's the trouble?"

"A message for you. The commissioner wants to see you at two o'clock," Mary Jane informed him. "So hustle up here. And don't wear your uniform."

"Two o'clock? Tonight?"

"Naw. This morning. It's past midnight now. And it's urgent."

"But what about?"

"I'm not the commissioner, Ruddy. You understood what I've said?"

"I got it."

"You sound like you were dead to the world."

"I was sleeping like a log. I was dreaming. I was coaching a rookie to direct traffic."

"Traffic? I bet it was flowing north and south! Ha, ha!"

"You dirty-minded gal!"

"Ha, ha! See you, Ruddy!"

Click!

He hung up and stared into space, vaguely aware that his wife had flooded the room with light.

"Who was that, Ruddy?"

"Mary Jane. The commissioner's secretary."

"Why in God's name is she calling you at this hour?"

"It's her duty, honey. I got to go in at the commissioner's at two . . ."

"Tonight?"

"It's morning, darling. It's urgent, she said."

"She shouldn't call you like that."

"She's doing what she's told."

"But she never called you before at this hour."

"I know. Don't know what this can mean."

"Didn't you ask her?"

"Yeah. I did. But she won't tell."

"Well, I never. You're a captain. They shouldn't rouse you out of your sleep like that."

"Something's up," he said, idly scratching his chest, vaguely sensing the vivid dream he had had fading from his mind. Was it the Maybrick case? No—that was settled. *And don't wear your uniform!* "She said I was not to come in in uniform."

"*Why?*"

"The commissioner's order, she said."

"That sounds fishy to me."

He turned and looked down at his wife's dimpled, peach-colored face, the deep brown eyes clouded and heavy with sleep.

"Now, Agnes, don't you be a little kitten and start scratching at Mary Jane. She's not trying to lure me out of the house for her sake . . ."

"I didn't say that," Agnes mumbled sulkily.

He glanced at his wristwatch; it was twenty minutes past midnight. He leaned over to his wife and lifted her head with his left palm and kissed her. Gently, he eased her face from him. "You go right back to sleep. I'll get dressed."

"When will you get back?"

"I really don't know, honey. Something's up. It's been years since I got a midnight call to come in . . . say, what's that?"

"What?"

"That noise? Jesus . . . Tommy's typing. And at this hour. Doesn't he ever sleep?"

"He's studying for his exams, Ruddy."

"Goddammit, he's overdoing it. A boy his age ought to be sleeping."

"He sleeps enough. You'll call me as soon as you know?"

"Sure thing, kitten."

"And no uniform? Maybe they've got a plainclothes assignment for you and—"

"Naw. Those guys are a dime a dozen."

"Maybe you're being assigned to guard some bigwig?"

"Could be. But they've got hundreds of guys to do that stuff. And I'm the man who assigns 'em. Couldn't be that." He rose, yawned, and stretched. "I won't wear my uniform, but I sure will take my gat."

"You do that," Agnes said

"I'll shower," he said, turning as a knock came on the door.

"Dad."

"Yeah, Tommy. What is it?"

"Come on, Tommy," Agnes called.

The door swung in and a tall, slender brown youth of eighteen poked his head and half of his body around the doorjamb.

"I heard the phone and heard you two talking," Tommy began.

"I'm summoned to headquarters," Ruddy said lightly, poking his feet into his house shoes. "You still up?"

"Cramming," Tommy said, twisting his lips in a self-effacing smile.

"You ought to get your sleep, son," Ruddy said. "When I was your age, I was either playing baseball or chasing gals."

"He knows what he wants to do," Agnes said.

"A big crime case coming up, Dad?" Tommy asked. He now showed his right hand, which held a smoldering cigarette. He lifted it to his lips and drew smoke deep into his lungs.

"Don't know, son. Got to report at two. Say, you look damned tired," Ruddy scolded softly.

"Oh, I'm all right," Tommy mumbled with a jocular kind of lofty indifference. "See you." He went out and closed the door.

Ruddy stared dreamily before him, not speaking. Agnes kept her eyes upon the flowery patterns of the quilt.

"I wish I knew what was going on in that boy," Ruddy said.

"He's studying for his exams," Agnes said. "I told you."

"Yeah. I know."

"Darling, kids are not now what they were when you grew up," Agnes reminded him.

"It's not that," Ruddy said with tense lips.

"You seem worried. Tommy's all right."

"I hope so."

"Ruddy, what do you mean?"

"Nothing. Just old-fashioned, I guess. Gee, I got to bathe, dress, and get out of here. . . . See you in a sec."

He hurried to the bathroom and turned on the shower, testing the temperature of the water with his hand until it was right, hearing all the while the sharp tapping of his son's typewriter. "What's wrong with that boy?" he asked himself out loud. For example, that way in which he had said: "Oh, I'm all right." It had had a strange ring; it had reminded Ruddy of some of the queer characters he had had to handle at the city jail. Why wasn't Tommy more straightforward? Agnes could not see anything about Tommy. She was the boy's mother and defended him each step of the way. He paused, stripped off his pajamas, realizing that his condemnation of his son was far severer than any objective evidence warranted. "I'm just nervous for 'im, I guess," he said, edging his body under the needle-sharp strings of tepid water and seizing the bar of soap. He washed leisurely, lathering his huge, bronzed body, mulling over his son, his own childhood, trying to still a deep and secret worry gnawing at his vitals.

Ruddy was intelligent enough to realize that there was something in him that was clouding his vision of his son, and that no matter how hard he had tried, he had never been able to erect the kind of healthy father-and-son relationship he had always dreamed of and wanted. "Goddamn, everything else in my life is straight, except that," he grumbled. And there was no doubt that there slumbered deep in Tommy a resentment of him. "But why?" he whispered despairingly through the beating waves of water. "I've given 'im every damned thing he ever asked for." Yet that was not it. In fact, Tommy always accepted what was given to him with a slight attitude of mockery that robbed the gift of its intention. And Ruddy was as sure as he was of anything on earth that there was some secret behind that smiling irony of his son. "But why doesn't he tell me everything?" he asked himself.

He stepped from the shower, cut off the water, and began drying himself with a towel, feeling that his thoughts and feelings were muddled. How much of what he felt he knew of his son was he misinterpreting? But what worried Ruddy was that he could not help but regard his son somewhat in the same light that he held the criminals he questioned each day. He paused, staring. Goddamn, that's a hell of a thing to feel about one's own son. Yes, but it was true. There was that withholding of something vital from the outside world that Tommy shared with the lawbreakers Ruddy dealt with day in and day out.

"Oh, hell, I'm just a stupid, middle-aged father," he chided himself. "Tommy hasn't ever done anything wrong." But that very assurance bothered him. That was just it. Tommy had not ever done anything wrong. He remembered hearing the fellow officers at the city jail complain of their sons:

"Here I am catching hoodlums everyday and my own son seems to be turning into one."

Indeed, on one occasion, James Hill, his closest friend on the force, had had to talk with his son in jail and watch him being tried in court for car stealing. It had all turned out for the good in the end; the boy had been paroled to the father, who had promised the judge: "If that boy ever touches a car that doesn't belong to him, he won't get as far as this jail, Your Honor. I'll take care of 'im."

And Jim Hill had. But that episode had been the talk of the department for months.

"You see, even a cop's son can go wrong."

"Hell, a cop's boy is human like everybody else."

"Who the hell says that an officer's son won't steal, when

officers themselves steal," Commissioner King had observed one day.

Well, maybe that was true. But he, Captain Rudolph Turner, had never broken the law in any form or fashion in his life. So there was no earthly reason for Tommy to get into trouble. He stared unseeingly at his underwear. Here I am thinking of the boy as though I knew that he was guilty of something. . . . "I'm crazy," he said, stung with guilt. I mustn't treat that boy in a way that will make him go wrong. He realized that there was a danger in that direction. I don't want to treat that boy in a way that will make him act exactly in a manner that I don't want. He understood that kind of thing well enough. In his early days on the force he had once been assigned to a juvenile bureau and he had seen how stern action on children would make them rise to the challenge, make them turn brutal, make them defiant. But, hell, nothing remotely like that had ever happened between him and Tommy. Guess I'm worrying about nothing, he tried to soothe himself, hearing the nervous tapping of his son's typewriter. And after all, he had once had a long talk with Father Joyce about his confused feelings for his son; time after time the good Father had questioned him about Tommy's behavior and he had not been able to say a concrete thing against the boy, and the Father had counseled him to let the boy be. How ashamed he had been over that.

"Don't you love that boy?" Father Joyce had asked.

Tears had come to Ruddy's eyes, and he looked reproachfully into the old priest's eyes. He had not been able to answer. He could still remember with gratitude Father Joyce's reassuring pat on his shoulder as he left the church.

"Have faith, son," Father Joyce had advised. "And remember that more than you or I watches over our sons. God loves us all."

After that, he had kept his worries to himself. Only to Agnes had he allowed them to become articulate, and now he was finding it hard even to talk to her. Yeah, maybe I'm dumb, he thought, trying to smile, pulling on a shirt. How light and undressed he felt without that heavy uniform! And it was more than just the weight of that blue woolen cloth that gave him a sense of protection; it was the sight and symbol of it that mattered. His function in society was marked out by it, and even the bronze tint of his skin was redeemed by it. When he had donned his gray suit, he was clothed but felt naked still, somehow, some way. Only the presence of his service revolver on his hip served to act as an anchor to his threatened personality.

Dressed, he went to the door of the bedroom, which now stood ajar. The light had been turned out. He hesitated, then called in a whisper: "Agnes."

There was no sound. As he pulled the door to, he heard her give a sigh.

"Agnes," he called again, softly.

She still made no reply. He eased the door shut and passed down the hallway, the sound of Tommy's typing coming louder as he neared the stairway. He paused, glanced at his watch. He had plenty of time. In any case, he might be able to flag down a squad car heading toward headquarters. Then the sheer intensity of the typewriter keys pounding upon paper gripped him. It gave him a strange sensation to know that the man concentrated in thought and feeling behind those flying keys was his son. *But what was he studying so furiously?* Then it struck him that maybe that was what was wrong; he had no way to get into the secret center of his son's life! Maybe I'm just jealous. . . . Naturally, the boy would have a life of his own, be preoccupied with ideas of another world and another generation. I've got to accept that, he told himself with a pang of contrite guilt. Yes, he'd give the boy a glad hand. He knocked against the shut door and the sound of the racing keys grew still.

"That you, Dad?"

"Yeah, Tommy."

"Come on in, Dad."

He entered the smoke-filled room and found Tommy turned smilingly toward him, his fingers lifted just above the level of the typewriter keys.

"Headquarters bound, hunh?" Tommy asked, the cigarette dangling from his lips flopping as he talked.

"Yeah."

That was what he did not like. Tommy always seemed to anticipate what he would say, always defined the relations between them before he could. There was no doubt that the lad was sharp, too sharp almost. But who am I too judge?

"Mama sleeping?"

"Oh, yeah. Say, this place is smoky. You're a regular chimney."

"Ha, ha. I smoke like that when I'm on the homestretch for an exam," Tommy said, rising now from the machine. "Kind of odd, their calling you like this."

"Yeah. Something's up. Something always is. What's the exam about?"

"Sociology."

"Oh. Like it?"

"Oh, yeah. It's all about this South Side of Chicago." Tommy seemed suddenly effusive, open. Class stratification, poverty, color consciousness, family disorganization . . ."

"Tommy, that's deep stuff," Ruddy said with heartfelt admiration.

"No. Not really. Once you get into it, it's really simple, almost obvious. People who have no family get lost and go bad. People who make money develop airs and manners of other people and become strangers to their own. It's the women in the setup who catch hell."

"If that stuff is so easy, why do you grind so hard at it?" he asked Tommy in spite of himself.

"I've got only another hour's work here and I'm through," Tommy defended himself. "I can sleep until noon."

"Yeah. Guess so. But you ought to knock around a bit, kid. Relax some. You've got plenty of time. You're ahead in school now. Don't work too hard."

"Dad, it's not work to me," Tommy said with an offhanded laugh.

There was silence, Ruddy felt offended. This was the core of the difference between them. Tommy had judged him. Had spoken from a core of meaning beyond the scope of Ruddy's life. And that which was beyond the core of Ruddy's life was either superior to it or inferior to it. And since he could not imagine that his son could be in some way his superior, he felt that he was, well, not exactly inferior but different, something like those tough young men who were picked up pimping or housebreaking.

"Say, Dad, I've been so busy—and so have you—that I've not had a chance to ask you about the execution of Thompson," Tommy said.

"Thompson? Which one was that?"

"Don't you remember?"

"Oh, that one. He went last month."

"Remember what I predicted about him, Dad?"

Ruddy frowned. Somehow, for a reason he could not express, he resented Tommy's keen interest in crime.

"Can't say I do, son."

"I said he wouldn't confess," Tommy reminded him.

"Yes. I remember. In fact, he didn't."

"He didn't do that job, Dad," Tommy said.

"Oh, hell, Tommy. There you go. You're pitting yourself against the police and the courts and—"

"Oh, no. It's not that, Dad. Look, you and I both agree that a guilty man usually confesses when he's facing that chair. Hunh?"

"Yeah. There's no use in holding back then. It's over for him. And they usually confess. But that Thompson didn't."

"And you know why, Dad?"

"I wouldn't know, Tommy."

"Because he didn't do it, Dad. He wasn't guilty."

"Oh, Tommy. You're off, boy. They had the goods on 'im."

"But he didn't confess."

"That's right. You get hard ones sometimes."

"But he wasn't hard. . . . Dad, do you want to know why he didn't confess?"

"What are you talking about? You just said that you felt he wasn't guilty; if that's the case, then what could he confess?"

"That's not the point, Dad. The guy wasn't guilty. I'm convinced of that. The police didn't believe his alibi, but I did." Tommy sat now, and words poured out, passionate words that held Ruddy spellbound. "That woman told the truth. Of course, she was a drunkard. That's what made the police reject her story. Thompson was never near that place. . . . Now, Dad, when you get a guy in jail—a guy like Thompson, illiterate and scared—and sentence him to the electric chair, he gets to feel guilty. And Thompson would have confessed to that crime, but he simply didn't know how to do so."

"Aw, Tommy, that's crazy," Ruddy rejected the theory with heat. "You just said that he wasn't guilty—"

"He wasn't," Tommy said. "Dad, I went and talked to that woman. She told the truth and—"

"You never told me you talked to her!"

"I was doing fieldwork one day near her flat," Tommy explained. "I went in. I told her I was a social worker. She told me everything. She was scared to death. Thompson was in her flat when that robbery was taking place—"

"But what's this about Thompson wanting to confess and not being able to?" Ruddy asked, blinking.

"Dad, he wasn't guilty of that job," Tommy went on to explain. "But when the law grabbed him, and when he was facing that chair with no hope of getting off, he really wanted to confess to something. Now, you say, at the very end, he tried to confess to some minor jobs in hope of getting the death sentence commuted. You said that the police rejected those confessions. I don't think he was lying. *And if he had really done that murder job, he would have spit it all out.*"

"Tommy, I don't know. I don't follow you, son," Ruddy mumbled, scratching his head. This is what he did not like. This son of his holding forth about the vital heart of his police work and with undaunted authority. This is what had made him demand of Tommy that he never talk like this before his fellow officers, who sometimes came to the apartment. "I just don't believe that there are people who are crazy enough to confess to something that they never did." He glanced at his watch, and though he still had plenty of time, he felt like fleeing the disturbing presence of this strange son of his.

"Ha, ha . . . I know you don't get me, Dad," Tommy said with that cool, superior laugh of his. "We'll talk about it some other time. I know you got to go now."

"See you, Tommy," Ruddy said, doubling his fist and playfully placing it at his son's chin.

"I got you blocked," Tommy called out, lifting his elbow just in time.

"Your reflexes are quick," Ruddy said, glad to change the subject.

"You bet," Tommy sang.

"See you, boy," Ruddy called.

"Okay, Dad," Tommy said, turning back to his machine.

As Ruddy went down the stairway, and even when he was upon the rain-wet front steps, he could hear the diminishing whir of Tommy's typewriter keys. "Goddamn, if that boy's right, then I'm crazy," he muttered half-aloud to himself. A man wanting to confess to a crime that he did not commit just because he is in jail and is ignorant. "Goddamn," he railed at himself and at his strange son. "I wish to hell he wouldn't talk like that."

CHAPTER 2

Ruddy was relieved to plunge into the faint drizzle of warm rain that greeted him when he stepped into the street. Hazy blobs of yellow streetlamps gleamed to the left and right of him and not a single soul could be seen. "Quiet neighborhood," he appraised the quarter in which his two-story stucco house stood, in keeping with his officer's rank. Yes, all in all, *he*—Rudolph Turner, captain of police, colored, Catholic—had made it. His neighbors were white; he did not have to fear hoodlums loitering about his premises. He had at once, as soon as he had purchased his property, joined the neighborhood protective association to guard the interests of all who owned property in the area, and he had been accepted with enthusiasm.

To his neighbor, Mr. Stonewell Britten, vice-president of the Greenlawn Bank and Loan Association, who had greeted him the morning he had moved in with "We're damned particular about who lives around here."

Ruddy had said heartily: "I'm glad to hear that. Now that I'm here, I'm particular *too*."

Yes, things were all right with him. His son was in the university, and in a few months, Ruddy would retire. Maybe he would join a private detective agency; no fewer than five had already spoken or written to him, offering inducements. Well, he'd decide when the time came. He strode on, feeling his limbs strangely vulnerable in his civilian suit but feeling comforted by the weight of his gun on his right hip. Now, he could take a taxi to police headquarters or he could take the subway. No, he'd call and see if there was a squad car in the area. As a captain of police, he had the right to commandeer squad cars for his transportation, but he had rarely availed himself of the opportunity. Yes, tonight, being summoned at two o'clock in the morning to the commissioner's office, he felt that he not only had the legal right to command a squad car but the moral imperative to do so. And what the hell does old Commissioner King want with me at two o'clock in the morning? he asked himself as he neared the end of the block and came in sight of a police alarm call box. He should have worn his raincoat, dammit. The thin rain was thickening to strings that gleamed like lead in the glare of the streetlamps. And in this rain, I sure would be a fool not to ask for a squad car. A short, thick-necked white youth passed him and threw him a quick glance. Run along, buddy, he mentally advised the man. What could you be doing out in this residential neighborhood alone at this time of night? And he felt the weight of his gun again, nestling against his hip. As he reached the box, the youth went from sight, around a corner. Ruddy jiggled the hook of the telephone and at once heard a sleepy masculine voice: "Police Headquarters, Squad Car Detail. Sergeant Simmons speaking."

"Sergeant Simmons, this is Captain Turner speaking."

"Oh, yes, Captain. What can I do for you?"

"Is there a squad car prowling about this area?"

"Just exactly where are you, Captain?"

"At the corner of Ninety-first and Blue Ridge Avenue."

"Lemme check, Captain. I think Jock Weidman ought to be

somewhere near there by now," Sergeant Simmons said. Ruddy noticed with gratitude the respect that had at once crept into Simmons's voice. *He ought to be glad to help me—I endorsed him for promotion. Good boy, that David Simmons. Never hurried, never excited.*

"Hello, Captain."

"Right here, Sergeant."

"Jock Weidman is about six blocks from you. Shall I call him to pick you up?"

"Right."

"I'll do that. You have an appointment for tonight."

"Yeah. I know. What's it all about?"

"Wouldn't know that, Captain."

"Say, is it raining in the city?"

"Not a drop of rain falling here. Is it raining there?"

"Yes. Just a drizzle, but it's thickening."

"I'll tell Lt. Jock Weidman to rush over."

"No rush. I can wait under an awning."

"Won't be but a minute, Captain."

"Righto."

He hung up, went to the entrance of a clothing store, sheltered himself under an awning, and lit a cigarette. That was one advantage that plainclothesmen had over those in uniform; they could smoke when and where they pleased. But never in twenty-five years on the police force had he been summoned to see the commissioner of police at two o'clock in the morning. *What could that man want?*

Was he to be reprimanded? No, hell—if that was the case, why, he'd have got it in writing, as was the usual routine. . . . A decoration? No, he had had six. And by all fair means, he was certainly not due for any more. Then what? The nearer he came to seeing the commissioner, the tenser he got. *But there's nothing to worry* about, he told himself. But he worried. Oh, maybe an officer had been slain? Yeah, cop killing always got the force all worked up. The commissioner always said, "For every cop killed, always kill a crook, no matter how. That's the only safe way." And Ruddy agreed with that, for he carried a scar under his right arm where the doctors had to dig out a .38 bullet which a second-story punk had once put into him. "It could have been me," he muttered aloud each time he remembered that close call of death. He pulled on his cigarette and scanned the streets. Empty. Everything's quiet. Too quiet. Yeah, they say cops are like mothers: when their children are too quiet, they get more worried than if they were making a lot of noise.

His ears caught the faint and distant sound of a police siren. Yeah, that's Jock. What a guy. Who'd ever think a man with a sense of humor like that would be on the police force? And what a tender heart. What a practical joker! I'll bet Jock's driving tonight. Jock was a guy who wanted to do everything. He had been married four times. His first wife died, his second ran off, and his third killed herself. And everybody swore that none of it was Jock's fault. He was still with his fourth wife. "After her, I don't want no more," Jock was wont to say, shaking his head and waving his right forefinger. Some guys just have hard luck. And Jock was straight. He was an ideal guy to command. He obeyed orders without question, looking you straight in the eye. If I were ever a commissioner, I'd sure have Jock at my elbow, Ruddy muttered, hearing the wail of the siren's volume growing and swelling through the rainy air. "Jock, take your men and surround the building. Have your tear gas ready," Ruddy mentally issued orders to a waiting and eager Jock. "Yes, Captain . . . yes, Commissioner." A gust of rainy wind swept the budding daydream away. Far down the avenue came two gleaming yellow eyes and one red one, seemingly swept along by a sharp siren wail. Ruddy left the awning and stood at the curb ready to toss his cigarette away and step into the car when the door was flung open for him. The car slowed, then a swift and blinding light hit his eyes. "What the hell," Ruddy muttered, feeling anger rising. Then he saw Wade Williams's white teeth showing in his black face.

"Escort the prisoner to the car, men," Wade ordered, tossing back his head and rolling naughty eyes.

"You bastard," Ruddy said. "You want me to get soaking wet in this rain?"

"Hey there, Ruddy?" Wade asked.

"Hey," Ruddy said as the rear car door swung open.

"Get on in here, Gangster," Jock called.

"I'm reporting you for this, Officer," Ruddy said, grinning, edging his long, lean frame into the car. "Well, well, the car's full tonight. What's up? Wade, Jock, Bert, and Ed . . . Who are you guys looking for? Dillinger?"

"Yeah," Jock said. "And we got 'im. Get on in here. We're taking you down to headquarters. The commissioner wants to see you."

"But, Mister, I was just walking along the street. I ain't done nothing."

"The hell you haven't. What were you doing coming out of that shop there?" Jock demanded.

"I just went in there to have my suit repaired." Ruddy fell into the spirit of play. "I got the receipt here. Want to see it?"

"Show me," Jock demanded, flashing his electric lamp full onto Ruddy's face.

Ruddy's left hand went into his inner coat pocket and then it snaked out and he said with a full throat: "BOOM! Got you, cop!"

The car exploded with laughter.

"You're dead, Jock," Wade yelled.

"Jesus Christ, Jock." Ruddy chuckled, ruffling Jock's shock of blond hair. "Hell, you fell for the oldest trick in the books. Now, lie down there and be dead."

"You really got me that time," Jock admitted. "You see, I wasn't expecting a guy as well dressed as you to pull a rod on me."

"Hell, you've got to be careful with all of 'em," Ed said.

"Ruddy, we're taking you to headquarters anyway," Wade said. "They got the goods on you this time."

"What kind of goods?" Ruddy demanded, imitating a surly criminal.

"We dug up those government bonds you buried in your backyard," Wade announced triumphantly.

"I got an 'out,'" Ruddy threatened.

"Nothing won't help you this time, big boy," Wade cautioned. "You're going up for twenty years this time."

"No. I'm going to turn state's evidence," Ruddy said. "You forgot that the other half of those bonds are buried in *your* backyard."

"Aw, nuts," Wade muttered. "Forgot that."

"Well, we're going to book you anyhow and put you in tomorrow's lineup," Ed spoke with mock frustration.

"You can't put a finger on me," Ruddy warned. "I got an alibi."

"We got your dame too." Jock stalled off Ruddy's confidence.

"I ain't got no dame," Ruddy told them. "I'm a homo. Didn't you know?"

The car again roared with laughter.

"Jesus, you're clean." Ed sighed. "Well, we'll have to hold you on suspicion of bothering minors."

"Oh, that," Ruddy said blithely. "I ain't really no homo."

"But you just said you were," Jock reminded Ruddy.

"You stay dead, Jock." Ruddy sneered. "But when I said I was a homo, you guys didn't really understand me."

"The hell we didn't," Ed said. "We're witnesses to what you said."

"But, Mister, I don't see my boyfriend but three times a week, and that don't make you no homo," Ruddy wailed in mock rage.

The laughter was so general and spontaneous that the car slowed at a curb.

"That's the best one I've heard yet," Jock moaned, lolling his head.

"But that's a true one," Ruddy spoke seriously. "I heard that one last week in the lineup with my own ears."

"No kidding?" Ed asked.

"I swear. You can ask Captain Drake."

"Jesus Christ," Wade murmured. "Those punks'll say anything."

"What's that down that side street?" Jock leaned forward and pointed.

The four of them focused their eyes on a dark, slight figure carrying a bundle.

"Aw, that's only Wang, the Chinese laundryman," Ruddy explained. "I know 'im."

"What's in that bundle he's carrying?" Ed asked.

"Slightly soiled ladies' drawers, I'd suspect," Ruddy said.

"What's he going to do with 'em?" Wade asked.

"They usually wash drawers in laundries," Ruddy said softly.

"He ain't going to wash 'em before he's smelled 'em," Jock said.

Once again the car exploded with laughter.

"*Who* said that?" Wade asked, peering into the back seat.

"Who do you think?" Ruddy asked. "Old Jock-strap, of course."

Wade stepped on the brake and the car jerked to a halt. Laughter roared in the car.

"Jock, you'll never live that down," Ed predicted.

"That one hit me between the eyes," Jock admitted, his body shaking with mirth.

Ed was now talking softly into the squad car's telephone: "Squad Car Number 147 reporting. Suspect seized at Ninety-first Street and Blue Ridge Avenue. He's armed with verbal artillery and is dangerous."

"Don't forget to report that you lost one of your officers in the first burst of gunfire," Ruddy said.

The squad car was now entering traffic and the officers grew quiet. Ed lit a cigarette and offered one to Ruddy, who accepted. The tires of the car whirred on the wet asphalt.

"What's new?" Ruddy asked in a guttural tone.

"We're pulling in the same small fry," Wade said.

"How's that Tommy of yours?" Jock asked, clapping Ruddy on the back.

"Good. He's studying hard for his exams," Ruddy said.

"Fine chap, that Tommy," Ed said. "We'll need him on the force."

"I don't want 'im in the service," Ruddy growled.

"Why? That's the very kind of idealistic chap we do need," Ed was emphatic.

"He wants a profession," Wade said. "I don't blame 'im."

"If he turns cop, I'll shoot 'im," Ruddy warned darkly.

"What in hell have you got against cops?" Jock demanded.

"Guys like me," Ruddy said.

"You're a good officer," Ed said. "The force draws its best men from the families of officers."

"I know," Ruddy said. "But I don't think Tommy's mind runs toward our kind of work."

"Why not?" Ed demanded.

Ruddy was silent, thinking, annoyed. The car had now entered State Street, and Wade let out the siren in order to make headway.

"I'm going to let that boy have his head," Ruddy said. "I don't want to force 'im."

"Nobody's saying you ought to," Ed reminded him. "Say, did I tell you that I know Tommy's professor at the university?"

Ruddy whirled and stared at Ed. Ed was known as the intellectual among the cops, a man who knew ideas and how to make them clear and simple for other officers. Ruddy did not know if Ed was really pulling his leg or paying him a compliment.

"Really? What does he think of my boy?"

"He's great, that Tommy," Ed said reflectively. "He's on to the new idea about crime. Ruddy, that boy of yours is ahead of us."

"What new idea is this?" Ruddy asked in a doubting but playful tone.

"Well, it's rather deep stuff," Ed ventured. "The idea now is that criminals ought not to be punished—"

"Oh, that bullshit." Wade sneered.

"We just let 'em go?" Jock asked softly, staring.

"Oh, no. That's not it at all," Ed corrected Jock.

"Punishment is the only thing that a criminal understands," Wade said.

"No one says that we ought to open the prisons and let murderers out," Ed told them. "The real aim of penal law is to protect society."

"Okay, wise guy," Wade said. "Ain't we doing that when we lock up a killer for twenty years?"

"No," Ed said coolly. "Look, just last month, Baby-faced Bruno came out. He served fifteen years for murder. He was out four months and he killed again. Was society protected?"

"Well, hell, we're going to lock 'im up again," Wade declared indignantly. "This time for good, maybe. Perhaps he'll get the chair."

"But his getting the chair doesn't bring back the life of that old man he killed to get fifty dollars," Ed scored.

"That's right," Ruddy agreed. "That cold-blooded bastard should not have been let out the first time."

"But Baby-faced Bruno is just one among hundreds of thousands who go free to kill and steal again." Ed stated the full scope of the dilemma.

"What are you driving at, Ed?" Jock asked.

"Putting a criminal in jail is not a way of protecting society," Ed said.

"Well then, you tell us how we are to do it," Ruddy said.

"They are sick people," Ed said. "They have to be treated."

"What kind of disease have they got, Doc?" Ruddy was sarcastic. "Show me those germs under a microscope."

"It's not that kind of sickness, Ruddy," Ed contended. "It's emotional."

"Tell me how are we going to know when a punk is emotionally sick," Jock demanded.

"You can tell," Ed said. "Those psychologists can tell."

"And you say that Tommy goes for that stuff?" Ruddy asked.

"Yes, he's deep in it."

"Maybe I'm emotionally sick," Jock said slyly. "I've got woman trouble all the time. But I never killed or stole anything."

"It's not that simple," Ed said. "There are questionnaires you can give a kid and find out when he is on the wrong track. You can do that long before he ever kills."

"What are some of the things that make you know he's going wrong?" Ruddy asked. He felt a sense of uneasiness.

"Attitudes," Ed said. "Things like that."

"Give me one attitude," Ruddy insisted. "Just one idea about how to spot a bad egg without breaking it open."

"Well, there's one thing the psychological guys are always

talking about," Ed began cautiously. "When kids rebel against authority, that's the start of trouble. You can find it in the home, at the dinner table."

"Oh, that kind just needs a damned good spanking," Wade said angrily.

"What kind of rebellion against authority?" Ruddy asked.

"All kinds," Ed said. "Long before a boy shoots one of us, that boy has killed his father in his mind by rejecting him."

"That's pretty slippery logic," Ruddy commented. "You just praised Tommy. Now, Tommy doesn't agree with me. Does that make him a future killer?"

"I'm speaking of emotional rejection and rebellion," Ed insisted. "Not just a boy's right to discuss with his dad."

"Oh," Ruddy said, and he was surprised at the amount of relief he felt. "I don't get all that. It's something for the professors."

"Ditto," Wade said.

"I say get the bastards who hurt and kill others," Jock said.

Was Tommy really against him? Ruddy tensed as he sat and stared unseeingly at the gold of the streetlamps on the black wet asphalt. That boy is locked away from me; he lives in another world. He longed to ask Ed more questions about how to spot a potential criminal, but he dared not, for he did not wish to betray his own worry. *His own worry?* Was he worried about Tommy or about himself? That was the question. Yeah, I got to think about this. He too, Ruddy Turner, had his problems, but he had solved them. Or had he? Yeah, I'm all right. And the mental tone in which he said that reminded him of Tommy's constant and almost make-believe lightheartedness. A stitch of fear snatched at Ruddy's heart. Yeah, that boy's like me. If that were true, then everything would turn out all right? But what if Tommy's kind of problem could not be resolved as he had resolved his own?

Ruddy too was lighthearted, and yet he well knew that that was his mask for others, for his wife, his pals on the force, his superiors, and, above all, for the criminals he caught. The car tires whirred like his wheeling thoughts. Sometimes he would like to have a good heart-to-heart chat with old Ed.

Ed Seigel was Jewish, and Ruddy was a black Catholic, and he had always kept a kind of distance with the Jew boy. He liked him, yet he feared that if he had too much to do with him, people would think that he was too intimate with an unpopular minority. And Ruddy loved being with the majority; he respected the wishes of the community; indeed, he loved the laws and rules of the community with an abiding and intense passion. He lived, after all, by enforcing the laws and wishes of that community. But if he talked a bit to Ed, nothing would seem amiss. And Ed knew so damned much. Why was it that the guys who were outside of the majority group seemed to be so smart, knew so much? Yeah, there was something devilish about that. But why not seek advice in some other quarter? Father Joyce? No. He knew without trying that the good Father would shunt him off with meaningless assurances, would imply that he was losing the faith.

Well, in a few months, he would be retired and then he would get next to that boy of his. What better plan could he devise than that? What better proof could there be of his sincerity than his resolve to devote his life to his son? I'll just be a stepping-stone to that boy and help him on the way up. And Ed had said that the boy's professor at the university had said that Tommy was a genius. But what was a genius? The very word disturbed him. All too often he had heard of criminals about to be executed and the doctors had said that they acted and talked like geniuses. No! Let Tommy be just like any other boy. Let him play baseball, basketball, shoot pool, get a gal. . . . And keep away from too much gnawing into those goddamn books.

Yet Ed's claim had something in it. Ed knew more than he knew and that bothered him. He could not refute Ed; he could only listen and offer feeble objections. That was as it had always been. And the other officers, he knew, felt more or less the same way about old Ed.

"We're on the homestretch," Wade said, letting the car shoot forward with speed.

"What the hell are they dragging me down here for at two in the morning?" Ruddy asked in a tone that sought to convey that he was peeved about his loss of sleep.

"Something rather important if the commissioner demanded it," Ed commented.

"Something that he did not wish to let wait," Ruddy said.

"Old King gets a bee in his bonnet sometimes," Jock said.

"But bees don't act up at midnight unless somebody bothers them," Wade pointed out.

"Right," Ruddy seconded.

Wade turned and slowed at a wide gate at which a uniformed guard saluted; the gate swung open and the car rolled forward into a vast court-like interior in which hundreds of other cars were parked. Two minutes later Wade stopped before a door under a glass shed and an officer armed with a submachine gun came forward.

"We got something hot here; be careful!" Jock called warningly.

The submachine gun lifted its muzzle.

"Are you trying to get me shot?" Ruddy asked Jock and pushed his shoulder as he opened the door and began edging himself out. He found old Greenwood advancing with the machine. Then Greenwood stopped, stared, his lips parting.

"Who's that?" Greenwood asked. Then, without waiting for an answer, he intoned: "It's the captain . . . Captain Turner!"

"Put that thing away, Greenwood," Ruddy cautioned. "You never know; it might go off."

"Aw, hell," Greenwood grumbled. "I thought they were bringing in a killer."

"He is a killer . . . of *crooks*," Ed said.

"Hi, Ruddy!" the voice of a passing officer that Ruddy did not see greeted him.

"Hi," Ruddy responded with a hand wave.

"If you need an alibi, we're it," Wade said, pulling away from the door.

"I'll remember that," Ruddy said.

Ruddy pushed his way past a milling throng of policemen.

"Hi, Captain."

"Hi, boys."

"What're you doing here tonight, Captain?"

"Don't know, really."

It was twenty minutes to two; Ruddy was undecided whether to get a cup of coffee in the main swing-room or to go right up to Commissioner King's office and wait on the bench in the hallway. Not feeling like chatting idly, he took the self-service elevator to the tenth floor and found himself surrounded by other officers of varying grades.

"What's up?" Ruddy asked a young rookie.

"Haven't you heard?"

"No."

"Chief Mo Branden was killed last night—about half-past eleven," the rookie explained.

"Jesus, no!"

"Yep."

"Poor Mo Branden."

"He was a fine officer," the rookie said.

"A wonderful officer," Ruddy murmured. "What happened?"

"A shotgun blast . . . don't know the circumstances yet," the rookie said. "You'll know before I do. It was on the police radio shortly after it happened."

"I was asleep," Ruddy said. "Can't listen always."

"I know."

"My Lord," Ruddy breathed.

Mo Branden had been the chief of police in the suburban area south of where Ruddy lived; he had not known the man, but his reputation was high. Mo Branden had been intimate with all the higher-ups, his daughter having recently married a stockbroker. And he had been police chief in an area in which a few wealthy Negroes had recently installed themselves. But had he, Ruddy, been called in about this? Could there be racial trouble out there? And why had the rookie not disclosed a single incident about the slaying? Ruddy looked about. There was not a single officer he knew, but he saw a few eyes weighing him, watching him. "Something really big's cooking," he muttered under his breath and sat on a bench whose back rested against a granite wall. Jesus, anything could happen in police work. Beside him lay a discarded copy of the *Chicago Tribune*, but, when he examined it, there was no news of the Mo Branden slaying. "No, it's too early for that," he said. He glanced idly around. A plainclothesman passed him, nodded slightly, and hurried on. Was he imagining things? People were paying more attention to him tonight than usual. In fact, that policewoman was smiling at him as she passed. "Something's up," he muttered yet again to himself, leafing aimlessly through the newspaper.

"Ruddy Turner!"

He whirled his head. Jack Watkins, a South Side Negro politician, was bearing down on him. Ruddy leaped to his feet and took off his hat.

"Hi, Mr. Watkins," he said.

Watkins was running for the city council, and it was always safe to be friendly with men like that.

"That Branden killing shocked 'em all," Watkins said.

He was a short, hard, brown man with curly hair. He had long ago given up a high military position in the Illinois National Guard to enter politics and he was still rising fast.

"What happened?" Ruddy asked with a tone of voice that implied that all confidences would be respected.

Watkins did not reply at once; his eyes roved over Ruddy, judging, weighing. "What are these guys looking me over for?" he asked himself desperately.

"Looks like it was a revenge killing," Watkins said slowly.

"None of our people involved?"

"No. A bank robber . . . Somebody Branden sent up years ago," Watkins explained. "He got out last week. Hunted Branden up and let 'im have it."

"Cappy Nelson?" Ruddy asked.

"That was the boy," Watkins said. "They riddled 'im. But it was too late."

"Good Lord. Looks like putting 'em in jail doesn't help much, does it?" Ruddy found himself remembering Ed's question and Ed's interest in Tommy's ideas.

"It helps only as long as they are in jail," Watkins said. "When they get out, they always kill again."

"You know, I helped to capture that bloke," Ruddy explained.

"Yeah. The commissioner knows that," Watkins told him. "I know he sent for you. There's a crowd in there now. He'll be seeing you soon. Fine man, that Commissioner King."

"Wonderful man," Ruddy chimed in.

"Got to rush on home now, Captain." Watkins excused himself. "I'll be seeing you around. I know."

"Good night, Mr. Watkins," Ruddy called to the retreating man.

Well, one thing was true. Everybody seemed to know that the commissioner had sent for him. And it was dollars to doughnuts that it had to do with the Branden killing and the retaliatory killing of Cappy Nelson. "Maybe identification matters," he mumbled. He tensed. Cappy Nelson had been a university man who had gone wrong; he recalled that Cappy Nelson had spread a trail of terror in bank crashing across the nation until he had come to a bad end in Chicago. And, at the time, the newspapers had been full of long articles asking why would a man upon whom so much money had been spent to educate him resort to crime. Cappy Nelson had been called "The Mad Bulldog." After a long and expensive court trial, in which alienists had testified to Cappy Nelson's emotional state, a sentence of fifteen years had been passed upon him. "Nobody ever really found out what was wrong with that guy," Ruddy told himself. "I remember that he looked like a matinee idol. Quiet, too quiet. Almost sweet. Spoke beautiful English. Ha, ha. . . . In fact, he once corrected the grammar of the district attorney! And they say he was the best teacher of English at the prison university. Jesus, Ed may be right, after all. It would take God Himself to figure out guys like that. Cappy Nelson grew up with everything. Was a football hero at the University of Chicago. Was engaged to marry the daughter of a well-known something-or-other when he was caught robbing his first bank. Was let off through high influence, let off on parole. Then he started his terror. Well, that's about all I remember of the guy." He frowned. The image of his own quiet Tommy came compulsively into his mind. "Oh, hell. Tommy's not that kind." He folded the paper and flung it aside. "And why in hell do I keep on thinking of Tommy in relation to things like that?"

He felt guilty. Maybe some kind of warning was sounding deep in him? Was he superstitious? No. But why was his worry about Tommy sucking, like a down-circling whirlpool, all the worries of police work into its funnel? I'm nervous. . . . Been working too hard.

Slowly, Ruddy began tapping his left foot against the marble floor, a sign that he was really nervous. He felt one of the old nervous crises coming over him, the kind he had when he first joined the force. God, how scared he had been in those days! When Ruddy, twenty-five years ago, had joined the police force, Chicago's South Side had been relatively a small community, deeply race-conscious. Indeed, it could not be strictly said that he had, on his own volition, joined the force. He had been "taken in." Being an assistant Republican precinct captain at a time when a Negro ward committeeman had been given the honor of submitting the name of a Negro to become a member of the police force, turned out to be the opportunity. Just from Memphis, young, big, raw, hard, silent, and willing, Ruddy Turner had been called in to see "Scooty" Peterson, the ward committeeman, who had asked him: "How'd you like to be a cop?"

"What's in it?" Ruddy had asked, completely bewildered.

"I don't want you to be a grafter," Scooty had warned. "In fact, you'll be on trial. You'll have to walk a chalkline. You'll make enough money to live on. You can retire on a pension after twenty-five years. There are chances for promotion. And you'll be a credit to your race. What do you say?"

"What do I do to get it?"

"You take an exam. You'll have my endorsement," Scooty said.

Ruddy was out of work. Gee, here was a chance. But he did not like the idea of being shot at.

"Just what kind of work is it?" Ruddy had asked.

That question had almost lost him his chance. "Scooty" had risen and glared at him as though he were crazy.

"Shit, what do policemen do, man? You catch crooks. You kill 'em, if necessary. And you remember your friends, see? You direct traffic. You keep crowds from collecting. You protect property. You reckon you could do that?"

"Maybe I could. Just never thought of being a policeman," Ruddy had mumbled.

"Well, what is it—yes or no?"

"I'll try, if you want me to."

"Do you want to be a policeman?"

"Sure, sure. I'll take the exam."

"Then you're in."

"Don't be too sure of that," Ruddy had warned. "I'm not too good at head work."

"I know that. All you'll need in this job is a strong back and good feet. And the ability not to look scared. I think you have those qualities. Here're the papers. Show up at that address after a good night's sleep and do your best. If you hear from the exam, come and see me. The rest will be arranged."

And that was how it had all started. When Ruddy had gone that morning to take the examination, he had felt more like a criminal himself than a man who was seeking the mandate to track them down. The examination had been easy, so easy that he had felt that the examiners were slighting him and he was sure that he had failed. "I'll never get into this game," he had consoled himself. Yet, while waiting to hear the results of the examination, he had had several nightmares. He dreamed of men tracking him down, of his facing black roustabouts who wielded razors at his throat, of his trying to arrest prostitutes who laughed at him and refused to follow him.

Just what frightened Ruddy about the job, he was never able

to tell. He was a colored man, poor, alone, not too well schooled; and he felt that the world in which he lived was so much better than he was. How on earth could anybody ask him to help run and protect that world? Then there had been times when he had been a boy when he had hated the authority of that world, had thought several times of violating its laws. Though he had never been arrested, he had been with gangs of boys who had raided school premises at night, just for the hell of it. He had played hooky from school to go fishing; he had ridden the roads from Memphis to New Orleans and back again; and somewhere down in a far Arkansas town he had left a girl with a baby. He felt guilty, and yet he knew rationally that those foolish boyish pranks could not and did not make him a criminal. Literally, he had had no life before him when he had taken the examination for the police force, and the sheer void of his existence was a thing that made him feel more guilty than any deed he could remember.

But there was another and deeper buried kind of guilt that slumbered in him, a guilt which now he could not think of without sweating. He had been seethingly race-conscious in those days, and while hunting jobs that did not exist, he used to curse the look of a world that excluded him, damn it to hell for the mental tension it evoked in him, and he used to long to collar the smooth, smug, clean-shaven white men who passed him with their well-fed bodies. He had had wild daydreams then; he was the head of a black invading army who would conquer a city like Chicago and then as the head of that army he could be merciful and inform the population that his sole aim was racial equality for all people. And maybe there would be a few diehards who would reject his regime and he would have to order them shot at dawn. Yet Ruddy knew while he was deep in these hot daydreams that nothing like that would ever happen, but there was left in him, nevertheless, a sense of guilt. This was a guilt for deeds he had never done but had wanted to do. And he knew in his heart that that was the worst kind of guilt, for he could never tell anybody about it. It sounded too silly, too much like the talk of children. He had never confessed these things to his Church; in fact, while talking to the priest in the confessional, no such "crimes" had ever occurred to him to confess, and, had he done so, the priest would perhaps have been shocked. How did one talk of a guilt that came from not doing the things that one wanted so much to do? Each day during those years a drop of guilt dripped into his emotions until they were full like a dam; but there was no leak, no way to drain off the rising tide of guilty poison. And this guilt was nameless, without a face, without solidity. That was the awful thing; one could not speak of it to one's friends. Yet one felt it in the pores of one's skin; it sweated itself out in the blackness of the night; it shimmered in one's nerves when one was alone; it hovered invisibly tense when one was performing one's duty. How well he had hidden that guilt during all of these long years on the police force! Of that he was proud. He was known far and wide as a fearless police officer. Yet the containment of that tension had been his greatest achievement, an achievement greater than his having aided in the capture of Cappy Nelson, greater than his single-handed capture of the gang of silk thieves during the early part of 1934, greater than the cold-blooded decision he had made to give that kidnapper the third-degree until he had confessed. Yet no decorations had ever been given to him for that silent and enduring courage, for it could not be seen or guessed. He was its only audience, and only he could tell the price paid to maintain a front of calm, of smiling cooperation.

As Ruddy had progressed in his police work, he had found, to his amazement, that it was this hidden sense of guilt that aided him in ferreting out breakers of the law, and the more lawbreakers he caught, the calmer he became. How the two guilts, the outward and the inner, fitted together! When he nabbed the guilty, he felt a deep degree of moral satisfaction. When he pounced upon the guilt of others, he felt that he was stilling the silent raging of his own secret, hot guilt. Indeed, his being a policeman had been the paying of a kind of debt to society, a debt which he had gladly paid. Could old Ed ever suspect a thing like that? And there was Ed talking of emotional illnesses! All you had to do was master yourself; others could do what he had done. It was easy. And so confident was he that he could say, with deep satisfaction, when looking at a black man gone wrong: "There but for my watchfulness, go I!"

And there had been none of that standing outside of society, which Ed had said was the secret hallmark of the criminal rebel; for even when he had been yearning to take a smashing potshot at society, he had wanted to be a part of that society. "No, I was never feeling like a criminal," he comforted himself. "The proof is that when they gave me a chance to enforce the law, I did, by God!"

He glanced anxiously at his watch; he could go in now. He rose, pushed through the swinging doors, and faced a gum-chewing Mary Jane at the switchboard.

"Hi," he greeted her. "Can the commissioner see me now?"

"He's still tied up," Mary Jane said, smiling, glancing at the big green door over which was stenciled: COMMISSONER OF POLICE—WILLIAM J. KING.

"This is the first time I've been called in at this hour in years," he commented, trying to evoke some information from her.

"There's a first time for everything," Mary Jane said.

"Too bad about Branden," he murmured.

"Wasn't that awful?" Mary Jane echoed. "I couldn't believe it. I still have goose pimples." She sighed and looked at the ceiling. "How do you policemen stand it? That Cappy Nelson was a mad dog, if ever there was one."

"He should've got the chair the first time," Ruddy said.

"We're too easy on 'em," Mary Jane complained.

"What's cooking in there?" He shot his question quickly, trying to take her off-guard.

"Ruddy, you know better than that," she chided him. "Me? I don't leak anything. I'm a boneyard."

"You sure are," he told her. "But the Bible says that bones will speak someday."

"Not these bones," she said. "Take it easy. Everything will come out all right, Captain Turner."

He stared. The inflections in her voice had been teasingly meaningful. She had not called him Captain Turner in years.

"Mary Jane, you've been around here a long time," he said.

"You came on the force in the year in which I was born," she told him significantly.

"You're smart," he complimented her. "How do you know that?"

"We keep records in the police department," she told him.

Aw, she knew why he had been called in. His curiosity was now at fever heat. Why would she not just give him a hint?

"I guess I've goofed something." He spoke with simulated despair.

"Don't be a dope," she said.

Well, at least it was not bad news. And his record had been taken out and pored over. But for what? He paced slowly to and fro.

"How's Agnes?"

"Fine. Fit as a fiddle."

"Men are funny," Mary Jane said. "When they are worried, they pace the floor. And they are worried about their wives having babies and their work."

Yes, he had been called in about his work. Some irregularity?

But it was useless to ask Mary Jane. She would not let a word slip that could be construed as having told. Yet she had bade him be of good heart.

"Thanks," he said, pulling down the corners of his lips.

"You're welcome," she sang, turning to answer a buzzing on the switchboard, listening intently, then plugging switches into electric holes.

"The crowd's leaving now," she announced.

"Through the other door?" he asked.

"Yes."

"Public figures?" he asked, cocking his head.

"You're warm," she admitted.

At that moment the big green door swung open and Commissioner King's huge bulk filled it. He was a man over six feet in height, lean and hard as a rail, yet with a florid complexion, blue eyes, bushy white hair, and a hawk-like face dominated by a long nose. He wore an expensive gray suit, double-breasted, a polka-dot tie with a diamond stickpin, and carried a cigar with an inch of ash in his left hand. His blue eyes widened gladly at the sight of Ruddy and his mouth flew open in a wide, soundless greeting. He rushed forward, shooting out his right hand. Ruddy was on his feet, his face lit with expectation and smiles.

"Ruddy, you old skunk! Been ages since I've seen you," the commissioner exclaimed.

"It's been a while," Ruddy admitted. "My, but you look like a million dollars."

"I'd better look it, for I'll never make a million in this lousy job," the commissioner said. "I'm sorry to have kept you waiting."

"It was nothing. I'm at your orders, Commissioner," Ruddy said.

"You're at my orders, Ruddy?" the commissioner asked with meaningful inflections.

"That's right."

"Well, I'm ordering you to march straight into my office and sit right in front of my desk," the commissioner declaimed.

"Right," Ruddy said, walking ahead.

"And I'm ordering you"—the commissioner pointed to Mary Jane—"not to bother me until I'm through with Ruddy."

"I understand, sir" Mary Jane said.

When Ruddy overheard those words, he knew that he was in for an exciting session, whether it meant ill or good for him. He advanced toward the commissioner's desk, sat as ordered, and glanced around. Commissioner King was standing and watching him. He crossed to a cabinet, took out a bottle, and said: "I now order that both of us have a drink."

"I always obey." Ruddy smiled and watched the amber fluid flow into two glasses.

The commissioner handed Ruddy his glass and then lifted his, intoning: "Ruddy, here's to you, one of the finest officers we ever had on our staff."

"You're a wonderful man to say that," Ruddy mumbled, overcome, rising.

"No. Stay in your chair, Ruddy," the commissioner said. "Because I'm going to tell you something that will make you hold onto your seat."

"Yes, sir."

"Here's to friendship among true men," the commissioner said, tilting his glass.

"And here's to the finest officer I ever served under," Ruddy said.

They drank.

"How's the wife, Ruddy?"

"Fine, Commissioner,"

"Ruddy?"

"Yes, sir."

"From this moment on, my name is *Bill*."

Ruddy started; his eyes grew misty. God, what's this?

"Thanks, Bill."

They both rose and shook hands.

"H-how's your family, Bill?" Ruddy asked.

"Wonderful, except my wife, Kitty, is a bit sick," the commissioner said. "Say, I've been hearing some wonderful things about that son of yours. Seems like he's burning up those classrooms at the University of Chicago."

"He's going ahead, Bill," Ruddy said. "I'm so proud of 'im, I'm kind of scared. Didn't think I could have a son like that."

"Be proud of 'im," the commissioner said.

"I want to be worthy of 'im," Ruddy said with a thick voice. Deep down, he wondered why so many were asking about his son these days. He felt a keen pang of guilt for not having seen and appreciated Tommy's great qualities.

"Ruddy?"

"Yes, Bill."

"I want to tell you something that's going to change the whole of your life."

"Yes, Bill."

"From this moment on, you are the Chief of Police of Brentwood Park," the commissioner stated in slow, ponderous tones.

Ruddy's breathing stopped. For a split second, a kind of paralysis went over the whole of his body, then he felt a kind of heat glowing on his skin. Good God! A promotion to the very top! Brentwood was the suburban area in which poor Mo Branden had been police chief until tonight. And already the wheels had turned, and he had been selected to fill the slain chief's shoes. Gratitude flooded him; his eyes not only misted this time; he wept; he felt tears coursing down his cheeks.

"No, Bill," he whispered hoarsely. "I'm not worthy of that. That's not for me. Just let me retire and—"

"If you keep babbling like that, I'm going to get up from here and clip you one hard on your goddamn chin," the commissioner threatened.

"I-I . . . you s-see . . . Bill, I'm colored . . . and I will be the first . . . You s-see. . . ."

"Shut up, dope." Bill soothed Ruddy by placing his arm about his shoulder.

"But I'm not w-worthy of that kind of job or honor," Ruddy protested.

"Are you questioning the wisdom of the community?" Bill asked. "If we say we want you there, then there you go. If we say that you're the man for the job, then you're it."

Ruddy tried to answer, but his lips were twisted.

"All right. Cry it out. I know this is a shock. And I know that this was the last thing on earth you expected," Bill went softly on. "But now, I want you to dry those eyes, get into your new uniform, and start enforcing the law in Brentwood Park. I want a swift and hard cleanup out there. I want this kidnapping wave stopped. I want all this molesting of young children by perverts stamped out. I want housebreaking cleaned up. I want the streets of Brentwood Park so calm that a six-year-old girl can roll her hoop down the main street without fear, singing her little nursery song. I want every hoodlum and pander and crook run out of that area, Ruddy. I want it so that a housewife can go to the grocery store and leave her door unlocked. Can you do that for me, Ruddy?"

Ruddy's lips opened twice before words came. Then he whispered fervently: "Bill, I'll do it for you or die trying."

CHAPTER 3

An hour later, Bill and Ruddy were sitting side by side upon a huge brown leather sofa before which was a table holding the bottle of Scotch and half-filled glasses. The tension and excitement had gone out of Ruddy, and now he was the officer of old—alert, eager, attentive—his hard black eyes staring into the blue mist of cigar smoke, his quick brain grasping the situations which Bill was now swiftly outlining. On the left wall a round clock ticked slowly, its pendulum moving with ponderous grace; on the right wall was a map of Chicago, showing the various wards outlined in bright red. Behind them was a glass case in which were revolvers, machine guns, and shotguns captured from slain gangsters. The commissioner's desk was far in front of them and, to the left of it, was a teletype machine from whose slitted mouth a tape of white narrow paper regurgitated and curled itself in a pile upon the dark, blue-green rug. The whirring noise of the teletype emphasized the quietness of the huge room.

"Ruddy, I want to give you a rundown on Brentwood," Bill began with squinched eyes. Now, the DA's office and the police files are full of the goings on out there, but those files do not tell the whole story and—"

"Oh!" Ruddy exclaimed softly.

"You'll know why later," Bill told him. "The Brentwood crowd is not my kind or your kind. They are rich, with a sprinkling of artists and professionals: bank presidents, plant managers, corporation heads, newspaper owners, some politicians, and a lot of social register fools. For the most part, they do as they like in their big houses surrounded by their servants. There are a lot of children out there; I'll come to that later. The rich can afford a lot. But the children out there are more in visible evidence than in a Chicago ward. They run wild. But, as I said, I'll get to that later.

"Ruddy, those folks are powerful. All of their brushes with the law are not contained in the official records. That's the way they want it. They don't want their daughters' misdeeds written down in black and white to be used against them later. And when a rich son out there gets in trouble, there's a million dollars to help him get out of it. So, officially, Brentwood is one of the nicer areas in America—spotless, clean, ranking high in all the vital statistics. But there is another and unwritten record about Brentwood, and that record is in our heads. We police officials remember what they do not wish us to write down. And, for the most part, police officials respect their wishes. And why not? Those people can make you or break you."

"But, Bill, why do you want me to go there?" Ruddy asked with deep concern. "I've got six strikes against me. I'm new, colored, unknown . . ."

"That's just why I'm insisting that you go there," Bill said emphatically. "Look, Branden was married into that crowd. He was a good officer. Don't overlook that. But he was too close to them. I don't think Branden ever did anything wrong, except maybe now and then he closed his eyes to something he ought to have looked straight at. It's hard to move against your friends or to see them objectively. That was Branden's trouble. It was not all of his making, but now that I've a chance to change all that, I'm doing it—in the interests of society—in the interests of those people out there.

"Ruddy, when a rich man's in trouble, he comes running to the law, demanding help, action," Bill outlined. "But when *he* breaks the law, he will stare you right in the eye and dare you to touch 'im, reminding you that he can hurt you. Most times, that trick works. The law is made for everybody, and the whites and the blacks, the poor and the rich, native-born and foreign-born ought to observe it. That's my view, Ruddy."

"That's mine, too, Bill," Ruddy concurred.

"And that's why you're going to Brentwood." Bill underscored his determination.

"What are they bothered with out there—housebreaking?" Ruddy asked.

"That's the question of a good officer," Bill approved. "And housebreaking is what you'll see written in the official reports. But housebreaking is not what is wrong in Brentwood. Look, most of the housebreaking out there comes from aggrieved servants who are no longer in their employ. We've established that. They know where the valuables are, and they sneak back at night and get them. But we trace almost all of that stuff. That's kid's play. They can't sell the stuff without our putting our fingers on it, and once the stuff is spotted, the nabbing of the thief is not far off.

"Strangely, the turnover in servants out there is heavy," Bill went on. "Why that is, I really don't know. But our questioning of their maids and cooks and butlers makes me feel that the servants feel out of place out there. In the last six months, there were eighteen cases of housemaid pregnancy—eighteen were reported. How many really took place and did not come to us, we'll never know."

Ruddy whistled. "Rape?" he asked.

"Ruddy, when a rich man does something, it's done in a manner different from what a poor man would do," Bill recited. "There's liquor, presents, parties—too much of everything. Wives sleeping around with everybody. Is it any wonder that the husband or son gets the notion of tumbling the maids? A dress, a ring, a twenty-dollar bill, plus a bit of alcohol, and a maid is in bed with her clothes on, not quite knowing what is really happening to her. We can't call it rape. It's just delinquency. Ruddy, I call it crime.

"But that's not what is really wrong out there," Bill said, twisting down his lips. "If it were, I wouldn't be wasting time talking about it. The big crime in Brentwood is the sexual violation of children—"

"*What?*"

"You heard me," Bill snapped.

"But I thought that that took place mainly among poor folks, sleeping six in a room," Ruddy breathed.

"No—it takes place in families where there are five people sleeping in sixteen rooms too." Bill's voice was rasping and cynical.

"Jesus Christ," Ruddy sighed.

"You can say that again," Bill agreed.

"No leads on the perverts?"

"Plenty."

"Aw . . . Influence. Protection. Higher-ups."

"Right."

"Did this have anything to do with Branden's being slain?"

"No. It didn't. Branden's death was a revenge slaying," Bill explained. "Ruddy, the police chief who wouldn't haul in the guilty rich was killed by a guilty poor man. I don't say that that's justice, but it happened."

"Bill?" Ruddy's voice called out insistently, though he was staring at the ceiling.

"Yeah?"

"I ain't no fancy cop," Ruddy rumbled angrily. "If a man's guilty, I grab 'im, no matter what. Will the department stand by me?"

"Not only the department but the DA's office will back you up," Bill assured him. "Ruddy, I wouldn't be talking to you here tonight if I didn't know you were square straight. Now, don't go and get poor Branden wrong. He was straight, but he went blind, so to speak. You can't be with the law and have friends whom you admire who break the law. Those things can't mix. Branden loved the big, rich boys and felt sorry for 'em when they went wrong. And when they spent big money to hide their crimes, Branden wouldn't insult 'em by insisting upon looking too hard at 'em. He was going to run for country sheriff, and then he was going to try for the mayoralty."

"Wheew," Ruddy whistled. Then he rolled his hard, brown eyes at Bill. "There's a ceiling on my ambitions."

"There's a ceiling on every honest man's ambitions," Bill amended Ruddy's statement. "Ruddy, I came from as far down as you. I'm Micky Irish. My people were more than dirt-poor. They had lice on 'em. I had 'em once too. But I'm clean now, and I'm clean in more ways than one."

"Spill a little more on this child-violation stuff," Ruddy asked softly.

"Most of the records on that are in my head," Bill said. "When a rich man's daughter is molested sexually, he wants it kept under cover. He doesn't want his property soiled in the public eye, get it? Now let me start backward. Last month two girls, ages six and eight, were raped in Brentwood. We know that from hospital reports."

"Any leads?"

"Two general leads," Bill stated. "We know the boy who violated one child. And we know the girl who violated the—"

"A girl?"

"Lesbian."

"That place is rotten," Ruddy growled.

"Straight through to the core," Bill affirmed. "We've got a good notion as to who the boy is and also the gal. But—"

"But what?"

"Ruddy, it'll take a million dollars a piece to convict 'em," Bill said sadly. "They paint pictures of all kinds of neuroses and complexes, and they'll end up by making the world feel sorry for the poor rich boys and girls."

"If the courts are powerless, what can I do?" Ruddy wanted to know.

"You can harass 'em," Bill jerked out. "You can let 'em know that they are corrupting youth. You can make 'em feel wrong. By God, you can educate the public with 'em. The press'll be behind you—that is, in the main. The common people are with you. You want to try it?"

"Bill, I've nothing to lose," Ruddy said, smiling bitterly. "I thought I was going to retire in a few months and pal around with that boy genius of mine. But I can't shrink from this. Bill, I'm a bulldog cop. If you say, 'Sic 'em,' then I'm going after 'em."

Bill stood and clapped Ruddy on the right shoulder. "Good."

Bill went to his desk and flicked a button and spoke into the office intercommunication system. "Mary Jane, tell Watkins, that corporation lawyer Jacobs, and those two witnesses to come in here. I'm swearing Ruddy in right now."

Ruddy heard Mary Jane's voice coming with metallic musicality: "The press is here, Mr. King."

"Tell 'em to go to hell," Bill snapped. "I'll talk to 'em to-morrow afternoon. I'm confronting the entire city with a *fait accompli.*"

Ruddy stood facing Bill and they were both silent for a moment.

"Nobody has ever trusted me this much before, Bill."

"I'm trusting you as though you were my own son," Bill said with a sigh.

Ruddy's old tension was now reborn in him, that tension that had dogged his footsteps when he had been a rookie. But there was a difference now; that tension was modified. He was no longer a lone colored man with a gun but a well-known and respected one who was being given a mandate to enforce the law among the lawless. Yet he had never regarded the men of wealth and power as being lawless. What Bill had told him had stunned him, not so much for its revelation of moral turpitude but for the seeming guiltlessness of the people whom he would rule, or, to put it another way, for their apparent guiltiness. It all depended on how he looked at them and felt about them. Did he feel identified with the lawless people of Brentwood Park? No. But there slumbered deep in him a sneaking kind of admiration for their strength; he had the feeling that they were somehow right in doing what they did, even if their deeds were against the law. Yes, Branden had no doubt felt that way, and he had agreed with Bill in condemning Branden's blind wayward-ness. Yet those people—were they not merely feeling and having their way in an objective manner while he, Ruddy, had had his guilty way years before in a subjective manner? If that was true, why was he being called upon to condemn them? Ruddy had never thought of this before, and had it not been for his pending induction into a new job, he would never have dreamed of it. There was no doubt that there was an attractive and alluring image in the actions of rich people who did as they liked. Did not everybody want to do that? Was freedom to be denied only to the poor or only to the frightened poor? For Ruddy, a policeman, knew quite well that there were many poor people who had and were taking their way with blazing guns. It seemed that only at the two extremes of society, the very top and the very bottom, could there be seen or felt any real freedom. What was freedom then? And what was law?

Ruddy was a policeman because he was a man who had once loved freedom so hotly that he had become guilty in the pores of his being by dreaming illicitly of freedom, and his becoming a policeman had been a manner in which he had escaped being cast into an ocean of guilty emotion. He had eased the burden of guilt he carried by seeing and trapping it in others; he had earned the right to live with himself by being able to handle the guilt that seethed in him in an objective manner in the lives of others. Now he was being called upon to check and put down that freedom in others that he had once yearned to have. Did he at heart merely regard the poor and weak as being guilty—as being guilty because they were poor and weak? And did he really feel an admiration for the strong because they could be free with impunity? The clock on the wall ticked loudly in the quiet room and beads of sweat, tiny and glistening, oozed out upon Ruddy's bronzed brow.

"Don't worry, Ruddy," Bill said, moving nervously about. "It's not my aim to give you time to reflect."

They grinned at each other. What would Tommy think? And Agnes? Their lives would be different now. And the pledge that he had given them that he would have plenty of time for them after his retirement would have to be withdrawn. Never would he be so busy as he would be now. He would be facing the supreme test of his life, and he would give a strict account of himself, of his office, of his duties, of his zeal. But those rich whites? How would he face them? Would they, too, try to get next to him? And he a black man? He smiled wryly. If they wanted to continue to carry on their mischief, they would certainly try to do that. Yes, that was why Bill was pushing him into this job. His smile grew.

"You see what I'm doing?" Bill asked.

"I see it all," Ruddy murmured.

"A good idea, hunh?"

"I must say it is, Bill. It's just like you."

"Depend on me to fuck 'em good, Ruddy," Bill snarled.

Ruddy felt a flash of power surge through him as he recalled that he had been thinking all along in terms of his facing them as one individual. No—he would have a staff.

"Bill?"

"Yeah. Speak what's on your mind. In a few moments it'll be too late."

"I have some police administration experience," Ruddy spoke slowly.

"I know it."

"The responsible work of a staff of policemen is done by a small hard-driving nucleus," Ruddy spelled it out.

"Right."

"I want the right to name the men directly under me."

"You're cooking with gas. Name 'em and they're yours. I'll list them right now," Bill said, lifting an ornate ink pen and poising it over a clean sheet of paper.

"Jock Weidman."

"One of the soundest officers on the force. He knows the work from A to Z, despite the fact that his personal life is a mess," Bill murmured, writing. "Who else?"

"Ed Seigel."

"A good man," Bill murmured. "An all-round man. A little cracked on ideas, maybe. But you might find him useful out there among all those rich eggheads. Okay. Who else?"

"Captain Drake, for protocol and general work," Ruddy said.

"Damn good. Go on."

"Wade Williams, as my bulldog," Ruddy said.

"He's as stubborn as black paint," Bill sang as he wrote. "Go on."

"You're going to object," Ruddy warned.

"No."

"Mary Jane Woodford, as the boss of the office," Ruddy boomed fearlessly.

Bill lifted his head and stared at Ruddy. He bit his lips then.

"That's all I need as a core of a team," Ruddy stated.

"Okay, boy. You can have 'em. Sorry to part with Mary Jane. She knows more about police work than I do," Bill said with a sigh. "You've just picked the cream of our police force."

"That's what I'll need." Ruddy was definite.

"When the mayor sees who's helping you, it will help him to defend what I'm doing," Bill said with a grin.

"I know what you mean," Ruddy sympathized warmly.

"I'm not scared," Bill let out.

"Nobody ever said that Bill Joseph King was a scared man," Ruddy stated with calm judgment.

The buzzer sounded. Bill picked up the receiver of the intercom: "Yes?"

"They're here," Mary Jane said.

"Send 'em in. What're you waiting on? And *you* come in too, Mary Jane," Bill instructed.

"*Me?*"

"Yes. I'm changing your life, too, tonight," Bill said, then slammed the receiver on the hook. He rose, opened a drawer and took out a big black Bible, and laid it upon his desk just as the door opened.

Watkins entered first, grinning, his arms stretched wide.

"I'm presuming that everything's working," he said, pausing, glancing at the commissioner, who nodded, and then embracing Ruddy.

"Something big's happening to you tonight," Watkins sang.

"Thanks, Mr. Watkins," Ruddy said with a choked voice and eyes clouded with emotion.

"I'm Hymie Jacobs." A short, plump man with white hair introduced himself to Ruddy, extending his hand. "I'll congratulate you after I've sworn you in."

Two other men, both of whom Ruddy knew by sight and name, followed into the room. Mary Jane, her eyes baffled, came in last.

"Ruddy, you know Johnny Welch." Bill made the presentations perfunctorily. "And Dick Donovan. Johnny's been my assistant for well-nigh ten years. And Dick's the head of the plainclothes squad and is our liaison with the DA's office." Bill took Ruddy's left hand and placed it on the Bible and then turned to Hymie Jacobs, lifting his eyebrows.

"Will you raise your right hand?" Hymie Jacobs asked Ruddy.

Ruddy complied silently, his temples throbbing.

"Rudolph Turner, do you solemnly swear that you will discharge the duties of the office of Chief of Police of Brentwood, Illinois, and that you will defend and protect the Constitution of the State of Illinois, and that you will, without mental evasions or reservations, defend and protect the Constitution of the United States of America, against all enemies, both foreign and domestic, to the best of your ability, so help you God?"

Ruddy took a deep breath and said, "I do."

A sigh went around the room. Bill came forward with his

right fist clenched, then extended it and clapped into Ruddy's right hand a golden star.

"Good luck, Chief," Bill said.

"I owe you a debt that I feel I can never pay," Ruddy sighed.

"Forget it," Bill said.

"Congratulations," Jacobs said, shaking Ruddy's hand again.

There were congratulations all around, including those of Mary Jane, whose eyes were round and moist.

"Mary Jane," Bill began, "from tonight on, you are the chief clerk in the office of the Chief of Police of Brentwood."

Mary Jane's blue eyes widened. "Oh," she exclaimed, staring at Ruddy.

"And here's the list of Ruddy's private staff, who will flank him all the way," Bill said.

"Jesus, everything happens," Mary Jane murmured. "I don't deserve this promotion."

"It's no promotion," Ruddy said. "You're just hired. And you'll work until your tail drags."

"I'll *work* for you," Mary Jane declared fervently. She stared around the room with open lips.

"I don't want to be rude," Bill said. "But now that the formalities are over, Ruddy and I have a lot to talk about in a short space of time."

There was an aimless milling around, more congratulations, and then the swearing-in personnel, including Mary Jane, retreated, leaving Bill and Ruddy alone once more.

"Sit down," Bill said. "I want to show you something."

"Sure," Ruddy said.

Bill extracted from a drawer a large dossier, then sat beside Ruddy again.

"I want to show you some of the horrors of Brentwood," Bill said in a faraway voice.

CHAPTER 4

Ever since its incorporation as an independent municipality, Brentwood Park has been in trouble. It was conceived in corruption; the aim was to avoid and evade city taxes. Had the men who had this idea in mind not been rich, the charter would not have been granted. But our state legislature could not refuse the requests of bankers, brokers, and industrialists. Though the rich sheltered and protected Brentwood, the first house that was erected there turned out to be a hideout for Blacksnake McClusky, the famous bank robber. How he wriggled that, we never learned. The real estate men who sold him the plot swore that they did not know his identity, and it is useless now to probe into that. We got Blacksnake McClusky—shot 'im down in Dallas . . . but he was the first rotten apple in the Brentwood Park barrel.

"You might wonder why the lawbreakers permitted a crook like that to live next to them. Well, Ruddy, it was gambling. And where there's gambling, as you well know, there's always easy money. And then there was Prohibition. Illicit liquor and gambling formed the basis of entertainment life for the rich men who worked all day in the Chicago offices.

"Add to this the ideas of rich boys and girls who spend their time in university classrooms, commuting to and fro in high-powered sports cars. Of course, there was swimming, tennis, dancing, and all-night parties. That was natural. At first all of this took place in restricted clubs, but as time went on, everybody in the whole area, regardless of age or sex, was welcomed. It was then that trouble started. That was in the twenties. Then you had all kinds of wild ideas in the air. Sexual experimentation. Communism. Ether parties. Booze. 'Advanced ideas'—whatever that is. And all kinds of foreign notions about life's not being worth anything unless you could wring your share of experience out of it.

"The first semi-criminal death occurred among a group of students. You recall the Kennedy case? Three students decided to commit the perfect crime. One actually offered himself as the guinea pig and helped plan his own murder so that the police would never find out."

"Yeah. I remember that case," Ruddy drawled.

"Now, the odd part of that was this: Charles Kennedy, the murderee—if you'll permit my calling him that, for he did offer himself as a victim—thought that he would somehow be alive after they had killed him and would enjoy the bafflement of the police in trying to solve their perfect crime. We proved that John Davis and Harris Potts, the murderers, had no such beliefs and that they knew that Kennedy was mentally off, so they took him and killed him in a manner that did actually baffle us for a while. It was only because Davis and Potts seemed too anxious to help the police that we finally suspected that they had a hand in it. The moment we touched 'em, they confessed.

"How did you try a case like that? Nobody could make head or tail of it. The defense contended that there had been no murder, for the murdered man aided in his own death! Had actually asked that he be killed! But the state and the court ruled that he had been murdered, even if he had asked to be murdered, and the men who had carried out Kennedy's crazy instructions were murderers. But when the defense got through describing the mental and emotional state of those boys, the jury declared them guilty of manslaughter. The judge sentenced them ten years each; they were transferred to insane asylums for treatment. Five years later they were declared sane and now they are out—in Europe.

"The Kennedy case set the frame for the style of crime in Brentwood Park for the next two decades. As I told you before, housebreaking, forgery, stickups, etc., were never very prominent there. The crimes committed had a 'family' air about them. Get what I mean, Ruddy?"

"You sound a bit like old Ed now," Ruddy chided Bill.

"And that was why I so heartily approved your selection of Ed to your staff," Bill went on. "Truth to tell, maybe Ed could give you a better rundown on all this than I can. If there was ever a locale where emotional factors rather than pure greed figured in crime, it is in Brentwood Park. There are no poor folks in Brentwood, and therefore no so-called class struggle. The divorce rate is high, yet they have a lot of children. One wiseacre said that married couples in Brentwood were swapping husbands and wives about. Well, he forgot the children; what he should have said was that they were swapping the children about, and that makes for emotional troubles—or so the social workers tell us.

"Though Brentwood Park's been messy, from a policeman's point of view, we had more or less kept track of all their crazy doings until about a year ago," Bill went on. "Then a crime wave struck the place, and we've never been able to figure it out. You recall the kidnapping of Roberta Southern?"

"Sure."

"That was never solved. The child was found dead—like they always are. We still suspect that that was an inside job, for the ones who did it got cold feet and never did try to get the ransom, even when it had been left for 'em.

"The next 'snatching' was plainly a professional job," Bill recited. "We knew it the moment we entered the case. It was done in a workman-like manner and we anticipated every move. The ransom letter came; the money was picked up; the body of the stockbroker, Symons Jordan, was found dead—just as we expected. But he was killed to prevent identification, we suspected. And he was. We traced the ransom bills and finally caught up with the couple who pulled that job. They were executed.

"You see, no doubt the Roberta Southern idea was proving contagious. But it took professionals to carry the crime to its conclusion," Bill analyzed. "Now come three crimes, the last ones committed, for which we do not have a single clue. I don't believe in perfect crimes. Yet so far we seem to have three on our hands, and Branden professed himself completely stumped. This time all indications point to its being a Brentwood job, or the crimes were committed by somebody who knew Brentwood well.

"Last March a Protestant clergyman, Ernie Hindricks, was killed. Try as we might, we could not scrape up one iota of a motive for that murder. Hindricks had no enemies. Even the Catholics in the area admired and emulated his tolerance. This is one of the cases we need you to focus on."

"I recall the case," Ruddy said, frowning. "It was followed shortly afterward by the murder of Father Byrnes—"

"And not a single clue," Bill asked. "We want you to concentrate on these cases we cannot afford to close—and another one as well."

"What's the population ratio out there, in terms of Catholics and Protestants?" Ruddy asked.

"About equal, give and take a bit," Bill said. "We exhausted that angle, and it led us nowhere. As in the case of Hindricks no hint of a motive, as we know and understand them. We combed the political radical groups and could get nothing. Stools were sent into that Brentwood area on all levels and could get absolutely nothing. Rewards were offered but to no avail. Father Byrnes was killed in June. Three months lapsed between the two killings. We waited. There seemed to be a kinship between the two murders, and if so, we could expect a third one. We tried to speculate upon whom would fall the next blow. Since two men of the cloth had been done in, we wondered if the killer would not next choose a man who had donated much money to both religious causes in terms of aiding their charities. But nothing happened in that direction. It was as though the murderer was watching us, following our line of reasoning. Then, in October, he struck again—at the son of one of the detectives investigating the two crimes. That baffled the hell out of us.

"You would have thought that it would have been the detective himself who would have been the target," Bill argued. "And when the news came in, we actually construed that such had happened, and it was only hours later that Detective Heard called us himself and said that it was his son, and not he, who was the victim."

"Do you think that they could have been trying to scare Heard away, that the murderers felt that he was getting warm?" Ruddy asked.

"We thought that once," Bill said sadly. "But Heard said no. He had no notion as to who could have done it, and had anybody thought he was 'warm,' they would have gotten him, not his son. We went into Charles Heard Jr.'s death—he was shot with a .38—as we've never gone into the killing of anybody and we got nothing."

"But you feel that the three crimes were linked, maybe committed by the same person or persons?" Ruddy asked.

"Exactly," Bill admitted. "But that is only a hunch, an intuitive guess."

"It's mine too," Ruddy said.

"Now, the psychologists are arguing that this is a new kind of murder," Bill said, with a rising inflection of voice, an inflection that showed irritation. "I don't know what they mean; I don't understand 'em. They contend that the motives in these three crimes are extraordinary. Maybe they are. But a murdered man is a dead man, and that started with Abel."

"What kind of motives did they dope out?" Ruddy wanted to know.

"Well, as close as I could understand 'em," Bill related, "they felt that these crimes were semiphilosophical."

"Bullshit," Ruddy spat.

"Right. But in the absence of anything else, we had to go on that," Bill complained.

"What kind of so-called philosophy did they talk about?" Ruddy demanded, wrinkling his brow.

"Well, they claimed that the murderer was killing because he had never killed—"

"Jesus Christ!"

"That was the theory," Bill affirmed. "They further contended that he was to be found right in Brentwood—"

"That's possible," Ruddy said. "But what about the killing of Heard's son? Did they say that was because the killer had never killed? Why he had killed two men before that."

"Well, about that they had an even crazier idea," Bill reported. "The psychoanalysts contended that the man who killed Heard's son did so because he wanted to be caught for the other crimes."

"Brother, deliver me from those screwballs," Ruddy railed.

"Ruddy," Bill said, rising and flipping the dossier toward him, "those three killings are your first task. See what you can unearth about 'em. I don't say that it'll be easy, but your coming in from the outside might give you a new slant on 'em. The machine that Branden has set up out there ought to be able to take care of the run-of-the-mill stuff. So you are free to go after the big fish."

"You mean the whales," Ruddy said.

"Of course, when you catch this whale, you'll find that he is a guy five feet tall, with a tendency to blushing and sweaty palms. And, above all, he will have sent beautiful cards to his mother on Mother's Day."

"And he's going to expect that we kiss him and forgive him." Ruddy sneered.

"I'll forgive 'im," Bill wailed. "I've give 'em twenty thousand hot volt right up his rear end."

"Make it forty—the extra twenty's from me," Ruddy said. He stood and looked off. "I'd like to phone home, Bill."

"I was expecting that." Bill smiled. "Tell Agnes the big news." He strode from the office, whistling under his breath.

CHAPTER 5

Dawn was breaking when Ruddy emerged from police headquarters. He bought a copy of the *Chicago Tribune* and saw his picture on the front page; he balled the paper into his fist and frowned. He did not wish to know what the press said; he had a job to do. Though he had promised Agnes over the phone that he was coming right home and would explain everything to her, he now was bitten by another idea. He commandeered a detective squad car and ordered that he be driven through the Brentwood Park area. He wanted a glimpse of the domain that he was to rule in the name of the law.

He was alone in the car with a police chauffeur. The car was unmarked, and he sat up front where he could get a good look at this fashionable area.

The chauffeur grinned and weighed Ruddy out of the corners of his eyes. "Glad to have the honor of driving the new chief out to his area."

"Thanks, fellow."

"Looks like you're taking over screwball land," the driver said.

"Is that what they call it?"

"That's it."

"To tell you the truth, I can't make head or tail from what I've heard about the place," Ruddy confessed.

"Nobody can understand that Brentwood Park area," the driver said. "Any particular place you want to go, Chief?"

"Just drive around, then go to the top of Andeley Hill and let me get a good look at the whole joint."

"Right, Chief."

They entered the shopping center, bustling with super-markets, drugstores, three big department stores, sports stores, hardware and clothing stores, and movie houses. At the main intersection two big banks, the First National and the Brent-wood Park Trust, faced each other. Northward was the dark bulk of the pine-covered Andeley Hill and southward stretched the main boulevard, flanking the wide sweep of gleaming lake sand. Eastward rose the section of immense private dwellings where the main body of the rich people of Brentwood Park lived. To the southwest were tall gleaming apartment build-ings, sparkling in the early morning sun, rising ten, fifteen, and some even twenty stories into the cloudless blue sky. To the northwest were sundry scattered dwellings belonging to civil servants, doctors, and skilled and domestic workers. Opposite the railroad station stood the post office in an inconvenient lo-cation that had been the subject of many bitter local editorials. Toward the beach were side streets filled with cafés, restaurants, bars, laundries, amusement arcades, etc.

"An artificial town," Ruddy commented.

"An easy money town," the driver said.

"What's the population here now?" Ruddy asked.

"One hundred and thirty thousand when I last heard," the driver answered.

"Wheew," Ruddy whistled. "That many? What a jump. I would've said about ninety."

"Most of 'em are up in those apartment hotels and buildings," the driver explained. "They tell me the poor people around here complain that there's nothing for 'em to do when they quit working."

"There're plenty of bars," Ruddy pointed out.

"Too high for 'em," the driver said. "How can a maid shell out two dollars for a sniff of Scotch?"

"They've got it all planned," Ruddy commented, thinking of how such tactics had long been used against the people of his own race to keep them out of certain restricted business establishments.

"Look, Chief! See that Piper Cub?" the driver said, pointing to a plane zooming low over the town.

"Looks like it is going to land," Ruddy observed.

"That's right, Chief. The landing field is atop that hill."

"Let's get up there," Ruddy ordered.

"Right, Chief."

The oar turned and made down a wide side street and then followed a rising curve. At once tall pine trees flanked both sides of the road and the air felt cool. Ruddy saw many footpaths leading off the roadway into the dark denseness of the pines, some of which were even large enough to admit cars.

"Lovers' lanes, eh?"

"Yes, sir. I expect that's what they call 'em," the driver said. "But you know, sir, most of the crimes committed around here were never staged in the forest."

"They took place in the hotels and private homes, eh?"

"Yes, sir."

"Millionaires don't want to get their feet muddy," Ruddy grumbled.

The trees grew darker and denser as the car mounted the narrow asphalt road, and even flecks of fog began to form on the windshield. Ruddy saw a few people wandering amid the paths in the forest, and he saw that they were well dressed.

"This town was built to give people an excuse to spend money," Ruddy stated. "There's nothing here they could not get in any other small town."

"That's right, sir," the driver said. "But that's our country. We've got to find a way to spend our money and keep busy. At the first sign of a depression, the people will start flocking out of here as though there was a smallpox epidemic."

"Right," Ruddy sighed.

Yes, Ruddy felt that he was on alien ground; this was no Black Belt, Irish shantytown, no Little Paris filled with jabbering Frenchmen, no make-believe Berlin choked with Germans; this was native-born America, rich, proud, free. Could he ever understand these people? At once the image of his Tommy flashed into his mind. Yes, Tommy would and could help him here. Not that he would ask Tommy to work on the force; no—he would ask Tommy questions about this place, for the studying of such areas was Tommy's main interest in life. Aw, maybe my boy will be close to me, after all, he thought with pride.

"One more turn and we'll be at the top," the driver said.

Three minutes later they were rolling along a road that gave a vast sweep of Brentwood Park far below.

"Stop here, fellow," Ruddy ordered.

"Yes, sir."

Ruddy alighted and lit a cigarette, offered one to the driver, who accepted eagerly. Puffing, Ruddy stared down at the long strip of houses, sand, apartment hotels, and streets. Far out, the bosom of Lake Michigan gleamed and sparkled.

"Well, the main approaches are from the north and south," Ruddy observed. "Anybody wanting to make a quick getaway would not come up here. The roads are too narrow. Of course, somebody might hide out in that forest for a time. But big-time crooks would get away by the highways, the lake, or that airfield over there."

"Looks like the highways would be the thing," the driver said.

"Of course, somebody on foot could come over this hill," Ruddy said. "But I'd rule out bank robbers, kidnappers, and gangsters using these hill roads. That leaves the highways and the lake and the airfield."

"Well, not much doing on that lake since rum-running days," the driver said.

"Right. And I don't see anybody pulling something and flying off in a Piper Cub," Ruddy said. "They couldn't get far. And the noise of the motor would be heard. And I'm sure each plane there is accounted for."

"That's right, sir."

"So whatever happens here is mostly bound to take place with all the players living right down there, barring an occasional joker creeping over this hill at night," Ruddy said.

"That simplifies it." The driver grinned.

"And makes it more complicated," Ruddy growled. "Those goddamn inside jobs are a headache. Everybody seems guilty, and everybody swears they are innocent, and everybody calls on everybody else for an alibi. Well, goddamnit, we'll see. Let's get back down, fellow."

"Right, Chief. Where to?"

"Take me home. 9890 Elm Street."

"Okay, Chief."

CHAPTER 6

Ruddy rang his doorbell and waited for Agnes or Tommy to answer. When no movement or sound came from within the house, he let himself into the front hallway with his latchkey.

"Agnes!" he called.

His voice echoed hollowly and there was silence. He took the steps four at a time, calling "Agnes! Tommy!"

He halted amid silence in the upper hallway. Agnes's door was open. He whirled to Tommy's door; it also stood ajar. Where in hell were they? Then his ears caught a strange sound. "Static! My radio's on . . ." He descended the stairs and went into what he was wont to call his den, and there the radio crackled, emitting no voice of music. He scanned the room and finally spied what he knew he would find—a note. He snatched it up and read:

Darling:
We got the news on the radio. Tommy and I are off to look at Brentwood Park. We'll see you for lunch! How awfully excit-ing it all is! Incidentally, Tommy is soaring up into the air,

for he specialized in the social stratification of the Brentwood
Park area last year! Imagine! He's just dying to talk to you!
Darling, congratulations and tons and tons of kisses. There's
so much to talk about.

Yours,
Agnes

So they were gone. Hell, you'd think that they had been appointed Chief of Police of Brentwood Park. They're taking over my own job. He sighed, folded the note, and put it into his pocket, then changed his mind and laid it on his desk. He clicked off the radio and slumped into an armchair. Well, wonders never cease . . . *he was a chief of police!* How did chiefs of police feel? He did not know. But he was one and he ought to know. "How do I feel?" he asked himself out loud. "Well, I feel tired, and just like I felt yesterday morning. Only I'm sleepy." He poured himself a jigger of whiskey and downed it. He'd be getting his pension and also a chief of police's pay. He'd be on easy street, money-wise. Okay. That's settled.

The phone shrilled. Agnes, no doubt. He picked up the receiver.

"Chief Turner . . . Is he there?"

He swallowed and answered: "Chief Turner speaking."

"Chief Turner, this is Captain Snell speaking. I've been the acting Chief of Police until I was notified a few moments ago that you'd been sworn in," the voice rumbled. "First of all, Chief Turner, my warmest congratulations!"

"Thanks a lot. That's kind of you, Captain."

"Look here. I heard from Commissioner King that you were planning to plunge right into things," Captain Snell said. "Shall we send a car for you? Is there anything we can help you do?"

"No. Look, thanks a lot. I was planning on taking nap and dropping over tonight and—"

"I could come by later and give you a rundown on everything," Captain Snell offered.

"Say, that's not a bad idea," Ruddy agreed, accepting. "It would help me to know what's what when I get there."

"That's the idea, sir," Captain Snell said. "You name the hour."

"What about three o'clock?"

"Fine."

"I'll be seeing you, Chief. If you want to contact me, I'm right here on tap."

"Are there any urgent problems pending, Captain?"

"Nothing that won't keep."

"Right."

As soon as he hung up he heard Agnes's and Tommy's voices calling from the downstairs hallway: "Ruddy!" "Dad!"

He rushed to meet them, hugged them both at once.

"Wow!" Tommy said, jumping up and down.

"Darling, darling," Agnes murmured, kissing him clingingly.

"Okay, okay, give me some air, folks." He chortled, edging away and waving his hands.

"This is tops for you, darling!" Agnes screamed, her face radiant.

"Dad, I don't want to sound like a know-it-all," Tommy yelled. "But, tell me, do you know what a chief of police is?"

"No, son. You tell me," Ruddy said.

"You are going to be a Little Caesar in that Brentwood Park police station. Your discretion is almost unlimited. Gee, nothing like this ever happened to us before. Hot diggity dog!"

Ruddy doubled his fist and nudged it tenderly under Tommy's chin.

"Take it easy, boy. You know I'm no Hitler!" He grew serious. "Folks, come in and sit down. We've got to hold a family council."

"Goody, goody," Agnes crooned, dancing into Ruddy's den.

"Dad, I got a million questions to ask," Tommy announced.

"And I've got a million questions to ask you," Ruddy said, grinning, pushing Tommy into a chair.

"Darling," Agnes asked, "did you expect this? Had you any notion when that Mary Jane called this morning?"

"I knew nothing," Ruddy said, sitting. "To tell you the truth, I thought I was being called on the carpet about something. I didn't care, really, though. I thought my record'd save me."

"But what *happened?*" Agnes demanded.

"I'll get to it," Ruddy soothed her. "Let me tell it my way. You see, what happened was this: Branden was killed . . . and—"

"We heard that," Tommy and Agnes chimed together.

"Well, Commissioner King really tricked me," he admitted. "He was making me accept it before I knew it. I knew nothing when I got to headquarters." He leaned forward in his seat and smiled at his wife and son. "I hope you're not angry. I—"

"You're crazy," Agnes sang.

"Dad. *Dad*! Chief," Tommy murmured.

"Thanks, folks," Ruddy sighed. "The board of directors votes me a dividend—"

"And elects you chief," Agnes said, smiling mistily.

"Now, I got to work," Ruddy said. "Look, I—"

"Let's leave your father, Tommy," Agnes began.

"No, no!" Ruddy checked their standing up. "For once, my work starts in my family." He paused and stared at Tommy. "My first conference as Chief of Police of Brentwood Park is now coming to order. Tommy, they tell me that you studied that region last year and—"

"I'm still studying it, Dad," Tommy declared, looking at the floor.

"Oh! I see," Ruddy said. He laughed. "They'd call it graft if I put you on my payroll. But I must ask you some things. For instance . . . what the hell's happening in Brentwood Park?"

Tommy stared at his father, bit his lips, and then rose again and walked the floor.

"I don't want to sound off," he said, obviously trying to control himself. "Maybe you'll think I'm crazy. 'What's happening in Brentwood Park?'" He repeated Ruddy's question. "Life, Dad. Life's happening there."

There was a long silence. Agnes glanced from her husband to her son and leaned forward tensely.

"Yeah. Go on. Explain it. I'm waiting," Ruddy said.

"Who can explain life?" Tommy countered.

"Aw, son. Come on. Get down to brass tacks," Ruddy chided him. "I've got to deliver. I can't say that to the commissioner."

"I know that," Tommy agreed. "And that is what makes it so difficult. I'm not trying to dodge. I'm trying to find a way to tell you what's happening so that you can give the higher-ups a hint, a glimpse, see? Now, Detective Heard's son and I went over that joint with a fine-tooth comb—"

"You knew 'im?" Ruddy shot out, a policeman now, even though he was talking to his son, his flesh and blood.

"Yeah, Dad" Tommy grinned. "He was a personal friend of mine."

"I know that," Ruddy said.

"Really? How? Who told you? When?" The questions came tumbling eagerly.

"The commissioner told me," Ruddy said.

"Oh!" Tommy exclaimed and stared off. "How did he know?"

"From Ed Seigel, another detective," Ruddy said.

"Oh! I see."

"Now, how did Heard's son die?"

"How did he die?" Tommy repeated the question. Then he grew solemn and self-conscious. "He was killed—they say."

"Why?"

"I don't know, Dad."

"How well did you know this Heard boy? Charles was his name, wasn't it?"

"Yeah, Dad. I knew 'im well. Very well. We worked together, as I told you."

"But why would anybody want to kill 'im?"

"Gee"—Tommy scratched his head and stared off—"I don't know." Tommy looked at his father, then his mother. Then he broke into a loud and long laugh.

"What're you laughing about?" Ruddy demanded sternly.

"Excuse me, Dad. But you see, in our studies, we don't study such questions."

"What do you study?" Ruddy asked and did not know that he had asked it. His mind was suddenly lost in a region that was alien and frightening to him.

"We . . . w-we s-study about why hasn't he already been killed?" Tommy said stammeringly.

"*What?*" Ruddy echoed.

"What do you mean, Tommy?" Agnes asked, her lips parted.

Tommy sighed, laughed again, and sat down.

"Dad, what I'm going to say to you will sound wild and crazy," Tommy began. "In school we are trying to understand things just as they are. You ask me: 'Why was Charles killed?' And in our studies we asked: 'Why is Charles not being killed?' Sounds crazy, eh? Well, it is simply because you've not heard the question put before. Now, wait—does that mean we are advocating

Charles being killed? No, no. There's more meaning in that question than you think, Dad. The question is: '*What is it that keeps people from killing Charles?*' That takes us into history, into law, into the ideals by which we live." Tommy paused.

Ruddy stared, looked nervously toward the bottle from which he had taken a drink, but did not move.

"Yeah," Ruddy said dryly, "go on."

"Dad, do I make any sense to you?" Tommy asked with eager passion.

"The law that I uphold, that I swore today to uphold, says that you must not kill." Ruddy spoke slowly, heavily. "That's the law I took an oath to keep."

"But who's behind that law?" Tommy asked with breathless passion.

"What? Who's behind it? Hell, it's the law," Ruddy bellowed.

"Okay, okay," Tommy agreed. "But where did it come from?"

"The people made the laws," Ruddy said.

"Sure, sure," Tommy readily agreed. "*But what people?*"

"The American people, you dope!" Ruddy shouted.

"Okay, okay," Tommy murmured, smiling, looking off. "I see what you mean. Look, Dad, this is the first time we've talked about this. That's why I'm going easy, see? Sure, I know the people made the laws. They elected people to represent them, and those people made laws that the people accepted. But how long ago was that? Do the people who now live under those laws believe in them? Was there ever a time in the whole history of the human race when murder was more popular? Was—"

"What in hell are you taking about, son?" Ruddy demanded.

Tommy giggled and sighed. He looked at his father and said, "This is going to be hard. But you're my father and you'll *have* to listen. *I'll make you listen.*"

"*Tommy, shut up! You're crazy!*" Ruddy shouted.

"Tommy, you never told me about this," Agnes stammered.
Tommy rubbed his hand nervously over his mouth.

"Back of law are people," Tommy began, "and back of people
are the beliefs of the people. Those beliefs come down the ages
and most people are unaware of how they come and what they
mean. Even when people stop believing in their beliefs, they still
walk around repeating them but negating them by their actions.
Now, now, take it easy, Dad. I know: we're talking about Brentwood Park. I'm talking about it, too, but in a general and abstract
way. I'll get to those murders later on. Every now and then in history men meet, argue, fight, and finally embalm their so-called
beliefs in great documents. The Bill of Rights. The Rights of
Man. The Magna Carta, and so on. But history rolls on. Slowly
time, usage, progress, saps the meaning of those documents.
And men are unaware of that sapping. Now, when those men
created those documents and forced kings at the point of death
to honor them, those men felt that those documents embodied
not only what they felt deep in their hearts but also what the
universe endorsed. God wanted those documents enacted, those
men felt. Now, the time that sapped the meaning and validity of
those documents was impersonal. No cynic destroyed the meaning of those documents. Gangsters had nothing to do with it.
Thieves did not plot it. Forgers did not tamper with the writing.
Inventions, discoveries, etc., made those documents useless. *But
the people did not know it.* So they went on living by the word of
those documents while they really obeyed the living spirit of their
times. Now, let's get to Brentwood Park. Something happened
over there that runs counter to the laws that you just swore to enforce. Who's breaking those laws? Bad men? Gangsters? Thieves?
NO! The men whose forebears made those laws. Why? Because
they don't really believe in those laws anymore; they don't feel
the need for them. The laws don't serve their interests anymore.

They have outlived the usefulness and meaning of their laws. So that is why I asked: Why should not Charles Heard be killed? I'm not advocating his death. I'm simply calling to your attention that there just does not now exist in this state or nation any real hindrance to the killing of the thousands of Charles Heards. That's my point, Dad."

In the silence that followed, Ruddy sighed, rose, and walked about the room with steps so heavy that he jarred the parquet. He paused, stared at Tommy, whose eyes avoided his, whose lips drew deep and nervously upon a cigarette.

"If I felt like you, I couldn't be a chief of police," Ruddy said.

"Dad, it's going to be hard for you in Brentwood Park," Tommy told him. "It'll not be like enforcing the law in a Black Belt area. There, the folks believe in the law even when they violate it. They do it sneakily, in the dark, sweating and trembling. They know they are doing 'wrong' when they do 'wrong.' But in Brentwood Park the law is violated in the light of day, in the sunshine, with hundreds looking on."

"They're criminals just the same," Ruddy ruled.

"No. They're just folks having a good time," Tommy corrected his father. "They feel no guilt. That's the main thing. It's hard to catch a criminal who has no sense of guilt."

"All I've met so far have felt guilty," Ruddy said uneasily.

"In Brentwood Park you meet some who don't," Tommy said.

"Well, you oughtn't try to discourage your father," Agnes said in a troubled voice.

"He's not bothering me any," Ruddy said too loudly. "Ha, ha! Looks like I'm going to have some help right in my home this time with my police work. Tommy, I'll test out some of your ideas." He rubbed his palms together to indicate an eagerness that he did not feel. "Well, wife, how about some grub? How do you expect a starving man to do a decent job of being a chief of police?"

CHAPTER 7

The late breakfast was filled with laughing chitchat; Ruddy felt sleepy and even the strong black coffee did not help him much. And beneath his hunger and lack of sleep the job he had to do slumbered stirringly.

"Tommy, when did you start visiting the Brentwood area?" he asked, pushing back his chair from the table and lighting a cigarette.

Tommy hesitated and nudged his father in the ribs with his elbow. "Am I a suspect?" he asked, grinning.

"No. I'm wanting to know how well you know the place," Ruddy said.

"Oh, about a year ago," Tommy said, shrugging.

Ruddy's lips opened as if he were about to ask another question, but he remained silent. He yawned.

"I got to lie down and try to sleep," he mumbled.

"Come, darling," Agnes coaxed. "Let me tuck you in."

"What're you doing?" he asked her gruffly. "Trying to baby the chief of police?"

"That's exactly what I'm going to do," Agnes said. "Your poor eyes are heavy with sleep."

"Okay. Lead me to that bed, baby." Ruddy grinned meekly. "See you, Tommy."

"Take it easy, Dad," Tommy called out in a seemingly false voice of joy.

With her arm affectionately entwined about her husband's sturdy waist, Agnes led Ruddy into the bedroom.

"Tired, darling?" she asked in a whisper.

"Yeah. And excited too," he confessed.

"Pull off your clothes and lie down and—"

"Naw. Just my shoes. Captain Snell's coming at four o'clock."

"Want a sleeping pill?"

"No, no. Just a little relaxation."

He slipped off his shoes and eased himself onto the bed; Agnes sat beside him and put her cool, soft palm on his brow.

"What a day," she whispered to him.

"You can say that again," he murmured, eyes closed.

"Are you glad?"

"Yes and no."

"Why no?"

Ruddy was silent for a long time. Agnes moved her hand and stood.

"Sleep."

"No," Ruddy said quickly, opening his eyes and lifting himself up on an elbow. "Say, Agnes, when did Tommy start doing this fieldwork in Brentwood Park for his course in sociology?"

"Oh, I don't know," Agnes said, frowning. "Oh, yes. I think it was at the beginning of February—the beginning of the first semester. I'm sure of it."

"Why? How?" Ruddy asked, the policeman in him forcing him to demand logic from his wife.

"Why? Because it was—"

"Right after that affair he had with that girl, wasn't it?" Ruddy asked excitedly.

"Yes, that was it."

"Agnes."

"Yes."

"What in hell happened with Tommy and that girl? Do you know?"

"No more than what he told me," she said.

"He was engaged to marry her," Ruddy summarized. "And then he broke it off. Or she did. What happened?"

"He wouldn't tell me," Agnes said.

"Goddamn," Ruddy growled. "I don't know that boy of mine. He's my son and I don't know a thing that is happening with him."

"Oh, don't say that, darling," Agnes protested. "You know him as well as I do. Tommy's right here every day and—"

"I don't know 'im!" Ruddy almost shouted.

"No, darling. Don't shout. He'll hear you and—"

"I'm sorry." Ruddy was suddenly contrite. "But don't you see what I mean? He was engaged to marry. Then it's off. And I couldn't get a goddamn word about it out of 'im. Now, tell me, didn't he say something to you? Didn't he tell you anything?"

"Nothing, Ruddy," she said. "I didn't want to press 'im. He was in such a state. I thought I'd make 'im feel worse. A father maybe could get it out of him better than I could."

"I told you he wouldn't talk to me," Ruddy complained. "All I could get out of him was that he didn't want to speak of it. That he was all right. Always he said: 'I'm all right.' I don't like that. Look, think back. That morning he went to buy that marriage license . . . what happpened?"

"Nothing. He went out. Just before he left, he told me confidently that he was going to get the license. He was smiling, eager, excited, and all . . . then he left. Two hours later he came back. He looked green, pale, sick. I was scared. I asked him what was wrong. He said, 'Nothing. But that marriage is off.' That was all. I kept at 'im and he started yelling. 'Leave me alone!' That was all. I touched him. He was as cold as ice. He was sweating. He had had a shock of some kind. There was no doubt about that. And soon after that was when he said that he had quit his field studies in the Black Belt and was working with that Heard boy in Brentwood Park, wasn't it?"

Agnes stared, then started. Then she forced a laugh.

"Good Lord, Ruddy," she exclaimed in a whisper, "you're not linking Tommy's doing that with the murder of that Catholic priest?"

"I didn't say anything about that," Ruddy protested quickly. "I just want to know when he began studying that area, that's all."

"Oh, I thought it was about the girl you wanted to know," Agnes said innocently.

Ruddy gaped. Yes, deep in him there had been stirring a vague thought about *that*. Ruddy had quit his studies in the Black Belt right after his marriage was put off, and it was soon after that he had begun frequenting Brentwood Park.

"If Tommy was studying in that area about that time, then he could tell me a lot about the atmosphere and attitude of the people there," Ruddy said, rationalizing his mood.

"But he knew nothing about that murder or the other one," Agnes said stoutly.

"Yes," Ruddy said. "It is not about those killings I want to ask him but about the population, see?"

"Oh."

"And he knew that Heard boy when he was killed," Ruddy maintained.

"Yes. He told us of it before we read it in the papers," Agnes remembered.

Ruddy felt a desire to ask Agnes if she recalled the exact date and time of his son's speaking of that third crime, but he desisted. No, that would make Agnes feel bad. Goddamn, he was acting too much like a cop about his son. Yes, he would talk to him. But that talk would have to be different from the one he had had a little while ago.

"He's a stranger to me," Ruddy burst out.

"Who?"

"Tommy."

"Oh, no. Don't say that. You sound angry," Agnes chided him.

"But, dammit, a father ought to know his own son—"

"We all have our secret places, places that we don't want others to touch or poke," Agnes said. "Something that hurt him happened with that Marie. I know it. I feel it. And I think the best thing to do is leave it alone."

"But he ought to be able to tell his father," Ruddy contended. "I'm not only his father. I'm his friend."

"But he does not want to talk of it," Agnes insisted. "I know."

"Why doesn't he wish to?"

"I don't know, Ruddy, some people are like that. So one leaves 'em alone. Oh, he's all right. I'm sure he is."

"Maybe." Ruddy sighed.

"Darling, are you really worried about something? About Ruddy?"

"I was planning to pal around with Tommy before this new job came up," Ruddy said. "Now, I seem further from 'im than ever."

"Look, honey, now you and he will have so much more in common—you with this new work of yours," Agnes told him. "Look at it that way."

"Yeah."

"You say you want to get close to 'im," Agnes argued. "Then

rely upon him more. Ask him his opinion. He's very sharp. He'll feel more confidence in himself. I know how young people feel."

"You reckon that'll work?" Ruddy asked.

"I'm sure of it. You'll see."

"You might be right." He sighed.

"I'm glad that you think of him so," Agnes said. "But do be patient. Take time. He's so young and sensitive. He's not self-made like you are. He'll come around. You'll see."

Ruddy stared. Though he had heard his wife, his mind was grappling with something else. Maybe Tommy might have a hunch worth listening to. All the experts had failed. *And Tommy had known Charles Heard intimately!* By God, yes. He would milk Tommy for every iota of information about that murdered boy. His ideas. His habits. Whom he knew. Strange, but the police had questioned Tommy only casually about Charles Heard. Well, hell, he'd reopen the whole damn case. Maybe the information, the clue he sought was right here under his own roof. His skin tingled. That seemed unreal, too odd. Yet an element of irrational danger seemed to breathe upon him, as though he were watching a strange cloud of drifting poison gas, gray in color, seeping toward him, and he could see one whiff of it straying toward him, with the vast, formless mass of it, the rest of it, following.

"I'll see," he said softly.

"You'll try to sleep now?"

"Yes," he lied, stretching out on the bed again.

"I'll see you soon. I'm leaving now. There's chicken for lunch. You'll want to eat again before that captain comes, won't you, darling?"

"Yes," he said vaguely.

She went out and he was still. He lay a moment with closed eyes. Deep down beyond the reach of his conscious mind was a rising storm of feeling, making him restless. No, he could not

sleep. He rose and paced the room in his socked feet. Footsteps
sounded in the backyard, and he peered out to see Bertha, the
maid, hanging up clothes; then there came to his ears the faintly
echoed clang of a pan in the kitchen. Yes, Agnes, giving a hand
to Bertha, was starting lunch. But he was not hungry and the
mere idea of food was repugnant. Thoughtfully, he scratched
his chin, staring into space. Then a third sound floated to his
ears: the tapping of Tommy's typewriter. Yeah, I'm going to
talk to that boy *now*. Yes—that was the decision he had been
trying all along to make. And the split second he had made
it, he felt better, organized, pointed with purpose. He slipped
into his shoes, tied the laces, and went down the hallway. Before Tommy's door he halted, his knuckles lifted to knock. But
ought he? He was on the point of turning back when he caught
a pause in the typing. He rapped. There was a long silence.

"Yeah?" came Tommy's voice, carrying a trace of annoyance.

"It's me, son," he said.

There was another silence, then the door was flung abruptly
open.

"Come in, Dad," Tommy invited carelessly. "I thought you
were sleeping."

"No. Just stretched out a bit," Ruddy said, feeling guilty
and foolish. "Terribly busy?"

"Not *too*," Tommy pouted, then he smiled.

Yeah, he's nervous. Goddamnit, he suspects that I want to
talk to him. And, by God, I will.

"Mind if I sit down and talk a bit?" Ruddy asked.

"No. Oh no. Take a chair, Dad."

"Thanks."

Ruddy took the armchair and stretched out his long legs,
crossing them. Suddenly he felt the gun pressing almost pain-
fully against his right hip.

"Hell," he growled, "this damned gun." He unbuckled the holster and laid the gun across Tommy's bed. "Get sick of carrying that damned thing."

"Y-you always carry it?"

"Sure. Regulations."

"How does it feel to walk around with a death-dealing instrument always on you?" Tommy asked in a quiet, confidential voice.

"Oh, you get used to it."

"You really forget it's a *gun*?"

"Kind of. It becomes a part of you."

"B-but you don't think of it as something with which you can kill others?" Tommy asked with a forced smile.

Ruddy stared. Here it was again. Those damned tricky questions.

"No. It's something with which I defend myself," Ruddy said.

"Others don't see it like that."

"How do they see it?"

"You carry something that can kill them instantly," Tommy stated.

"Not unless they do something," Ruddy corrected him, modifying his role.

"Only upon policemen has society conferred the right to kill," Tommy said.

"Aw, hell, Tommy," Ruddy exploded. "We kill only to protect life and property."

"Did you ever shoot a man to protect property?" Tommy asked.

Ruddy thought a bit. Then shook his head: "No."

"To protect life?" Tommy asked.

"Yes. Mine."

"Never other people's lives?"

Again Ruddy reflected. "No."

"Then there is really no need to carry that gun to protect lives and property, other than your own life, is there?"

At last anger flashed full and strong and clear in him.

"Goddamn, Tommy! Where are you getting these crazy ideas from? Who's been talking to you?"

"Nobody."

"This stuff you ask . . . you get it out of those books at the university?"

"Not books at the university." Tommy smiled. "Just books and books. You can find 'em everywhere."

"Tommy?"

"Yeah, Dad."

"Are you *against* me?"

"What makes you ask a thing like that?" Tommy was shaken.

"I just want to know. Your questions and remarks bother me."

"No, Dad. Not *you*. I'm just curious about the system of society in which we live. My questions are not directed to you. It's the kind of questions we ask at school every day," Tommy argued.

"Don't you believe that my profession is respectable?" Ruddy demanded.

"All social functions are respectable. They spring from mutual needs." Tommy evaded him.

"Tommy, what in hell's wrong with you?" Ruddy demanded openly.

"Does something seem to be wrong?" Tommy countered.

"Can't you answer me straight?"

"We just don't understand each other, Dad," Tommy sighed.

Shame and guilt choked Ruddy. Hell, this was no way to to talk to one's son. He was treating Tommy not only as an equal but as a kind of dreaded superior. Yes, he would have to change his tone, attitude, and approach.

"Son?"

"Yeah."

"I want to ask you some questions."

"Sure, Dad. I'll tell you anything I know about Brentwood Park and—"

"No, no. It's not about that. . . . It's about you."

"Me?"

"Yeah."

"What?"

"I didn't want to bring this up now, but something in me keeps hammering at me about it," Ruddy began nervously. "Son, I don't want to probe into your private and personal life. I feel you are a man like me and you've got your rights. But I want to know you. After all, I'm your father. You're my son. Isn't that right?"

"Sure."

"Well, Tommy, last year . . . that girl you were going to marry. It didn't work out?"

"No. I told you that."

"What happened?"

"I didn't want to talk about that."

"Might be good for you."

"Ha, ha. You mean, confession is good for the soul. If the criminal unburdens himself, he'll sleep better."

"Aw, come off it, Tommy. You know I don't mean that. Tell me this: Did you break it off or did she?"

"Does it matter?"

"Yes, it does. You're my son. I want to know what's happening with you."

"She did nothing. And neither did I."

"Did the family interfere?"

"No."

"Then what interfered?"

"Society?"

"What? What do you mean?"

"Dad, I don't wish to talk of this," Tommy wailed.

And Ruddy saw pain in his eyes. Yes, goddamnit, there *is* something wrong. And though he was tempted to desist, he knew he had to go on.

"Tommy, I'm waiting for you to tell me what happened," Ruddy said.

"Talking about it isn't going to help!"

"Let me decide that. You said 'society' stopped you. How? Why?"

"It's all crazy," Tommy muttered.

"Maybe. But tell me about it."

"No."

"I'll find out, then," Ruddy threatened.

"How?" Tommy's eyes were truly fearful now.

"I'm an officer," Ruddy said. "I could find out."

"Aw, no, Dad," Tommy pleaded.

Ruddy felt that he was near his quarry. The detective in him urged him not to let up; his feelings as a father spurred him on. It'll be for his own good if he tells me, he told himself.

"Well, I'll find out," Ruddy said. "I'll not stop until I do."

"Dad, don't meddle in this," Tommy warned.

"Marie was colored," Ruddy spoke aloud. "So when you say 'society' stopped you, it could not be a question of race. Then what was it?"

Tommy's whole body seemed to grow rigid, and Ruddy saw beads of sweat on his forehead. Jesus Christ, I got to make this boy unburden himself.

"Tell me about it, son?"

"Goddamn, no!" Tommy suddenly screamed.

Ruddy ran to the boy and put his arms about his shoulders.

"You can say anything to me, Tommy."

"Goddamn this world—and everybody and everything in it," Tommy sobbed.

"Okay. Okay. Cry a bit. But tell me," Ruddy insisted.

"Leave me alone," Tommy begged, speaking, it seemed, more to himself than to his father.

"Give me your burden, son," Ruddy pleaded quietly, compassionately. "I can understand. Trust me. You're too much alone."

"I want to be alone," Tommy sobbed.

"No. I'm going to be with you—"

"Stop, Dad," the boy hissed through his teeth.

"I won't stop until you talk to me," Ruddy said, squeezing his arm about his son's shoulder. Experience had taught him that this personal, physical touching was a good art in extracting a confession. It helped to divert the resistance of the overburdened heart. "Talk, Tommy."

Then Tommy could not speak, for his throat was racked with sobs as he gasped for breath. Ruddy waited, holding him, knowing that he had won but feeling somehow fearful of his victory.

"Dad . . ."

"Yes, son."

"It wasn't her fault, or my fault," Tommy breathed.

"You loved her?"

"Yes, a lot . . . more than anything."

"Who interfered?"

"I-I have to start at the beginning. Dad, I don't know if I did right or wrong, honestly. But, in the end, I did what I felt I had to do."

"I see. I'll understand it, if you tell me."

"Marie was a good girl, Dad," Tommy said. "Her father is a carpenter. Her mother keeps house. They're converted Catholics."

"I know. John Wiggins is law-abiding. And Marie is beautiful."

"We'd been going together for quite a bit," Tommy whispered, his voice still charged with dread. "She is in a class just below mine, and I helped her a lot. We were together night and day—almost all the time. Her family trusted me. She was mine. That is how we felt. Well, you know . . . It happened one night. We knew we were going to marry, so it was not something terribly serious. But I was careful." Tommy looked defiantly at his father. "She was not pregnant. I'm Catholic. She's Catholic. And we knew how to be cautious. Well, this went on for a year. Then we decided to get married. I told you and Mama, and you both said it was a good thing. Marie's parents said so too. The wedding was all set. Then we went to the doctor to get our blood tested."

"Yes?"

"I handled all that for her," Tommy said. "That is, I took her to the doctor with me. And I arranged to go and pick up the blood tests."

There was silence. From far off came the faint wail of a police siren.

"Yes, son?"

"Well, I went after four days for the blood tests," Tommy resumed with a weary sigh. "The doctor handed me mine. 'Yours is okay,' he told me. I waited. The doctor sat there staring at me. And I said: 'And where's Marie's?' And he asked me: 'How well do you know this girl?' I thought that that was a funny kind of question. I said, 'I'm going to marry her.' The doctor stood up and began to pace the floor. He said: 'I know you want to marry her. That's why you came to me for these blood tests.' Then he sat down. 'There's something wrong with that girl,' the doctor said. I kind of froze. I could not imagine what he meant. 'What do you mean?' I asked. 'She's sick, real sick,' he said. 'What's the matter? What has she got?' I asked him." Tommy's head sagged low and his lips hung open. But no words came.

"Yes, son? What was it?"

"Dad, the doctor told me, 'Son, this girl has four-plus syphilis!'"

Tommy's body shuddered and Ruddy felt the boy's skin grow ice cold. Ruddy felt for a second that he could not breathe. Good Lord.

"Jesus, Tommy . . . What happened?"

"I don't know," Tommy murmured.

"Was . . . s-she a virgin?"

"That's the odd part. She was. There was nothing that she did and nothing that happened to her that gave her that disease."

"Then how did she get it? Oh, this is horrible . . . oh, Tommy, I'm so sorry . . ."

"I asked the doctor and he said that he would talk to Marie," Tommy related. "Dad, I left that doctor's office a blind man. The sun was shining, but I could not see it. I don't think the world will ever look or seem the same to me. Well, I waited for the doctor to call me. He did; he asked me to come in. I went. He told me, 'Son, this is tragic. Your girl has congenital syphilis. She inherited it. This is the first case of this kind I've ever had.' Then, Dad, I knew that it was true. You see, the doctor had the report checked, had the test done over again, just to make sure that there would be no mistake. I hadn't eaten for four days, practically. And now I knew the worst. I felt a kind of cold night come down over me. Then the doctor asked me, 'What are you going to do?' Strangely, Dad, I hadn't until that moment thought of what I was going to do. I was numb. Yet—" Tommy paused, then continued, whispering. "I knew what I was going to do. I had already done it. I was going to ditch that girl. I couldn't marry her. One night I even dreamed that I killed her. I couldn't blame her for what had happened, but I was hurt, hurt as I had never been hurt in all my life. I asked the doctor, 'What can I do?' I asked him that just to make sure that he had told me the truth. 'We could cure her,' he said. 'How long would that take?' I asked. 'I don't know,' he said. 'And I would have to wait while that happened, wouldn't I?' I asked. 'You can't, under the law, marry this girl while she is ill,' he said. 'You slept with her, didn't you?' 'Yes,' I said. Then a new fear—one I had until then not allowed myself to think of—swept down over me. The first fear had been a cold one. This second one was as hot as fire. Had I caught syphilis?" Tommy's body gave a long shudder. "I asked the doctor and he said, 'I don't know. We'll test you.' I sat and sat. Dad, I could not move. Then I asked the doctor, 'How did she take it?' He said, 'She collapsed. She was hysterical. I've never seen a girl go to pieces so absolutely. She tried to get drunk but could not. She wept for three days. Haven't you seen her?' I told the doctor that I had not, that I could not. 'What are you going to do?' the doctor asked me again. Then I blurted out what I knew I had to say: 'Can't marry her!' Oh, Dad, I didn't decide. Something in me decided. It was *moral*. I felt unclean. Polluted, contaminated, poisoned. I swear to God. Oh, you'll never know. Each time I walked the streets, I trembled with each step. I felt the world would dissolve, melt, fade away before my eyes." Tommy bent forward, his body shaking, and he sobbed. "Dad, I did wrong. But I couldn't help it. I went back and asked the doctor: 'I don't have to marry her, do I?' He said, 'No, of course not. But I can cure her.' I said, 'No, I don't want her now.' It was true, Dad. I couldn't ever have slept with that girl again, no matter what."

"Did the doctor ever find out how she got it?"

"No. It was congenital, he said," Tommy related.

"What's happened to Marie?"

"Dad, I don't know," Tommy cried. "I've never seen her. I know you're going to say I'm wrong, hard-hearted. But I can't see her. That she was sick, wasn't my fault. The doctor said so."

"Good God," Ruddy murmured. "And you lived with this all to yourself?"

"Yes."

"And you? Did you have tests to find out if you had been contaminated?"

"Yeah, hundreds of 'em," Tommy confessed. "I went crazy for a while, I guess. I went for a Wassermann each month, until the doctor said he would send me to a mental clinic if I could not believe that I had nothing, that I was clean. Oh, Dad, you'll never know. I sent Marie my savings, told her she could sell the ring."

"What did she say? Did she cry?"

"I talked to her by phone, Dad. I never saw Marie again, Dad," Tommy whimpered.

"Why?"

"I just couldn't bear to look at her . . ."

"Good God. That poor girl."

"I know, I know . . . you're going to say that I was a shabby man. *But Dad, I couldn't*. That's all, I *couldn't*."

"I knew that something had happened to you," Ruddy declared, justifying his insistence.

"After that, Dad, I changed my outlook on everything," Tommy said.

"What do you mean?"

"That's how I got to know Brentwood Park," Tommy said in a low voice.

"What do you mean, son?"

"Don't you see, Dad?" Tommy asked wailingly. "I could no longer do my fieldwork in the Black Belt. It was contaminated. Poisoned. I told my professor I had to quit. I begged off and asked to change my thesis. He consented. I was assigned to Brentwood Park."

"Oh, I see. My God," Ruddy said.

"I've never been in the Black Belt since. I fled it, Dad. I never want to go back into it. What kind of a world is that? How could a thing like that happen? I ride past the Black Belt now. Whenever I walk the streets there, I feel like I'm going to faint, fall down."

"You're sick," Ruddy said.

"Only when I'm there, am I sick," Tommy contended.

"Good God Almighty." Ruddy rose and stared at his son.

"Dad, do you blame me?" Tommy begged.

"You did what you felt you had to do, didn't you?"

"Yes. But would you have waited for her and married her?"

Ruddy hesitated a long time, then mumbled, "Don't know, son."

"I couldn't," Tommy insisted.

"What did the doctor say?"

"He said I was acting within my rights."

"He didn't say anything about the 'right' or 'wrong' of it?"

"No," Tommy said and choked.

"And you've lived with this since that time?" Ruddy asked.

"Yes, alone, each day and night," Tommy confessed. "Until I felt I was going crazy . . ."

Yes, that was why Tommy had always acted so casually, so detatched, with such a ready smile. He had been hiding all this. Ruddy embraced his son and mumbled as he wept. "I'm sorry for you, son. You must have been through hell."

CHAPTER 8

Never had Ruddy felt more deeply protective toward his son than now. To realize that Tommy had gone through that whole stormy period alone, saying not one word! He should have told me! Yet what good could he have done? And not even Agnes had guessed at what was wrong. He must have sweated, Ruddy said to himself.

Yes, Ruddy felt that Tommy was, in a manner, a better man than he was, for Ruddy surely would not have been able to endure such an agony without confiding in somebody. He just sweated it out alone. Ruddy's past experience in police work now enabled him, without his knowing it, to judge Tommy a bit objectively—but not all the way. At this moment he felt that peculiar kind of need that a doctor feels when a member of his family falls sick; he yearned to call in one of his colleagues for help, somebody upon whose objectivity he could rely. But, no, not for something like this. The dreaded disease that Ruddy had mentioned was as morally loathsome to him as to his son, and he easily felt how stunned poor Tommy had been. Jesus, I must get that kid a gal, for I don't want 'im to develop any crazy complexes. Just because one gal is contaminated does not mean that they all are, he reasoned. Yet, deep down in him, he blamed Tommy for having abandoned the girl, and yet he could not have said that he wanted him to marry her. And Tommy had slept with the girl. Thank God he didn't give her that disease and thank God he didn't catch it himself, he prayed half-aloud to himself. Congenital? Yes, the sins of fathers were visited upon the sons and daughters. A tainted stream of life had run close past his door and actually brushed itself against his own flesh and blood. A dreadfully damaged girl! A rotten girl—though rotten through no fault of her own—who would pass her rottenness on to others—and especially to her children! Jesus God. He sank upon his bed. No, he, too, would not tell Agnes. Tommy, in a way, had been right; no woman ought to know of such. It was as though, if Agnes knew of it, it would somehow communicate itself to her.

Yeah, he knew how Tommy had felt, why he had gone again and again to that doctor for tests; he had been trying to prove to himself a cleanliness deeper than that of blood. Ruddy's processes of reasoning stopped. Good Lord, the poor boy had been so shaken that he had fled the Black Belt! The sense of uncleanliness he had felt had been extended to the entire area. How awful . . . The Black Belt must look to him like a coiled rattlesnake, Ruddy thought. What a crushing blow! Now, more than ever, he had to be near that boy. Yes, he would take Tommy with him as much as possible into the Brentwood Park police headquarters and let him see that all areas had their tragedies, that all areas had their poisons, their sources of contamination. Tommy had to see this thing in a balanced way. Ah, he could pretend that he wanted Tommy's advice about the crime in the area; that was a way of bringing Tommy near him, placing the boy in a position where he could regain his confidence.

Should Tommy have married that poor girl? Frankly, Ruddy

did not know. He adhered to his religion, but he had never met the problem in a form that brought his religion so much into play. He was sorry for the girl, but ought a young man to saddle himself with a girl that ill? True, there were miracle drugs on the market. But how could you marry a girl whom you were afraid to touch? Aw, that's why that kid has veered from the girls around us! Jesus, that's it. And I never dreamed. . . . How goddamn complicated life is. And, oh God, you see how right and just law was! He would point out to Tommy, next time they talked, how wonderful it was that there existed a law that compelled him and that girl to take blood tests. Why, if he had been in some of the backward states that had no such law, he would have found himself married to a tainted girl! And, years later, when children were born, or when the disease had broken out in him, the girl would perhaps have said that Tommy had given her the disease! Ruddy's brow grew hot and damp. Jesus, that was a close shave. And to have children in whose blood seething spirochetes would be raging, and those poor doomed children would, in turn, pass it on to others! And God help 'em if they were girls!

Ruddy stood at the window and stared out, feeling that maybe Tommy ought to have stood by the girl, gotten her well, and then married her. But could you build a marriage on such foundations? Suppose Tommy had done that and suppose in the years to come there had risen arguments between Tommy and the girl—could not Tommy have, in a moment of blind fury, hurled an accusation against the girl? And would not the girl have been emotionally crushed and wounded beyond measure? Yeah, that's always a risky business, Ruddy breathed. Sometimes one ought to be noble and forgiving, but one's feelings won't let one. Hell, after all, according to the doctor, the girl had not been at all at fault. It was she who had sustained the brunt of the brutal shock. Would she ever get over it? Her marriage had gone glimmering for no reason or fault of her own. Would she not always feel that she was a damaged girl? Not worth what other girls were worth? Somehow excluded? But how could such a girl presume that a man should overlook her affliction and marry her and save her? Jesus, what a moral problem! Never had he heard anything in the law about a situation like that. It was something, really, that went beyond the law. Ruddy grew tense. Was that why Tommy had been talking of men who lived beyond the law? Men who acknowledged no laws? Men who just acted according to their own notions of having a good time? No, no, he was not talking about that, Ruddy told himself uneasily. Two vague ideas simmered in Ruddy's mind: the wildness of lawless Brentwood Park and the desolate emotional state of his son, but though his feelings linked the two things in some way, his rational mind pushed the two things apart. After all, nobody's asking Tommy to be Jesus Christ and marry that girl, and if he felt wounded in his heart, he had a damned right to be. But how wounded had Tommy been? That was a question he could not answer. Maybe even Tommy did not know how much he had suffered. You had something untoward hit you, and the blow was so vast and powerful that you felt numb all over and you turned and fled, never being able to gauge or judge correctly just how much you had been wounded. *I've got to save my boy*, Ruddy wailed inwardly.

And from now on he would raise no more questions with Agnes about Tommy; he would take the poor boy's part from now on. How much strength Tommy could muster would depend upon how warm and loving and understanding his home was. And a woman need not be told about such horrors. Yes, it would be something just between him and his son. I'll send that boy to Europe, to Asia, to Africa. I'll make 'im forget that sad experience. I'll make it up to 'im. That's what a father's for, goddamn. He won't have to go it alone with a festering wound like that in him. And, he would, unknown to Tommy or Agnes, seek out that poor girl and try to help her! That was it. One could not expect poor Tommy to have done that. He was too carried away by his loss, a loss that could not be blamed on anyone, a loss that had shattered him, had taken away the sights and sounds and color of the world in which he lived. Yes, I can imagine how he felt. He was like an ox hit between the eyes by an axe.

"Ruddy," Agnes was calling.

"Yeah?"

"Lunch is ready," Agnes said.

"Coming. Shall I call Tommy?"

"Tommy had to go," Agnes told him up the stairs.

"Oh."

So Tommy had gone. Okay. He would not raise any questions about it, but he strongly suspected that Tommy had chosen to be out, not to eat lunch with them. Maybe it's for the best. Maybe he wants to get hold of himself. When Ruddy descended to the table, he found Agnes already seated and Bertha standing, ready to serve.

"Feeling better?" Agnes asked with a compassionate smile.

"A lot," he lied.

"Did you sleep?"

"Well, no. Not exactly."

"I heard you and Tommy talking," Agnes said.

He shot her a quick glance; she was smiling confidently.

"Yeah. Look, we've got together," Ruddy said.

"I told you there was nothing wrong," Agnes said triumphantly.

"Nothing that a father couldn't help with," Ruddy said.

"Did he mention Marie?"

"No. Not directly."

"What did he say?"

"They had a spat."

"Oh, a lover's quarrel," Agnes said knowingly. "They'll get together yet. You'll see."

"Maybe," he said and sighed.

"How is his mood?"

"Okay. He's studying real hard, that boy." Ruddy sought to cover up for his son.

"Now, darling, promise me you'll not fret over Tommy," Agnes asked.

"I promise," he said. "And I was glad that I talked to him. I'm going to lean heavily on him for information about Brentwood Park."

"Good! A father-and-son team!"

"No. Not quite that," Ruddy corrected her.

"But anyhow, you'll get closer, won't you?"

"That we will, darling," Ruddy pledged.

"I'm so happy," Agnes sang, heaping her plate with food. "What a day! You're a police chief. And my husband and my son are friends!"

"I want to be the best friend that boy ever had," Ruddy declared with passion.

CHAPTER 9

Smiling urbanely, his eyes holding a light of respect and ready obedience and yet a kind of manliness, Captain Snell was punctual. His left arm bulged with a stack of brown-covered police dossiers. After they had shaken hands, Ruddy asked him, "How are things over there?"

"All right," Captain Snell replied. "We're all very happy that you're going to be with us, going to be our chief. I came up through the ranks myself, and I want you to know that I'll be personally proud to serve under you, sir."

"Thank you," Ruddy said. "I'll be in in the morning." He paused, sizing up the captain. He liked him, liked the manner in which the captain readily surmounted all jealousies and racial feelings and put police work utmost. I'll keep 'im. . . . "Is there anything requiring my urgent attention?"

"No, sir. Just routine stuff, Chief. I'm sure you've heard tall tales about Brentwood Park. We do have a backlog of unsolved murders."

"Yes, Captain," Ruddy informed him. "The commissioner dumped all that into my lap during the first hour I was in office."

"If there are any orders about those cases—"

"No. Nothing for the present. And there'll be no special orders into things until I've had a look-see," Ruddy said with a smile.

"Poor Chief Branden was a fine man," Captain Snell sighed.

"An A-1 officer," Ruddy agreed, knowing that all this was more or less protocol, that they were feeling each other out.

"Chief Branden was regular," Captain Snell began.

"I'm regular too," Ruddy hastened to assure the captain. "There's only one thing I'm asking for. I want my own personal staff."

"That's reasonable," Captain Snell said, relieved.

"I'm bringing in Ed Seigel, Jock Weidman, Mary Jane Woodford for the office, and a few others."

"They're all first-class people," Captain Snell said, nodding.

"But I'm pushing nobody out," Ruddy told him.

"That'll be deeply appreciated," the captain said, nodding still more emphatically. "And we'll be with you until the curtain comes down, sir. Now, I tried to anticipate. . . . These"— he pushed the bundle of dossiers forward— "are the three 'lulus.' The DA's on our neck about 'em. I thought you'd like to see 'em first, give 'em a glance."

"Thank you, Captain. I do. But tell me, were you in on those three 'lulu' murders?"

"All the way, sir."

"Good—now maybe you'd be so kind as to summarize 'em for me," Ruddy requested. "Not too many details, but the general sense."

"Glad, sir," Captain Snell said. "Well, like reporting on all unsolved stuff, maybe I'll not be giving you the cases in the most concise order or manner. One does not know what is relevant or irrelevant, you see? It may well be that we've overlooked the heart of it, the most essential things."

"That's always the case with an unsolved crime," Ruddy agreed, nodding. "You have to grope."

"Right. Now, all three of these crimes were what we call 'bushwhackers.' They took place at night in the woods that rise to the west of Brentwood Park. Late one night, between ten and midnight, Rev. Ernie Hindricks and Eva Landsdale were killed with point-blank shots from a .38. They were both seated in the front seat of Rev. Hindricks's Oldsmobile. A light rain was falling. No one heard the shots. The car was found next morning with the door next to the driver's seat open. Rigor mortis had set in. There was not a single clue or motive to that shooting. There is no evidence that Eva Landsdale knew the reverend or that he knew her. Even how they met is a mystery. There is no evidence that they had known each other. It was as though somebody had dropped them down there in that car for them to be murdered. Absolutely nothing that we could determine had been stolen from either body. It was the consensus of opinion of all who examined those bodies that they had not been touched. It was the opinion of the medical experts attached to the district attorney's office that no sexual intercourse had taken place between Rev. Hindricks and Eva Landsdale or between the murderer and Eva Landsdale. There was not a footprint, a cigarette—nothing was left as a clue on the scene of the crime.

"We traced the movements of both deceased for forty-eight hours before the crime. Nothing suspicious. The reverend was at home preparing sermons the day before the crime, and on the day of the crime, he played handball with two of his young sons. He seemed to have had a happy married life. Eva Landsdale was unmarried and worked as a social worker. Her work never brought her into Brentwood Park, and we have no evidence that she had ever been seen there. On the night she was murdered, she is supposed to have gone alone to a movie near her apartment. But she was not seen there by anybody who attended that movie that night. Maybe Eva Landsdale met Reverend Hindricks somewhere. Undoubtedly they did. But where? There's absolutely no information about that.

"Though there's no evidence to support any lover's rendezvous, the newspapers made a big noise about that angle of it. There is a lot of foliage around there, and it is possible that neither of the victims knew that a murderer was lurking nearby. We don't know if the killer stopped them, that is, flagged down their car and ordered them into the woods or not. At the best of times, these hit-and-run killers are hard to track down, but when it is seemingly done by somebody who really plans it, then it is almost impossible to size up what kind of killer it was.

"We dug back ten years into the lives of each of the victims and found nothing that linked them to each other or to anybody who would have wanted to kill them. Robbery could not have been the motive, for Reverend Hindricks carried some four hundred dollars in cash in his wallet. There were twenty dollars and some odd cents in the woman's purse, which, incidentally, seems not to have been touched. It was known that the reverend was to visit a travel agency the morning after the murder and pay for a railroad ticket that covered a lecture tour he had agreed to undertake. That accounted for his having the money. He took the money out of a Loop bank at ten that morning. Nobody but the bank teller knew of it; the teller's movements were checked and his character studied. Nothing came of it. That teller knew no crooks. (And if he did, it is doubtful if he'd be involved in a $400 robbery-killing.) Now, it was surmised that maybe the killer panicked and was too frightened to search his victims; in fact, that theory was widely believed at the time, but when the killing of Father Byrnes came about and under vaguely similar circumstances, that theory was abandoned.

"The character of the reverend's wife was carefully checked on the grounds that maybe she had a secret lover, but she was without blame. And Eva Landsdale had no boyfriend to seek vengeance. Chief, there it is. Just that. And nothing more.

"Six separate investigations have been launched into the Hindricks-Landsdale slaying, and nothing has come out of them. The case has never been closed, and the $5,000 reward offered by the National Baptist Church Council has not been withdrawn.

"Now and again vague rumors crop up and we check them, but they turn out to be duds. Every crackpot in Chicago tried to butt their way into the Hindricks-Landsdale slayings. Sixteen psychopaths came forward to confess that they did it, and when their 'confessions' were checked, they could be placed nowhere near the scene of the crimes."

"Hmmnnn . . ." Ruddy sighed, frowning. "Did you ever notice, Captain, that there is a kind of crime that brings these confessing psychopaths out like flies?"

"Yes, Chief," Captain Snell agreed, nodding his head. "Especially those crimes with violent death, a hint of sex, and mystery in them. Many people get terribly wrought up."

"Why do you think some crimes have that power?" Ruddy asked.

"Well," Snell said cautiously, "one of our psychologists said that such crimes make people think that they could have done it, and from that possibility, if they are inclined to feel generally guilty, they leap to the delusion that they did it."

"Maybe," Ruddy said, scratching his head. "But why would they feel generally guilty?"

"That beats me, Chief," Captain Snell said, smiling wryly. "I think I'd be a miserable man if I felt like that."

"I would too," Ruddy declared. "Well, it takes all kinds to make a world."

"Right. Now, Father Byrnes's and Sister Karn's slaying stood out clearly in many respects: it was like the Hindricks-Landsdale murders but with a kind of cleanness, if I can use that word. What I mean, there was no hint of sex, we knew what Sister Karn was doing with Father Byrnes that night, we knew where they were going, and we knew why they were in those woods."

"I see. That's interesting."

"Sister Karn was visiting her family that Thursday evening. It had rained hard, and the sky was black. A strong wind was blowing. Sister Karn's aged brother came down with a heart attack. He was a devout Catholic. Naturally, Sister Karn wanted a priest to administer extreme unction. Now, the rainstorm had blown down telephone lines. They could not summon a priest by phone. They consulted the telephone directory and found that Father Byrnes was the nearest priest. Sister Karn went into the wet streets, found a taxi cab, and went directly to Father Byrnes's house. The priest was in. He agreed to come with her but told her that it was not necessary to take the cab back, that they could take a shortcut across the woods and be at the house of the Karns in five minutes. Now, Sister Karn knew nothing of the paths in those woods. But she agreed; she was not fearful. She felt perfectly safe, being with a father of the Church.

"They set out. That was the last ever seen of them. When Sister Karn did not come home, and when Father Byrnes did not return to his apartment, a search was made. Toward five o'clock that morning, a party of searchers found their cold and wet bodies in the woods. Both had been shot to death with a .38. Now, it so happened that in falling, Father Byrnes fell across the body of Sister Karn, and that odd incident was what made the press pour out tales of a tryst of love between a Catholic priest and the nun. But there was not a single detail at that scene that suggested such.

"They seemed to have been ambushed suddenly by somebody standing in their path with a gun. What really happened, nobody knows. They seemed to have been shot at point-blank range, twice, through the head and then through the heart. Both of 'em. And no clues. Not a match, a footprint, a cigarette, a strand of hair . . . nothing, nothing, nothing. The killer vanished. His race, his sex, his social standing, his profession—nothing is known about him. The slaying of Father Byrnes and Sister Karn proved that the other killing really had nothing to do with blackmail, jealousy. I say that by assuming that the same killer killed both times and—"

"Why do you assume that?" Ruddy asked.

"I told you that in relating crimes in which there are no clues, one might relate things that are not germane to the crime," Captain Snell said apologetically.

"I understand, Captain."

"It's perfectly possible that a different killer killed both parties," Captain Snell went on. "That both parties were killed at night, that the parties were a man and a woman, that no robbery took place, that the bodies seemed not to have been touched. All of this might well be merely a coincidence. But, Chief, there is something in the popular imagination that did not let the public or the police believe that. Queer, isn't it?"

"I agree," Ruddy said. "I said with what you have said."

"Crimes seem to speak." Captain Snell smiled wryly. "One

of the men from the DA's office said that. Those crimes had a smell about them. They seemed to have been linked, not so much objectively but subjectively, in some killer's mind. Odd, hunh? But you couldn't escape feeling like that.

"Now, the same investigatory procedure that was employed in the Hindricks-Landsdale murders was employed in the Byrnes-Karn murders. We traced everything—and I mean everything—and we drew a blank. We are inclined to believe that those people were thrown together that night accidentally and were killed by a crazy 'bushwhacker.'"

"You are assuming that he is always in those woods, that 'bushwhacker,'" Ruddy said.

"I know, I know," Captain Snell admitted an irrational element in his report.

"Maybe the 'bushwhacker' was there more times than one," Ruddy speculated. "Maybe he was waiting not for the particular victims he did kill but for somebody or someone who fitted his notions of being a good victim."

"That's possible too," Captain Snell admitted.

"In that case, then, he frequents those woods," Ruddy said.

"We came to that conclusion," Captain Snell said. "And that theory leads me to the third crime, for it came out of our trying to test that theory. Detective Heard and Policewoman Jenny Saunders were assigned to the case—in a sort of long-term proposition, see? We gave them plenty of latitude. They were in plainclothes. They came to live in Brentwood Park. Heard was married, a son in the university, and—"

"My son knew Heard Jr.," Ruddy told Captain Snell.

"No!"

"Yes."

"He's given you any ideas about it?" Captain Snell asked.

"Nothing of any value," Ruddy said. "You know how it is. Laymen don't know how to observe. They get all wound up in wild abstractions when they try to think about crime. But go on."

"Well, as I said, Heard and Saunders frequented that wood," Captain Snell went on. "And they contrived to let it be known that they were investigating. We circulated rumors that we were near a solution to the crime, that we almost knew who did it."

"A come-on," Ruddy said. "A provocation, so to speak."

"Right. Well, nothing happened all summer. Heard and Saunders were in those woods night and day, in their car, afoot, and once they even slept in a tent there. They met many people who eyed them and passed on. But nobody—and I mean nobody—molested them. At this time crime waned in Brentwood Park and we wondered if it was because of Heard's and Saunders's presence. But we could not tell.

"Then one day Charles Heard Jr. went to find his father for some urgent reason," Captain Snell reported. "He went into the woods. He never came out. A party of picknickers found him shot to death. Heard was in a state of collapse. And this death forced us to believe that there was one killer in the series of murders."

"You would have thought that the killer would have slain Heard and Saunders," Ruddy said reflectively.

"Exactly," the captain said.

"But they got his son," Ruddy said wonderingly.

"That's the only fact that knocks the theory of the single killer," Captain Snell pointed out.

"It does. Now, could the killer have made a mistake?"

"How?"

"By killing a victim he thought was somehow allied with what had made him kill the other two?"

"We'll ask 'im if we ever catch up with 'im." Captain Snell permitted himself a cynical joke.

"Maybe the killer was taunting the detective," Ruddy suggested.

"Why?"

"Well, he—"

"If it was a 'he.'" Captain Snell emphasized the mystery.

"Yeah. We really don't know if it was a 'he' or a 'she,'" Ruddy agreed. "There were many women in the last war and they were taught to shoot."

"That last killing was what really threw us off," Captain Snell confessed, running his fingers through a shock of curly blond hair. "If we accept the theory of a single killer for all three crimes, then this last killing seems to indicate a change of outlook on the killer's part, another perspective, even a kind of exasperation."

"What could 'he' or 'she' have been exasperated about?" Ruddy asked.

"Don't know. It was just a kind of hunch that made me say that," the captain admitted.

"Now, the commissioner told me that there was a sharp decline in crime in Brentwood after that," Ruddy stated. "How do you account for that?"

"I don't account for it." The captain was honest. "Again we can only guess, Chief. Out of all the wild talk, the many speculations advanced, somebody said that maybe those three crimes were so horrible, so brutal and cold-blooded, that the amateurs were chilled into inaction."

Both men laughed sheepishly.

"Were there many anonymous letters after the Heard killing?" Ruddy asked.

"Bushels of 'em—like always," the captain reported. "And

filled with the usual tommyrot. Only this time there were accusations that the police themselves had a hand in the killings. We had those letters carefully analyzed by psychologists, so desperate were we for facts, any kind of facts. But nothing came of that."

"And were there many voluntary confessions this time?"

"There was not one voluntary confession for the Heard slaying," the captain pointed out. "It was odd and made some of us think that we were wrong in trying to link all three crimes together."

"There was no sex angle in the Heard killing," Ruddy said. "Maybe that made the psychopaths silent."

"Maybe."

"It's weird," Ruddy said, sighing, standing. "There seems to be a secret buried out there in Brentwood Park. And, by God, I'm going to try to dig it up."

"I'm at your service, Chief," Captain Snell said. "Do you want me to leave these dossiers?"

"No. Ed Seigel ought to be reporting—"

"He signed in just before I left this afternoon," the captain said.

"Good. Dump these dossiers into Ed's lap and tell 'im to be ready to give me his impressions in the morning," Ruddy ordered.

"Yes, sir. Anything else?"

"Nothing at the moment. I'll be here all afternoon. I'm fagged out. No sleep last night. I don't want to come into the job half fuzzy-minded. I must get some sleep. I'll be in in the morning—at about nine."

"Right, sir."

"If anything comes up, I'm here."

"Right, sir. We're happy to have you with us."

"And I'm glad to be with you. Listen, any man on that force has the right to come in and talk to me at any time. I'll see no politicians sent by officers. I'm straight, regular. No string pulling, no shake-ups. Just straight police work."

"That'll get the loyalty of every man on our force," the captain declared. "Good-bye, Chief."

"Good-bye, Captain."

CHAPTER 10

Ruddy felt that his nerves were drained, taut, tired, but he knew that sleep or rest was no cure for what ailed him at that moment. He felt that he lacked exercise—yes, that was it. He ought to go down to the police gym and have a hard workout, let pouring sweat empty the accumulated poisons out of his body. But, no. He wanted to think, to resolve all the mass of contradicting facts that had been poured into his mind during the past ten hours. In his office he paced to and fro, like an animal behind bars, staring unseeingly. He had as yet—despite the commissioner's, despite Tommy's, and despite Captain Snell's reports and descriptions—failed to get the "feel" of Brentwood Park. Something was missing, some vital link had not been uncovered, some handle was out of sight—a handle that he had been trained to take hold of and work with. And what was hovering tantalizingly beyond his reach were not the "facts" of the case but a meaningful interpretation of them, an angle of vision from which to see and weigh them.

Had he made an error in allowing Commissioner King to persuade him to accept the chiefship of Brentwood Park? Had he let the commissioner persuade him against his better judgment? No. Police work was his profession. Yet had he refused, he could have, in a few months, been retired and on his own, fishing, traveling, attaching himself to some private agency at a fancy salary. And he could have had the comradeship of Tommy, who, God knows, sure needed it now. Yes, there was no doubt but that he needed a rest from all the hurly-burly of crime, from all the hordes of killers and thieves; he needed to be around people who were not tracking down crimes or criminals who were trying to escape the meshes of the law. He yearned to see a clean sweep of sparkling blue water and feel a sharp, clean wind blowing on his face. That would do him a world of good. One got stale facing and probing into the same old problems. Yet there was something about Brentwood Park that challenged him, whetted his police instincts.

"Ruddy."

"Yeah, Agnes."

She opened the door and smiled compassionately at him.

"You're not sleeping. And you're not resting," she chided him.

"I'm not sleepy."

"Your eyes look tired."

"I know."

"Why don't you lie down?"

"Don't know. Just restless, I guess."

"That job has got you by the throat," she said. "Look, darling, I have a bridge party. . . . When will you want to eat?"

"I'm not hungry, Agnes."

"But if you go to bed on an empty stomach, you'll be ravenous before morning," she told him. "I know."

"I couldn't eat anything now."

"Listen, I'll leave you a ham sandwich, a glass of chocolate milkshake, and a slice of pie on a tray."

"Good, I'll take a bite later."

"Why not go to a movie? It'll relax you."

"Say, I might. If I can find something good."

"Try that, dear." She kissed him. "Take it easy."

"Okay."

When she had gone, he tried to convince himself that he wanted to see a movie, but he knew deep in him that he really did not, that he would have looked at the screen and not understood the flowing sequence of images. Then suddenly what he wanted to do struck him with thunderous force: he wanted to find that girl that Tommy had not married! That was it. Yeah, I'll find that Marie. He did not know why he wanted to do that, yet he felt compelled toward it. Slowly, thoughtfully, he changed into his uniform, then felt into his suit pocket and found the chief of police badge that Commissioner King had given him, and pinned it on his chest. After he had tilted his visored cap above his large, dark eyes, he surveyed his reflection in the mirror. Yeah, he looked formidable. It was said that some men looked like cops and some did not; and he was one who did, powerfully. The boys had always said that he looked more like a general than a policeman—well, he was geting there. He was a chief of police now. And when he had his new rank service stripes sewed onto his new uniform, he would look like the nearest thing to a general. He found himself becoming debonair, smiling, slipping into an organized, official mood. As he went out to his car, he realized that he did not know where Marie Wiggins lived. He doubled back to the telephone, lifted the directory, and leafed through the pages. Yeah, he had heard Tommy talking to her many times over the phone, and undoubtedly she had one. Then he saw in fine print, memorizing it as he read it, as he had been trained to do: 6499 Woodlawn Avenue.

Ten minutes later Ruddy was rolling through the April

twilight. Suddenly the streetlamps flashed on. He drove slowly, his watchful eyes glancing officially about without his being aware of it, noting which cars were obeying or violating the traffic code. He observed a big Buick overtake another car in the crowded traffic and pass it with but inches to spare. "I wouldn't've done that," he told himself. At a street intersection where he had the right of way, he stopped and waved a woman across—a woman who was pushing a baby buggy. She smiled at him and he nodded. This courtesy was now automatic with him. In the dim past, when he had once been assigned to a traffic detail, that was what he had always compelled other motorists to do. As he drove on, he looked up and glanced at his face in the rear-view mirror. Yeah, that was a policeman. On duty. Alert. On guard to observe if the law was being obeyed. Yes, he was the Chief of Police of Brentwood Park, Illinois.

He reached the South Side and found Woodlawn Avenue. This was a foolish errand. Suppose she was not in? He ought to have called her first. Okay, if she's not in, no harm's done. He saw from the names above the mailbox that Marie Wiggins lived on the first floor. He pushed the bell. There was no answer. He rang again, long and steadily. A buzzer sounded at the vestibule door.

Now that somebody had answered, Ruddy had a momentary doubt about the wisdom of his visit. What could he say to the poor girl? He let himself through the door and saw a dark form waiting for him at the end of the first-floor hallway.

"Yes?" a small feminine voice called.

He advanced, trying to see who had spoken, not replying.

"Oh, you're a policeman!" the feminine voice half-shouted in terror.

"Miss Wiggins?" he asked.

"Yes," the voice said.

He could see her now. It was Marie herself. He stopped just short of her and he looked down into her upturned face—a face twisted with fear, a face whose mouth was hanging open.

"I'm Tommy's father," he told her. "Ruddy Turner."

"Oh!" Her voice came low and relieved.

"Could I speak to you a moment?"

"Oh, yes," Marie said, backing through the opened door and into a dim room.

He advanced after her, sorry now that he had come. Never had he seen a girl in so cringing a posture.

"Don't be afraid," he told her.

"You're not coming to arrest me?" she asked, shaking her head from side to side.

"God, no," he told her.

She switched on a light. She wore a housedress, bedroom slippers; her hair was in curls. She was much thinner than he remembered her having been, and there were lines from her nose to her lips. They stared at each other for a few seconds, then she burst into loud weeping.

"Don't be afraid," he consoled her. "I'm not here to hurt you. I came to see how you were."

His voice only increased her sobbing. It was as though now she knew that she was not going to be arrested—for what, she had not said!—her feelings were free to give way to sorrow and the consequences of disappointment. He reached out his right hand to take her shoulder to lead her to a chair, but she quickly twisted out of his reach.

"No," she sobbed.

"Sit down," he said.

"I know . . . I know that you think I'm poisoned. You're just like all the others," she wailed.

He understood now why she had shied away from him. She

had felt that had he touched her, he would have afterward regretted it. Oh, God, she must have been through the mill. Yes, poor Tommy had had his share in making her feel this way.

"Do you feel well enough to talk?" he asked her softly.

"I-I g-guess so," she stammered, her sobbing letting up a bit.

"Sit down," he said.

She sat in an old chair and he edged himself upon the side of a bed.

"Are you here alone?" he asked.

"Yes. My family is upstairs. I didn't want to stay with them. Papa rented this kitchenette for me," she related in a sigh.

"How are you?" he asked.

There was a momentary pause, and then she whispered: "I'm alone . . ."

He had asked about her physical state, and she had answered in terms of what mattered most to her, that is, her state of emotional abandonment.

"Are you seeing the doctor?"

"Yes, yes . . . the police told me to . . . I . . ."

"I understand."

She had thought that he was an officer coming to check on whether she was having the prescribed treatments for syphilis. Goddamn . . . He had not wanted to do that to her.

"I'm sorry," he told her. "I was not sent here by the police. I came on my own."

She lifted startled, disbelieving eyes to him and a tiny relaxation came into her face.

"Everybody hounds me," she complained in a hopeless voice.

"I'm not here for that," he said. "You've suffered enough, God knows."

"It was not my fault," she whimpered. "I swear. I didn't know I had anything. I-I only s-slept with T-tommy . . ."

"He told me," he said.

There was a long silence. Ruddy could hear a rumble of an El train in the distance.

"D-did he g-get it from me?" she asked.

"No, no," he assured her.

"Aw, I'm glad." She sighed.

"It was not contagious," he told her.

"The doctor told me," she said. "But I was not sure. I'm not sure of anything anymore."

"You know, you must not let this break you down." He tried to put some courage into her.

"It already has," she said, sobbing again.

His instincts told him that she was already beyond any emotional help that he could give her. Never in all of his police work had he seen a criminal more abject than this girl, more claimed by a sense of guilt, more ready to accept all that could be said against her.

"I'm bad," she moaned. "Rotten . . ."

"No, no," he spoke vehemently.

"I am! I am! It's all written down in the medical reports," she wailed. "I want to kill myself."

"None of that," he rasped at her. "Your life has been shattered, but you must now try to rebuild it. You are taking treatments?"

"Yes."

"How often?"

"I see a doctor three times a week."

"Is it expensive?"

"Y-yes . . . you see, they won't let me work. It's charity. And what my father can do. My mother . . ." Her voice trailed off.

"How is she?"

"All right. You see, she is convinced that I caught it running

around with boys . . . men . . . drinking. I can't make her realize that that's not true. Then she thinks that Tommy ought to
have married me. I told her that it was only with him, you see?
She can't believe that he didn't give it to me. Oh, God, it's all
mixed up, Mr. Turner. *Nobody believes me.*"

"I do," he said.

"D-did Tommy send you?" she asked timidly.

"No."

Another long silence. "How is he?"

"Oh, all right," he informed her. "Marie, you must realize
that I didn't come here to hurt you any more than you are already hurt. But I must tell you that Tommy was hurt too. Terribly. That is why he has never been to see you. He too was caught
up in awful emotional reactions. He didn't blame you. You see,
Marie, something happened to both of you that was too big for
both of you, and you could not really react to it. You were both
hit, you harder than he. And he was just cold and numb. He too
felt awfully guilty. He didn't know what to do."

"I don't blame what he did," she whimpered. "He did what
anybody else would have done, I guess."

Aw, there was a tiny bit of doubt in her voice. She still felt
deep down that Tommy should have stood by her. Yet she knew
that she could make no claim on him. God, where was the right
and wrong in this? Could a boy be blamed for doing something
that his most powerful feelings had prompted him to do? The
boy had run and the girl knew that it had been her physical
state that had set him fleeing. And the girl knew that the world
would have sided with the boy had all the facts been publicly
known. How much could one ask of another in the act of love?
Could one be demanded to embrace exactly that which turned
the impulse of love into loathing?

"Are you still at the university?" he asked her.

"No, no," she said quickly, shaking her head. "They told me to stay away . . ."

"Oh, God." He sighed.

Her life had been shattered, all right. And whose fault had it been?

"What did the doctor say, Marie?"

"I inherited it," she said, picking nervously at her dress.

She had said it in a strange tone of voice; she had told him that she was not really guilty at all, and yet she had all the stigma of guilt.

"I'm crucified," she moaned.

"Oh, no," he objected feebly.

Yes, she had been. And she still was. His mind leaped toward the future, and he could see no way out for her. Maybe she would be cured and then she could flee to another city, change her name. But even then maybe her past would catch up with her—like the past of criminals caught up with them. And how could she ever really know that all the contamination had been cleaned out of her blood? Maybe she would never know, not until she had had children.

Ruddy rose and walked nervously about. Yes, Marie's life had been poisoned at the very springs of it. The past had cast its black shadow upon her, and that shadow might well throw itself into the future and fall across the lives of whatever children she might bear.

"Don't you go out?" he asked.

"No," she mumbled.

"Oh, you must, you know," he said. "You look pale."

Indeed, she looked like those prisoners who spent a lifetime behind bars; there was a greenish pallor about her skin.

"I don't want to," she said. She was staring off into space, then began biting her lips. "I hope Tommy's all right. I hope

that he's not too bitter toward me. After all, it was *not* my fault.
Yet I can't and don't blame 'im. For a month I felt dead. I could
feel nothing. I tried drinking, but I couldn't get drunk. I can't
read anymore. I don't like movies now. I used to play tennis, but
I dare not now show up where I used to go. I just stay here." A
sob caught in her throat. "Blind people are not shunned like I
am. When I walk down the street, I feel that people are shying
away from me. I—"

"People you know?"

"No. Just all of them."

"Marie. That's not true. It can't be true."

"I know, but I can't help it."

The chief of police sat stumped. What could he do? A burning compassion for this girl came over him, yet he could not
still in him a raging revulsion. Goddamn! He knew now why
Tommy had fled. To flee was natural, and Tommy's feelings had
been natural. As natural as his were.

"Marie."

She did not answer; he could see the muscles quivering in
her throat.

"Marie, listen to me."

"Yes," she whispered.

"I want to help you," he told her.

"No. Leave me alone. Just leave me alone."

"No. Listen. I've just been appointed chief of police in
Brentwood Park," he told her. "And I'll have extra money. I want
to give you twenty dollars a week, money enough for your treatments, see?"

"No."

"Yes. Don't be foolish."

"Why are you doing this?"

"I want to help," he declared.

"Did Tommy send you?"

"No. He doesn't know I'm here."

"Does his mother know?"

"No. No one knows but me."

She sat silent.

"I'm no good," she breathed.

"You are. We must save you," he swore.

"Just leave me alone. When I see those I used to know, I feel that I'm being unjustly judged," she whimpered. "Oh, why did this have to happen to me? What have I ever done? This hurt fell on me for nothing?"

"Marie, did you ever try to trace with your father and his father how you could have caught this?"

"Yes."

"What happened?"

"My father's father had it. My father has it."

"Your mother?"

"Strangely, no."

"Is your father being treated?"

"Yes. But maybe it is too late for him."

"What did the doctor say about you?"

"I'm being cured," she said.

"There. You see. Everything will come out all right." He tried to encourage her. "Now, look, I'm"—he ran his hand into his pocket and pulled forth some money—"I'm giving you this now. Two hundred dollars. Enough for twenty weeks. After that—"

"You shouldn't do this, Mr. Turner," she objected. "You make me feel even worse."

"I want to do this."

"Is Tommy getting married?"

"Not that I know of."

"Has Tommy told anybody about this?"

"No. Not even his mother. And he told me only yesterday, when I forced him to."

"Oh." She sighed.

Ruddy understood. Marie was thinking that his offer of help was a bribe for her to remain silent for the sake of Tommy's future. A stab of pain stitched at his heart. Dirt bred dirt. Jesus Christ. Yet, in her sense of abandoment and degradation, it was a natural thing for her to think. It was as natural for her to think that as it had been for Tommy to flee from her presence.

"I'm giving you this because I want to help you," he spoke simply. "I know it's hard for you to believe that, but it's true."

"If I thought otherwise, I'd hate you for the rest of my life," she said with sudden, hard bitterness.

"You'd be right," he said. "But this money is clean. It's from my heart."

"All right," she said.

He laid the roll on the bed, not daring to wish to put it into her hand.

"Oh, Marie, life is hard," he half moaned, feeling hot tears stinging his eyes.

"I wanted to kill, just to kill anybody, everybody, when I knew what had happened to me," she said.

"Medicine now can cure you." He tried to encourage her. "It is not like in the old days when illnesses like that were thought of as horrible. It is a moral feeling—"

"It is *horrible,*" she insisted. "I saw it in Tommy's eyes. I see it in yours. And in my mother's eyes. Everybody's eyes."

What could he say to her? She was right. No matter how quickly she was healed, she was poisoned in the minds of others and, above all, in her own mind. Never in one lifetime could it be gotten rid of. And how contagious was the feeling that she had in her. That feeling was composed of germs more powerful than the ones that flowed in her veins. It made one shrink, in spite of one's self. Hovering in Ruddy's mind was an allusion that Marie had made to crime. She had said that what had happened to her had made her want to kill. God, no. But, maybe, yes. When you were unjustly condemned by those around you, you wanted to hit out at everybody, at a world that held and nourished and poisoned your life. Yes, but that was only a temporary reaction, he told himself. How lucky Tommy escaped. Suppose he had married the girl and had then found it out? That boy would have gone crazy, he thought.

"Thank you, Mr. Turner," he heard Marie whispering.

"It's nothing," he said. "I only knew about it today. Or I would have come sooner. You and Tommy are children. You were hurt, through no fault of your own. I'd have been here sooner, had I known. You must learn to trust life again, Marie. All is not over for you. You'll be cured. I'm certain of that. Then I want to see you and try to help you figure out a life."

"Thank you," she said, her eyes lowered.

"And if you ever want anything, call me at my office in Brentwood Park," Ruddy told her.

He stretched out his hand to her. He saw her staring at it, then she took it, without rising, and pressed it, then let it fall.

"Good-bye, Marie," he said.

She did not answer. He went out, and when he reached the dark, lamp-lit streets, he seemed to be entering a world filled with bright sunshine. He knew that this illusion was caused by the deep sense of oppressive suffocation that he had had when talking to Marie. He seated himself behind the wheel of his car, and for a reason he did not know, he lifted from the glove compartment an insignia of the police department and affixed it to the windshield. Why had he done that now? He was frightened and he wanted the protection of the power of his office. He drove slowly on, not in any particular direction. What a goddamn rotten world, he muttered between his teeth. It'd make you kill, for sure. Kill like that killer in the woods of Brentwood Park. He slowed the car and pulled to a curb. Why in the name of God had he thought of that? I'm nervous, he said. I'm acting now as though I was sick. He shook his head and swallowed. Never, since he had been in the service of the department of the police, had anything like this even remotely touched his life. And he admittedly did not know how to react. Until now he had always found some way to convince himself that those who were caught in the meshes of the law or who were in trouble, had only themselves at bottom to blame. But how could he blame Marie? Or Tommy? No, he could not. God-damnit, life is tough sometimes.

CHAPTER 11

Chief Turner's usually unruffled feelings had been swept by a dark storm of emotion that left him wondering and half afraid. His traditionally rigid view of the world, a view outlined and buttressed by the law, had been shattered in a manner that did not allow him to set it right again. Here was no simple question of man against the law but of suffering inflicted by vast and mysterious powers outside of and above the law. It was not a question of the so-called unwritten law that was bothering him but maybe of a higher law that overruled or could overrule the law he knew and executed. Who or what was responsible for what had happened to Tommy and Marie? Ruddy understood the so-called acts of God, such as storms, tidal waves, earthquakes, and he knew that most people were prepared, however reluctantly, to accept them, to bow their heads before them, to mumble a silent yes with teary-eyed sorrow. He now remembered something that Tommy had years ago said to him; he had asked Tommy some question about how a man could suffer so silently and Tommy had said, quoting an English poet—what had been his name? Black, Burke, Blake, or what?—that "a hurt worm forgives the plow." That was true. But in the give and take of human life, what on earth was a plow? A storm? Something that came from outside human life and society? Or could it be something that flowed with the blood in human veins and was transmitted in the act of life, the defenseless act of giving with arms wrapped about a desired body? It was that "love" aspect that presented the problem! The hurt that had come had descended not with violence, not with assault, not with theft, but when all human defenses were down and the heart was open. A man who had dealt unfairly with you, had caused you suffering, loss, and pain, could perhaps be understood and maybe, under some circumstances, be forgiven. Insurance companies indemnified you for damages sustained when storms struck you or fire wiped out your home. But who was to blame for the hurt sustained by the Maries and Tommys who innocently and buoyed by love were made victims of forces beyond their control? "It's the goddamnest thing I ever heard of," he spoke aloud. "Glad Tommy escaped being infected . . ." His throat tightened. But Tommy had not escaped. He had walked around the physical disease, but he had undoubtedly been touched and tainted by the aura of evil that wafted that disease along. Tommy had not been ill and Tommy had not married the girl. Tommy had left the girl alone to fend for herself, and he had been too ashamed to tell even his father what had happened. No, Tommy had not escaped, not really. "Tommy would have done wrong no matter what he did," he muttered. "It's goddamn unfair." His unblinking eyes roved unseeingly upon the passersby thronging the sidewalks. Well, he had done what he could for poor Marie, and he could and would do more. When she was cured and able to mingle again with people, he would help her to get a job somewhere. She was bright, and a good job with good pay would help her to become emotionally fit and would help

her to forget. Forget? Could she ever forget that? Never heard
of an accident like that. Tommy did not deserve that. It must
have made him burn inside . . . or freeze.

He sighed. "Don't know what I would do in a case like
that." Ruddy's fingers, tan and stiff, gripped the steering wheel
with murderous intensity. Gradually his emotions cooled and
calmed. Well, he'd go home now. No, he did not want to. And
he didn't wish to see a movie either. He was tired but restless,
nervously taut but not sleepy. And he did not relish seeing or
talking to Agnes just now. Then, from out of the depths of him,
there flashed the vague and comforting image of an office, *his*
office, the official home he had out there in far-off Brentwood
Park. He glanced at his wristwatch; it was a quarter past nine.
Yeah, I'll drop in there. And I'll go by way of those woods above
Brentwood Park.

He reversed the direction of his car at an intersection and
rolled swiftly forward. He was now psychologically organized
again, a policeman on duty, an efficient officer upholding the law,
an officer on a mission, on guard, alert. Twenty minutes later, he
turned and took the road whose sign read: BRENTWOOD PARK, 10
MILES. The road rose in the warm spring night, stretching ahead
between far-flung and rising yellow streetlamps, whose glow was
misty like blobs of shimmering gold. Ten minutes later he was
atop the vast and sloping hill, staring down at the oblong shape
of the town of Brentwood Park, its outline marked by yellow lights
that glimmered. He slowed, turning, following the roadway, and
began the long descent till the streetlamps were no more. Yeah,
I'll get this place lit up; that's the first thing I'll order done. How
fine the air smelled up here! How cool and clear was the scent of
the looming black pine trees! And how calm and silent were the
woods! It seemed impossible that three atrocious murders had
taken place in these surroundings, that five people had lost their

lives. Yet the thick foliage made him know that such a landscape offered criminal possibilities galore. What was a paradise for some was a hell for others. Yeah, a bushwhacker could thrive up here. He slowed the car to five miles an hour; yes, he could see a few people out strolling even on this dark, starless, moonless night. Couples arm-in-arm passed him, talking in low tones. "Even five murders can't help 'em out of here," he mumbled in amazement. Everybody thought that they could not be killed; their neighbors could be, their friends, even their fathers and mothers, but they themselves were immune. Ruddy was familiar with that feeling in his police work. Cops never really believed the bullets of the killers would reach them, for, if they did, they would be as frightened as the killers. A sudden impulse made him pull his car over onto a stretch of wide gravel that soft-shouldered the road and stop. He doused his lights, sat back, lit a cigarette, puffed, but hid the glowing tip between each inhalation and exhalation. He was still about two minutes when he heard a sound; his ears pricked up. Footsteps were slowly approaching his car—the kind of footsteps that bushwhackers used. His right hand snaked lightning-like to his gun, and in a second he had it in readiness and was peering about over his shoulder while he crushed out his cigarette into the car's ashtray. Yeah, somebody was creeping toward him. *Was this it?* He strained his eyes. God, it was a *white* face! And though he did not know it, he was surprised to know that the possible attacker was a *white* man. Who in hell is this? The face came closer and closer. Ruddy flung open the car door and demanded harshly: "Stand where you are!"

"Hey, what're you doing here?" the white face challenged him.

"Who are you?" Ruddy demanded, swinging the police spotlight round and full into the man's face.

"Hey, you're blinding me . . . don't do that!" the white face shouted.

"Put your hands up and come closer," Ruddy snapped softly. "I've got you covered with a gun. Be careful." He sighted along his revolver straight in the direction of the man's heart.

A pair of long arms lifted into the darkness and the blinking white face came nearer.

"Who are you? What're you doing out here?" Ruddy asked.

"I'm Dr. Louis Redfield," the man stammered.

"What're you doing sneaking up on my car?"

"I-I t-thought you were a prowler," the man stammered.

"That's hot," Ruddy said, relaxing. "A prowler prowling at cars and looking for prowlers, eh?"

"But . . . I . . . who are you?"

"Come closer," Ruddy ordered. "And keep your hands *up!*"

"Don't hurt me, Mister," the man begged in a trembling tone.

"I'm a policeman," Ruddy informed him, alighting from the car now. "I'm not satisfied with what you told me about sneaking up on my car."

"Oh, you're the police," the man said in a tone of deep relief. Ruddy took the spotlight out of the man's face now. "Aw, yes, an officer. Thank God. I thought you had cornered me. You see, sir, we've got an unofficial posse patrolling these woods at night since all of those terrible crimes were committed. We're searching for those murderers."

"An amateur detective, eh?"

"Sort of," the man apologized with a sheepish smile.

"Where do you live?"

"92 Edgeware Avenue, Brentwood Park."

"Where do you work?"

"I teach at the University of Chicago."

"You're a professor there?"

"Yes, Officer."

"You know, I can check that."

"I'm assistant head of the department of sociology there," the man explained.

"Oh!"

"It's true," the man insisted.

"Did you know Detective Heard's son, who went to school there?" Ruddy asked.

"I heard of 'im," the man said. "He was not in any class I taught."

"Step closer to me and still keep your hands high," Ruddy ordered.

The professor came so close that Ruddy could feel his hot breath on his cheek. Then Ruddy quickly patted the man's pockets, hips, and felt along his legs for weapons.

"Okay. You can drop your hands," Ruddy said.

"I'm not armed," the man protested.

"They all say that."

Ruddy slid his gun back into its holster.

"I was really looking for—"

"I think you ought to go home and go to bed," Ruddy told him. "And leave law enforcement to the police department."

"Yes, Officer."

"You own a car?"

"Yes."

"Where is it?"

"About half a mile from here."

"Show me your driver's license."

The man fumbled in his pockets, and Ruddy pressed even closer to him, so close that if the man had suddenly drawn a hidden gun, Ruddy could have seized his arm.

"Here it is, sir."

Ruddy examined the document and handed it back.

"Okay, Professor. I think you can go home and tell your friends, if any are out here, to go home too," Ruddy said.

"Yes, Officer."

The man started off.

"Say," Ruddy called.

The man turned and walked back.

"You said that you were in the department of sociology."

"Yes, Officer."

"Well, I want to ask you a few questions. You know this town well?"

"Oh, like a book. In fact, I've written a book on it."

"You know these woods well?"

"Absolutely."

"You know all the paths leading in and out of here?"

"Everyone of 'em, Officer."

"Could anybody get into these woods without coming through that town?"

"Sure."

"How?"

"There's one narrow path that comes up over the rocks and across a brook."

"Oh."

"It's about two miles back there."

"Where does that path start?"

"It takes off in a railroad yard—just beyond Brentwood Park."

"I see." Ruddy was thoughtful. "Professor, I want you to report to police headquarters at ten in the morning and—"

"But I've done nothing," the professor protested. "I was only trying to hunt for murderers. I—"

"You will come, won't you?"

"Will I be arrested?"

"If you don't come, I'll take you in now," Ruddy threatened.

"Sure, I'll come," the professor said. "But I haven't done anything. I—"

"We just want to ask you a few questions."

"Sure. I'll come."

"Okay. Go on home," Ruddy said.

The man walked off with quick and nervous steps, making loud echoes on the gravel of the soft shoulder.

"He's no bushwhacker," Ruddy said to himself. "He'd wake the dead with those feet of his."

He got into his car and rolled toward headquarters. "Lay detectives . . . my God. It's a wonder there aren't more people killed in this world."

Ruddy nosed his car into the gate of police headquarters and was confronted by an armed officer.

"Who's that?"

Ruddy poked out his head and grinned. "Chief of Police, Rudolph Turner," he called.

There was an astonished silence. "Yes, sir! Come in, Chief. We weren't expecting you tonight. Roll straight ahead and you'll find the main door over that red light."

"Right."

Ruddy heard a shrill whistle behind him and at once a sergeant loomed before him as he slowed the car. The sergeant saluted.

"Good evening, Chief."

"Good evening, Sergeant."

The sergeant opened the door and Ruddy stepped out and looked around.

"You want me to show you to your office, Chief?"

Ruddy looked at the eager man and smiled. He knew that officers liked calmness and deliberateness.

"I would appreciate that," he told the officer.

"Right this way, Chief," the man sang.

"Thanks, Sergeant."

He followed the officer, who was a tawny-haired, chunky lad of about twenty-three. Irish maybe. Seems eager to serve. He strode along walls of marble, and he knew from the smell that the air was conditioned. The hallway was carpeted thickly with red plush material into which his feet sank. Plush . . . swank almost. Well, this was the top of his career. He had been sent in here to clean up crime. By God, he'd do it. They were lifted upward in an ornate elevator four floors and he fronted a huge open door, which bore gilt letters: THE CHIEF OF POLICE—BRENT-WOOD PARK

"Officer Ed Seigel is in your office, sir," the sergeant said, flinging wide the big doors.

"Good. I'm looking for 'im."

As Ruddy went through the door, his eyes swept what was to be his office.

"The staff is gone, sir," the sergeant said. "But if there's anything that—"

"I won't need anything tonight." Ruddy dismissed the man.

"Good night, sir."

"Good night."

Ruddy stood still as the door closed behind him. Yeah, there was old Ed Seigel seated at the side of his desk, his head lifted toward him in a cone of light shed by a desk lamp. Ruddy said nothing for a long moment, his eyes sweeping the office. It was huge, some thirty feet by forty feet, with a huge desk, beside which was a teletype machine, now silent, a wall map of the city of Chicago and its environs, and then various watercolors. Three sofas of red leather adorned one end of the room and a huge table stood at the center. The big portrait of the mayor of Chicago, Mayor Denin, occupied the left wall and an American flag of fifty white stars was on the right. Ruddy looked and pulled down the corners of his lips.

"The taxpayers are good to me," he mumbled.

"Damn right," Ed smirked.

"What are you butting in for? Work, you bastard!"

Ed laughed, rose, and ran his fingers through his graying hair, his left hand resting on the open dossiers that Captain Snell had given to him.

"What in hell you think I'm doing?" Ed came from around the desk and stood facing Ruddy. "Ruddy, you didn't forget me, did you?"

"Drop dead," Ruddy said, embarrassed.

"I'm grateful for the first promotion I've had in fifteen years," Ed said with a husky voice.

"You deserve it," Ruddy said.

"Why did you do it?"

"Do *what*?"

"Bring me here? Promote me . . . ?"

"I want your help, you dope!"

"But I thought you didn't believe in my ideas," Ed protested.

"Maybe I don't," Ruddy snapped.

"Then why am I here?"

"To give you a chance to convince me that you're wrong," Ruddy said with heavy irony.

"You're a straight guy, Ruddy," Ed said.

"You're straight too, Ed. You've been a friend of mine ever since you came on the force."

"That's natural."

"Sometimes."

"With me, friendship always comes natural."

"Why in hell do you think I've got you here if I didn't know that?" Ruddy asked.

"Look, did you see this gold eagle here?" Ed pointed out. "That's to go on your cap."

Ruddy lifted the golden insignia and studied it.

"Eagles have claws," he said absentmindedly.

"Yeah. To grab crooks with," Ed reminded him.

"And to scratch out the eyes of officers who are insubordinate." Ruddy chuckled. He slumped into the seat behind the desk, then looked down at a mass of papers.

He read out loud: "Inauguration ceremony at two P.M. Staff meeting at four P. M. Bullshit. Ed, have you been over those dossiers?"

"Just finished 'em, Chief."

"Listen, Ed. Cut that 'chief' shit with me, see?"

Ed grinned his appreciation. "Okay, Ruddy."

"Now, tell me. What do you make out of those reports?"

"Ruddy, you have to read this stuff in order not to believe it," Ed stated.

"Now, what do you mean?"

"I can't tell you about this unless I fly off into the clouds," Ed complained. "And that's what I don't want to do. I want to start my job right. But, Jesus, I can't make head or tail of this."

"First, one straight question . . ."

"Yeah, Ruddy."

"Did you find anything amiss with the conduct of the police in those dossiers?"

"Nothing. If there's any monkey business here, I can't spot it. Branden was a house on fire, but he was straight, regular. He did what any policeman would have done."

"Good. That means that we can look for crooks," Ruddy said. "And we don't have to be scared of our shadows."

"You've got enough rope to proceed?" Ed asked, arching his eyebrows.

"I wouldn't be here if I hadn't," Ruddy snapped. "Ed, I won't get any more promotions. I'm at the top. So I'm not scared of making mistakes or stepping on anybody's corns. I'm out to do a job. Come hell or high water."

"Good. A thing like this comes once in a lifetime."

"What do you think of my team? The commissioner gave—"

"I saw the list," Ed said with a grin. "I peeped into your papers."

"Before I did?"

"Yeah. I'm a spy."

"Look, I'm the chief. Not *you*."

"Just helping, Ruddy. You asked what I thought of your team, your staff . . . first-rate. All except one. And that's me. I can't judge myself."

"Nobody's asking you to," Ruddy said. "Now, tell me what that nightmare report gave you. What impressions?"

"Nightmares," Ed said, sitting, stretching out his legs. "Honest to God, we are out to catch a phantom."

"Do you think there was one or two or three or more murderers?" Ruddy asked.

"One."

"Why?"

"I don't know," Ed confessed.

"Just hunches, guesses?"

"Something like that," Ed said. "There isn't enough here for me to go on for me to make any other kind of statement. These are terse facts, and they do speak a kind of cryptic language."

"Okay. Just relax and let me hear what you think and feel,"

Ruddy said. "Don't hold back anything. Remember that you are going over ground where all the experts failed. So don't be bashful."

"Ruddy, we're dealing with something out of the ordinary here," Ed began.

"Is that all you got to tell me?" Ruddy countered.

"Wait. Let me get into it," Ed protested. "Now, look, this murderer—"

"Man or woman?" Ruddy interrupted.

"I think it was a man," Ed said haltingly.

"Why?"

"Well, in the light of what we got to go on," Ed began, "it's a kind of psychological guess, you see. A preacher is killed with a woman. Then a priest is killed with a nun. Then the detective's son is killed—alone. Now, Ruddy, I've been sitting here trying to put myself in that murderer's place. It's hard. Now, that preacher, that priest, and the detective's son represented something to that killer. Ruddy, a woman is an earthy kind of creature. If she hates you, she kills you. And there is always an understandable reason. But a man kills in a funny kind of way. First of all, those whom he kills have to be kind of transfigured in his mind . . ."

"What?"

"Made bigger than life, see?" Ed hastened to explain. "That priest was not just a priest. That preacher was more than a man of the cloth. And that detective's son was more than merely some man's son."

"What were they?"

"Symbols of something hated," Ed said.

Ruddy sighed, looked at his shoes, and then at Ed. "I'm the craziest chief of police in the whole United States," he said slowly.

"Why?"

"I'm sitting here and letting you talk to me," Ruddy grumbled.

They both laughed.

"Well, if you think somebody else can talk with more sense, then—"

"Go on with your theories," Ruddy ordered.

"Now, this transfiguration business," Ed observed. "It needs explaining—"

"I'll say it does," Ruddy scoffed playfully.

"Say, Ruddy, were you ever in love?"

"Yeah. But what has that got to do with it?"

"Plenty. Do you recall how you felt when you were in love?"

"It was great, man. It was out of this world."

"Good. Now, can you recall just how the girl looked to you."

"Great, I told you."

"No. What was there about that girl that made you love her?"

"Gosh, everything. Whenever she looked at me, she sent me. That's all."

"Okay. But that didn't happen to others around her, did it?"

"No. I guess some other guys were after her, but *I* won her."

"Do you think her mother saw her as you saw her?"

"No. Her mother wasn't in love with her the way I was," Ruddy pointed out.

"And her brothers?"

"No. They didn't see her like I did."

"Her other relatives?"

"No. They were not as excited as I was."

"Good. You transfigured that gal," Ed stated.

"Now, just what in hell does that mean?" Ruddy demanded.

"Psychoanalysts call it overestimating the object," Ed explained.

"What? To me she was worth more than she was to others?"

"You could put it that way."

"Ed, are you being cynical?"

"No. Factual."

"Now, how was this priest, this preacher, and this detective's son worth more to somebody—so much more than to others that he killed 'em?"

"What I'm getting at, Ruddy, is that hate also transfigures," Ed said.

"Oh." Ruddy snickered. "I thought you were going to say that I was the murderer."

"You're murdering my logic," Ed complained. "Now, do you get what I mean by overestimating?"

"Yeah. I get you. Go on."

"Now, Ruddy, men do that more than women," Ed said. "That's why I'm settling on a man for our murderer. Women don't write Bibles. Not many women write novels."

"Thank God."

"Men are the crazy creatures who want to go to the moon, not women."

"I see."

"The world's great painting comes from men."

"Hunh huh."

"Men are always imagining something bigger, richer, more powerful than it is, and then going and trying to grab it," Ed analyzed. "A woman would have cussed out that preacher and had done with 'im. A woman would have gossiped about that priest and left 'im alone. A girl would have cried about Heard's son and suffered in silence. A man acts. He's compelled to. The world a man sees differs drastically from that seen and felt by a woman."

"Okay. I buy that, Ed. I felt all along that a man did it, maybe more than one. I don't know. The reason why I asked you to keep on theorizing was that I wanted additional facts to go on," Ruddy rumbled. "Now that we are looking for somebody in the masculine half of the human race, you might try to narrow our search by trying to plumb the motive for those murders."

"Wheew," Ed whistled. "All that in one evening?"

"Yep. You're being paid—"

"This is overtime," Ed grumbled, grinning. "Well, what kind of motive? That's hard. Here we have three separate murders, five victims, and no evidence. We have to find a motive that fits all three crimes. Now, for the sake of simplicity, let's rule out those women who were killed. They seemed to have been there by accident. There were two different women in two different slayings. But there were three men in three slayings. And each time there was a murder, the women seemed to have dropped out of the clouds to be at the side of the men victims. My feeling, based on those facts, is that the murderer was not after the women at all. But how could he kill his intended victims and get away without killing the women. So, in looking for a motive, I'm ruling out the fuss and noise of the newspapers, that is, that the priest and the preacher were surprised in love trysts, see? After all, there was no molesting of the bodies of the women. That's strange. In a lot of cases the muggers will at least lift the woman's skirt and get a look. They always have time for that. Some even make 'em lie down and submit before killing 'em. But there's absolutely no evidence in that direction. All right, the man or men wanted to kill only the men; the slaying of the women was incidental.

"Now that brings us to a queer problem. What kind of motive will fit those three killings? Could the same woman have been in love with both the priest and the preacher and the detective, taking revenge on his son? Could she have hired a man to do all three killings? It is too far-fetched. I can't think that any such thing has happened, not knowing life as I do. If such happened, then it was indeed something weirdly coincidental. I don't think it happened.

"Was there an anarchist with a grudge against men of religion?—and I'm now saying that the killing of Heard's son was to forestall his finding the real murderer. If it was an anarchist, why didn't he go for heads of states? Why religious people? I would rule out anarchists. Their acting in such a manner is atypical.

"Communists? No, I don't think so. They go for the tools of production. Why kill religious men and bring down on their heads a full tide of terror? The Communist always deals with masses of people, not individuals. If a Communist had a grudge, he would have gone to the slums of either the Black Belt or to the trade unions to preach his message of revolt. Rarely do they bother with the bourgeoisie, and most surely not preachers of either of the two big branches of the Christian religion. The Communists are rivals of the Church, so why would they do something that would stun and horrify the followers of the Church? No, they wouldn't. Instead, they would try to show those followers that it was the *Church* that was committing the horrors. I'd think that the fascists would follow the same general course, only they'd be preaching myths instead of ideology. But there was no preaching in these murders or even the hint of them—"

"You spoke of these murders being a kind of language," Ruddy reminded Ed.

"Yeah. I'm keeping that in mind," Ed said. "These murders were shock tactics. They were designed to make masses of people both take notice and recoil. Notice how crime fell off sharply after the murders? That was one of the aims."

"Jesus, Ed," Ruddy complained, "how could you or anybody know that?"

"I don't say the murderer or murderers consciously aimed

at that," Ed conceded. "Maybe deep down they were aiming at it unconsciously—"

"I was waiting for that goddamn word, 'unconscious,'" Ruddy spoke scornfully. "I'm a cop and don't deal with that in my work. I can't talk to the DA about 'unconscious' motives, see? Let's be clear about that."

"Okay. I'm not submitting stuff for the DA," Ed said. "I'm trying to get a line on these crimes, see? That's all. I still insist that, if my theory holds until now, there was something that the murderer wanted to say."

"To whom?"

Ed rose, jammed his hands into his pockets and paced the floor.

"I'm trying to keep my feet on the ground," he grumbled. "S-suppose his audience was the w-world . . . m-mankind."

"Aw, Ed," Ruddy slapped his hand derisively toward him.

"No, no. Calm down," Ed pleaded. "Take your time. And follow me."

"Talk concretely," Ruddy insisted. "What goddamn audience?"

"That's the problem," Ed said. "I could possibly feel what kind of audience, but I cannot describe it. Strange, eh?"

"You mean that the murderer didn't have his audience visually in mind?"

"Yes and no. He sensed it," Ed explained. "It was so obvious to him that he did not have to picture it out clearly."

"But it was toward something," Ruddy insisted. "Or your theory is nonsense. If I even hinted that to the DA, he'd say I was trying to supply the murderer with a defense of insanity even before we caught 'im."

"I know, I know," Ed admitted. He began to speak in a low, pleading tone: "Ruddy, who made our laws?"

"The people, they say," Ruddy replied, lifting his eyes.

"And when I mention the word 'religion,' what comes to your mind, Ruddy?" Ed pursued his aim.

Ruddy sighed, looked distrustfully around the huge office. "Must I play this game?"

"Yes. Just try it. What have you got to lose?"

"Nothing, I guess. Just my time and taxpayer's money," Ruddy said with a silent laugh in his voice. "Religion . . . well, it brings to my mind churches, temples, organs playing, dim cathedrals, candles flickering, stained-glass windows, choirs—"

"No definite image of certain people?"

"No."

"Now, try to imagine the banking system . . ."

"Heaps of money, vaults—"

"No definite people?"

"No."

"Armies, military might? What comes to your mind?"

"Guns, planes, tanks, missiles—"

"No images of certain people?"

"No. Vaguely I think of generals."

"What generals?"

"None in particular."

"Now, Ruddy, we talked of law, the church, banks, armies— and no people came to your mind in a concrete way." Ed followed the thread of his argument. "Most people think like that. Yet people and people alone make those realities real. Now, why should criminals think any differently of them?"

"I see what you mean," Ruddy said in a dubious tone. "But how in the world could we ever know what was in that murderer's mind?"

"We got a damn good clue," Ed insisted.

"What?"

"The corpses—that is, if we rule out the murdered women."

"Oh. Religious men, two of 'em. And a detective's son," Ruddy recited.

"Now, what do they mean?"

"The Church. And policemen."

"Yeah. Now, let's translate what the Church means. It is religion and religion is law. And from that law we get the law that Heard's father was executing. So it was law that the murderer struck at."

"Now, you are reversing the argument," Ruddy pointed out.

"Right. Churches and policemen stand for people who operate them. Churches and policemen hold law in their hands. When Churches and policemen are attacked, the law is attacked. Now, you can start either with the Church or with the police. You end up in the same place, with the same image."

"So, we've got a vague motive." Ruddy was tentatively accepting the theory to see what it would yield. "A man against the law—"

"In the deepest sense," Ed reminded him. "He had in mind the origin of law and those who explained it and those who executed it."

"A cop hater, hunh?"

"No. It was deeper than that—if my theory is at all true," Ed said.

"What could that murderer have been hating, then?" Ruddy asked slowly.

"Well, let's again reverse the argument, the procedure," Ed suggested. "We don't know what he really hated. We know it was the law in abstract. The moral impulses behind the law and the men who wrote that law and the men who executed it. Now, let's try to imagine what kind of event happened to such a man that would make him go hunting for men who represented that law."

"And we're leaving the women out of it?" Ruddy asked. "Completely?"

"Yes and no. It's possible that that murderer had a yen to polish off those women," Ed admitted. "But I don't think he went into those woods just to hunt and kill women. Maybe at first he did not go into those woods to kill at all. Maybe he just went for a walk—because he was distracted and wrought-up, see? Then he came upon that preacher and that woman. Then his complexes were set off."

"Humnnn . . ."

"But . . . let's get back to the point we had in mind," Ed spoke with a voice full of self-scolding. "We said we would try to imagine what kind of event or events made him kill. Now, we're on quicksand—"

"We've been in quicksand from the beginning," Ruddy muttered.

"Number one: Let's imagine a young medical student doing scientific experiments. He's put all his money into the thing," Ed outlined. "He's worked night and day for years and years. At last he thinks he's found something. He goes and presents it to his superiors. They examine it and find one tiny meaningful flaw. He's out. He had thought that he was made; he had banked all his moral capital and material capital on it. He's floored. He's mad. But at whom? He walks out, blind, into those woods to cool his hot brow and—"

"I'm sorry for that sonofabitch." Ruddy grinned.

"Okay. Number two: Let us imagine a young man, nominally religious, Catholic or Protestant, in the French Foreign Legion, stationed in North Africa. Let us imagine that one day this young man receives a cable that an old and rich uncle of his is dying and that that uncle wants that boy near him. The military authorities permit the boy to visit the uncle. The boy goes, finds that the uncle has somewhat recovered but is still ill. The uncle tells the boy that he will make him his sole heir if the boy remains by the side of the uncle and aids him. The boy decides to desert the Foreign Legion, sticks close to the bedside of the ailing uncle. But the uncle does not die at once. He lingers. The old bugger is stronger than even the doctors think. The boy lingers on, helping, hoping. But he dare not try to speed the uncle's departure. He's much too devout for that. He waits and waits. The uncle grows slowly feebler. The boy acts now as a kind of nurse. He empties bedpans. He bathes the uncle, who won't let others touch 'im. With the boy at his bedside, the old uncle begins to relive his life. He tells the boy of his youth, of his old hopes and plans. He is passing on his torch to the younger man whose blood is still hot and pulsing. One day the boy has to go down to shop. The old man, feeling stronger than he really is, gets out of bed to make a cup of tea in the kitchen. He stumbles in his nightgown and falls, and in falling, he yanks out the gas tube of the gas stove. He's too weak to rise. He calls weakly for help. His head swims. He knows what has happened to him; he struggles up and tries to walk to the wall to shut off the gas and his legs become entangled by a fallen chair and this time he plunges down, hitting his head against an edge of the stove. He's temporarily stunned, out. The escaping gas is now filling the kitchen. Lying prone, the uncle is asphixiated. The boy returns and finds the apartment filled with gas. He rushes in, but he is too late. He calls for help. The uncle is dead and cannot be revived.

"That boy is crushed. He had given up all for the sake of the inheritance and he has hopes that he'll get it. But he feels guilty, as though he had killed his uncle. The uncle is buried; then the will is read. *The Uncle, feeling that he had longer to live than he had imagined, had failed to revise his will and the boy is penniless.*"

"Goddamn, Ed, did that ever happen to you?" Ruddy demanded, laughing ruefully.

"Hell, no. I don't know what I'd have done, if it had," Ed confessed. "Now, penniless, the boy, after the reading of the will, stumbles out of the house. The only thing left him is to return to the Foreign Legion, where he will be punished for desertion. He wanders into the woods above Brentwood Park . . ."

"I see it," Ruddy said, lighting another cigarette.

"He could kill in a fit of pique or rage, helpless, hopeless rage," Ed stated.

"Yeah," Ruddy agreed, rubbing his left palm over his eyes. He looked unseeingly around. "Any more ideas?"

"Well, let's imagine another one. Number three: Now—"

"What about a woman?" Ruddy interposed. "A woman jilts a man . . ." He saw poor Marie as he asked the question.

Ed pulled down the corners of his lips.

"You know, Ruddy, the role of woman has been dreadfully overestimated in this world," Ed said. "Oh, yes, they are the mothers of the race. We know that. They bear us, give us the breath of life. But we don't think of that much. We take it for granted. And after all, women want to do that. All right, a girl jilts a boy. He's sad. He mopes. Or he kills himself. Mostly they kill themselves if they do anything at all. Now and then, in Latin countries, they kill the girl. But, hell, here in the good old U.S.A. or in England, where women are to be had and where, in spite of all, we have a rough kind of sexual democracy, would he kill himself or the girl? 'There's always another one, just like the other one,' goes a childhood song."

"All right, get on with Number three," Ruddy coaxed Ed.

"Number three. Let's imagine a young man who grew up as a model son in a family. He loves his parents. His parents love him. One day he learns that his mother is not his mother, that his father is not his father; he learns that he is an adopted orphan. That he came from some slum way down in the social heap. Let us imagine that not only does he learn this but all his friends learn it. He feels cut off, let down, and betrayed. He does not know what to do. He is obsessed in wanting to find out who his real parents were. For those parents now assume a mythlike and legendary quality for him. He is intelligent; he pores over records in police stations—"

"This is interesting," Ruddy murmured, lifting his right hand and brushing away a film of dampness from his forehead.

"He finds that his father was a murderer," Ed went fiercely and relentlessly on. "He finds that his mother perhaps even then did not know who the 'real' father was. That boy is stigmatized in the very depth of his soul. Oh, if only he could destroy those records! Wipe them out! He feels as he walks along the street that everybody knows his shameful secret. He can't sleep, can't eat, can't work. He dares tell no one what he really knows, for it is far worse than what they already know about 'im. That boy walks the streets at night. He finds the woods above Brentwood Park, wanders in then . . . for no definite purpose. He finds Reverend Hindricks and a girl in a car. He has a .38 on him, to kill himself perhaps. He uses it on impulse. He shoots them."

"Yeah." Ruddy rose and walked to and fro in the office. "Could be." His voice was high-pitched and tense. "Anything could be," he added, hoping to wipe out any untoward meaning that might have crept into his voice.

"But, Ruddy, do you get the kind of 'feeling' that might have been in our slayer?" Ed asked. "I need not continue to spin out these hypothetical situations."

"I get it," Ruddy said crisply.

"Now, how do we start looking for such a man?" Ed asked.

"Beats me," Ruddy growled. "I'll have the newspapers searched for any untoward happenings of an odd nature." He kept his voice neutral. "You never can tell what'll turn up."

"Right," Ed said, scribbling on a pad of paper.

"We'll have the high school and university examination records in this area gone over to see if there were any failures that had a bad emotional reaction upon the student," Ruddy said.

"Right," Ed agreed, sribbling again.

"I'm going to have all bankruptcy proceedings in this area looked into," Ruddy added.

"Not a bad idea at all," Ed said. "Since we have nothing, something just might turn up."

"And we must leave no stone unturned to trace that .38," Ruddy said.

"It was odd about that gun," Ed said reflectively. "It was the same gun used in all three murders. That's another fact that convinces me that there was one murderer."

"I want all suicides checked into again," Ruddy said. "Not only might the fool have killed himself, but he might have left traces of evidence in his life that could lead us to a solution."

"Right."

"I want all of those psychopath confessions reexamined," Ruddy ordered.

"Right."

"I want the correspondence, signed and anonymous, relating to this case reread and reassessed," Ruddy ordered.

"Not bad."

"As discreetly as possible, I want to check, in some way or other, all psychiatric records of those appealing for help at the various hospitals and mental clinics," Ruddy said.

"Good."

"In order to facilitate our work, we must somehow determine if our murderer lives in Brentwood Park or not," Ruddy said, remembering the Professor Louis Redfield he had met a few hours past.

"Yes," Ed murmured. "That's baffling."

"Ed, there is a secret—no I oughtn't say that—but a little-known path leading into those woods—"

"No! How do you know?"

"A professor at the University of Chicago told me that," Ruddy said softly.

"There's no mention of that in these dossiers," Ed said.

"It seems to have been overlooked."

"Looks like a lot has been overlooked in this case," Ed sighed. "Say, where does that path begin?"

"From a slum area near the railroad tracks," Ruddy explained. "It mounts over a huge rock, then leads to a creek, across which it is not difficult to negotiate, and then on into the woods."

"Goddamn."

"Ed, I want to start backward in this case," Ruddy went on. "Forget the preacher. That priest. Let's start with Heard Jr. We will be able to determine quickly if the cases are linked. If we get any lead on how Heard was killed, then we'll know if the others were linked to him. That'll save us time. And Heard's case is closer to us in time."

"Right."

Suddenly the teletype machine began to whir clackingly. Ruddy's and Ed's eyes turned to it. Ruddy picked up the jutting and sliding tape of paper and began to read it. He was interrupted by the shrill ring of the telephone. He lifted the receiver.

"Chief Turner speaking."

"Chief, this is Lieutenant Parrish reporting. A report from Officer Only says that a workman has reported to him that the body of a young woman has been found dead in the woods above Brentwood Park. Shot to death. We're holding the workman, though he seems to be telling a straight story. I've notified the medical exaiminer's office. Three squad cars have responded to calls and are on the way."

"What part of the woods is the body in?"

"Near the center," Lieutenant Parrish said. "Your official car's ready for you if you plan to go."

"Right. I'll be right down," Ruddy said, slamming down the receiver.

"What's up?" Ed asked.

"Looks like we won't have to bother about starting the investigation of this goddamn case in reverse," Ruddy said. "It's opened again, it seems."

"No?"

"Yeah. The body of a young woman, shot to death, has just been reported as found in the center of Brentwood Park."

"Crawling Baby Jesus Christ," Ed exclaimed.

"Let's go, Ed."

"Hell, yes!"

Not another word was spoken until the two officers had rushed down and gotten into the waiting car, their lips pursed tight, their eyes stony and hard and unblinking.

CHAPTER 12

Midnight was striking on all the town's clocks as the police-car's siren screamed into the balmy April air. Amidst high purple scudding clouds, a few faint yellow stars were visible. The car's resilient springs jolted them like a pitching ship as they sought to equalize the rutted streetcar tracks. Ruddy and Ed were alone in the back seat and two officers were in front—one of whom was a chauffeur at the steering wheel, his face hunched grimly forward. Ruddy and Ed sat hunched forward, tense, their fingers holding smoldering cigarettes that they had lit and had forgot.

"It's the goddamnest thing," Ed commented.

"Yeah."

"If it's the murderer again, then it rules out some of your suggestions," Ed said.

"Don't want to sound sadistic," Ruddy muttered, "but I'd not be sorry if it is the murderer. At least then we'd get a line on 'im and maybe keep 'im from killing again."

"Yes. Since this girl's dead already . . . and we were just thinking about starting with Heard's son—"

"Hunh?"

"It's strange, this new killing. Wonder if it is really linked with the others?"

"Hard to tell. We'll know something soon."

"Sleepy?"

"No. You?"

"No. But you didn't get a wink of sleep last night."

"I was a bit dopey. Earlier today. But I'm more wide awake now than I ever was in all of my life."

"It's always like that," Ed sympathized.

"Say," Ruddy asked of the chauffeur, leaning forward, "is your radio-telephone working?"

"Yes, sir. It's right before you, down a bit toward the floor-board."

"Oh, yes."

"If you pick up the receiver and wait till the light flashes green, you'll get a line."

"Thanks." Ruddy lifted the black receiver, and when the light glowed green, he asked the operator amid brittle static for Commissioner King's office. When put through, he was told that naturally the commissioner was not in but that he could leave any messages he wanted. Ruddy informed the secretary that she must tell the commissioner: he was canceling the inaugural ceremony, scheduled for two o'clock in the afternoon, and he was also postponing the slated staff conference, which was to be held at four P.M.; that he would be absent in the field, giving his reasons as "the urgent nature of the new developments that were taking place in Brentwood Park."

He hung up, feeling free now to give himself over without reserve to what lay ahead.

"Gosh, you weren't an hour too soon, Chief," the chauffeur said as Ruddy hugged the car handle, balancing himself against the tight pull of a steep curve.

"Looks like it," Ruddy mumbled in an uncommunicative tone. "No facts as yet on this new find?"

"Nothing, Chief. Just what came over the wire about finding a girl's body."

"Hummn . . ."

"A workman found the body?" Ed asked.

"Yes, sir. But he seems on the level."

"Funny, eh? It comes just a bit after you took the oath of office," Ed commented.

"I was thinking about that," Ruddy said almost defensively.

Ten minutes later, both Ruddy and Ed, following an officer with a flashlight, plunged into high wet grass and thick tree leaves and struggled toward an area ahead, which was illuminated by blinding spotlights. Yeah, a regular paradise for muggers. The cuffs of his trousers were becoming heavy and waterlogged from the limp, dew-wet grass.

"We must map out this little-used path in these woods right away," Ruddy growled angrily.

"Yeah. This surely ain't it," an officer volunteered.

"Why in hell would a young girl come in here?" Ed asked, more of himself than of Ruddy.

"You got me there. I'd rather walk a mile on asphalt than wade through here," Ruddy said. "But some people have odd ideas."

"Her body must be somewhere near that path one keeps hearing about," Ed hazarded.

"Maybe."

"These damned wild woods are more frequented than we imagine," Ed observed.

"People who live in cities dote on savage places like this," Ruddy said.

"Looks like it."

Far ahead, through wet leaves, Ruddy could glimpse bits of dazzling yellow light.

"Not far now," the officer grunted.

"I see the lights," Ed announced.

A minute later the officer said, "Here we are, sir."

He pulled aside a bunch of slender tree branches so that Ruddy and Ed could step into the full glare of the circularly grouped spotlights. A dozen or so officers and plainclothesmen stood in a rough semicircle. Ruddy pressed forward and a few officers made way for him, calling out softly: "It's the Chief; let 'im in."

Ruddy halted abruptly. He stood gazing down at the prone body of a young girl who lay half on her stomach and half on her side, as though her body had twisted itself while in the act of pitching headlong toward the ground. The girl's body pressed down wet weeds more than two feet tall.

"Has anybody seen that path?" Ruddy called out.

"Yes, sir. It's about half a mile from here."

"Then she was running, trying to dodge somebody," Ruddy said. "Even a damn fool wouldn't *walk* in here."

"That seems about it, Chief," somebody chimed in.

A cheap, white handbag, the handle of which was still clutched in the still, waxen, stiff fingers, lay partly opened with most of its contents spilled out: a handkerchief, now wet and soggy; a brown comb with a few strands of blond hair; an address book, swollen from humidity; a gilt-colored lipstick; a powder case; a cheap paperback love novel, now swelling with dew; a billfold fairly thick with what seemed like paper money; a few opened letters; a batch of keys; and other odd items. A light wind was still blowing and it was agitating the girl's cheap skirt, which was pulled a few inches above her right knee, revealing a short sweep of white thigh. The girl's tiny hat was still on her head, tied by a pink ribbon under her chin, the knotted bow out of sight now. Both of the nylon stockings had been ripped. The long blond hair, worn loose and tied in a ponytail at the back of her head, was tangled and wet about her face and shoulders. A tiny band of gold ring—not a wedding ring—showed in soft glints around a dim blue stone on the middle finger of the girl's left hand. Ruddy had to stoop and peer in order to study the girl's face, and he saw a bullet wound high in the middle of her forehead.

"Felled like an ox," he breathed.

"Done at point-blank range," Ed said.

"Exactly like the other wounds," Ruddy said.

"A .38?" Ed asked, looking up.

"Yes, sir. Seems like it."

"Identification?" Ruddy asked.

"Yes sir, Chief." The voice was that of Captain Snell.

"Oh, Captain. You're there," Ruddy complimented the man.

"And I'm amazed to see you here, knowing you had no sleep last night," Captain Snell said. "We've been into the handbag. Her name is Janet Wilder. Aged twenty. We got that off her Social Security card. She lives at 931 Beachcomb Street—in Brentwood—that's way over where there's a new housing development. She worked as a wrapper, it seemed, for Swift's, in the stockyards."

"Any signs of sexual molestation?"

"No sign of any. Of course, the coroner will be able to tell definitely. But I'd say no, from the looks of her clothes," the captain reported.

"Anything seems to be missing?"

"Doesn't seem like it so far," the captain said. "We're going to check to find out what she had on her, besides what we see here. It seems that she's just been paid off. Her paycheck is here—calling for eighty-one dollars and sixteen cents, minus income tax. And there is four dollars and forty cents in cash in the handbag."

Ruddy stood and pulled off his cap and felt the cool night air on his hot forehead.

"What was she doing in these goddamned woods?" Ruddy demanded with savage compassiion.

"Looks like she was taking a short-cut, Chief," somebody said.

"She took one." Ruddy was wild with impotent grief.

"We just heard about that path tonight," Ed murmured.

"Any idea when she died?" Ruddy asked.

"The coroner's rough estimate is about two P.M. this afternoon—that is, Chief, yesterday afternoon, for it's after midnight now. She must've died at once. Rigor mortis is beginning to set in."

"No signs of a struggle?"

"None whatsoever."

"No clues?"

"No, not yet. About five of our officers are fanning out with flashlights and beating the bushes. We'll be able to see better tomorrow morning."

"This is undoubtedly a repetition of those three past murders," Ed stated stoutly.

"Seems like it," several voices sounded at once.

"Captain Snell, get to her home and notify her kin and pick up whatever you can from 'em," Ruddy ordered, sighing.

"Yes, sir, Chief."

"Photos have been taken?"

"Yes, sir. They just finished, sir."

"Go over that handbag for fingerprints—just to make sure that we don't overlook any bets," Ruddy ordered.

"Yes, sir."

"Any sign of footprints at all?" he asked of the assembled officers.

"None, sir," Captain Snell answered. "You see, this grass here is now wet with dew. Whatever could have been seen is now gone. The dew made it rise and take its old stance again, and the leaves, if they've been pushed aside, have also gone back to their original position."

"Yeah. I see that." Ruddy sighed. "We never seem to be in time for our killer."

"Here comes somebody," Ed announced, pointing to an advancing cone of yellow light that wobbled in the darkness, a wobble that indicated a man walking.

Jock Weidman pushed forward, bareheaded, his face red and streaked with sweat and wet and showing scratches and bruises where tree twigs had whipped about his cheeks.

"I lost my cap somewhere," he said idly.

"Anything, Jock?" Ruddy called.

"Hi, Chief," Jock answered. "I've found something. A hole . . . freshly dug . . . about a quarter of a mile from here. Looks to me like somebody was digging up a buried gun. In fact, there seems to be the shape of something that looks like a .38 molded into the clay there."

"Jesus . . . let's get there!" Ruddy yelled.

"A clue of some kind at last," Ed yelled.

"I want a cast made of that hole at once," Ruddy ordered, plunging forward.

"Chief, the dew is still falling," Jock said.

"That's why we must shelter that hole," Ruddy said.

"I did, Chief," Jock said. "I put newspapers over it."

"God, good for you, Jock," Ruddy thanked his man.

"Get that plaster guy here quick and let 'im take a cast of this," Ruddy called.

"Yes, sir," an eager chorus of voices answered.

"Don't know if there is any chance of fingerprints," Ed spoke pessimistically, panting as they half ran and half walked.

"Maybe not," Ruddy agreed.

Jock was at their side, puffing, for he had been over this route and was now retraveling it. Ruddy saw that his coat was sticking to his skin.

"Jock, get to a car and get your clothes changed as soon as you show us this hole," Ruddy advised.

"It's nothing, Chief."

"No backtalk. Do as I tell you," Ruddy scolded him. "Don't want any of my men getting sick on me."

"Okay, Chief." Jock's voice held a note of gratitude.

Five minutes later they stood over a gaping brown hole amid tall grass.

"Goddamn," Ruddy breathed. "Now, what made 'im rush here and dig up that gun?"

"We won't know maybe till we catch 'im," Captain Snell murmured.

"Captain, get to that girl's house, like I told you," Ruddy snapped.

"Yes sir, Chief," Captain Snell answered and vanished.

"Not much of a chance for any kind of prints there." Ed spoke studiedly. "Sometimes a print will adhere from one object to another. But that clay is already losing its shape. This is a goddamn luckless case."

"Well, take a mold quick, anyhow," Ruddy pressed. "You can never tell. Maybe that .38 has certain defects that'll show. Now, we've got to find that gun. The killer has it. No wonder we could never find it—with its being buried here. Who in all hell would've thought of digging in this godforsaken wood for a .38? *But what is he going to do with it?* He's got one victim with it already, but he did not dig it up for that. He's going to use it. He thought enough of digging it up to risk being seen, for he knows we're looking for 'im high and low." Ruddy looked at the circle of officers flanking him. "Men, we are looking for a desperate killer. He's reached into our force and laid low the son of one of our men, Detective Heard. Before that, for some fantastic reason, he killed four times, twice each time he struck. Now, this is the sixth killing. I'm canceling all leaves. The search for this killer has priority over everything. And I'm asking Commissioner King to make it priority number one for the whole city of Chicago! Our police department is not going to rest until this killer has been had by the heels!"

CHAPTER 13

Having dispatched the station's standing corps of stool pigeons to the city's four corners to listen or snoop for possible leads or information; having assigned the squads of detectives to their various chores; having issued strict orders to keep all developments out of the press for fear of tipping off the murderer that his victim had been found—in short, having seen to it that all the traditional and routine aspects of the investigatory apparatus had been set in motion, Ruddy, instead of going home to sleep, sat alone in his new office, feeling the powerful tug of fatigue but somehow gripped by an irrational urge to resist resting.

The thought—that until now he had not dared to let himself think—was standing up full and imperative in him. It had not risen suddenly, that question, yet it could not be said that it had stolen upon him. Long before this murder case had broken, and long before he had had any notion that he would ever be a chief of police, there had slumbered in him a secret fear for Tommy. But that fear had been nameless, intuitive, tugging tentatively at his heartstrings, and he had never been able to tell why. Whenever he thought of Tommy, he thought of his own young manhood and there was an unbridgeable gap between them; there were no kindred parallels upon which he could rely. He had always consoled himself with the thought that he had not given the boy enough of his attention, and that in this modern world too great a distance of experience and attitude loomed between the generations of fathers and sons. But what he was looking at now as a possibility was no distance; it was an absolute pouring out from another world governed by other laws.

The hard kernel of that question had been sown in his mind by Ed's long and highly speculative analysis of who the murderer could possibly be and what motive could have sustained such cold-blooded and brutal slayings. And that was why, when Ed had talked and argued, an anxious sweat had broken out upon his brow. At first he had merely stared noncommittally at the magical logic of Ed's suppositions, as though peering into the wrong end of a telescope, sensing and feeling the horror of a remote possibility; the whole idea had hovered somewhere between his subconscious mind and his rational outlook, and then, as he had stood there above the dew-damp body of that slain girl, he had wondered who on earth was close enough to him to have known that he had become the head of the police of Brentwood Park, who on earth close to him had had in his past experience that shock of living that would have made him feel outraged toward all the moral and institutional laws of the world?

The question was: Was Tommy, his son, his flesh and blood, the murderer he sought? And Tommy—for reasons Ruddy had no cause at the time to suspect—had not been at home for lunch yesterday! Why had he rushed off into the unknown after their first long talk, a talk in which the boy had confessed having sustained an unbearable shock? Tommy had been missing at the very moment that the girl had been fleeing the demon who had slain her.

No, no, that could not be. He was tired, too tired to think; his nerves were overwrought. He was letting the responsibilities of his job weigh him down and cloud his better judgment. There was no reason on earth why a horror like that should so much as touch his life. No, it could not be true; it was crazy. *And he was crazy even to think it!*

But Ruddy was not completely his own master; years and years had gone into the making of him into a policeman and he could not control the cold and logical workings of his own mind. Given a certain set of hard facts, given a possible motive, given a cold and stiff corpse, his mind, in spite of his feelings, leaped inevitably toward guilty possibilities.

Just how badly had Tommy been hurt? "Maybe not much, or he would have talked to me about it," he muttered half aloud. Yet he knew that there were some shocks too deep for speech, that left the heart and mind numb, that sent one's tired and restless legs wandering down lonely black night streets. In his talking to poor Marie he too had felt the shock, the senselessness of what had happened to her and Tommy, had been swept by a blind surge of fury against the very foundations of the sentient universe. And if he had felt that, what must poor Tommy have felt?

Yet no matter how much logic appeared to be in it, it just could not be true. It could not possibly happen to him or to any member of his family. Did not his hands hold the law? Had he not done his part as a father and a citizen? Sure, there were freakish accidents in life, but they always visited other people, people who had somewhere deep down in their lives something to be corrected, some justice due them, some debt that they had not paid society or their fellow men or their God. But, in the very split second of thinking this, Ruddy knew that it was nonsense. First of all, he knew nothing of such matters. Only the Church knew. But he could never go to Father Joyce with this kind of story. Why not? Well, one just did not. Something in him told him that he could not trust the Church even in matters of this sort.

"But I've no proof," he growled out loud. "What the hell's wrong with me?"

Yet he knew that in any other case, had he had as much suspicion as he had regarding Tommy, he would have been in action; he would have been at the home of the suspect, examining his shoes, firing one question after another, poking into attics and basements for that .38. And here he sat, paralyzed. Yes, he knew now why doctors always called in another doctor when members of their family were ill; they had to have objective opinions. Should he talk to Ed? God, no! He was Ed's boss. And he had been on this job less than twenty-four hours. To be named chief of police and to ask one's neighbor if one harbored a murderer in one's family was insane, unthinkable, crazy, wild!

No, he needed sleep. He looked at his watch. It was seven o'clock. He rose and adjusted the Venetian blinds, letting in the soft light of a murky April morning. He had told the male secretary on guard to inform Agnes that he was being detained by urgent duty. Yeah, he'd go home. No. He had an appointment with that Professor Louis Redfield! Yeah, he would have to stay.

In a sleepy drawl, Ruddy ordered coffee, orange juice, and toast, and when an attendant served his breakfast, there was a batch of morning papers. Good God! Tall black headlines swept across the tops of the front pages like shouting borders of mourning:

NEW BRENTWOOD PARK MURDER

ANOTHER CORPSE IN BRENTWOOD FOREST

BRENTWOOD FOREST CLAIMS SIXTH VICTIM

NEW POLICE HEAD FACES GRIM TEST

HOW SAFE ARE WE NOW? ANOTHER SLAYING IN BRENTWOOD

ARE OUR POLICE ASLEEP?

BRENTWOOD PARK GHOUL STRIKES AGAIN

And in all the papers were photographs of Janet Wilder, some showing her in a bathing costume, others placing her in a picnic gathering amidst trees and wildflowers, and in one she stood with her arms about a young man's shoulder. Yes, it was all calculated to rouse the most intense horror, to cast doubts upon the efficiency of the police, and to make one stare suspiciously at one's neighbor. But, luckily, so far as he could see, no vital information had been leaked to the press, and for that Ruddy was grateful. He thrust the papers aside and ate mechanically, scarcely tasting his food. Yeah, I'm in the soup, all right. They are demanding that I deliver before I'm hardly on the job. He was determined not to let the press worry him, for he knew that the favorite sport of newspaper reporters was to bait and browbeat the police, who could not make a rebuttal. He knew how the public loved it when the press was rapping the police across the knuckles! It made the taxpayer feel that he was at last getting his money's worth. I'm not going to let 'em bother me. Yet, as soon as he had finished his cup of coffee, he picked up the papers again, turning to the front page editorial in the *Chicago Tribune:*

We live in the twentieth century. Piracy is supposed to be dead. Gangsterism is allegedly on the decline. We pay high taxes to make our streets and highway safe. Yet murder after murder occurs in our midst? How? Why?

How long must we law-abiding citizens tolerate lawlessness? How is it possible in our day and age for a murderer to strike again and again with impunity? Are we helpless in the face of those who would make a mockery of law and order? Is our law-enforcement machinery breaking down? It is time we asked these questions and had some frank answers!

During the early hours of this morning a workman came across the body of Janet Wilder, aged 20, lying amid weeds in the woods just east of Brentwood Park. A .38 bullet had shattered her skull. The slaying of this innocent young working girl brings the total of victims to six for Brentwood Park within the space of less than a year!

And the police tell us that they have no clues, no motives, no ideas, and no solution! What are police for? Why are not the woods of Brentwood Park patrolled? Why are not lights strung out along the highways traversing those woods?

The public is demanding action, results, not excuses, evasions. We want to see the criminal in the dock. We want no more corpses! And we demand action now. If not, then let us have a police "shake-up."

Ruddy gritted his teeth, crumpled the paper into a ball, and flung it from him. Goddamn! What a cheap way to win sympathy with the public! He could wring the neck of the fool who wrote those lines. Yet Ruddy felt those words in that newspaper stinging him. He was sensitive to public opinion; he knew that many thousands, yea, hundreds of thousands would take their

cue from that editorial. He snatched up a phone and asked for
Lieutenant Hawkins of the riot squad.

"Lieutenant Hawkins, Riot Detail."

"Chief Turner speaking. Listen, I want you to establish roadblocks on all highways leading in and out Brentwood Park,"
Ruddy said crisply. "Now, don't discuss this with me. I know
we can't catch murderers that way, but we must do something
to reassure the public. Put our police force out there where the
public can see 'em, see?"

"Yes sir, Chief. I get it."

"Okay. Get moving!"

"Right, Chief!"

Ruddy slumped back into his chair. Thirty seconds later
he heard the riot gong clanging and a few moments later there
came the sound of sirens as one squad car after another sped
from the station house. I can't give 'em a criminal, so I give 'em
a circus. He smiled cynically.

The phone rang. He lifted the receiver.

"Chief Turner speaking."

"Ruddy? Bill speaking."

"Hi, Bill!" Ruddy's face came alive, his eyes shone.

"Are you on top of things out there?"

"So far, yes. I've not got a wink of sleep since I saw you."

"Hell, no. Is that true?"

"Brother, this place is hot, I mean *hot*."

"Take it easy. Now, look, I'm calling about the press this
morning."

"I've seen it."

"Now, don't take that seriously. I know how it feels to read
stuff like that when you're the guy they are shooting at."

"I can't put the guy who wrote the editorial in the *Tribune*
in the electric chair for life," Ruddy growled.

"I know, I know," Bill said soothingly. "But forget it."

"Look, Bill," Ruddy explained. "I've sent out roadblocks. Just to show the public our men. I can't catch murderers that way. You know it. But I want them to know that we *are* on the job."

"I was going to suggest that you do that," Bill said. "I knew you'd be on the job. Don't let 'em shake you, Ruddy. I told the reporters this morning that we'd given Brentwood Park the best officer we had and that that officer would do his best."

"Thanks, Bill."

"And get some rest, boy."

"I've an appointment at ten, then I'm going home to hit the hay."

"Nothing new?"

"We found the hole where the gun was buried. No doubt the murderer went there to dig it up. That Wilder girl surprised 'im and he let her have it," Ruddy said.

"Oh! So there is something," Bill approved.

"But keep that on ice," Ruddy warned.

"I get it."

"Everything that can be thought of is being thought of, and all that can be done is being done."

"Right. You have my absolute confidence, Ruddy."

"Thanks, Bill."

"I canceled all that gold-braid stuff, as you suggested."

"I thought you'd understand."

"By the way, have a chat with the mayor, when you can."

"I'll do that, Bill."

"Bye."

"Bye now, Bill."

He felt good. His boss trusted him. *And he had made a tiny bit of progress!* At least we know the murderer is still active, still around. And—

The phone tingled again.

"Chief Turner speaking."

"Chief, your son's here to see you."

Ruddy froze, his lips becoming tense. He swallowed, then said, "Send him right in."

Mechanically, Ruddy hung up the phone, feeling mesmerized. Instead of his carrying the initiative to Tommy, Tommy was taking the issue to him! He felt cornered. Was Tommy deliberately coming to see him to prove that he had nothing to fear, to hide? Or was he so bold that he was coming to see if Ruddy suspected anything? Or was he, Ruddy, falling victim to his own imagination? He had wanted to be able to question Tommy without his suspecting his reasons for doing so. Instead, Tommy was maybe coming to question him with hidden reasons? Then, before he could sufficiently collect his thoughts, before he knew what line to take, the door opened and a beamingly radiant Tommy breezed into the room, clad in sweater and slacks, carrying a tennis racket under his left arm. At once, every morbid suspicion that had been rankling in Ruddy's heart fled and hid in shame.

"Hi, Dad!"

"Hi, son!"

"Gee, you look like a million dollars with that golden star on you," Tommy exclaimed, his brows lifted.

"That's my badge of authority," Ruddy said.

"You look tired. You didn't sleep at all?"

"Just a wink or two—there on that sofa," Ruddy murmured, yawning. "I'll be home this afternoon and catch up."

"Gee, Mama and I were thunderstruck at this new development," Tommy rattled on, sitting on the edge of Ruddy's desk. "Imagine, finding a corpse right off. Any line on who did it, Dad?"

"Nothing, nothing *yet*," Ruddy said.

"Gosh, what an office," Tommy said in an awed tone.

"Sort of nice," Ruddy agreed.

"A real teletype?"

"Yep."

"Just like in the movies," Tommy marveled.

"Yes and no. Looks like the movies, but things are much more humdrum here," Ruddy said.

"Not with a murder on your hands," Tommy disputed him. "But I guess it's old stuff to you. Say, Dad, why did they kill her?"

"We don't know, son."

"Did they rob her?"

"Not that we can tell."

"Molest her sexually?"

"The coroner says she wasn't touched."

"Then why was she killed?"

"We know nothing."

"And the papers said she was only twenty years old."

"Yep."

"How horrible," Tommy breathed, looking off into space.

"It's life" was all that Ruddy could say. "Look, I wanted to talk with you more yesterday. You ran out on me."

"Had a date," Tommy said.

"A new gal?" Ruddy forced a smile.

"No. Went over to see Charles's mom and dad," Tommy said in a preoccupied voice.

"Oh. He lived here in Brentwood Park, didn't he?"

"Sure. Just a few blocks from here."

"He was a good friend of yours, hunh?"

"A straight guy. I liked 'im."

"A lot of horrible things happen to a lot of innocent people." Ruddy sighed, thinking of both Tommy and Charlie as he spoke.

"Yeah. That's true," Tommy mused. "But, shucks, Dad, you fellows on the police force get hardened to all this. I'm surprised to see you so wistful."

"Nobody gets used to death, Tommy," Ruddy said.

"Yep. Guess not. Say, how was that gal killed?"

"Shot."

"And no motive? No clues? Nothing?"

"Nothing."

"Do you think it's tied in with all those other killings, Dad?"

"We're going on that assumption."

"Quite a lot of senseless killing," Tommy murmured, shaking his head.

"It'll make sense someday, son," Ruddy said, trying to keep an edge of bitterness out of his voice.

"Dad, is it really true that there are a lot of murders that are unsolved?"

"A few."

"I suspect that there are more than the police want to admit," Tommy declared.

"Why do you say that?"

"One has to assume that all murderers are caught," Tommy reasoned. "Or why would we have a police force. But what about the murders that are not detected at all? There must be some. . . . Not all criminals are stupid."

"Not many get away with it," Ruddy said.

"Perfect crimes are not even known about," Tommy said. "I'd bet that the police only stumble on the blunderers."

Ruddy eyed his son, cleared his throat, and asked: "You don't like police, do you, Tommy?"

"As people, yes. As a force out to catch other people, no."

"Why?"

"I like constructive activities," Tommy said, replying and yet evading.

"You haven't told me why."

"It's the role of the profession, Dad," he said. "I like to ask questions. For the profession of law enforcment, one has to assume that one knows, really knows all the answers."

"I don't see—"

"Dad, I'm talking in philosophical terms," Tommy said, laughing suddenly. "Maybe I don't make much sense to you. You know, police work is exciting. I see that aspect of it."

"Don't you see that we are defending and protecting people, Tommy?"

"Dad, do people really want to be defended and protected?"

"What do you mean?"

"Look, obviously, the man who's spreading all this terror in Brentwood is not scared," Tommy said. "And I'd suspect that he could be found if people really wanted to find 'im badly enough."

"What do you mean?"

"Dad, I feel that what keeps us from getting all the criminals is that we would have to act and feel like them in order to catch 'em," Tommy said.

Ruddy blinked; he felt anger growing in him.

"You're talking rot," Ruddy spat.

"Dad, is there any law against cannibalism in this state?" Tommy asked.

"Not that I know of. Why?"

"We don't have such laws because we don't want to think of such," Tommy stated.

"So you think that there is a vast horde of people getting away with everything, eh?"

"No. Not at all. Just a bold few," Tommy said, grinning.

"The average man does not commit crimes simply because he does not think of it."

"And that's a damn good thing too." Ruddy laid down.

"But let the notion get into a man's head, and he goes to town."

"Like the guy who killed Hindricks, Father Byrnes, and that gal last night?"

"Oh, that . . . you know, I suspect that most of that killing was done by accident," Tommy said, laughing.

Ruddy wanted to order the boy from the office, but he kept still.

"I'd hate to let the taxpayers hear you talk like that to me," Ruddy muttered.

"Oh, I've got better sense than that," Tommy assured him.

"Why do you think those killings were accidental?"

"They were done so perfectly," Tommy said. "If they'd been planned, there'd be traces of clues all over the place."

"Maybe there are some clues," Ruddy suggested teasingly, looking off.

"No. You said there weren't."

"The police don't tell everything, son."

"So there were clues this time?"

"We've pretty well reconstructed this last killing," Ruddy said, realizing that he was not giving anything away by putting Tommy wise to what had happened. After all, only the police knew so far.

"Then what happened?"

"Some man went into that wood to dig up a gun," Ruddy related. "He got the gun. A .38. This girl came upon him accidentally . . ." He paused and was struck by the word *accident.* "The man shot her; it was the only thing he could do. Then he got away."

"Didn't I say it would be accidental?"

"Yeah, you did. Why did you say it?"

"Accidents have something free and pure about 'em," Tommy said eagerly. "They drop out of the blue. And you can never tell what direction an accident takes." He narrowed his eyes. "Did they find the gun?"

"No."

"Then how do you know it was a gun he dug up?"

"The shape of it was still in the wet clay."

"Oh." Tommy mused a moment, then said, "Maybe he's going to use it again."

"Maybe."

"You know, I bet that guy thought that that gun would be found," Tommy said in a voice of slow amazement.

"What do you mean?"

"He knew that a new investigation would take place with a new police chief, and he dug it up. He was scared of its being found—"

"In all that wet grass? We wouldn't've found that gun till kingdom come."

"Yeah. He should have left it there," Tommy said loudly, laughing. "Funny."

"What's funny?"

"How much you can find out about something by just juggling the facts in a logical way," Tommy said. "If that guy ran to dig up that gun, it means that he was in a panic. And that means that he was not as intelligent as the kind of killers I have in mind."

"Tommy."

"Yeah, Dad."

"Only stupid people kill."

"That's a big generalization. I wonder if the police know enough to assume all that?"

"We do, son."

"I can see the necessity for assuming such," Tommy said, nodding affirmatively. "I guess most people live and act on that."

"You've started thinking quite a lot about crime recently," Ruddy said.

"Yeah."

"Why?"

"Dunno."

"Did it have anything to do with what happened to Marie?"

"No. Why? What has Marie done?"

"Nothing."

"She was just a victim, Dad."

"I went to see her, Tommy."

"Oh!" Tommy stared at his father, than sat down. "How was she?"

"Pretty bad, emotionally. Look, I let her have some money—"

"She hates me, doesn't she?"

"No. I wouldn't say that. She's just hurt, crushed."

"Dad, I did wrong about her."

"I wouldn't say that."

"I did wrong, but I couldn't help it," Tommy said with a quavering voice. "That was the crazy part about it. I never thought your deepest feelings could make you do wrong. I just dropped her. Killed her."

"*Killed her?*"

"It was like killing, Dad."

"What do you know about killing, son?"

"I know something about it from what I did to Marie. I left her when she needed me most. I said I loved her. Then I threw her to the dogs."

"I don't think of that as 'killing,'" Ruddy said, his voice full of scared wonder.

"It was killing," Tommy insisted, his voice breaking. He

bent forward and buried his face in his hands. "I don't ever want to see her again." He sobbed. "I can't help it."

"God, but you've dramatized this much too much," Ruddy said.

"You saw her," Tommy said, lifting his eyes. "You said she was crushed. Her life is blighted. *And I did it.*" He swallowed. "You see, I was told in school and church that love was the greatest thing on earth, that it could conquer all. . . . Hell, it didn't and it can't. What can and will conquer are fear and hate. You can be fearful before you know it; you can hate without thinking."

Ruddy was moved. No, the poor boy was suffering. How had he ever suspected him?

"You mustn't get morbid, Tommy," Ruddy chided. "You're a man, you know."

"What is a *man*?" Tommy asked of the whole huge office.

"Tommy, you're letting this throw you," Ruddy accused with compassion.

"Maybe. I'm just human . . ."

"You've got to forget this." Ruddy was stern.

"I can forget," Tommy said. "I can forget Marie. But I cannot forget what it meant to me to drop her. Dad, there's in us something more powerful than love. That was the shock. I left that poor sweet girl like I'd lift a flyswatter and kill a fly."

"No, no. You didn't," Ruddy pointed out. "You have been brooding over her."

"No, not about her. But about how easy it is to be disloyal," he cried.

"There's no goddamn disloyalty involved," Ruddy stormed. "Now, stop that goddamn nonsense."

"It's all right just to drop people and leave 'em?" Tommy asked, caressing his tennis racket with nervous fingers.

"Tommy, sometimes there are things too big for men,"

Ruddy began. "That's why we have friends. One can't stand alone in life in everything. One needs help. Especially in matters like this. You've commited no crime."

"I feel I have," Tommy insisted.

"Look, play tennis, swim—hell, have a good time and get that morbid rot out of you," Ruddy advised again.

"That's easy to say," Tommy murmured.

"Say, why don't you talk to Father Joyce?" Ruddy suggested.

Tommy lifted his head with a jerk, stared at his father with tear-wet eyes, then broke into a snickering laugh.

"What the hell are you laughing about?"

"I know what he's going to say."

"What?"

"He's going to forgive me."

"Right. And that's what you *need*."

"I don't want to dodge anything," Tommy growled. "Hell, what I'd like for him to tell me is what law I violated."

"Law?" Ruddy asked with an echo.

"Yeah. You admit that it was wrong. Then what made it wrong?" Tommy demanded. "I feel it was wrong. I willingly and passionately did a wrong thing."

There was a long silence. Tommy stared at his father and the father stared at the son.

"Tommy, you and I must talk," Ruddy said.

Tommy stood and wiped his eyes, then playfully swung his racket to and fro.

"There's nothing to talk about," he said in a normal voice. "I'm late for my game. I'll be all right." He forced a smile. "See you later—today, tonight?"

"Yeah, son."

"And get some sleep, Dad," Tommy called gaily, going out the door.

"Okay," Ruddy said. He bent forward and bit his lips. "Something's wrong and I don't know what to do."

He started as the phone tingled at his elbow.

"Yeah?"

"Professor Redfield is here to see you, Chief."

"Send 'im in in about ten minutes," Ruddy said.

"Yes, sir."

He wanted a few seconds in which to get himself together. He was much too fatigued to think clearly. And Tommy was still worrying him. Had that boy come to see him for some reason other than to say hello? He was sure of one thing: he had to "get at" that boy, find out what was seething deep down in him and why. Above all, he had to turn that boy's mind from too deep and constant a preoccupation with morbid matters. "He's all right," he mumbled half aloud. "It's what happened to Marie that upset 'im." Yet, in some way, Tommy had seemed to manage to get him to talk of matters relating to the murder of Janet Wilder—things that only the police knew so far. "No harm's done. He's not involved in this. God, I'm actually thinking and feeling as though I really suspected Tommy!" The more he thought of Tommy's reflections on the Janet Wilder case, the more he felt that maybe the boy was right. Why had Ed not mentioned the possibility of the role of "accident" in the three murders that had taken place—the Hindricks-Landsdale, the Byrnes-Karn, and the Heard cases? After all, far-fetched coincidences like that did happen now and then. Didn't a four-year-old child, only last week, fall out of a ten-story window and survive, with only slight bruises? Why then could there not be four different murderers who had struck, for various reasons, at four different times and places in the woods east of Brentwood Park? Aw, no. He was now, and he knew it, trying to build up a case in which it would be impossible for Tommy to figure! Hell . . . and there was yet another thing that made the role of "accident" impossible: there was that .38! A .38 had figured in the first three cases and was figuring in this most recent one. Of course, it had to be proved that it was the same .38 in all four instances. But he was almost persuaded that it was. Yep. The four damned cases seemed linked by that gun. But in the Janet Wilder case, couldn't some poor fool of a boy have stolen a gun, a .38 and, when he read in the papers that an intensive investigation into the Brentwood Park murders would take place, have gone and buried that gun, and then, in a panic, thinking that somebody would stumble upon it, have rushed out there and dug it up, and Janet Wilder comes upon him while he's doing so? No. That was much too far-fetched. Tommy had been right. The best thing for the murderer was to have left the gun alone, left it where it was, buried in those high weeds where there was one chance in a million that anybody would find it. Aw, hell . . . I don't get it.

The door pushed in. Ruddy rose, smiled.

"Good morning, Professor. It was good of you to come."

"Good morning, Chief," Professor Redfield said. "Really, I must apologize. I didn't know you were the head of our police department in Brentwood Park. I must have acted kind of silly to you last night."

"Forget it, Professor," Ruddy said. "I just wanted to chat with you."

"I feel honored to help in any way I can," the professor said.

"That's kind of you," Ruddy said.

"I see that you've thrown up roadblocks," the professor said. "You're really on the job. We could never get Branden excited about this thing. He was a good officer but kind of placid."

"Well, Professor, don't expect too much from those road-blocks," Ruddy said with a wry smile. "Just between you and me, it's done more to reassure the public than anything else."

"I suspected that," the professor said, nodding. "But it has helped. The people feel that something is happening."

"You say that you've studied this town, Professor?"

"Yes. Extensively."

"I don't want to ask too much of you," Ruddy said, smiling apologetically, "but I wanted to get an idea of how you see this place. You see, it would help us in trying to track down a solution to these crimes and give us a bird's-eye view of the town for general purposes."

"Well, I'll share with you what we know," the professor said. "Just what do you wish to go into?"

"Since we are at present clueless about these crimes," Ruddy began, "I'm anxious to find out, if possible, whether the criminal is from Brentwood or not. It'd help to narrow down our search."

"I couldn't tell you that exactly," the professor said cautiously. "But I *could* give indications—"

"Signposts, general directions," Ruddy told him hastily. "That's all we need. Before you speak, let me tell you something about criminal investigations. In general, people have very high-flown and romantic notions about criminal investigations. But that kind of stuff is for books, not life. Criminals and crimes run to types, like diseases. A competent officer can usually tell in ten minutes what kind of crime and criminal he's dealing with. Now, criminals do not realize this. If they did, we would be hard put to it to catch them. Each little crook, when he hatches out a job in his stale brain, thinks that it has never been thought of before. Usually, it has, many times. And we know at once in what direction to go to look for him. Maybe, like the measles, there may be complications in this or that crime; then we take that into consideration, and we make the necessary deductions or inductions. Now, our law-enforcement machinery and our criminal investigation network is geared to do just this. And it does it very efficiently. We know, for example, that certain crimes stem from various social groups. We know that 'bushwhacking' is a poor man's way of robbing. We don't look for a millionaire's son for 'bushwhacking.' Criminal assaults on children are a bit more complex; there we have got to take into consideration a set of bizarre psychological factors that might lead us into any social layer. Housebreaking stems almost always from a floating population, paroled convicts, young punks, etc. And we know where to look for them. Bank robbery is highly specialized, and the known number of crooks who can do it well are few; and we have our nets already spread to sniff out traces of them when they try to spend the stolen money.

"But, Professor, now and again there comes a crime with all kinds of elements wrapped into it," Ruddy explained, "and we are at a dead end. These Brentwood forest murders are like that. They resemble 'bushwhacking,' but they manifestly are not. Nothing is ever stolen and we can't trace any goods taken from the victims. The opportunity for sexual molestation was present in three of the cases out of four, yet it did not take place. And we cannot, as yet, find any traces of marital jealousy, of blackmail, etc. No political motives seem to be implied. And though two victims were churchmen, we have absolutely no clue in that direction. All we know is that our victims were shot at point-blank range with a .38. The murderer vanished. Now, to begin with, could you make a guess as to whether that murderer came from Brentwood Park or outside of it?"

The professor sighed. He opened his briefcase and began spreading out a folding sheet that held huge outlines of city streets.

"I don't *feel* (I emphasize *feel*, because no real proof is at hand) that these are Brentwood Park crimes," the professor began. "I'm not trying to defend Brentwood Park just because I live in it. I'm a scientist and try to be objective. If I say these crimes do not smack of Brentwood Park, it is because of the population structure and function here."

"That's exactly what I want to hear about," Ruddy said.

"I'll show you how this town grew up, and out of what it grew," the professor said, spreading out and smoothing his long maps. "First of all, there are no natural resources here except fresh air, sun, water, sand, hills, and pine trees . . . And that does not account for this being a town at all. You might say that no sensible person would make a town here. This town is a surplus, something artificially made by people with too much money." The professor laughed. "That does not include me. I just sneaked into the place to take advantage of it after it was built.

"Now, back in the early twenties, this used to be a kind of rough-and-tumble camping area—Boy Scouts, Girl Scouts, Nature Friend groups, etc. In fact, this place didn't even have a name, except that that jutting point of rock on the lake front was called Brentwood Point. Then bootleggers started using this spot to take their wares ashore. Again, the choice for Brentwood was purely accidental. That jutting rock was a good place to lay in a ship so that prying eyes couldn't see it too easily."

"Bootleggers, eh?"

"That's right, sir."

"Do many people know that?"

"Don't know," the professor said. "Maybe some of the old-timers remember it."

"Hummmn . . . that rook touches onto that path, doesn't it?"

"Yes."

"The contraband angle hasn't been looked into," Ruddy said, jotting upon his pad.

"You think that could—"

"I'm not thinking at all, Professor," Ruddy said quickly.

"You've just brought in another angle that we had not thought of. It's possible that somebody's still contrabanding, not liquor now but other things. They could have been surprised and had to eliminate those who had glimpsed them. But go ahead, Professor."

Professor Redfield pointed his forefinger to a shaded sector of a map showing an oblong strip along the coast of Lake Michigan.

"Right after World War I, a real estate shark, Stanton by name, came up here and bought up an area twice the size of what is now Brentwood Park. That area then included the forest that rises to the east of the town. (I'll talk about that forest later.) Stanton had surveyors up and a town was mapped out. Even the streets, more or less as they now run, were plotted out. The main highways were projected; the present railway track was indicated; a water system was designed; even a site for an electric power station was designated; and then lots were put up for sale. A lot of ballyhoo accompanied all this. You know the kind: whispered rumors that fortunes were to be made if you got in on the ground floor and—"

"Was there much actual cheating done?"

"Strangely, no. Stanton was a shark, but he always kept just within the law," the professor explained. "At first, the sales of lots for houses were brisk. Brentwood Park was advertised as a summer colony, and some building actually took place. Then came the Depression and, almost overnight, Brentwood was a ghost town. Stanton, who was operating on a shoestring margin, went into bankruptcy—"

"Aw," Ruddy exclaimed, "how did that work out?"

"Not badly," the professor replied. "You know how those things ago. Stanton lost everything and so did a few others who did not have enough cash on hand to tide 'em over. Stanton's

outfit went into receivership and was taken over by a moneyed
crowd who felt that they could make a going concern of it in
the future."

"What happened to Stanton?"

"He's dead. Died about five years ago," the professor
declared. "There was a lull of about five years during which
Brentwood rose and fell. There was a huge turnover in land and
houses. But many of the original buyers hung on; they liked
it here. Then the group that bought Stanton out was in turn
bought out by a group that eventually set up the Brentwood
Park Bank and Trust Company. They had capital, and they had
water, electricity, and gas brought in. Brentwood Park was on
its feet at last—and that was when I bought me a lot here. But
Brentwood Park showed nothing exceptional in growth; in fact,
compared to other new settlements, it lagged. Then came World
War II and a lot of easy money gotten out of war contracts. A
boom hit Brentwood and it hasn't stopped yet."

"Were there any outstanding claims against Stanton that
went unsettled or were settled in a way that left sour memories?"
Ruddy asked.

"No. You see, Chief, the Brentwood Park Bank crowd
changed the idea of Brentwood Park. Instead of a summer colony, it was turned into a fashionable suburb. Everybody was
happy. Over here"—he tapped a red sector—"one big house after
another went up, one family trying to outdo the other. Then
word got around about the advantages of anchoring yachts off
Brentwood Point—and that did it. The big money came.

"Then came the erection of a whole series of big apartment
hotels along the shore. Skyscraper studios were talked of, and
Scottwood, the painter, came. A whole army of other artists of
all descriptions followed him. Almost overnight, Brentwood

Park became famous for its parties, nightlife, and the big, sleek yachts anchored off Brentwood Point. The town began to protect itself; restrictive covenants were drawn up and—"

"They excluded who?" Ruddy asked.

"Well, Jews, Negroes, and what they lumped together as the 'undesirables,'" the professor mumbled.

"Have there been any cases of racial trouble about Negroes wanting to come in? Or Jews?"

"No."

"Why not?"

"No Jews or Negroes ever sought to live here," the professor explained.

"Are you sure?"

"Positive."

"How can you be so sure?"

"I see your point," the professor said. "You're thinking that maybe some disgruntled Jew or Negro was on the loose, feeling a rankling from being rejected and was killing—"

"I'm not *thinking*," Ruddy said testily. "I'm hunting around for disgruntled people who might have a grudge to kill you or your friends."

"No. There are no cases of that."

"Go on, Professor."

"Now, I told you that Brentwood Park was originally twice the size it is now. In settling claims against him, Stanton gave up the whole forest area to a textile millionaire, Wilson, who took over the area and, later, made a gift of it to the town—stipulating in his will that it was to be left in its savage state."

"That's why there are no buildings or lights up there, eh?"

"Right," the professor agreed. "Now, the hotels are beginning to fill up for the summer. Crowds are beginning to surge in from all over. That'll bring Brentwood Park's population to its peak." He shifted his finger to another area. "Here, beyond the hotels, are the big houses. That's the heart of Brentwood."

"The winter population?"

"About one hundred thousand."

"And the summer?"

"Between one hundred thousand and one hundred seventy thousand"

"Now, professor, does much crime come out of that area of big houses?" Ruddy asked. "You know as well as I do, rich people have a way of taking care of themselves. Much of what would go on the police blotters as being criminal never comes to the police station in places like this. Now, those big families— the Thurstons, the Runleys, the Hines, the Cooks, the Beltons, the Vassers—they'd never send an erring boy to us. You know what I mean?"

"Certainly. Well, from what I could get by my field-worker students, many of whom come from here—I'd say that abortions are fairly high. After all, they feel that they can afford it. The doctor tipped us off to that. A great deal of juvenile delinquency is handled strictly in private, between the heads of families. No one would think of calling in the police and subjecting a wayward boy to having a police record. Now, there are an unusual number of suicides—"

"For any outstanding reason?"

"Ill health among the fairly aged seems to account for eighty percent of it," said the professor.

"They don't like to suffer much," Ruddy observed.

"No. They can't take it."

"Just curious. What ailments crop up mostly?"

"Cancer."

"And what else causes suicide?"

"Money troubles. But not too much of that now."

"Now. Homicides . . ."

"We've had a few triangle killings," the professor said. "The Tablet-Curry case, the—"

"Yeah. I've heard of 'em."

"A lot of housebreaking in the winter," the professor went on.

"Any old feuds here?"

"No. Not that I know of."

"Now, what goes on in those smaller houses—off there to the left, where the poor people live?" Ruddy asked.

"Mostly Irish and Hungarian, second generation," the professor answered without hesitation.

"And their incomes?"

"Personal services, public services. You see, many of your officers come from that group." The professor smiled. "A few professionals."

"From what I can tell," Ruddy said, "they seem to be a pretty law-abiding group, both of 'em."

"Yes. They have their problems, but they live in pretty stable family groups. Not too much disorganization among 'em."

"Now, Professor, let's keep the Irish and Hungarians in mind," Ruddy began. "Without referring to your notes or charts, can you recall any unusual crimes that were newspaper-worthy among those groups during the past ten years?"

The professor pursed his lips and stared at the ceiling.

"The Hungarians produced a young gangster," he said. "The Hyjicks family. Funny thing. They were Roman Catholics. Mother, father, and eight children. Jim Hyjicks was the oldest. We never did find out what went wrong with 'im; none of the other children ever ran afoul of the law. Of course, young Hyjicks could not be classed as a gangster as we know them today. He started out by being behind in his classes in school. (You

see, we made a detailed study of him.) He was sent to psychologists but to no avail. He was arrested the first time with a gang
of young toughs who had stolen property in their possession.
Hyjicks swore that he was innocent; nevertheless, he was sentenced to a reformatory. He came out bitter; six months later,
he was caught in the act of burglarizing one of the summer
houses that had been boarded up for winter. He went 'up'—I
don't know why we call it going 'up' when we send 'em down
to Joliet!—for two years. He came out this time real mad. He
organized a gang and tried to muscle in on taking over truck
driver's unions. He shot a man, who recovered. He went 'up'
for five years this time. When he came out, he shot a policeman
while he was in the act of robbing a filling station—"

"Where is he now?"

"Joliet."

"And his brothers and sisters are all straight? Nobody tried
to avenge Jim Hyjick?"

"No. His family rejected 'im," the professor said. "Did all
they could for 'im, but there was no social or political sympathy. I'm sure none of the Hyjicks tried to get even in any way."

"Any other cases stick in your mind?"

"Two years ago we had a lot of trouble with the daughter of a postal inspector," the professor related. "Compulsive
shoplifting. Some kind of psychological yen, it seemed. She was
caught several times, got her name in the newspapers, and was
let off. She's married now and living in another state. She fled
Brentwood Park—"

"Her name now?"

"Evelyn Sorkin."

"And she's living—?"

"Somewhere in St. Louis, the last I heard."

"Any other memories?"

"I recall one pathetic case," the professor said. "A Miss Devin, a schoolteacher married a young fellow who was also a teacher, a chap by the name of Wintry—Robert Wintry. Wintry was ailing all the time but rarely complained about it. He was drafted into the army over the protests of his wife and physician. Three days after he was inducted, he died of heart failure. The wife went wild, ran amok in the truest sense of the word. She took Wintry's hunting rifle and tried to knock off a few cops—"

"Wait! What year was that?"

"In 1944."

"She didn't kill anybody?"

"No. Her aim was bad."

"And where is she now?"

"In Brentwood. She's remarried. Has four children and is quite normal," the professor stated.

"We'll check, just to make sure," Ruddy muttered. "Sorry to press you, Professor, but do you recall any others?"

"One rather unusual case comes to mind," the professor resumed. "Owen Calan was chief teller in the Brentwood Park Bank and Trust Company from its opening. He had an ailing wife—cancer. Hopeless case. Well, it seems that Owen Calan took more than fifty thousand from the bank by juggling the figures; he used it to try to cure his wife. A bank examiner discovered it and Owen Calan quickly and honestly owned up to it. He had even saved every medical receipt. He pleaded guilty. Was sent up for four years. He is out now—good behavior, you know. His wife died while he was in prison."

Ruddy stared hard and unblinkingly at Professor Redfield. Had that Owen Calan felt about his wife in some way that Tommy had felt about Marie? But Owen had stolen to help his doomed wife, while Tommy had fled his doomed girl.

"Where's this Owen Calan now?"

"Don't know."

"We'll trace 'im and check," Ruddy said. He rose. "You are very kind to submit to all this. We're really searching for a needle in a haystack, and we mustn't overlook anything, no matter how far-fetched. Maybe there's nothing in all of this, but you never know. And many thanks for your masterful description of how this town grew up."

"Not at all, Chief," the Professor said, smiling. "Any time my department at the university or I can be of service to you, don't hesitate to call on us."

"Thanks, again. And good-bye."

Ruddy was dead tired. But the image of that compassionate Owen Calan stuck in his mind. He ordered his car, drove home, and went straight to bed, taking a sleeping pill; he slept like a rock.

CHAPTER 14

Ruddy slept unbrokenly for twelve solid hours, and when he did open his eyes, he stared unseeingly, lying stone still; this was his habit of awakening. It was as though he distrusted his very bed and wanted to play possum a bit and see what would happen, if any movement that had been in action while he slept would resume itself. He yawned softly and could tell, without looking at his watch, that it was early morning, for the noises that came to his ears were distant, muffled, and infrequent. He turned his head; Agnes breathed deeply in sleep at his elbow. She had long ago grown used to these marathon stints of duty that so often claimed him and she had known better than to awaken him when she went to bed.

Then, as he surged slowly toward full consciousness, his body began to tense. The world was something with which to grapple. There were malefactors about who had to be caught; there were invisible threats in the very air. He suppressed a threatening yawn and wondered if Tommy was in his room. He must be asleep; I don't hear that damned typewriter . . . Jesus! He gritted his teeth. Am I spying on the movements of my own family in my own house? A sense of self-disgust filled him. But his mind, now awakened, was well launched into its merciless logic. That bank teller, Owen Calan, had had a case that was psychologically parallel to that of Tommy's! Calan had quietly and calmly, as though he knew deep in him that he had the right, disregarded the law made by men and had tried unsuccessfully to obey a higher one, felt in his own heart, in the effort to save his doomed wife. But in the end he had lost her in the worst way possible. She had died while he was serving his prison sentence for theft, and he had not even been allowed to attend her funeral! What had Owen Calan felt when he had been freed? Had it been something akin to what Tommy had felt when he had learned that his beloved Marie was tainted and was beyond his pale? Had he wanted to lash out at a world that mocked even his best efforts? Yeah, a guy like that could have come back here and tried to get even with this damn town. Yeah, he would send out an investigatory tracer on him first thing this morning.

But . . . if he had the right to suspect Calan, had he not the duty to suspect Tommy? Was it not unfair of him to set in motion an investigation about Owen Calan on the mere notion that the man had suffered a horrible shock, and not do the same for his own son? But Tommy hasn't, I *know*, done anything! But how did he know? He didn't. And what had he done to check on Tommy? Nothing. But just how did one go about checking on one's own son? Ruddy suddenly frowned, blinking; he suddenly realized that he did not know much about his son. Strange, how one took one's own for granted. What were Tommy's habits? Tennis? Anybody could play tennis. And, for example, he never would have thought that anything as traumatic as Tommy's desertion of Marie could have taken place without Tommy's having told him about it. Aw, I've nothing on that boy . . . and he was amazed that he had used the police terminology about his son. He had "nothing" on his son!

Yet, in a strictly moral sense, did he not have as much on Tommy as he had on that Owen Calan? *I'm losing my grip,* he chided himself at his inability to stop the relentless march of his policeman's thoughts. *Maybe I ought to have retired.* No, police work was his work, his life, his law. His mind and feelings hit a blank wall. He sighed, glanced at Agnes's sleeping face, and then at his watch. It was three-thirty. *I'll get up.* He loved being up and thinking and working when all the rest of the world was asleep. He was the true policeman then; he was a real guardian when others slept and he kept watch. He eased from bed without disturbing Agnes and went into the bathroom. Half an hour later, he was dressed in his uniform and was seated at his desk in his office, furiously scribbling upon a pad an outline of projected action for the coming day. He wrote a note to Agnes, telling her that he would be in for lunch, and then went into the hallway. The door to Tommy's room stood slightly ajar. *That's odd.* Had the boy gone out? He went to the front window and peered out toward the garage: Tommy's roadster was not in its accustomed place. *Now was the time to get a quick look into the boy's room!* No! He bit his lips. Yes! Why not? Had he not, after all, said that he wanted to get closer to that boy? Well, here was an opportunity to make a start and find out something about his son. But what did snooping on one's son have to do with establishing a fatherly relation with him? Hell, no matter what Tommy's involved in, I've got a right to know. *I must know!* For my own peace of mind. He slipped a note under the door of the bedroom and then tiptoed to Tommy's door. He froze. Suppose the boy was there and found him snooping?

"Tommy?" he called in a whisper, trying to establish an alibi if caught.

There was no answer. He pushed the door in, calling again in a louder whisper: "Tommy!"

He could see plainly into the room now; the boy had not yet come in. A murky dawn blue light filled the room. He entered, feeling the skin on his body prickling. Never before in his life had he even associated his son with the thought of crime, and in his determination to spy into Tommy's life, he felt a sense of guilt that was as deep as any he could ever possibly find in his son.

How orderly the room was! Not a book, not a chair, not a scrap of paper out of place. The pencils were neatly lined up at the top of the desk; the typewriter had its plaster cover neatly covering it. Last night's newspaper was laid on the night table near the bed. Even the ashtrays were shining and clean. Almost too orderly. Ruddy stood over the desk and peered down at a book whose title read *Studies in Hysteria* by Joseph Breuer and Sigmund Freud. Humnnnn. Too deep for me . . . psychological stuff. He sure goes for that. Ruddy glanced at the pictures on the wall: a scene from Venice showing canals and gondolas in bright sunshine; the Tour Eiffel with a Paris background; the photograph of a vividly black African mask. . . . He turned to Tommy's clothes closet and opened it, then felt gingerly for the bottom of trousers. Yeah, here they were; he felt tightly, squeezing the cuffs, feeling for dampness, seeing vividly in his mind the high dew-wet forest above Brentwood Park. Dry as a bone, he said to himself with a degree of satisfaction. He bent down and lifted a pair of tan shoes. They were dry too. He picked up another pair and found them dry. His tension was ebbing. He poked about in the pockets of the coats, finding a few coins and a half-smoked packet of cigarettes. Then, in the inside coat pocket of Tommy's Harris tweed suit, he felt what seemed to be a letter. He drew it out, switched on the light. Yeah, a letter from Marie! He opened it, pulling forth the sheet of paper . . . God, he oughtn't do this. Yet his police mind was driving him on. He bent and read:

Darling Tommy:

I hardly know how to write this. God, I feel so sorry for you. What have I done to you? How did I do it? Darling, all I can say is that whatever has happened is not my fault; I think the doctor told you that. I keep walking the floor and asking myself what can I do to make things right again? I've been thinking of taking my own life, but, as stupid as it sounds, I just don't know how to go about it. I don't blame you for not coming to see me, or telephoning, or writing. I know how you feel. Though you did not know it, I saw you yesterday and I knew from the expression on your face that you were suffering . . . Tell me, Tommy, what can I do? I'll do anything you say, even to going and jumping into the lake. I'm feeling that I'm through living without having even started. Darling, I'm not asking that you come to see me; I know you don't want to do that. But you can write. Can't you? Won't you? Just one word to let me know that all this tragedy is real and is not some nightmare that I dreamed up all by myself . . .

> *Your brokenhearted*
> *Marie*

Ruddy sighed. Goddamn . . . even that letter did not make him get in touch with her! Jesus, he must have been in some state. Ruddy glanced at the date; it was the twelfth of March last. Humnnn . . . just a few days before that Hindricks-Landsdale murder. Aw, hell! Why do I keep thinking of that? He put the letter back, carefully, so as not to rumple the suit. He was about to shut the closet door to leave the room when he saw a pair of tennis shoes, dirty and water-stained, lying where they had been seemingly tossed against the rear wall of the closet. He lifted one and found it damp; his heart began pounding. He paused, thinking: yeah, he played tennis yesterday. But there's been no rain around here in days. His eyes narrowed. Had Tommy been wearing these tennis shoes yesterday when he had come into his office? He could not recall. He lifted the shoes and looked closely at them. Mud? No. It was a whitish something sticking to the heels and soles of both shoes. Plaster? No, it was too gritty for that. Aw, I bet that this is cement. But where on earth would he be walking in wet cement? No wet cement around here. Aw, maybe it scraped off the tennis court onto his shoes? But, no, tennis courts don't have wet cement on them. And neither was there any wet cement, that he knew of, anywhere near the forest of Brentwood Park. Hell, it's nothing. He might have picked up that wet cement on his shoes anywhere.

He jerked as the corner of his eye caught a flickering dart of light. Tommy was coming! He flicked out the light and flung the shoes back into the closet and closed the door. In a flash he was out of the room. Should he stay and meet Tommy? No. He felt too guilty to do so. Oh, yes, there was Tommy now coming toward the front door. He would duck out the back way. He went hurriedly into the hallway and down the backstairs to the yard. It was almost daylight now. Had Tommy seen the light on in his room? Damn. Ruddy walked slowly and noiselessly to the garage and looked up to Tommy's window just in time to see the light come on. He sighed. He got quickly into his car and was about to put the key in the ignition when he felt a grittish lump on his right thumb. Aw, that cement from Tommy's shoes had stuck to his hand. Quickly, he opened the glove compartment and took out a sheet of paper and carefully wrapped the bit of cement into it. Yeah, he'd send that wad of cement to the laboratory for an analysis—to find out if it really was cement; he might even find out where it came from, the type of cement and sand used. Hell, I'm crazy, he said bitterly. This is no way to act. As he drove out of the driveway, he felt thoroughly ashamed of himself for having probed about in Tommy's room, yet all the while he was wondering where had Tommy been coming from at this hour of the morning. Was he trying to find Tommy guilty? No, he was searching for peace of mind. But suppose his peace of mind could come only as a result of his finding Tommy guilty? He shook his head, rolling through quiet dawn streets toward police headquarters. I've got to settle this one way or the other, he told himself. Can't do any harm to find out definitely.

And, Jesus, what a pathetic letter Marie had written to that boy! A letter like that must have driven him almost crazy. But it wouldn't make a man kill, would it? Frankly, he did not know. Anything might make a man kill under certain circumstances.

He passed the policeman on duty at the night switchboard and went directly to his desk and began to pore over an immense pile of reports that had been left for him. The top dun-colored folder read:

JANET WILDER CASE, DEC'D

UNTRACED, ANONYMOUS, UNIDENTIFIED

TELEPHONE CALLS

APRIL 14TH, 19—

11:02 P.M.:

An unidentified male voice reported from Kenwood region seeing a man fleeing with what appeared to be a woman's red handbag at 39th Street and Drexel Boulevard. Informant said that the "suspect" had a wildly suspicious look and is certain that the "suspect" was involved in the Janet Wilder slaying.

11:06 P.M.:

An unidentified woman's voice reported seeing a man in Huggins's Poolroom at 51st Street and Giles Avenue wearing a blood-stained shirt and coat, with trouser legs torn, as though they had been ripped or shredded in flight.

11:30 P.M.:

An unidentified woman's voice reported from far South Side that her twelve-year-old daughter had seen a man at 42nd Street and St. Lawrence Avenue walking with a pronounced limp; informant's daughter is convinced that this "limp" was simulated by the "suspect" and is certain that the man was wearing a disguise and might be the "suspect" sought in the Janet Wilder case.

01:23 A.M.:

An unidentified woman's voice with Southern accent reported seeing two young Negroes, at 91st Street near the Pennsylvania Railroad tracks, in a scuffle over an object that resembled a wallet, and informant is certain that the wallet came from the handbag of Janet Wilder. Informant reported seeing the two Negroes vanish in the direction of the Fat Man's Tavern.

02:30 A.M.:

An unidentified, high-pitched man's voice informed us that for $5,000, he will be willing to reveal the name and address of Janet Wilder's slayer. Reported he would call back in half an hour after we had considered his offer and would tell us where to meet him. No call came.

02:39 A.M.:

An unidentified man's voice reported from the near North Side of having seen a mysterious light in an abandoned warehouse window at 12th Street and Roosevelt Road. Squad Cars 144 and 96 went immediately to the scene and found nothing suspicious.

Ruddy grunted impatiently and then leafed hurriedly through the rest of the reports of anonymous telephone calls.

"Crackpots," he muttered. It was funny how people got all worked up over a murder that had been reported in the press. Ruddy recalled that one day last year Ed Seigel had cynically suggested that a mythical murder be printed in the press just to see how many innocent people would swear that they had caught a glimpse of the fleeing murderer! "That's why we can't let these fools enter a plea of guilty to first-degree murder," Ruddy said out loud. "Hell, innocent people would be slitting one another's throats for a chance to sit in the electric chair." Knowing the delusions of people, the law had wisely demanded that no unsubstantiated confessions for murder in the first-degree could be accepted!

"Ed, what in hell makes people do that?" Ruddy had once asked.

"They're projecting out their own buried guilt feeling," Ed had explained.

"But I thought that most people hid their guilt," Ruddy had contended.

"Not all of 'em, and not all the time," Ed had said. "The burden of guilt that some people carry is too much for them to bear. They yearn to confess but don't know what to confess to until something is suggested to them in the press. After they have confessed, they have some peace."

"But don't they know that they run the risk of being punished?"

"Not all the time. They feel that the suffering that they've had to put up with is more dangerous than the risk of punishment," Ed explained. "And you'll notice that each time they meddle in our crime cases, they manage to keep their identities hidden."

"I don't understand that kind of guilt," Ruddy had mumbled. "I don't get people who poke their noses into killings that don't concern them."

"Those killings do concern 'em," Ed had insisted. "You see, the killings that they read about in the papers evoke in 'em a mood of guilt that was repressed long, long ago. And, for a few hours, they can't tell the difference between the actual killing that they have read about in the papers and the mood of guilt that that killing brought on."

"We ought to have a law against that," Ruddy had said.

"That would only make it worse," Ed had contended. "You'd get even more meddling with the law. What we need is more crime novels, crime movies."

"Then, goddamnit, let's lock up everybody," Ruddy had yelled in hot anger.

"Fewer people than you think would object," Ed had told him.

And, deep in his heart, Ruddy knew that that was true.

"People are nuts!" he had spat.

"In a human sort of way, yes," Ed had agreed.

The office door swung open and Ed stood revealed in it.

"Think of the devil," Ruddy called out.

"You get some sleep?" Ed demanded.

"Yep." Ruddy tapped the dun-colored folder. "I wonder do people realize how much of their own money they toss away when they make us officers go through crap like this?"

"Oh, that," Ed said, pulling off his cap. "If that's got you down, wait until you hear some of the confessions to the Janet Wilder murder I've got for you."

"No kidding?"

"Murderers everywhere," Ed sang, "but not a goddamn criminal."

"Well, I'm in a mood to listen to one of 'em," Ruddy said, smiling.

"Ring the 'pen and tell 'em to bring 'im in, Andrew Gordon," Ed suggested impishly. "You'll learn something from him."

"What kind of gag is this?" Ruddy countered.

"It's no gag," Ed said. "It has nothing to do with *this* murder but with murder in general."

"Ring the 'pen yourself," Ruddy said.

After Ed had phoned for Andrew Gordon, Ruddy asked, "Any new developments?"

"Nothing—not so far." Ed shook his head. "Captain Snell called in after you left. He was at a building site on the far South Side. Seems that a piece of gun handle was found in a concrete mixer and—"

"What? A .38?"

"Don't know yet."

"They can't identify it?"

"It's only a fragment . . . not enough to definitely establish what caliber. The foreman in charge of making the concrete called in about four this morning," Ed explained. "It's an eighteen-story building going up, and three shifts are being used. They're working around the clock. Seems that the concrete mixer got stuck, and when they stopped it and poked around in it, they came across a part of a revolver—just a piece of the butt. The foreman thought that it ought to be reported."

"I want to see that piece of gun when it comes in," Ruddy declared, alert to the fact that the cement mixer was reminding him of the cement he had discovered on Tommy's tennis shoes less than two hours age. Ought he to tell Ed of that now? No. Ed would think that he was batty. He'd wait until he saw what Captain Snell reported. And there certainly was no sense in his getting as worked up as those untraced, anonymous telephone callers had been. Yet he could not defend himself against a certain nervous tension that gripped his hands.

The intercom whirred and crackled.

"Lieutenant Parrish speaking."

"Yeah. What is it, Parrish?"

"Your son's here, Chief."

Ruddy rose and frowned. "So early?"

"It's nearly eight now," Ed said.

"Oh! Oh, yes, send 'im in," Ruddy ordered.

Goddamn! What was the boy doing? One thing was certain; that boy had not slept a wink last night.

"Hi, Dad!" sounded as the door was flung open, and Tommy, smiling confidently, sailed into the room. "Oh, hello, Mr. Seigel!"

"Hi, Tommy," Ed said, shaking hands with Tommy.

"When do you sleep, boy?" Ruddy asked curtly.

"Dad, guess what?" Tommy said breathlessly. "I think I got something for you on the Heard murder and—"

"What are you saying?" Ruddy demanded.

"Really?" Ed exclaimed.

"Look," Tommy said, seating himself and looking importantly from one pair of policeman's eyes to the other. "Last night I spent five hours talking to Charlie's parents. You know, Dad, something was overlooked in that Heard case. It seems that Charlie's father had three revolvers—a .22, which he let Charlie use for target practice now and then; a .38; and a .45. Well, last night I asked the Heards to look and see if all three of the guns were in the house. The .38 was missing."

"No kidding?" Ed asked.

"Good God, how could we have overlooked that?" Ruddy asked.

"This just might be the first real break in this case," Ed said slowly.

"What made you think to ask about that?" Ruddy asked his son.

"Yesterday you mentioned finding a hole from which a gun had been taken," Tommy said, his voice eager but natural. "I knew Charlie. I thought I'd ask them."

"When you were playing tennis yesterday?" Ruddy asked, eyeing Tommy sharply.

Tommy laughed. "I didn't get to play tennis," he said.

"Oh." Ruddy scratched his head. "Where did you go?"

"Oh, all round," Tommy said.

"But do the Heards know when that gun was missing?" Ed demanded. "Was it stolen?"

"Gosh, I forgot to ask 'em," Tommy said in a lame, apologetic voice.

"It won't help us much if that gun was missing after Charlie's death," Ed reminded Tommy.

"I see," Tommy said.

"Hunh." Ed grunted. "If that piece of gun found in that concrete mixer turns out to be a .38, and if a .38 was missing from Heard's home before Hindricks was killed, or before Father Byrnes was killed, and if it turns out that a .38 was buried in that hole in the Brentwood forest, then we might really have something."

"A gun was found in a concrete mixer?" Tommy asked, eyes round with surprise.

"Yeah. Seems like it," Ruddy spoke crisply.

"Gee. Things are popping. Do you think they might be the same gun?" Tommy asked.

"We don't know yet," Ruddy said coldly.

Had Tommy been around that concrete mixer? He wanted to probe into Tommy about his "long" walk yesterday, but Ed's presence stalled him.

"You weren't at home when I left this morning," Ruddy said.

"No. I was with the Heards, I told you," Tommy said. "And you had just gone out, it seems, when I got in."

"Lieutenant Parrish speaking," the intercom crackled again.

"What is it?" Ruddy asked.

"I have Andrew Gordon. Shall I bring 'im in, sir?"

"Yeah. Come right on." Ruddy turned to Tommy. "This is

something for you to see and hear. We have a man here who is going to confess to the Janet Wilder murder."

Tommy shot to his feet. "No! Really?"

"Sure thing. You just watch and listen." Ed smiled.

"So you've caught the murderer?" Tommy asked breathlessly.

"No," Ruddy said, looking off.

"Then who is this confessing?" Tommy asked.

"Just a bum with an uneasy conscience." Ed smiled.

"Jesus! Is that possible?" Tommy asked.

"It's very common, Tommy," Ruddy said. "We get dozens of false confessions in every well-known murder case."

"B-but what do you do with the confessions?" the boy asked, looking from face to face.

"We just listen to 'em, then send 'em home, or to the mental clinic," Ed said.

"Oh," Tommy breathed. He sat, his eyes shining. "This is something new to me."

The door opened and Lieutenant Parrish led in a thin, bedraggled white man of about forty-five years of age.

"So, you're ready to talk, eh, Gordon?" Ed asked.

"Yes, sir," the man said, nodding, looking with amazement around the huge room.

"All right. We're listening," Ruddy said flatly.

The man looked hopelessly about him, then demanded in a whisper: "Can I sit down?"

"Sure," Ruddy said. After Gordon had sat, Ruddy asked, "Anything you want?"

"No, sir," Gordon muttered.

"Well, you said you had something to tell us," Ruddy prodded the man.

"I killed her," the man said stoutly.

"Who? You killed who?" Ed asked.

"The girl whose picture's in the papers," the man declared.

"Yeah? Where?"

"In those woods."

"When?"

"The other day."

"Do you know the name of the woods?"

"No, sir. But it was in the woods."

"What did you use to kill her with?" Ruddy asked.

"A gun."

"What kind of a gun?"

"A-a rifle; it was a rifle," the man declared.

"Oh, I see," Ruddy said. "Now, why did you kill her?"

"She was no good," the man muttered darkly.

"What had she done to you?"

"She broke off our engagement," the man whispered.

"Oh, I see," Ed said. "Now, what did you do with the rifle after you'd killed her?"

"I-I threw it in the lake . . . right off Brentwood Point."

"Hunh hunh," Ruddy said. "And what did you do with her handbag?"

"I pushed it down in a garbage can," the man said.

Tommy was staring with glistening eyes at the man, his lips forming the man's words as they fell from the trembling mouth.

"And why did you violate her?" Ed asked.

"I wanted to get even with her," the man mumbled, looking down now.

"That's enough," Ruddy snapped. "Turn 'im over to the social welfare department. He may have to go to the hospital."

"Oh, no sir, Mister!" the man cried, leaping to his feet. "You're not going to send me to the psycho again!"

"Take 'im out, Lieutenant Parrish," Ruddy ordered.

"Yes, sir," Lieutenant Parrish said, gripping the raving

man's arm. "All right, now. Come along. You'll be all right. No-body's going to hurt you. Come on . . ."

Tommy rose without knowing it as the man was dragged from the office. "Dad!"

"Yeah, Tommy?"

"What was wrong with him?" Tommy wailed, his eyes moist with tears.

"He's just a lost man, son," Ruddy said.

"But he d-didn't do anything," Tommy said. "It was clear."

"Of course," Ed said.

"One of the duties of the police, Tommy," Ruddy explained, "is not only to catch criminals but to keep innocent people who feel guilty from destroying themselves."

"But what made 'im plead guilty to murder?" Tommy asked insistently.

"He read about the murder in the paper," Ed said. "He's something on his mind. Maybe it's only a memory. But it both-ers him. He's got what's bothering him all mixed up with the Janet Wilder case. You see, he doesn't even have the details right. He knows nothing about what actually happened."

"But why did he confess to that murder?" Tommy wanted to know.

"Maybe he can't really remember what he really wanted to confess," Ed suggested.

"He wants to be punished," Ruddy said.

"But he's done nothing," Tommy insisted.

"We know that," Ed said. "This happens quite often. Now, people say the police frame people. We wouldn't hurt that poor devil for anything in this world. He needs help. We could make him sign anything. But he's not guilty of what he confessed."

"Do they ever confess something that they really did?" Tommy asked.

"Very rarely." Ruddy smiled sadly.

"It really makes you think, doesn't it, Tommy?" Ed asked.

"Gee, you really have to understand people to do this job, don't you?" Tommy asked Ruddy with a note of awe in his voice. "Dad, do you think that some girl really once jilted him?" Tommy asked in a still, quiet tone.

"We don't know, Tommy," Ruddy said, "and maybe it'd take a psychologist six months to find out, if ever."

"Look, the motive he gave us is not important," Ed told the boy. "I once heard a man give five different motives in confessing to a crime he never committed, a crime he could *not* have committed."

"We call that 'shopping' for motives," Ruddy said with a forced laugh.

"They why . . . ?" Tommy's voice trailed off.

"What do you want to ask, Tommy?" Ed prompted the boy.

"I think Tommy's got a belly full of crime for one day," Ruddy tried ever so subtly to stall off his son's question.

"I was just thinking," Tommy said, as though speaking to himself.

"Yeah?" Ed echoed.

"Well, why in hell doesn't he just c-c-commit a crime?" Tommy asked with a stammer and at once blinked in confusion.

A silence fell upon the office. Ed laughed softly, then cocked his head at Tommy.

"You're getting close to something, son," Ed said, wagging his head.

"Don't go confusing that boy," Ruddy complained. "He's got too much in his head already."

"Well, if he feels that guilty, why doesn't he commit a crime?" Tommy insisted now, his eyes hard upon his reluctant mentors.

Ed cleared his throat, shot a glance at Ruddy, whom he felt did not wish to prolong the conversation.

"That happens more times than is imagined," Ed said softly. "In this particular case, my guess is that Gordon feels too acutely guilty to commit a crime. He's simply overwhelmed."

"Then he doesn't really wish to be punished," Tommy said in a voice that was half statement and half answer.

"I dare say that he wants to be forgiven," Ruddy said, entering cautiously into the discussion again. "Most of the people I've seen sentenced in court were grateful deep down in them."

"Something happens to people," Tommy said, sighing, his eyes vacant with dreamy thought.

"Ha, ha! You sure can say that again," Ed agreed.

"That man Gordon was trying to steal another man's crime," Tommy murmured.

"But he wasn't bright enough to do it," Ruddy said meaningfully.

"Stealing other men's crimes is a thing that can be done well only if it is done collectively," Ed said in a far-off voice. "It's done in church every Sunday when a mass is said."

"All right, all right . . . ha, ha. Ed, now you just get off of my religion," Ruddy chided, laughing.

"Well, let's say we all borrow other men's crimes on Sunday," Ed amended his original proposition.

"I didn't know so many people felt so guilty," Tommy said.

"If they didn't, we wouldn't be able to catch 'em all," Ed stated emphatically.

"Do you suppose there are many who don't?" Tommy asked directly of Ed now.

"I suspect that men who feel no guilt do not have enough imagination to commit crimes," Ed said. "Maybe Ruddy wouldn't agree."

"I wouldn't know," Ruddy said, looking off.

"So we are all kind of in prison," Tommy said and laughed nervously.

"It's the memory of the father, son," Ed said, winking at Ruddy.

"I've never been hard on my boy—have I, son?" Ruddy asked.

"No, Dad. You haven't," Tommy said.

"Oh, I don't mean that," Ed said. "I mean we all have a secret ideal which we obey. It's our image of what is most powerful in the world. Some call it God. Others call it—"

"Superego?" Tommy asked, arching his brows.

"You're sharp, kid," Ed said, laughing.

A crackling came from the intercom.

"Yeah?" Ruddy called with relief in his voice.

"This is Mary Jane, sir," a woman's voice called. "I'm reporting for work."

"Get on in here and let's get a look at you," Ruddy ordered, laughing.

"Yes, sir."

Mary Jane entered, smiling, demurely lingering in the middle of the office rug, her pencil and her shorthand notebook poised in her hand.

"Congratulations, sir."

"Can that," Ruddy sang. "This is a workhouse. How goes it?"

"Don't know yet," Mary Jane said. "But it's exciting here in Brentwood. It was never like this with Commissioner King. And the papers . . . the roadblocks . . . and, say, the mayor called. He wants to see you, sir. Seems that there is a mass meeting tonight."

"About the Janet Wilder case?" Ruddy asked.

"Yes, sir."

"That's a big help," Ruddy sneered.

"There they go," Ed said, shrugging.

"When shall I tell the mayor you'll receive 'im?" Mary Jane wanted to know.

"Oh, hell. Any time. Fix an appointment," Ruddy said. "I guess he wants to tell me how to run this office, eh?"

"I don't know," Mary Jane said.

The phone rang. Ruddy snatched it up.

"Chief Turner speaking."

"This is Captain Snell, Chief."

"Yeah. What about that gun part that was found? Anything to it?"

"It looks like it could be from a .38," the captain said slowly.

"Well, what about finding the rest of it?" Ruddy demanded.

"That's the problem sir."

"What's your problem?" Ruddy asked.

"Well, the cement has been poured and has been placed onto a floor of the new building," the captain said. "Now, it just may be that there are other bits of that gun in that cement. What do we do?"

"Well, tell 'em that I want that cement," Ruddy stated. "Ask 'em to cooperate with us. I suspect that that gun was broken up and put into that sand and cement. If that's the case, we'll lose a clue, our only clue so far."

"What do you suggest?" the captain asked.

"Can't they break up that cement?"

"Guess so. I'll ask 'em."

"Do that. If they don't want to, tell 'em I'll get a court order and take the floor of that damned building," Ruddy threatened.

"Could I ask 'em for the cement that they've poured?"

"Sure. We'll haul it here."

"I'll ask and report later, sir."

"Right. Do that."

Ruddy hung up, then swung to Tommy. "I'm afraid that you'll have to leave us, Tommy. Oh, Mary Jane, this is my son, Tommy."

"How do you do?"

"How do *you* do, ma'am?" Tommy looked pleadingly at Ruddy. "Must I really go? Gosh, this is exciting. You've found the gun?"

"Don't know, son," Ruddy said, pushing the boy with his voice. "Tell Mama I'll be along at lunch."

"Okay. 'Bye, Dad."

" 'Bye, son."

After Tommy had gone, Mary Jane exclaimed, "He's your very image!"

"Bright boy," Ed said.

"Yeah, he's bright all right," Ruddy said and swung to his desk and pretended to pore over a report. He glanced up at Ed and Mary Janet. "I'm having 'em send the whole floor of that new building over. Get in touch with the city cleaning department and ask 'em to lend us some trucks to haul that cement. And get some hammers ready. I'm putting this police force to work pounding rocks. We're going to dig out every bit of metal in that concrete."

CHAPTER 15

Ruddy felt feverish. Moment by moment a fear and a re-spect for his son was growing in him. Goddamn, if only Ed wouldn't egg that boy on. Yet he knew that it was not Ed's fault. The boy was fastened in his mind and emotions upon that Janet Wilder crime; hell, maybe he's been fastened on the other crimes too. He's too damned suggestible.

Ed had gone and Ruddy sat alone. He felt in his pocket for the wad of paper that held the bit of cement that he had pinched off Tommy's tennis shoes. Well, first, he'd see if that gun was the .38 that had been used in the Janet Wilder case. If it was, then it was a good guess that it had been used in the other three crimes. They would compare the ballistics of all the bullets and then have the experts decide if the bullets were fired from that .38. But, deep in him, Ruddy knew that the .38 buried in the cement was the gun that had been used in all four of the killings, and he knew that the cement he had taken from Tommy's shoes must have come from that building site. Well, if that were true, what was he waiting on? Why did he not confront the boy and get the misery over with? No. He was sure that some excuse would be found, that he was let-ting his imagination run away with him, that what he had so far encountered was a tiny string of amazing coincidences. "That boy wouldn't do a thing like that," Ruddy muttered. Yet Ed, for one, felt that intelligence had nothing to do with things of that sort, that the emotions and instincts were what ruled in such actions.

Then suddenly he sat back in his chair and stared at the wall, sighing. Two things were happening: the public was crying for a victim and his son was slowly becoming seemingly enmeshed in this damnable murder plot. And the mayor would be in to see him this morning, and tonight a mass meeting would be held. He had been thrown into a boiling pot of soup—there was no doubt about it. Well, he would leave no stone unturned to catch the murderers. After all, he, unlike all the others who had tried, had a clue, a real hard clue during the first twenty-four hours of his investigation. No one would say that he was placid, was letting any grass grow under his feet. Yet he did not wish to be pushed, pressured, panicked. "Nobody is going to make me make crazy decisions," he muttered, shaking his head. But the first thing he had to do was to have a showdown with Tommy. He could not go ahead in this investigation while looking over his shoulder at his own son every five minutes. He would face him and have it out with him. Was it true that a gun had been stolen from the Heard home, and when? Ruddy picked up the phone and told Jock to rush to the Heard home and get a final and definite picture. He called Captain Snell and found out that the building contractor had agreed to tear out the concrete into which it was thought a gun or parts of a gun could be and make a gift of it to the city. Good! As yet, the net of stool pigeons had reported nothing of worth. And the poring over hospital records, case records in mental clinics, or the checking on recently paroled prisoners had yielded nothing. "Our best bet seems to be that gun," he said. His roadblocks would be continued, mostly for public reassurance. Half an hour later Captain Snell called and reported that the slabs of concrete would be in the hands of the city officials that evening. Good! Good!

"Chief?" Mary Jane called him on the intercom.

"Yeah, Mary Jane."

"The mayor's on his way to see you. He'll be in in about ten minutes."

"Thanks, Mary Jane."

He rose, washed his face, and combed his hair. One had to look one's best for the real big boss. Not that he feared the mayor, but it would do no harm to look one's best when meeting an important politician for the first time. He had hardly finished changing his shirt when Mary Jane ushered Mayor Warren into his office.

The mayor was of medium height, thin-faced, had a pair of kind, reflective gray eyes, but his dress was flashy; the man was a contradiction—his bearing and manner seemingly indicative of well-born conservatism while his apparel marked him as a sportsman. Ruddy sized him up quickly: a politician and a good one. He knows how to deal with crowds.

"Good morning, Chief," the mayor boomed, advancing with outstretched hand.

"Good morning, Mr. Mayor." Ruddy was equally as effusive, pretending to be relaxed while weighing, judging. "Won't you sit down? This is quite an honor. I hope you didn't mind my canceling my inaugural ceremony. But I found work here that's kept me going night and day, and I felt the best service I could give Brentwood Park was to set our law-enforcement machinery into operation and—"

"No explanations are needed, Chief," the mayor said, waving his right hand, which gleamed with a diamond. "I talked with Bill King, an old, old friend of mine, and he told me all about you."

"Bill's a great guy," Ruddy sang.

"One of the best," the mayor chimed in.

Ruddy always felt at ease when he and a stranger found someone whom they could praise mutually, for it seemed to hint that if he and his just-met friend could like a third person, then it argued well that they would get along, with that third person acting as a sort of guardian angel.

"I want personally—and in the name of our city council—to welcome you to Brentwood," the mayor said.

"That's very kind of you indeed," Ruddy said.

"I'm sure that we'll be seeing a lot of each other in the coming days," the mayor said.

"I'm sure we will," Ruddy said, relaxing a bit.

"Branden was a wonderful guy," the mayor said, shaking his head. "What a tragic end he had. . . . His burial next week will be an official event, you know."

"Oh, yes. Like many of our officers, he went down in the line of duty," Ruddy murmured.

There was a silence. Ruddy offered the mayor a cigar, which he refused, taking a cigarette instead.

"We tried to build the most modern police headquarters in America here," the mayor stated.

"You did it; it is the most modern I've ever seen," Ruddy said. "And I'm proud to work in it."

"I'm glad you appreciate it," the mayor said. "I hear you've a wife and son."

"That's right, sir. You just missed my son. He went out fifteen minutes ago."

"We must have you over to the house," the mayor said. "Bill sent me your record—not that that was necessary. You've had quite some career."

"Oh, it was normal, natural." Ruddy deprecated his work. "There are a thousand officers with the same record."

"Now, don't be too modest," the mayor said. "Bill knows a first-rate officer when he sees one. You know, we telephoned Bill and asked him to send us the best man he had, regardless of politics. And he said without hesitation that you were one of the best and—"

"I would have retired in a few months," Ruddy put in.

"I know, I know," the mayor said. "All the more wonderful that you consented to come here with us. Your experience makes you more valuable for the job"—the mayor paused, stretched out his legs—"and I think you've got a job here, eh? This crime wave—"

"Well, *we* don't call it that," Ruddy cut him off softly.

"Yes, I know. That's newspaper stuff," the mayor agreed. "I'm glad you put up those road blocks. Impresses the public. Everybody was struck by it."

"I suppose Bill told you that we don't catch crooks with roadblocks—"

"Ha, ha! I've been around, Chief." The mayor laughed. "I know the ropes. By the way, any lead on who killed that Janet Wilder? That was an awful thing."

"Terrible. Horrible. Cold-blooded murder." Ruddy underscored the mayor's concern. "Yes, sir, Mr. Mayor, we've got a solid clue, and we're developing the investigation all down the line. We think we've got hold of the gun—"

"Really? Now, that's something. How—?"

"I'll give you a more detailed account in a few days."

"Take your time," the mayor said. "I respect a man's office, his function. You'll get no meddling from me, Chief. You just let your force work and we'll applaud."

"Thank you, Mr. Mayor."

"Now, look, I wanted to see you to tell you that there will be a mass meeting tonight in the old masonic temple," the mayor said. "I don't want you to let that worry you. It was the chamber of commerce that called it. I tried to head 'em off, but you know there's a lot of excitement in town. Maybe this meeting won't be a bad thing. But you must not for a second think that it's directed against you or the police department."

"I get you, Mr. Mayor," Ruddy said. "I'd heard about it. I'm calm."

"That's it," the mayor approved. "People have to let off steam some way. Now, tonight they may pass a lot of hair-brained resolutions over there—resolutions that can't naturally be carried out. Don't let it bother you. They too will be playing to the public. I'm a politician, and I understand such things."

"I get you, Mr. Mayor," Ruddy murmured. "In fact, I'll help the meeting along with a special detail to guard it, honor it, and protect it."

"Fine! You've got the spirit," the mayor said.

"I'm used to these things," Ruddy said.

"Chief, are there any developments on the Janet Wilder case that you care to mention?" the mayor asked. "Is it linked with the Byrnes and Hindricks cases? Is there any way for you to tell if they were Brentwood Park jobs or did they come from the outside?"

Ruddy lowered his head. As an honest officer, he did not like to overrate what he had found, for he was sure so far that he had touched the heart of the crimes.

"Well, let's say that the crimes were a bit of both," Ruddy said. "We're fairly sure that the criminal came from outside . . . but it seems that he may have had some kind of contact here. At least, we're now fairly sure that the gun came from here. In fact, I'm willing to stake my reputation that the gun used in all four crimes came out of Detective Heard's own home," Ruddy stated.

"No? Now, Branden's death had nothing—"

"It was completely separate from these killings," Ruddy assured the mayor.

"And Heard?"

"He was in no way criminally involved," Ruddy said. "Yet the .38 that we think was used in all four jobs was taken from his home by somebody. We're checking intensively on that."

"That is progress," the mayor stated. "Didn't think you'd gone that far."

Ruddy related that his theory was that the gun had been buried in the forest east of Brentwood by the murderer, that the murderer had gotten into a panic and had dug it up, and had been surprised by Janet Wilder, who was slain by him.

"We think that the murderer took that gun, broke it up, maybe with a sledgehammer, and then threw the pieces into piles of sand and cement at a building site on the far South Side. That is how we came across it. A bit of that gun got stuck in a concrete mixing machine and was dug out. That made us feel that the rest of that gun was poured into cement, which is now drying on the twelfth floor of a new building. That cement is being knocked out and will be brought here tonight. While that mass meeting is in progress, we'll be pounding up that cement to find the various bits of that gun, and we will assemble it. Of course, Mr. Mayor, this is confidential. We don't want the murderer to know that we've made this much progress or he'll flee."

"Fantastic!" the mayor exclaimed. "The commissioner's judgment in you is confirmed. What work! For the first time in more than a year, we have a real lead."

"That's right, sir."

The mayor smiled and stood. "Well, if there's anything my office can do, don't hesitate to call on me, Chief."

"Thank you, sir." Ruddy also stood.

"And depend on my keeping a stiff upper lip about your findings," the mayor said.

"Thank you, sir."

"And if you have any problems, personal or otherwise, don't hesitate to come to me," the mayor said.

"You're very kind, sir."

"Good-bye."

"Good-bye, Mr. Mayor."

They shook hands. After the mayor had gone, Ruddy sat and sighed. Well, that had not been too bad. He had nothing to fear from that direction. He took the wad of paper containing the bit of cement from his coat pocket and opened it and stared at it. Ought he to hand this in for examination now? No, wait until that gun had been assembled, that is, if the other parts of the gun were found. Then, as usual, his mind flew back to its preoccupation with Tommy. Each move he made seemed to be drawing or pushing him nearer to an obligatory showdown with that boy. He had to sit that boy down and fire some straight questions at him. Now, he knew that Tommy had long been a close friend of Charlie's and that he no doubt had had access to the Heard home. Had Tommy swiped that .38 out of the Heard home shortly after Marie's tragedy had occurred? He sighed. How logical it all seemed. Tommy had a motive. Tommy had a gun. Tommy had grown secretive. Tommy had had cement on his tennis shoes. Tommy was obsessed with the idea of crime. And a bit of a .38 gun handle, Captain Snell had said, was found in a cement mixer. When he had been made the chief of police, had Tommy gotten into a wild panic, rushed to those woods and unearthed that gun, and had he been surprised by that Janet Wilder girl, shot her, and then taken the gun on a long and crazy night walk, then found that building site, broken up the gun and pushed the pieces into sand, cement, and the concrete mixer? Could be? Could be.

Wearily, Ruddy issued orders for a detail of officers to guard the mass meeting scheduled for that evening, then he told Mary Jane that he was headed home for lunch.

"Don't give out any information to anybody," he told her.

"You know me, Chief," Mary Jane sang. "I'm as silent as a boneyard."

CHAPTER 16

Even while en route home for his lunch, Ruddy could not entirely shake off the cares and preoccupation of his office. Before quitting the premises of the police headquarters, he saw the first city truck enter the huge courtyard, piled high with huge slabs of white concrete, from the ends of which were sticking the rusted tips of iron bars of reinforcements. Those slabs of concrete had to be crushed to see if they contained the missing bits of the .38, whose piece of handle butt had been found by accident in the concrete mixer. "Either I'm a blind fool acting in panic, or the other pieces of that .38 are in those chunks," Ruddy told himself.

At the last moment, when behind his steering wheel, instead of driving directly to his home, Ruddy slowly circled the city, reading the freshly pasted billboards advertising the mass meeting slated for nine P.M. that evening. COME ONE AND ALL, read one poster, AND DEBATE YOUR SAFETY. Well, he'd be there, keeping in the background, trying to weigh and judge the temper of the populace. And he would have the stenographic department take down every word that was said. You could never tell. . . . "Hell, the murderer might even speak tonight," he muttered with a grim smile. "Stranger things have happened."

As he was leaving the city limits of Brentwood Park, he slowed his car to glance at the recently constructed roadblocks and to give a few stiff waves of his hand to his men, who seemed smartly clad and alert. Now and again his ears caught snatches of distantly wailing sirens. Yeah, the force was on its toes. He felt pleased. He would go and eat now, feeling that the investigation he had launched was well under way. He slowed at a newsstand and bought the late morning papers and glanced at the headlines:

MAYOR TO SPEAK AT TONIGHT'S MASS MEETING

SECRET DEVELOPMENTS HINTED IN WILDER CASE

POSSES COMB BRENTWOOD PARK FOREST AREA

POLICE HEADS WORK AROUND THE CLOCK

NEW CHIEF CRACKS DOWN ON LAWLESSNESS

POLICE DRAGNET SURROUNDS BRENTWOOD PARK AREA

NATION SHOCKED BY JANET WILDER MURDER

CONGRESSIONAL PROBE OF LAW ENFORCEMENT HINTED

CRIME SPECIALISTS CALLED IN JANET WILDER INQUIRY

NEW LEAD ON MURDER GUN IS WHISPERED

That last newspaper headline made anger surge in Ruddy. "Now, who in goddamn hell let that leak out?" he asked himself aloud. "Somebody's gonna get kicked or I'll have somebody's head today!" But as he read the article, he found that no real harm had been done; yet he felt that his strict orders for secrecy had surely been violated, implicitly disobeyed. "I'll check on that now," he muttered, lifting the receiver of the phone in his car. When the light had glowed green, he asked for Mary Jane and growled to her, "Mary Jane, ask Ed to find out how the *Globe* has gotten hold of that information on the gun! I got to know!"

"Yes sir. It wasn't from me!" Mary Jane protested.

"Didn't say it was," Ruddy snapped. "Now, get busy!"

"Yes sir, Chief."

"I want discipline among my men or I'm going to know why," he said, hanging up.

Agnes met Ruddy at the front door; she had been waiting for him.

"Hi, stranger."

"Hi, Agnes," he greeted her. "Forgot me?"

"Almost," she said, kissing him. "You do look a bit tired and strained.

"How are you?" he asked.

"When did you leave this morning?"

"Oh, around three, I guess."

"Good God," she sighed, then with sudden anxiety asked, "Say, where's Tommy?"

Ruddy stiffened; they were walking arm and arm toward the dining room. He ripped off his gun and cartridge belt and flung it onto a chair. He turned and stared at Agnes.

"Isn't he here?"

"No."

"He left my office a little while ago," Ruddy told her with baffled eyes.

"He didn't come here . . . and he didn't sleep here last night, either," Agnes said, her eyes wide.

"Yeah. I know." Ruddy tried to speak calmly. "He got in late. But I don't know why he wouldn't have come straight on here." He recalled with shame how he had hustled Tommy out of his office.

"And, Ruddy, he must have come into the house last night because—"

"I saw 'im coming in as I left," Ruddy interrupted her.

"Oh. Then look—he unpacked a box in his room," Agnes said. "It was a car radio. The kind that the police use. I suppose he's fitted it in his car."

Ruddy stared again. Now, what in hell was this? Tommy had put a shortwave police radio in his car! That was the limit.

"You know, police radios in private cars is against regulations," he said.

"What do you suppose he wanted it for?"

"To listen to police news, of course," Ruddy said, and possibilities leaped in his mind. Why in the world would Tommy want to hear police broadcasts?

"And the *Globe* called here this morning," Agnes told him.

"The *Globe*?"

"Yes."

"What did they want?"

"I don't know. I asked them and they hung up."

Ruddy's lips parted. Had Tommy told the *Globe* about that gun? Jesus . . . had he told of the hole in the forest or about the gun missing in the Heard home? But Tommy wouldn't do that . . . and Tommy had heard him this morning stress the secret nature of that gun business. And Tommy had never before meddled in his police work. I should've known better than to talk like that before him. Then Ruddy was thunderstruck. Aw, maybe Tommy had told the papers about the gun missing in the Heard home before he had come to the office? If so, why had he not mentioned it? No. Tommy had done nothing like that. Somebody else had done that.

"How are things going?" Agnes asked. "You are all over the papers."

"Yeah. I don't like that. When things are going right in police work, there oughtn't to be any noise in the press."

"That mass meeting—"

"It's nothing, really. I talked to the mayor, and he said—"

"How is he?" Agnes asked eagerly.

"Okay. He wants us over one evening."

"Oh, great."

Even when they had sat down to eat, Tommy had not arrived.

"I wonder what that boy's up to?" Ruddy asked as he out into his steak.

"At school maybe," Agnes said. "But he generally sleeps here, and he didn't last night."

Ruddy hated the idea of talking "crime" at home, and especially with Agnes. But since Tommy seemed involved in all this, he felt he ought to say something.

"You know, Tommy gave us a valuable clue in that Janet Wilder case."

"Really? How? I told you—"

"He found out that the gun used might have come from the Heard home."

"The gun in the Janet Wilder killing?"

"Yes. And we think that that gun was used in the other killings too."

"Oh! Then maybe Tommy might get part of the reward?" Agnes asked, her eyes shining.

Ruddy started! Gosh, he had not thought of that part of it. Was that what was egging poor Tommy on? If so, what a fool he had been not to suspect it sooner!

"Don't know. A .38 was used on the Wilder girl, and a .38 is missing from the Heard home."

"You know that Charlie was one of Tommy's best friends, don't you?"

"Yes."

"Maybe Tommy's at the Heards' now?"

"Hadn't thought of that. I'll try calling there after lunch."

"Oh, if Tommy has helped a bit . . ." Agnes mused, toying with her fork.

Ruddy was irked, but he could not afford to tell her why. Goddamnit, why didn't Tommy keep out of his business? And why in all hell had he put a shortwave radio into his car? He's going too damned far, he shouted to himself. He's not to meddle.

"Ruddy?"

"Yeah, darling?"

"May I and Tommy go to that mass meeting tonight?"

"I don't see why not. If you can find Tommy—"

"Oh, splendid!"

Ruddy was eating dessert when the phone rang.

"Get that, Agnes," Ruddy begged. "Every time I hear a phone these days I almost start out of my skin."

"Yes, darling. I'll get it." Agnes rose and went to the phone.

"Mr. Turner's residence."

"Oh, yes, Mr. Seigel. Yes, Ruddy's here. Just a moment." Agnes cupped the receiver with her palm. "It's Eddie Seigel, your friend. He says that it's personal."

"Personal?"

"Yes. He's waiting."

Ruddy went and picked up the receiver.

"Yeah, Ed?"

"Ruddy, I think you ought to get to headquarters as quickly as possible."

"What's up?"

"I can't tell you over the phone."

"Why?"

"No. It's best you got here."

"But what the hell's wrong, man? I'm the chief of police in that station?"

"No, Ruddy. It's not that. It's . . . you see, it's something personal."

"About *you*?"

"No."

"Then *who*?"

There was a long hesitation on Ed's end of the wire.

"No, *you*, Ruddy."

Ruddy swallowed, blinked, then asked, "What do you mean? Me . . . ?"

"It's your son, Ruddy."

"Oh! Where is he?"

"Here."

"*Where?*"

"At the police station."

"Why?"

"Look, Ruddy, do me a favor and get here as quickly as you can, see?"

Ruddy's scalp felt tight. Then his face flushed hot. He thought rapidly. Thank God he had not mentioned Tommy's name over the phone; Agnes would have no notion about what had happened. All that Ruddy could understand was that the police, his men, were holding his son! And what for? His head swam. How ridiculous. But Ed had said it was so, was true, and Ed was no man to lie or joke.

"Okay," Ruddy said soberly, "be right there. Hold everything."

"Right!"

"Do nothing. I'm coming."

"Right. You can depend on me, Ruddy."

Ruddy hung up, lifted his right palm, and brushed sweat from his brow. Good God, had the police beat him to his own son? He knew now why Ed had not wanted to say more over the phone; Ed had not wanted to talk with Agnes near him. Hell, it must be something serious. What in hell had that goddamn fool of a son of his gone and got himself into? Yeah, he should have cracked down long ago! He ought to have confronted Tommy about that concrete on his tennis shoes. And why had Tommy gone and meddled into that gun business at the Heard home? Oh, maybe the police had learned that Tommy had found out about the gun and had told the *Globe*? No, had it been only that, Ed would surely have told him about it over the phone. And the boy had had a police radio recently installed in his car. . . . Was it in connection with the Wilder murder and those other murders that Tommy had been picked up? What a sensation that would make: POLICE CHIEF'S SON BOOKED FOR MURDER! No, God . . .

"What is it, Ruddy?" Agnes asked.

"Nothing."

"You looked worried and shocked."

"Oh, they just want to consult with me."

"You've got a break in the case?"

"Something like that," he mumbled, strapping his gun again about his hip. If that boy's gone and done something wild and foolish, I'll break his goddamn neck. And a mass meeting was coming up tonight, a mass meeting about crime. That was a hot one.

"Don't you want your coffee, darling?"

"Haven't time, Agnes."

He kissed her, then squeezed her shoulders with both hands, tightly.

"See you later, hunh?" he said.

"Sure. Maybe tonight. If I find Tommy and—"

"Yeah, if you find him," Ruddy said and was gone like a shot out of the room, down the hall and toward his car.

CHAPTER 17

With screaming siren, with his head tight to the point of feeling that it would burst, Ruddy burned up the asphalt in getting back to headquarters. As he drove, swinging around curves, he felt that all along a premonition had been seething in him that something like this was about to happen. And it made him feel hotly guilty; what had he failed to do? What had he overlooked? And why hadn't Ed dared be more specific over the phone? The suspense was the thing that hurt him most now. That something had happened, he knew. But what? It was bad, or Tommy would not be in the clutches of the police. But how bad? And not once did Ruddy ever think that his policemen could have made a mistake. He was much too good an officer to think or feel like that. If the police got hold of you, then it was for a damn good reason. The police were not always right, but they were more often right than wrong. Then what had Tommy blundered into? There flashed through his mind the image of the weeping Marie, the shock that Tommy had sustained about her dreadful illness. And then came Ed's disturbing and speculative ideas about how some people would kill when their basic idea of the world had been shattered. No, nothing like that's happened with Tommy. It couldn't . . . yet he recalled how sickened and shocked he had been when he had talked to Marie. Was it possible? Had that boy let that thing throw him off balance?

He was speeding along the lakeshore now, and to his left whitecaps leaped as bright and sharp as his panicked thoughts. To his right, turning and fading behind him, were the tall sky-scrapers of Chicago. Well, something was happening that he had never thought would happen: the world of law was meet-ing and melting into the world of nonlaw. The force of law that he represented had reached its long and cold arm into his very home and snatched one of his blood kin. Goddamn . . . what would the commissioner say about this?

He turned a long, slow right curve and headed for Brent-wood Park, passing the first roadblock that he had ordered erected last night. Goddamn . . . his men looked at him and sa-luted as he passed. No, I don't think they know. Ed saw to that, I suspect. Thank God it was Ed who had phoned 'im. What an impression for the new chief of police's son to be hauled in while the chief of police was trying to throw out a dragnet to catch murderers. What ironical editorials the papers would carry. Yeah, hell, I'll resign . . . what the goddamn hell! "I oughtn't to have taken the damn job in the first place," he said bitterly.

When he swung into the big, guarded gate of the police station, with his siren blaring, he caught sight of Ed at once, waiting for him on the ramp. He halted the car about six inches from Ed's tight face.

"What's up, Ed?" he asked tersely, alighting from the car.

Ed did not speak; instead, he grimly caught hold of Rud-dy's arm and piloted him a few yards toward the door before he opened his mouth.

"Your boy was picked up after a filling station was robbed,"

Ed reported in an undertone. "Seems like he was part of a gang. The gang got away. Tommy was driving the car and—"

"What in hell are you saying, Ed?" Ruddy asked fiercely.

"He's *here*," Ed insisted. "Your boy . . . you talk to 'im. He broke down and confessed."

"He was armed?"

"No. He was driving the getaway car. I tried to get 'im to identify the others, but he refused. That's his out, Ruddy. Maybe you can get—"

"*Jesus Christ!*" Ruddy croaked as he went down the corridor.

"He had a police radio in his car," Ed said. "This is tough on you. Goddamn, it is!"

Ruddy stopped abruptly in his tracks, staring bleakly ahead of him, then he turned to Ed and asked, "Where is he?"

"Lieutenant Parrish is guarding him in your office," Ed said. "Look, you're new here. We've got to handle this in—"

"Can that," Ruddy spoke exasperatedly. "I'm an officer. The law will take its course. Come on. Let's get the hell up there."

"Gee, Ruddy," Ed murmured, shaking his head, his eyes bewildered and baffled.

"I'll break his head," Ruddy growled.

"Now, look—take it easy," Ed counseled.

"I've been waiting for this," Ruddy snapped.

"Didn't know you were having trouble—" Ed sighed. "He seemed so sharp to me. Bright and—"

"Too *damned* bright!"

They entered the big door together and stopped short before Tommy, who sat slumped on a sofa, and Lieutenant Parrish, who stood at his side.

"Hello, Chief," Lieutenant Parrish mumbled.

"Hi," Ruddy answered, his eyes hard on his son.

Tommy's eyes were bloodshot and his fingers were nervously picking at a torn gap in his sleeve. Ruddy moved closer, then stepped back. Then he sat before his son and lowered his forehead into his palm.

"Goddamn, you let me down," he moaned.

"Sorry, Dad."

"What have you got to say for yourself?"

Tommy did not reply. He shrugged, his eyes staring sullenly into space.

"I guess the best thing for me to do is resign," Ruddy said, looking from Lieutenant Parrish to Ed.

A tense silence fell upon the office. Lieutenant Parrish let his eyes rove from Tommy to Ed and then to Ruddy, with lifted eyebrows and a serious face. Ed frowned, sat, rose, and cleared his throat. His lips moved several times before he spoke.

"Ruddy, I want to talk frankly," Ed began. "You're our chief. You're the boss. What you say goes, with me and all the rest. You're going to do what you want; that's your right, your privilege. You can use your judgment and make whatever decisions you feel that you ought to make . . ." Ed's voice died, and when he resumed speaking, his tone indicated that he was thinking intensely, weighing many factors and probabilities. ". . . The decision you feel or you *think* you've got to make. There's only one thing I'm asking: let me question this boy. You're dealing now with your own family, and you're likely to get subjective about it. If you trust me, I'll try to get to the bottom of this. I'm not trying to sound partial to you, but if I know anything about police work, there's something goddamn fishy about this holdup—"

"What do you mean, Ed?" Ruddy asked, his face becoming pale.

"Will you let me question your son?" Ed said, asking for trust and latitude.

"Did you do it, son?" Ruddy asked, turning swiftly to Tommy.

"Yeah. Now, you know." Tommy spoke sullenly, his eyes avoiding his father's.

"Did they disguise themselves with handkerchiefs?" Ed asked Tommy in a quick stab of voice.

"Yeah, they covered their faces," Tommy said, sounding surprised and quick at the same time.

"Hunh huh," Ed said, nodding, his eyes serious. "And they used a .38, I suppose?"

"No," Tommy said, "they had a .32."

"Oh," Ed said. "And they ordered the guy running the filling station to back out of the front door, eh?"

"Yeah. He backed out and they rifled the drawer," Tommy said, nodding defiantly.

"How long were they in that filling station while you waited to drive 'em off?" Ed asked.

"Oh, I don't know. I was excited," Tommy said. "A few minutes . . ."

"And you weren't with the gang?" Ed asked.

"Yeah. I was with 'em," Tommy answered, yet evading Ed's question

"You went into the station?"

"I was in the car—"

"You said you were with 'em and—"

"We planned it together, you see."

"You haven't answered me, Tommy," Ed said, hunching his shoulders and tucking his head down, bulldog like.

"What do you want to know?" Tommy asked belligerently.

"Did you hold up that filling station?" Ed roared.

"I was with 'em," Tommy argued. "They asked me to drive the car."

"Oh, Tommy, why in God's name did you do it?" Ruddy begged in despair. "Haven't I been good to you? Haven't I given you everything you wanted . . . everything you asked for . . . everything you needed? You're in the university, and you go and mess up your life!"

"Did you go into that filling station with those boys?" Ed asked again, insistently.

"No," Tommy said, "they told me to wait at the corner . . . in the car . . . with the motor running—"

"Then why didn't you drive 'em away when they came running out?" Ed asked.

Tommy hesitated; his eyes held a look of terror.

"I told you the cops came too quickly," he fumed. "You see, they ran and—"

"Why were you waiting at the corner in your car?" Ed demanded. "That's more than a hundred yards away? The filling station attendant never saw you."

Tommy was silent, biting his lips.

"You said they drove the attendant out, didn't you?" Ed asked.

"Yes, sir."

"Well?" Ed asked.

Tommy was silent, his eyes glazed. Ruddy had looked from Ed to Tommy during this exchange of questions and answers, his eyes blinking.

"And what was going to be your split?" Ed asked Tommy.

"Even. We were going to split it evenly between us," Tommy explained.

"Now, tell me: where did you plan the holdup?" Ed demanded.

"In a drugstore—out on Stoney Island," Tommy said vaguely.

"What number?"

"I don't know."

"What's the name of the drugstore?"

"I didn't look. . . . I don't know—"

"Tommy, you're lying!" Ed shouted. "Now, tell us what really happened!"

"I'm telling you the truth," Tommy screamed, sweat beading on his face.

Ed laughed suddenly and sat down beside Tommy and then placed his right palm tenderly on Tommy's knee—a knee that shook.

"Tommy, stickups don't happen like that," Ed told the boy.

The office was so silent that the hard sound of Tommy's breathing could be heard.

"How do you know?" Tommy asked finally in a child's voice.

In the silence that followed, a soft wind of relaxation blew through the office.

"You want us police to tell you the secrets of our trade, eh, Tommy?" Ed asked kindly.

Ruddy slapped his thigh and stood.

"Well, I'll be goddamned," he sang in a harsh, throaty tone. He turned to Tommy and stormed, "I ought to slap you into the middle of next week!"

"Take it easy, Ruddy," Ed cautioned. "We haven't got to the bottom of this yet."

"Boy, are you crazy?" Ruddy demanded. "Making up a wild tale like that—"

"You see," Ed explained, "he heard about the call to the police over his car radio. What happened was this: he got there a few seconds before the police. The station attendant pressed an alarm. The boys took the dough and beat it. Tommy saw the attendant come out of the station after the boys had run. He made up the whole thing!"

"No!" Tommy screamed in shame.

"What are you doing, Tommy?" Ruddy demanded. "Why are you acting this way?"

Tommy stared at his father and did not answer. Ruddy felt he knew. But he had never dreamed that Tommy's reaction would assume this form of defiance. Then a feeling of relief came over Ruddy. Well, that meant that Tommy surely had nothing to do with the murders! Ruddy had been expecting some kind of blowup and had been afraid that it had gone in that direction.

"You see, this morning we were talking of 'borrowing' crimes," Ed said soothingly, keeping his hand still on the boy's trembling knee. "And then he went and did it. But the question is: Why?"

They were frozen and almost missed the tingling of the telephone.

"Chief Turner speaking," Ruddy mumbled into the receiver.

"Squad car 188 reports that the men who held up the filling station have been captured," Mary Jane reported.

"Thanks," Ruddy said, hanging up. He turned to Tommy. "Now, your partners who helped you have been taken in. Do you want to be tried with 'em? Will they agree that you helped 'em?"

Tommy stared in disbelief, then hung his head.

"They will laugh at you in court if you tell that tale," Ed told the boy. "Those guys would scorn to say that *you* helped 'em."

A tiny tinge of compassion crept into Ruddy when Tommy's eyes glistened with tears. But what had made the boy do it?

"If you insist that you did it, shall we take down your confession?" Ed asked softly.

Tommy squirmed, unable to take his eyes off the floor.

"Well," Ed sighed, turning to Ruddy, "the rest is up to you."

"I'll take care of 'im," Ruddy said in a tone of simulated confidence. "Okay, Lieutenant Parrish, you can leave 'im." Ruddy looked about in a disturbed manner, then drew from his pocket the paper holding the tiny wad of cement. "Say," he spoke to Lieutenant Parrish, "take this to the lab and have 'em analyze it. It's a bit of cement. I want to know what kind of cement was used, the quality of sand, and the ratio of cement to sand."

"Yes sir, Chief," Lieutenant Parrish said and left, looking lingeringly at Tommy.

When Ruddy and Ed were alone with the boy, Ed asked, "What happened, Ruddy?"

"Don't know. Leave it to me, Ed. I'll get the truth out of 'im," Ruddy said, crestfallen.

"Okay."

"Ed, I want you and Jock to take charge of those cement blocks that are being brought in," Ruddy directed. "Maybe you'll have to get some of the city prisoners to come over with sledgehammers and start pounding the stuff. I want every bit of metal out of that cement."

"Right."

Ed left, first patting Tommy's shoulder and looking compassionately at Ruddy. Alone with his son, Ruddy said nothing for long minutes. He sat at his desk, his cap still on, staring into space. Tommy sat huddled on the sofa, sniffing now and then, not daring to lift his eyes.

"Tommy, what's happening to you?" Ruddy finally asked.

The boy did not reply.

"You know, you're skating pretty near the edge of something that could ruin both you and me, don't you?" Ruddy prompted.

"I don't care," Tommy whispered.

"All of this started with what happened to Marie, didn't it, Tommy?"

Tommy still failed to respond.

"If you talk about it openly, maybe I can help you," Ruddy told him.

"Nobody can help me," Tommy mumbled.

"Aw, hell," Ruddy said. "Now, tell me, what has this pretending that you're a holdup man got to do with Marie?"

"Nothing," Tommy said.

"Were you trying to test out what Ed said this morning about people pretending to commit crimes—borrowing crimes?"

Tommy shook his head.

"Well, you were trying to pretend *something*."

"I'm sorry," Tommy sighed.

"And what does being sorry mean now?"

Tommy remained obstinately silent.

"Say, did you tell the *Globe* about a gun being missing in the Heard home?"

"No."

"Oh." Ruddy felt a bit more at ease. "They called you at home, the *Globe* did."

"I want to go away," Tommy said suddenly.

"You're going nowhere," Ruddy snapped.

"But I-I—"

"Shut up about it," Ruddy snapped. "If you keep talking like that, I'll have you sent to a clinic."

Tommy quailed and Ruddy knew that the blow had hit home. The boy bit his trembling lower lip, then lifted eyes that were flooded with tears yet showing a kind of desperate cunning.

"You w-won't tell Mama about this," he begged in a dying whisper.

Ruddy felt trapped, yet he had to marvel at the boy's sharp

presence of mind. He sighed, which was his sign of reluctant con-
sent to the boy's plea. Tommy knew how ardently he had always
sought to keep the sordidness of the world dealt with by the police
out of the home and from the feelings of Agnes. Indeed, his ada-
mant decree that police work was not to be too much discussed at
home was a kind of apology for his being a policeman. And now
he was feeling that maybe it was his being a man of the law that
had brought this turmoil down upon the head of his son.

"Tommy, are you fighting me in some way?" he asked, smiling wryly.

"No," Tommy said in a surly tone.

"Why do you answer like that?"

"Why do you keep asking me these *crazy* questions?"

"My questions are not crazy," Ruddy said. "I'm supposed to
be solving murder cases, and here I am taking up time to try to
talk some common sense into you. Son, this foolish thing you
did . . . it means that you ought to let somebody help you."

"I'll be all right." He leaned forward. "Will there be a r-re-
cord of this?"

"Luckily, no." He felt that he had spoken too quickly, too
lightly. "Not this time, at any rate." He had felt compelled to
toss a mild threat into his assurance. "Tommy?"

"Yeah."

"All this comes from what happened to you and Marie,
doesn't it?"

"No," Tommy snapped.

"Then where does it come from?"

"Don't know. But I'm all right now."

A possible solution struck Ruddy. Was it impossible? Why
not try it?

"Say, you know, Marie told me that she was cured. Son,
these modern miracle drugs—"

"No. I don't want to hear that," Tommy's voice rose for the first time.

"You said that you loved the girl and—"

"I do! And that's why I can't and won't *touch* her!"

"This is all in your mind," Ruddy said soothingly. "If you see her, then the image of the real Marie that you love will come back and—"

"I said no!"

Ruddy's mind protested against the boy's reaction, but his own feelings agreed, for he had had the same reactions when in Marie's presence. Yet he sensed that it was what he thought of Marie rather than Marie herself that had bothered him. God-damn, why had this happened to his son? And couldn't he find some way to rid his son of this wild and driving sense of repulsion? He could think of nothing.

"What're you going to do, Tommy?" he asked, and was suprised that he could pose the question so frankly, for it implicitly confessed his inability, his powerlessness to control the situation in which his son found himself, and he was admitting that he no longer felt any moral right to make demands in the name and in the fact of his being a father. Then there flitted through his mind the notion that he, too, like Tommy, was bowing to the force of another law more powerful than the one he administered and enforced each day. What he could not put into words, he put into his eyes as he lifted them and stared pleadingly at Tommy.

"I'll be all right." Tommy repeated his chorus of false courage.

"You keep telling me that and—"

"You can't help me," Tommy desperately cried out in a tone of accusation.

Ruddy knew that he had to keep track of what Tommy did from now on, but he did not wish to use the complicated and tainting forces of his office to do so. Then what could he do? Aw, Agnes could take the boy to the mass meeting tonight. That might not be a bad idea. Let the kid see and hear how others were worried about crime; let him feel how strong was the force of society that was pitted against the lawbreaker. That would surely make him know that stunts of a crazy nature like the one he had pulled this morning could never work.

"Say, your Mama wants to go to that mass meeting tonight," Ruddy said. "But she can't go without you. She doesn't want to be alone."

"What mass meeting?"

"Haven't you heard?"

"They're holding a meeting about the Janet Wilder murder, and other stuff that's happened here during the past year," Ruddy explained.

"Tonight?"

"Yeah. At the old masonic temple," Ruddy said. Then he was sorry, for the terror that came into the boy's eyes was truly terrible. "You don't have to go."

"I guess I ought to go," Tommy said slowly, as though thinking of many imponderables.

"You don't *have* to."

"I-I'll go," Tommy said.

"With your mother," Ruddy stipulated.

"Oh. All right."

"Then you're going directly home?"

"Yeah. But you'll not tell—"

"I won't say a word, son," Ruddy swore.

"Thanks, Dad. I don't know what got into me to make me—"

"Keep away from crime," Ruddy said sternly. "You know nothing about it. You can't fake a holdup or try to get yourself arrested for a stickup man. We know about that stuff."

"Yeah, Dad. It was silly, hunh?" He tried to laugh.

"This is nothing to laugh about," Ruddy reminded him.

"Don't worry, don't worry. I'll be all right."

"I hope so."

He went with Tommy to the door and let him out, watching his retreating back as he shuffled down the marble hallway. Aw, Christ, he sighed and turned back to his desk.

In a manner that he could not have explained, Ruddy felt that he had lost control not only of his son but of his relation to him as a father. What was really bothering him at bottom were those disturbing but beckoning ideas of Ed's regarding the overriding power of the notions of guilt. But what was guilt? Regret and remorse about something that one had done? Or the sensation of being crushed for something that one had not done? And then there was that outlandish notion of Ed's that said that guilt spurred people to commit crimes. How on earth could that be? Though his conscious mind could not answer that question, there lingered deep in him a dim notion that somehow things like that really happened.

He had a son who was reacting to life in terms that Ed had vaguely outlined, and if that were true, then he had to confess that he knew little or nothing of what was happening to that son and knew less about what to try to do about it. That being the case, and since Ed had helped him only this morning, ought he not take Ed into his confidence? Ed was a friend; he had the faculty of understanding what went on in the heart. But could he tell a friend anything that shameful? Could he talk about Marie to Ed? No. Marie's secret, her shame, her taint sprang from darkness, a darkness that seemed to draw him into its conspiring net, seemed to set a seal upon his lips, a seal as tight as the one that had kept his son so silent for so long. Had he been Ed's assistant instead of his chief, then he would have felt no qualms or hesitation in enlisting Ed's sympathy and wisdom. But he was Ed's chief, and how could he place his authority—even in a private manner—and his private life with all its dark aspects of shame, under Ed's moral direction? No, he could not. No, not unless he really had to, and if it ever really came to that, he would resign forthwith. And could he dare take Bill, the commissioner, into his confidence? God, no, not after having had Bill thrust this immense job and honor upon him. Why, Bill might well ask himself how could Ruddy handle the city of Brentwood Park if he could not manage the much simpler and nearer problems in his own home? And just as Tommy had quailed at the idea of talking to Father Joyce, so did he too now.

It had been bad enough to let Ed salvage Tommy from that stupid and pretended holdup this morning. To say that Ed's revelations had astounded him would have been stating it in terms far below their reality; he had sat in mute awe at what Ed's skilled questions had elicited and laid bare. He, Ruddy, had been much too subjective, too angry and ashamed to have so neatly plucked the truth out of Tommy's tangled web of make-believe. The truth of the matter was that he had believed the boy was guilty! He had believed him guilty even though he loved him deeply! In the end, to cover his own embarrassed shortcoming he had had to pretend—as Tommy had been trying to pretend!—that he had seen or guessed at Tommy's game all along. And now he felt a double sense of shame at having tried to fool Ed, for he sensed that Ed had not been fooled at all. And he knew that if another wild stunt like that ever came from Tommy again, he would not be able to pull off a make-believe knowing again. And in spite of himself, and in spite of Tommy's sullen assurances, he felt that soon still another and maybe other crises would surely erupt from out of the hot cauldron of Tommy's emotions.

What could he do? He had, and quickly, to get down to the bare bedrock of what was happening with his son. First, was Tommy really in any way linked with, say, the Janet Wilder murder? If so, had that anything to do with the other murders? And if that were ever proved to be true, then did that account for Tommy's wanting to be sent to jail for what he had tried to make-believe was a holdup in which he had had a part? Had he been, as Ruddy knew too well, trying to seek a haven of safety in jail for a lesser crime than the ones he had really committed? Or was he blunderingly and stumblingly trying to plead guilty—as that crazy Andrew Gordon had done—and as Ed claimed more people than one believed would like to do—plead guilty in a more general sense for something that had become displaced wrongly in his life?

And that gun that loomed just out of the reach of the police? That .38? Some instinct told him that Tommy had been too eager to unearth a .38 in this case. And how odd that he had found a missing .38 in the home of the detective whose son had been killed? By God, he had issued orders for Jock to investigate that angle. Just as Ruddy reached out to take up the phone, it tingled.

"Chief Turner speaking," he sighed into the instrument.

"Chief, Jock Wiedman speaking."

"Yeah, Jock. What's keeping you? Was just about to phone you."

"Well, I'm late, Chief," Jock reported. "I can't make head or tail out of that .38 story at the Heard home."

"Why? What's the matter?"

"Well, Mrs. Heard says she saw one. So what? Nobody knows when they saw it or when it was missed. Or its serial number. It seems that that gun fell into Detective Heard's hand from some killer and he was keeping it as a memento. Against regulations, yeah. But, so what? All we got is a missing gun. But we have no way of telling if that is the gun we want. Say, who got wind of this missing gun, anyhow?"

"Well, Jock, it was my son. He was a friend, you see, of Charlie."

"You want me to follow it anymore, Chief?"

"No. Drop it," Ruddy said. "Say, get over here. I want you to help supervise breaking up some concrete."

"Oh, that stuff from that building site?"

"That's it."

"Okay, Chief."

Ruddy hung up. Now, what did that mean? It meant, if his hunches were working right about Tommy, that for some reason Tommy wanted another .38 injected into the case. Why? What was Tommy trying to do? Draw a veil of mystery across the path of their investigation? To create confusing circumstances? Ruddy knew that at times even fairly dumb criminals could baffle the police, because their reasoning was so horribly childlike, so out of the ordinary, so downright obvious. Was Tommy's hand showing in all this?

"Goddamnit, if I had one-tenth of the suspicion about anybody else that I have in my heart about that boy, I'd have arrested 'im long ago," Ruddy growled.

No. Surely Tommy, if Ruddy pressed him, had some explanation to give not only for that pretended holdup but also for all his wild ideas, all this crazy talk, some excuse that had nothing even to do with Marie. But what on earth could that be? No. That was not true. He knew that boy's life. Maybe he had underestimated the Marie business, but surely there could be no other reality that was rousing him to dangerous pitches. But that wad of cement Ruddy had pinched off those tennis shoes? Could that be just a coincidence? Even in the face of a bit of gun handle having been found in a cement mixer?

Ruddy doubled his fist and softly but tensely pounded the top of his desk. He knew that, in spite of himself, he was deep down in his heart trying to make a case to exonerate his son. No. The world he defended could not make people feel like Tommy said he felt, even if there had been a mishap about Marie. What happened to Marie happened once in a thousand million times. And you could not go around acting as though your hair was on fire about it.

A Sergeant Grisby brought him a stack of reports—from stool pigeons, detectives, patrolmen, et cetera—which he looked over, finding out nothing new. Still another dun-colored folder brought him another deluge of anonymous phone calls at which he refused to glance. During the afternoon, Lieutenant Parrish told him over the phone, no fewer than eight derelicts had come in to confess to the Janet Wilder killing. "Mother of Mary," he sighed wearily. He could do with a drink, yet he dared not—no telling when some very important break would come and he would have to receive somebody of distinction.

Then he realized an omitted act; he phoned Lieutenant Parrish to take a bit off the new slabs of cement that were steadily coming into the police courtyard in city trucks and take it over to the laboratory.

"I want the same kind of analysis," he ordered.

He wouldn't go home for dinner. He would let Tommy meet Agnes alone, and tomorrow he would have yet another talking session with Tommy. By God, this time I'll make 'im puke up everything that's in 'im. . . .

And that .38? A teasing memory was stirring in him, had been trying to force its way into his consciousness. Why did he keep thinking of it? He stretched out on a sofa and closed his eyes. Tonight there would spew up a tirade against the police, but he could tell the reporters in the morning that he had been on the job for only thirty-six hours and already had accomplished something. Yeah, it was like that time that the hunt had been on for escaped parolee Edgar Kean. The wires had hummed; people had not slept; and it had been he who had gone into a movie and, even though off-duty, had kept his eyes peeled and had spotted Edgar Kean in the audience. He had followed the gangster to the door as he left and had grabbed him by both arms, and a .38 had clattered to the floor amid the gasps of passersby. Ruddy leaped to his feet. My God . . . the mystery of the .38 had been partially solved. The chief of police had given him that .38 as a memento, for he had nearly been killed by it. *Now, where was it?* He had kept it in the bottom of the desk drawer at home. Was it there now? Realization that Tommy might have taken it made his breath come and go quickly. Was that why Tommy had worked up that wobbly tale of Detective Heard's .38 being missing? Had Tommy unintentionally called his notice to his own .38, which could be missing? Yeah, that's the way people think, try to fool others. He ought to rush home right now and see if that gun was still there? No, that would tip Tommy off. Oh, yes—he would wait until Agnes and Tommy had gone to the mass meeting, and then he would make a swift trip to the house and investigate. That would tell the tale.

He sat at his desk again, his fingers trembling. Had he solved it? Yet he needed more evidence than that. But he was now willing to bet a million dollars that the .38 that was to be assembled out of the concrete was his gun, the gun he had kept for so long. But could it not have been stolen from him? That was possible but, in the light of the way things were developing, not terribly probable. The next move would be to make Tommy account for all of his moves on the nights when those murders had taken place . . . for if that old .38 was missing, then there was only one person in the world who could have taken it, and that was Tommy.

A distant melodious voice, like that of a movie soundtrack or like a fading calliope, made Ruddy lift his head, then he heard, after a pause, a voice coming as from a loudspeaker, growing nearer and increasing in volume. He went to the window and opened it wide and peered down into the traffic-clogged street. A sound truck decorated in bright yellow stood directly under his eyes; it had stopped for a red light and the words pouring from the loudspeaker crashed upward from eight stories below:

"Tonight at nine o'clock a public mass meeting is being held for the benefit of Brentwood Park citizens at the old masonic temple on Madison Avenue. Come one, come all. It's your city. Help to build and protect it. Members of the city council and other prominent citizens will be heard. Come and participate in plans to protect and defend Brentwood Park from lawlessness. The crime waves must be broken. Do your part!"

As soon as the voice stopped, a nostalgic and martial blare of music poured out; the red light winked to green, and Ruddy heard faint, scattered hand clapping. He shut the window, feeling that invisible coils were slowly drawing closer and tighter about him. Then his eyes caught sight of another city truck pulling through the gate of the police courtyard, and he saw Captain Snell and Ed Seigel flag it down. About twelve men, clad in prison gray denim, moved forward at once and began unloading the chunks of cement, piling them into wheelbarrows that were carted out of sight toward the police sheds. Ruddy now heard the faint sounds of whacking, and he knew that the prisoners were pounding to bits the slabs of concrete, searching for bits of gun metal. The clock on the wall of the office showed 6:17. He knew that he ought to eat, but he had no hunger. He was of half a mind to go down and watch the pounding of the concrete but desisted; it would make him seem too eager, too anxious, too lacking in confidence—a state of mind that did not lend itself to inspiring the best morale in his men. He had to be patient and wait. Yet his nerves tingled. He clicked the switch on the intercom and called: "Mary Jane?"

"She's off-duty, sir. This is Lieutenant Longhorn at the switchboard."

"Chief Turner speaking. Connect me with my home please."

"Yes, sir. Just a second, sir."

A few moments later the voice of Agnes sounded: "That you, Ruddy, darling?"

"Yeah. How are you, Agnes?"

"Okay. And you?"

"Fine. How's Tommy?"

"Tommy? He's not here. I was going to ask you—"

"Didn't he come in yet?"

"No. Did you see him?"

"Yes. He was here a while ago. He left, heading for home."

"Well, he hasn't come. Ruddy, what's he doing? For the past three days I've scarcely seen 'im. And don't tell me that it's his studies. He didn't come in last night at all and—"

"He was with the Heards, he told me. Look, he's all right. I talked to 'im. He did get in last night," he said, knowing that, above all, he had to sooth Agnes's worries. "But he went right back out. Something about a car radio . . . remember? That's the way boys are, Agnes. They get bees in their bonnets and can't keep still. Look, I'll be out in a quarter of an hour."

"Can you spare the time?"

"Sure thing. I can always spare the time for my wife and home. Ha, ha." He tried to make her feel that he was jocular.

"See you, then, darling."

Yeah, there was no getting out of it; he had to tell Agnes about Tommy. He had to prepare her for whatever shock was coming. And his going home would give him the chance to check about the .38 in his desk drawer. He was certain that it was gone, but being a policeman, he wanted to see its absence with his own eyes before mapping concrete plans of action. He adjusted his cap on his head, hesitated, then picked up the phone and asked for Ed Seigel.

"Yeah, Chief?"

"I'm off to the house for an hour or so."

"Sure. Look, nothing here. We're pounding hard. Got about six slabs pulverized and nothing but dust. Not a scrap of metal."

"Okay, Ed. Keep 'em at it."

"Okay, Chief."

He hung up and went out of the office, dropped to the first floor in the elevator and walked into a poignant April night—a night all the more poignant because its mauve sky and balmy wind contrasted with the horrible tension Ruddy felt. Now, what could he tell Agnes? He'd have to tell her the truth, if he was going to prepare her at all. He wanted to spare her too great a shock, but he flinched at telling her of Marie. He could even now see the horror that would well into her eyes, the tears that would flow, the grieving sorrow for Tommy that would bend her forward in sobs, her trembling hands lifting to quivering lips.

When he entered his driveway, he saw a dim light glowing in the bedroom window; as silently as he could, he rolled the car into the garage, then entered the house through the back door. The maid had gone, and he mounted to the second floor over a carpet that rendered his footsteps noiseless. An impulse to call to Agnes was checked as an idea captured him: he would look now for that .38 in his desk drawer, just to make sure that his theory was correct; he ought to do that before speaking to Agnes. He went noiselessly to his office, entered, opened the bottom drawer of his desk, and his head shot back and he gasped. The gun was there, shining dully up at him. He had been wrong. "Mother of Mary, what's wrong with me?" he asked himself. Now that his hypothesis had been knocked, he went to the opposite extreme: Tommy was innocent. . . . What had made him think otherwise? Then what about that stupidly pretended robbery that Tommy had staged? Where did it fit in? What about all of Tommy's wild babbling about guilt and nonguilt? What was bothering the boy? There was no doubt that he was being goaded and driven by some surging tide of black brooding. Goddamn, that boy will drive me crazy. Then shame flooded him in a sheet of hotness. Why was he and why had he always been so anxious to assume Tommy's guilt, to participate in it? The guilt that he had projected out upon Tommy now rebounded and engulfed him.

Was it something universal, elementary? Was it natural that one should feel somehow guilty before one's offspring? Then maybe that guilt came from not really wanting them? If so, then was it the infant helplessness of those offspring that drove repulsion out of one's mind, that replaced repulsion with compassion? Maybe it was even more elementary than that; maybe one simply resented the presence of any new appearances upon the earth, especially when those appearances assumed the physical guise of one's own kind? Did he hate his son? Distrust him? If so, why? These vague waves of questioning realization made Ruddy's body prickle with goose pimples.

"Ruddy?"

He started, leaped to his feet, and whirled. Agnes stood in the partly opened door.

"Oh," she said, "You're there. I didn't hear you come in, didn't hear your car . . ."

"Yeah," he breathed.

"What's the matter? God, you look pale. Ruddy, is there something wrong? Has anything happened? Where's Tommy? Oh, God, there *is* something—"

"No, Agnes." He tried to quiet her. "Come in and sit down." He had to talk to her now, tell her something and yet not tell her too much. He had to sort out what was real from the thronging fantasies that were storming his mind and feelings.

"It's Tommy!" she half sobbed. "I knew it. I felt it. I—"

"No, no, no." He stemmed her outbreak. "Tommy's all right," he lied to her. "Just a bit of confusion, that's all."

"But where is he?"

"He'll be in soon." He lied yet again, for he had no notion of what Tommy might be doing.

"Is he in trouble?"

"No."

"Then what is it?" she demanded insistently

"Sit down," he told her, guiding her by her right arm. "I'll tell you everything. Now, just sit and listen. Everything's going to be all right."

"Is Tommy all right?" she demanded, her eyes glued to his face.

"Yes," he said. "Agnes, you see, I didn't pay too much attention to what was happening to the boy. I was running night and day with my work, I should have had a better, closer relationship with 'im. What has happened is as much my fault as his, in a way."

"But what has happened? Please, Ruddy . . ."

"Just wait. No tragedy, darling," he consoled her. "I can't talk to you unless you promise me you'll be calm and listen. Unless you listen and understand, you won't be able to help. It's an odd thing that's happened. I didn't tell you. There was nothing that you could have done. Now, Tommy was all set to marry . . ."

In a low mumbling tone yet speaking with flowing fluency, Ruddy recounted the fantastic fatality that had befallen Tommy and Marie, how stunned and numbed Tommy had been in his reactions, how morally stupefied he had felt, how he had fled the girl he had loved too maddened and grieved to speak of it to anybody, too morally repulsed even to see the girl again; and of how crushed, whimpering, and outlandishly defensive Marie had been, how she had been morally denounced by her uncomprehending mother, how her father had been the really responsible factor, how cut off and lonely the girl had been. Ruddy managed to relate it all with a great deal of surprising matter-of-factness (his long experience as a policeman helping him amazingly here, for he had had to relate many times in his life the details of the tragedies of strangers that were just as heart-rending) that left Agnes pale and speechless.

"Oh, God . . . God, Ruddy, why on earth didn't you tell me?" Agnes cried out in a demanding and reproving wail from behind her lifted and trembling right palm.

"Agnes, I didn't know a word about all this until day before yesterday," Ruddy told her.

"Poor Tommy . . . and that poor girl, that poor child!"

"It was an act of God," Ruddy mumbled without conviction.

"Oh, Tommy must have suffered . . ."

"He was quite cut up about it, but kept a stiff upper lip."

"We must see that child, that girl, and—"

"I've seen her already, Agnes."

"How was she?"

"Numb. Sitting in a dark room . . . alone. She looked like the sky fell on her."

"We must help her."

"I did. I gave her some money to continue her treatments."

"Should I go see her?"

"Yeah. But give her a day or so. She's simply shattered."

"And no wonder. Aw, for a thing like that to happen to such a good girl. It's unbelievable. It's a wonder she didn't die. God, what a thing!" Unconsciously, Agnes crossed herself.

"Now you know why Tommy has been out-of-sorts. He tried to hide it by saying he had to stay. That's why he's been so shut off from us, so secretive, so aloof."

"Did he come to you and tell you?"

"No. I sensed something. I kept after 'im, and finally he broke down and told me the whole story. Remember I kept speaking of how he was acting? I felt something was wrong and it worried me. Now, we *know*." Ruddy's voice held a note of hollow triumph.

"We must help 'im," Agnes swore.

"Yeah. I'm doing all I can," Ruddy said.

"He mustn't let this throw 'im, turn him against things in life—like marriage, girls—"

"That's right. We've got a job to do."

"But how can we? What should we do?" Agnes asked in a despairing whisper, her cheeks wet with tears.

"It has bothered Tommy greatly," Ruddy said, feeling that that statement ought to cover the boy's preoccupation with crime, with guilt and nonguilt, and also his powerfully foolish attempt this morning to have himself arrested for robbery. "We've got to have patience with the boy."

"Of course. But, Ruddy, isn't there any hope for them to get together at all? How does Tommy feel about it? And Marie?"

"Tommy doesn't want it, not at all. And Marie has to accept Tommy's decision."

There was a long silence and then Agnes whispered in a barely audible breath: "Men . . ."

"Oh, darling . . . don't look at it like that. You can't force people's feelings. What happened to that boy was a shock, a shock that neither you nor I have ever faced."

"And what'll happen to Marie?"

"Well, I'll try to help her get a job later. You know, Tommy didn't want to run any risks, see?"

"But, Ruddy, you said that she didn't get that illness from running around," Agnes argued, desperately trying to save a situation in which she felt that she herself was involved. "She's a victim. She's innocent. She doesn't deserve that. It's not fair. She inherited it."

"I know, I know," Ruddy quickly agreed. "It wasn't her fault. Yet she's got it; she's had it. Agnes, marriage and syphilis simply don't go together. You can't think of 'em in the same second. You flinch. It doesn't matter that she got it from her parents."

"But you said that she said that the doctor had pronounced her as cured," Agnes argued weakly, half doubting, yet compelled to take the side of women in troubles of this sort.

"Agnes, in matters like this, you've just got to take people's feelings fully into consideration," Ruddy said. "You can't force things; you can't make 'em feel what they don't or can't feel. That's all. Tommy felt like he could not marry that girl. And if he had, what guarantee could anybody have that the marriage would have been successful? Couldn't he always, if there was a tiff, throw it up at her? And couldn't she always feel that she had come to him damaged? It's too great a risk for the emotions of people, Agnes."

"Yes, I guess so," Agnes assented uneasily. Then she continued, speaking in a voice that came from her heart: "Men are strange. Hummnnn. They look for fireworks, neon lights, rainbows, and shooting rockets in love. They're always making women something they are not and—"

"Well, you women help us," Ruddy said, smiling. "Lipstick, rouge . . ."

"Aw, Ruddy, men don't know what love is."

"Honey, what was wrong with that girl would have killed love in nine hundred ninety-nine thousand men out of a million. Look, suppose Tommy had married the girl and they had a blind baby . . . ?"

"Mother of God," Agnes murmured, crossing herself again.

"Look, Tommy was lucky in a sense," Ruddy argued, more confident of himself now. "Suppose all this had happened in some of those backward Bible Belt states where they don't ask for blood tests? Why, poor Tommy would have been had . . ."

"B-but don't say it l-like that," Agnes protested. "The girl didn't mean any—"

"Yes, but she had it," Ruddy said. "And Tommy's children might not have had it, and it would have passed on to his grandchildren."

"Oh, Ruddy," Agnes half screamed, her elbows pressing in repulsion against her sides.

"Tommy was thinking about all that." Ruddy pled his son's case.

"But he could have waited," Agnes contended. "The girl was sick, that was all. It was not all her fault. Why couldn't he have given her time. Why did he rush it so? Break off so brutally?"

"Agnes, he couldn't do anything but what he did," Ruddy insisted. "Even *I* can understand that."

"I can't," Agnes said. "I'm not saying that he should have married her. No, not unless he wanted to. But to leave her like that, so suddenly, all alone. And the way her family acted toward her . . ." She lowered her face into her hands. When she lifted her eyes, she asked, "But where's Tommy now? Won't he go with me to the mass meeting? He oughtn't to brood and sulk off by himself. We mustn't leave 'im too much alone, you know."

"Oh, he'll be along; he'll come," Ruddy said. "He said he would."

"I ought to go and see that poor girl," Agnes said. "And drop that mass meeting . . ." A look of self-accusation came into her eyes.

"No. Take Tommy to the mass meeting," Ruddy advised. "It'll be good for you and him. Stick close to Tommy for a bit until he gets his bearings."

"Oh, I will," Agnes said in a tone that hinted of self-defense.

There was silence again. Agnes's eyes danced with apprehension.

"There are miracle drugs now, you know," she said brightly.

"Agnes, it's not the purely physical part of it that shakes you," Ruddy explained. "It shakes you morally, sticks in your feelings."

The uncertainty in his voice was not being caused entirely by the facts about Marie that he was citing, or about Tommy's moral revulsion; he was seeing in his mind as he talked those rough slabs of white concrete that were being pounded to powder in the police courtyard by the hammers of sweating prisoners clad in gray denim.

"Say, I've got to get back to the office," Ruddy said. "When Tommy comes in, give me a ring, hunh? Just call up and say that Ed Seigel wants me to call him. Then I'll know that he got in all right."

"Yes, I understand," Agnes whispered.

"And go easy on Tommy," Ruddy counseled. "Don't get 'im worked up. I think it's best, for the time being, not to let on that you even know."

"Why?"

"He begged me not to say anything to you about it at all," Ruddy told her.

"Oh. All right. But I wish I could talk to 'im."

"If you take time and try to get really close to 'im, maybe he'll open up on his own," Ruddy explained. "That's the best way in things like this."

"I'll try," Agnes pledged.

When he went to her, she rose and kissed him gravely. "Don't worry too much," she said to him.

"I won't," he said. "Be easy with Tommy. 'Bye, now."

" 'Bye, darling."

As he drove, he felt more relaxed than he had felt for many days. The lamps flashed on in the early evening streets. Yet he knew that had solved nothing really. But he had at least brought out into the open the problem—that is, some of it, with Agnes. And that was something. He had to admit that her attitude had surprised him; she had been horrified, but she had encompassed the horror with the maternal instincts of a woman. "Those little soft women are really very strong," he said to himself as he passed the first roadblock that he had ordered thrown up. He glanced at his watch; it was a bit past eight. Gosh, that damned mass meeting would be getting under way in another hour. *But where in hell was Tommy?* Why had he not gone home as he had promised? No, he should have known better than to have let that boy go out alone like that. Jesus, it is hard to make decisions about your own flesh and blood. Though infinitely relieved, Ruddy knew that he had not solved anything. There was a solution to these gathering shadows that lay just beyond the rim of his mind; there was some way of juggling these slippery facts and making hard sense out of them, the kind of sense that he had learned in the police school he had attended. He could see clear now, he thought, why Ed's queer notions had had so deep an effect upon him; it was because he was at a loss, at sea, and, above all, because his own blood kin had been involved. Yet . . . yet that was not exactly true. Ed had ferreted out of Tommy, before his very eyes, the fact that the boy had pretended to participate in a holdup. That had been no illusion. Goddamnit, Tommy could tell me. But how could he make 'im tell? And where was he? Despite the fact that he had told Agnes to "go easy" on Tommy, he was resolved now that when he got his hands on that boy, he would squeeze him dry, open his little stomach and see what was bothering him.

As he swung into the big gate leading into the police court-yard, he saw Ed Seigel standing under the official parquet where only squad cars were allowed to halt. Ed waved to him and came rushing forward and was at the window of his car as it stopped.

"We got the murder gun," Ed reported.

Captain Snell moved forward, grinning. "Chief, that was a hunch in a million," the captain said.

"Chief, most of that gun was buried in the first two slabs of concrete we broke up," Ed said. "Now, I've jumped the gun a bit and—"

"What do you mean?" Ruddy asked.

"I've sent the chamber and barrel on to the lab for compari-sons," Ed said. "All the bullets fired in all four murders came from that gun we've got!"

"Well, we've got that far," Ruddy sighed. "But we've got to trace that gun—"

"The order's in." Captain Snell grinned.

"Good," Ruddy approved. Yet he was still far from his goal. The gun found could not definitely be traced or connected, as yet, with the gun missing from Detective Heard's home. And Ruddy's gun was still in his desk drawer.

"Any report yet from the lab on those two batches of con-crete sent over?" he asked.

"Not yet. But we'll hear any minute now," Ed promised. "Boy, we got a break in a year-old mystery. We'll crack this case; I'm confident of that now."

"You see," Captain Snell explained, "we've learned that the gang working on the building site took an hour off the other night. It was then that somebody approached the concrete mixer and piles of sand and cement and tucked those gun bits into them. Somewhere that gun had been pounded and broken with a sledgehammer. Chief, that murderer is still in Chicago. Hell, he might this very minute be in Brentwood Park. Come to think of it, he might even show up at that mass meeting tonight."

"I want the whole plainclothes force called in to cover that meeting," Ruddy ordered. "Let 'em mingle with the crowds and keep a sharp eye out."

"Yes sir, Chief," Captain Snell said.

"Three more loony confessions came in," Ed reported with a grin.

"Can that," Ruddy said. He studied the floor. "At least I can tell the mayor that we've located the murder weapon and that the wheels are turning as fast as possible to trace it."

"Right," Ed sang.

Ruddy suddenly felt that his aides' confidence was making him depressed; he felt empty, lost. Hell, he had to talk to somebody.

"Ed," he called softly. "I want to talk to you in my office," he said slowly.

Ed stared straight into Ruddy's eyes. "Okay. Whenever you want."

"Right now," Ruddy said. "See you, Captain. Incidentally, Captain, that's fine, quick work."

"Thank you, Chief." The captain beamed.

Ed followed Ruddy up in the elevator and into the office. Ruddy sat, pushed his cap far back on his head, and lit a cigarette. Ed stood watching his chief, his blue eyes somber.

"You've been worried for several days, Ruddy," Ed said. "What's the matter?"

"That boy did not go home," Ruddy opened up at last.

"What?"

"I don't know where he is."

"Tommy isn't home?" Ed demanded.

"No."

"Ruddy, I didn't try to keep up with 'im," Ed explained. "I thought you had 'im in hand, see? After all, it was a kind of family affair and—"

"I have not got my son in hand, Ed," Ruddy confessed and swallowed.

"I thought he was a model," Ed said in amazement. "That is, until this morning. But even then I thought that he was just caught in some wild gang of boys or something."

"Ed, I need your help," Ruddy said, his head low. "I can't figure things out anymore in my house, my own house."

"Spill it," Ed said. "You know I'll help. I thought you would be on top of the world now, being chief here. But you've had a vacant look in your eyes for days. What is it?"

Ruddy sighed. Impulse and counterimpulse clashed in Ruddy's mind. He wanted to tell Ed everything, but something— was it pride, shame, or defiance?—held him in, censored what he was about to say. In his mind he was staring hard at the whimpering features of Marie, but when he began to speak, he thrust her from his mind and feelings, changed the aspect of her, decided to alter what he would report about Tommy.

"Tommy's had a bad shock," Ruddy reported.

"Aw, now we're getting somewhere." Ed approved of the apparent openness.

"Doctor's call in other doctors when they have illness in their family." Ruddy's voice rumbled. "I'm calling you in."

"I'm here," Ed said with flat emotional adherence. "I caught wind of some emotional confusion in Tommy this morning, but I didn't wish to pry. What kind of shock has he had?"

"A girl jilted 'im," Ruddy lied, hoping that that would cover enough of what was happening in Tommy for Ed to help.

"Aw, I wondered," Ed said. "He's at the age. Nineteen, isn't he?"

"That's it. Soon he'll be twenty."

"This is not unknown," Ed said comfortingly. "That kid's between two families now: the one he wanted to establish and the one in which you are the head. He's kind of lost. That makes for guilt feeling, giddiness, confusion."

"But why in hell did he pretend to take part in the god-damn robbery this morning?" Ruddy asked raspingly.

"He was trying to evade some responsibility," Ed said.

"Ed," Ruddy called in a forlorn, hopeless voice.

"Yeah."

"I was not completely surprised when it was reported that a bit of gun handle had been found in a cement mixer," Ruddy said with a constricted throat.

"No?"

"Y-you-s-see I . . ." Ruddy swallowed. "Hell, here's what happened, goddamnit. I'm straight. I'm an officer. I'll go the god-damn limit. Ed, I found a bit of concrete on the soles of Tommy's tennis shoes the other night. Something made me take a pinch of it and wrap it in paper and keep it. Then came this report about the gun handle and the concrete mixer—"

The telephone tingled.

"Yeah," Ruddy breathed a sigh into the receiver.

"Chief, this is Lieutenant Parrish."

"Yeah. I'm listening."

"Those two samples of cement you sent over to the lab," Lieutenant Parrish reported. "Well, they are the same. There's no doubt about it."

"That's what I figured," Ruddy mumbled. "Thanks." He hung up and turned bloodshot eyes to Ed.

"I heard it," Ed said before Ruddy could speak. "You say you took that from Tommy's tennis shoes?"

"Yeah."

"And our lab reports that it is the same cement?"

"Yeah."

Ed's right palm lifted and clapped over his pursed lips. "*Mama mia*," he breathed.

Ruddy leaped to his feet and bellowed: "Ed, I'm going crazy! My son's no murderer! But the facts are here. Jesus, the chief of police's son is the criminal that is captured! Is this a joke? Is somebody playing a goddamn trick on me? Well, it isn't funny, goddamnit. Was that stunt about Tommy pretending that he was a robber *true*?"

"Yeah, it was true, Ruddy," Ed said sadly. "But I never dreamed about this angle. Good God. What are you going to do?"

"I'm an officer," Ruddy yelled bitterly. "I'll do my duty! Like I've always done!"

"Sure. Sure. N-nobody doubts that," Ed said in a mollifying tone, but his eyes were staring as though about to leap from their sockets. "But . . . what motive could he have had to do such a thing?"

Ruddy looked forlornly at Ed. "You know those things better than I do." Ruddy sighed. "Maybe he got mad with everybody because of that girl and—"

"Aw, no. Ruddy, that's as bad as that faked robbery this morning," Ed said. "I don't know of a case on record where a boy took a gun and went shooting people because a girl jilted 'im."

"He knows something about those killings," Ruddy contended sadly. "Or that cement wouldn't have been on his shoes. He had that gun; he tried to destroy it."

"Yeah, that seems true," Ed admitted. "But was anybody with 'im?"

"That Charlie Heard boy before he died?"

"We'll check. But I doubt it. I'm thinking of a homosexual linkup."

"Oh!" Ruddy was flabbergasted. "No."

"You're sure?"

"Positive. Nothing like that in Tommy."

Yet he was afraid. What did he really know of Tommy? Now that Tommy had pretended to have taken part in a holdup, and now that it was circumstantially proved that he had been at the site where the murder gun had been hidden, Ruddy was emotionally inclined to believe that maybe many others things had happened, that the worst could be true. "What have I done wrong?" he moaned to himself, sitting again and lowering his head into his hands. Then a ray of desperate hope came to him.

"Maybe that dead Heard boy led 'im astray?"

"We'll check," Ed said without conviction. "But I doubt it. Those crimes seem to be the work of a lone hand." Ed bit his lips. "This will not be good for you, if it breaks that Tommy was involved in this."

"I know. I'll be finished." Ruddy heaved up his words.

Ed paced the floor, daring glances at Ruddy's distraught face. "Where is this girl—Tommy's girl?"

The question caught Ruddy by surprise. He knew that Ed was wanting to question the girl, and that was the last thing that Ruddy wanted. He felt now as strongly as Tommy about her shame, her taintedness, and he felt that he had to mislead Ed.

"I don't know," he lied.

"Why did the girl reject Tommy?"

"He wouldn't tell me," Ruddy sank deeper into his deception, feeling horribly, hotly guilty.

"How long had Tommy known her?"

"Oh, about two years, I think."

"Goddamnit, if Tommy did this, then I don't think that anything that that girl did made 'im do it." Ed seemed to be talking out of a fund of knowledge beyond the ken of Ruddy.

"Don't know," Ruddy mumbled, siding now more and more with his guilty son but being unable to distinguish his own guilt from that of his son's. Then he opened his lips in wonder. Oh, God, how easily Agnes had said, "OK, but that's nothing . . ." Yeah, women were strong. Here he was trembling in the face of one of his best friends, and Agnes had taken what now was troubling him in her heart's stride.

"What does your wife think of this?" Ed shot at him.

"I-I haven't told her yet," Ruddy lied, hating himself as he did so. Oh, hell, why couldn't he trust Ed and tell him the truth? Yet he knew that it was hopeless to try. He now understood why Tommy had not been able to tell him. Yes, by God, he would see this through and resign.

"Ruddy?" Ed called in a questioning tone.

"Yeah, Ed."

"Let's understand each other," Ed began. "You're the chief. But insofar as your son's involved in this, let me handle it. I can be more objective than you about it. I'll swear that Tommy'll be protected as much as possible. I—"

"Don't protect anybody," Ruddy growled. "I won't try to defeat the law. You know that."

"I wasn't talking about that," Ed hastened to assure him. "It's precisely because you're in a conflict here that I'm asking the right to decide for you. You can't think or feel straight about this; your own flesh is involved. You might be too hard on the boy or on yourself. That's why I'm asking."

Ruddy thought hard. Maybe Ed might learn the truth about Marie. Perhaps. But he wouldn't tell him where Marie was and he was certain that Tommy would not. So, feeling that the shameful secret was safe, he said, "Okay. You take over."

"Yeah, okay. I'll take over. But I'll do it in a way that won't embarrass you, see?"

"Okay," Ruddy said, feeling relieved but also defeated.

The intercom crackled.

"Yeah," Ruddy spoke after flicking the switch.

"Chief, this is Captain Snell speaking."

"Yes, Captain. What is it?"

"I'd like to see you at once. Something urgent."

"Come right in," Ruddy said, switching off the crackling vibration. "Snell's coming. Something's come up, he says." Ruddy was now sure that even more evidence had come in against Tommy.

"I'm now sure that Tommy was trying to hide something this morning," Ed said serenely.

"Oh, yeah."

"The problem is: What was he trying to hide by pretending he had been in a holdup?"

"You've got me."

"He didn't kill those people because of a girl's saying no," Ed stated emphatically.

"Then what could it be? If he did kill them . . ."

"He would have told you, crying, weeping . . . But he would have," Ed stated confidently.

"But he seems as sure as hell involved," Ruddy pointed out. "That cement places him as having been in possession of that gun.

"Look," Ruddy said with sudden hopefulness, "maybe he's pretending to be involved in these murders like he pretended about that holdup this morning."

Ed pursed his lips and stared. "Maybe . . . but he's being spurred by something else. And that's what's troubling me."

Again Ruddy felt on the tip of his tongue the desire to tell Ed the truth, but he could not. And then he recalled the ease with which Agnes had taken Marie's plight, her simple and all-embracing phrase: "But that's nothing . . ."

The door burst open more unceremoniously than Ruddy had ever seen it, and Captain Snell came rushing in with a newspaper extended in his right hand. He paused before Ruddy and Ed, as though baffled as to what to do, then he asked softly, "Did you see this?"

"What're you talking about?" Ruddy asked.

"An extra . . . the *Globe*. It says . . ."

He did not finish; he could talk no more. He laid the paper upon the desk, then stepped away, as though disassociating himself from the tall black headline:

POLICE CHIEF'S SON CONFESSES TO MURDER WAVE

Ruddy half rose; his lower jaw dropped, then he sank down again. He lifted his open palms as if to cover his eyes, then froze, reached out and lifted the paper, and stared at the blown-up face of Tommy whose eyes were staring defiantly into his own.

"Jesus . . . oh, Mother of God," Ruddy intoned and slipped into his seat, his huge body seemingly crumpled.

Sensing his friend's consternation, Ed stepped purposefully forward and picked up the newspaper and stared fixedly at the headline; his expression did not change; his eyes did not blink, but the newspaper fell from his still and seemingly nerveless fingers and landed dryly upon the glass top of the desk. He turned as though to walk out of the room, then whirled and came back to the desk, but his eyes were sightless.

"Well, I'll be damned," he sighed.

The office was filled only with the soft, faint sound of the huge, electric clock on the wall and the breathing of the three men. Captain Snell avoided looking directly at either Ed or Ruddy, but his eyes darted in the direction of one of them and then the other, and finally rested upon the newspaper. He blinked his eyes and bit his lower lip. As though by telepathy, Ed would not meet Ruddy's eyes and Ruddy's would not meet Ed's. A decision was being made and tension and anxiousness made the three men silent; it was in this long moment that the scepter of moral leadership in the office of the chief of police passed from Ruddy to his friend Ed; it passed without a word, without a gesture.

"We've got to get hold of Tommy," Ed said in a low, determined tone.

"Yes, that's the first thing," Ruddy agreed.

"I wonder if that"—Ed tapped the newspaper—"*Globe* is holding 'im? I suspect that they paid him for his confession."

"My God," Ruddy moaned.

Paris, summer/fall of 1960

About the author

About the book

Insights,
Interviews
& More ...

Read on

A Chronology of Richard Wright

The Granger Collection, New York

For more
information
about the
Richard Wright
Centennial,
including
upcoming events,
visit www
.harpercollins
.com/
RichardWright.

1908

Born Richard Nathaniel Wright, September 4, on
Rucker's Plantation, a farm near Roxie, Mississippi,
22 miles east of Natchez, first child of Nathan Wright,
an illiterate sharecropper, and Ella Wilson Wright, a
schoolteacher. (All four grandparents had been born
in slavery. Father was born shortly before 1880, the
son of Nathaniel Wright, a freed slave who farmed
a plot of land he had been given at the end of the
Civil War. Maternal grandfather, Richard Wilson,
born March 21, 1847, served in the United States
Navy in 1865, then became disillusioned because
of a bureaucratic error that deprived him of his
pension. Maternal grandmother, Margaret Bolton
Wilson, of Irish, Scottish, American Indian, and
African descent, was virtually white in appearance.
A house slave before the Emancipation, she later
became a midwife nurse, a devoted Seventh-Day
Adventist, and the strict head of her Natchez
household, which included eight surviving children.
Mother, born 1883, married Nathan Wright in 1907
despite her parents' disapproval, and then gave up
school teaching to work on the farm.)

1910

Brother Leon Alan, called Alan, born September 24.

1911–12

Unable to care for her children while working on the farm, mother takes Wright and his brother to live with Wilson family in Natchez. Father rejoins family and finds work in a sawmill. Wright accidentally sets fire to grandparents' house.

1913–14

Family moves to Memphis, Tennessee, by steamboat. Father deserts family to live with another woman, leaving them impoverished. Mother finds work as a cook.

1915–16

Wright enters school at Howe Institute, Memphis, in September 1915. Mother falls seriously ill in early 1916. Grandmother comes to care for family. After grandmother returns home, mother puts Wright and his brother in the Settlement House, Methodist orphanage in Memphis, where they stay for over a month. Spends relatively pleasant summer at 1107 Lynch Street in Jackson, Mississippi, where maternal grandparents now live, before going with mother and brother to Elaine, Arkansas, to live with his favorite aunt, Maggie (his mother's younger sister), and her husband, Silas Hoskins, a saloonkeeper.

1917–18

After Hoskins is murdered by whites who want his prosperous liquor business, terrified family flees to West Helena, Arkansas, then returns to Jackson with Aunt Maggie to live with the Wilsons. After several months they go back to West Helena, where mother and aunt find work cooking and cleaning for whites. Aunt Maggie leaves with her lover, "Professor" Matthews, a fugitive from the law (they eventually settle in Detroit).

1918–19

Wright enters local school in fall 1918. Mother's health deteriorates early in 1919 and Wright is forced to leave school to earn money. Delivers wood and laundry and carries lunches to railroad workers. Family moves frequently because of lack of rent money; Wright gathers stray pieces of coal along railroad tracks to heat their home. Mother suffers paralyzing stroke, and grandmother comes to bring the family back to Jackson. Aunt Maggie helps care for mother, then takes Leon Alan back to Detroit with her; other aunts and uncles help pay for mother's treatment. ▶

A Chronology of Richard Wright (*continued*)

1919–20

Wright moves into home of aunt and uncle, Clark and Jody Wilson, in nearby Greenwood, Mississippi, where he is able to attend school. Finds household calm and orderly but his aunt and uncle cold and unsympathetic, and is terrified by episodes of sleepwalking. Returns to grandparents' home in Jackson. Mother begins to show signs of recovery from paralysis, then has relapse caused by a cerebral blood clot that leaves her virtually crippled. Her illness impoverishes the family, already hurt by the rheumatism that makes Grandfather Wilson unable to work.

1920–21

Enters Seventh-Day Adventist school taught by his youngest aunt, Addie. Only nine years older than Wright, she is a rigid disciplinarian often at odds with him. Wright rebels against the rules and practices of the religion, including its diet, which forbids eating pork. Finds himself opposed to his family in general, except for his mother, who is too sick to help him.

1921–22

Enters the fifth grade of the Jim Hill School in Jackson, two years behind his age group. Does well, quickly gains in confidence, and is soon promoted to the sixth grade. Begins friendships, some of them lasting into his adulthood, with a number of other students, including Dick Jordan, Joe Brown, Perry Booker, D. C. Blackburn, Lewis Anderson, Sarah McNeamer, and Essie Lee Ward. Takes job as a newsboy, which gives him the chance to read material forbidden at home because of religious prohibitions. Family life continues to be difficult, although his mother's health improves slightly. Travels briefly during summer in the Mississippi Delta region as "secretary-accountant" to an insurance agent, W. Mance. The trip allows him to know better the rural South, but he is dismayed by the illiteracy and lack of education he encounters among blacks.

1922–23

Enters the seventh grade. Grandfather Wilson dies November 8. After many arguments, grandmother reluctantly lets Wright take jobs after school and on Saturday (the Seventh-Day Adventist sabbath). Runs errands and performs small chores, mainly for whites. For the first time has enough money to buy school books, food to combat his chronic hunger, and clothing. Baptized in the Methodist Church, mainly to please his mother. Avidly reads pulp magazines, dime novels, and books and magazines discarded by others. Uncle Thomas Wilson, his wife, and their two daughters come to live with the family in spring 1923. Mother's health worsens. Wright works during the summer at a brickyard and as a caddy at a golf course.

1923–24

Enters eighth grade at the Smith Robertson Junior High School, Jackson (a former slave, Smith Robertson had become a successful local barber and a community leader; the school, built in 1894, was the first black institution of its kind in Jackson). Until he can afford a bicycle, Wright walks several miles daily to and from the school. Makes new friends at school, including Wade Griffin, Varnie Reed, Arthur Leaner, and Minnie Farish. Begins working for the Walls, a white family he finds kindly (will serve them for two years). Later remembers writing his first short story, "The Voodoo of Hell's Half-Acre," in late winter (story is reported to have been published in the spring as "Hell's Half-Acre" in the Jackson *Southern Register*, a black weekly newspaper; no copies are known to be extant). Brother Leon Alan returns from Detroit. Wright is initially pleased, but their relationship soon disappoints him. Works for the American Optical Company, cleaning workshop and making deliveries.

1924–25

Enters ninth grade at Smith Robertson Junior High School, and graduates on May 29, 1925, as valedictorian. Rejects graduation speech prepared for him by the principal and instead delivers his own, "The Attributes of Life." Works as a delivery boy, sales clerk, hotel hallboy and bellboy, and in a movie theater. Begins classes in fall at newly founded Lanier High School, but quits a few weeks later to earn money. Leaves Jackson for Memphis, Tennessee, where he boards with a family at 570 Beale Street.

1926

Works for low pay as a dishwasher and delivery boy and at the Merry Optical Company. Reads widely in *Harper's*, *Atlantic Monthly*, *The American Mercury*, and other magazines. Moves to 875 Griffith Place. ▶

A Chronology of Richard Wright *(continued)*

1927

Joined by mother, who is still in poor health, and brother; they take an apartment together at 370 Washington Street. After reading an editorial highly critical of H. L. Mencken, long noted as a critic of the white South, Wright seeks out Mencken's *Prejudices* and *A Book of Prefaces* and is particularly impressed by Mencken's iconoclasm and use of "words as weapons." These books serve as guides to further reading, including works by Theodore Dreiser, Sinclair Lewis, Sherwood Anderson, the elder Alexandre Dumas, Frank Harris, and O. Henry. Aunt Maggie, who has been deserted by "Professor" Matthews, joins family in the fall. In December, Wright and Maggie, who hopes to open a beauty salon, move to the South Side of Chicago, while mother and Leon Alan return to Jackson. Sees his aunt Cleopatra ("Sissy"), but is disappointed to find that she lives in a rooming house, not an apartment, and moves into a rooming house with Aunt Maggie.

1928

Works as delivery boy in a delicatessen, then as a dishwasher. Wright finds Chicago stimulating and less racially oppressive than the South, but is often dismayed by the pace and disarray of urban life. Passes written examination for the postal service in the spring, then begins work in the summer as a temporary employee at 65 cents an hour. Rents an apartment with Aunt Maggie and is joined by mother and brother. In the fall Wright fails the postal service medical examination required for a permanent position because of chronic undernourishment and returns to dishwashing. Disputes over money and his reading cause tension with Aunt Maggie. Wright takes another apartment for family and invites his aunt Cleopatra to move in with them.

1929

After undertaking a crash diet to increase his weight, Wright passes the physical examination and is hired by the central post office at Clark Street and Jackson Boulevard as a substitute clerk and mail sorter. Moves with family to four rooms at 4831 Vincennes Avenue, which allows him to read and write in relative comfort. Dislikes the post office bureaucracy, but becomes friendly with many fellow workers, both black and white. Among his friends are schoolmates from the South, including Essie Lee Ward, Arthur

Leaner, and Joe Brown. Writes steadily and attends meetings of a local black literary group, but feels distant from its middle-class members. Attracted by the Universal Negro Improvement Association, a group inspired by Marcus Garvey, but does not join it.

1930

Volume of mail drops in decline following the 1929 Wall Street crash; Wright has his working hours cut back before losing his job altogether. South Side sinks into economic depression. Works temporarily for post office in the summer. Mother suffers a relapse, aunt Cleopatra has a heart attack, and brother develops stomach ulcers. Begins work on *Cesspool,* novel about black life in Chicago. Enrolls in tenth grade at Hyde Park Public School, but soon drops out.

1931

Reads books recommended by friend William Harper (who will later own a bookstore on the South Side). Wright is particularly impressed by Dreiser and Joseph Conrad, and continues to write. Short story "Superstition" is published in April *Abbott's Monthly Magazine*, a black journal (magazine fails before Wright is paid). Through a distant relative, finds job as a funeral insurance agent for several burial societies. Also works as an assistant to a black Republican precinct captain during the mayoral campaign, and at the post office in December. Becomes interested in views of Communist orators and organizers, especially those in the League of Struggle for Negro Rights.

1932

Sells insurance policies door-to-door and works briefly as an assistant to a Democratic precinct captain. Family moves to slum apartment as Wright is increasingly unable to sell policies to blacks impoverished by the Depression. Asks for and receives relief assistance from the Cook County Bureau of Public Welfare, which finds him a temporary job as a street cleaner. Works at the post office during the Christmas season.

1933

Digs ditches in the Cook County Forest Preserves, then works at Michael Reese Hospital, caring for animals used in medical research. Recruited by ▶

A Chronology of Richard Wright *(continued)*

fellow post office worker Abraham Aaron to join the newly formed Chicago branch of the John Reed Club, a national literary organization sponsored by the Communist party. Welcomed and encouraged by the almost entirely white membership of the club, Wright begins to read and study *New Masses* and *International Literature*, the organ of the International League of Revolutionary Writers. Writes and submits revolutionary poems ("I Have Seen Black Hands," "A Red Love Note") to *Left Front*, the magazine of the midwestern John Reed Clubs. Elected executive secretary of the Chicago John Reed Club and organizes a successful lecture series which allows him to meet a variety of intellectuals. Gives lecture at open forum on "The Literature of the Negro."

1934

Hoping to consolidate his position in the John Reed Club, Wright joins the Communist party; is also impressed by the party's opposition to racial discrimination. Publishes poetry in *Left Front*, *Anvil*, and *New Masses*. Becomes a member of the editorial board of *Left Front*. Enjoys literary and social friendships with Bill Jordan, Abraham Chapman, Howard Nutt, Laurence Lipton, Nelson Algren, Joyce Gourfain, and Jane Newton. Grandmother Wilson comes to Chicago to join the family; they move to apartment at 4804 St. Lawrence Avenue, near the railroad tracks. Mother's paralysis returns after attack of encephalitis. Wright is laid off by the hospital in the summer, and again works as a street sweeper and ditch digger before being hired to supervise a youth club organized to counter juvenile delinquency among blacks on the South Side. Attends Middle West Writers' Congress in August and the national congress of John Reed Clubs in September. Dismayed by party decision to cease publication of *Left Front* and to dissolve the John Reed Clubs in 1935 as part of its Popular Front strategy. Meets Jack Conroy, editor of *Anvil*. Reading in Chicago by this time includes Henry James (especially the Prefaces to the New York Edition), Gertrude Stein (notably her *Three Lives*, with its portrait of a black character, Melanctha Herbert), Faulkner, T. S. Eliot, Sherwood Anderson, Dos Passos, O'Neill, Stephen Crane, Dreiser, Whitman, Poe, D. H. Lawrence, Conrad, Galsworthy, Hardy, Dickens, George Moore, Carlyle,

Swift, Shakespeare, Tolstoy, Dostoevsky, Turgenev, Chekhov, Proust, Dumas, and Balzac. Lectures on the career of Langston Hughes to the Indianapolis John Reed Club in November and contributes fee to new publication *Midland Left*.

1935

Publishes leftist poetry in *Midland Left*, a short-lived journal, *New Masses* ("Red Leaves of Red Books" and "Spread Your Sunshine"), and *International Literature* ("A Red Slogan"). Family moves to 2636 Grove Avenue. Begins submitting novel *Cesspool* to publishers (later retitled *Lawd Today!* by Wright; it is rejected repeatedly over the next two years, then published posthumously as *Lawd Today* in 1963 by Walker and Company). Wright attends the first American Writers' Congress, held in New York in April. Speaks on "The Isolation of the Negro Writer," meets Chicago novelist James T. Farrell, and becomes one of fifty members of the national council of the newly formed League of American Writers. Works on story "Big Boy Leaves Home." Publishes "Between the World and Me," poem about lynching, in July–August *Partisan Review*. Falls seriously ill with attack of pneumonia during the summer. Article "Avant-Garde Writing" wins second prize in contest sponsored by two literary magazines but is never published. First piece of journalism, "Joe Louis Uncovers Dynamite," describing the reaction of Chicago blacks to the Louis-Max Baer fight, published in *New Masses*. Grandmother Wilson dies. Family, with Wright still virtually its sole support, moves to 3743 Indiana Avenue. Wright is hired by the Federal Writers' Project (part of the Works Progress Administration) to help research the history of Illinois and of the Negro in Chicago for the Illinois volume in the American Guide Series. Discusses influence of Hemingway with fellow writers in federal project.

1936

Publishes "Transcontinental," a six-page radical poem influenced by Whitman and Louis Aragon, in January *International Literature*. Becomes a principal organizer of the Communist party–sponsored National Negro Congress (successor to the League of Struggle for Negro Rights), held in Chicago in February, and reports on it for *New Masses*. Transferred in spring to the Federal ▶

A Chronology of Richard Wright *(continued)*

Theatre Project, where he serves as literary adviser and press agent for the Negro Federal Theatre of Chicago and becomes involved in dramatic productions. Finishes two one-act plays based in part on a section of his unpublished novel. In April, Wright takes a leading role in the new South Side Writers' Group (members will include Arna Bontemps, Frank Marshall Davis, Theodore Ward, Fenton Johnson, Horace Cayton, and Margaret Walker). Takes an active role in the Middle West Writers' Congress, held in Chicago June 14–15. Because of what he later describes as a Communist plot against him on the Federal Theatre Project assignment, Wright returns to the Writers' Project, where he becomes a group coordinator. Story "Big Boy Leaves Home" appears in anthology *The New Caravan* in November and receives critical attention and praise in mainstream newspapers and journals.

1937

Publishes poem "We of the Streets" in April *New Masses* and story "Silt" in the August number. Breaks with the Communist party in Chicago, basically over the question of his freedom as a writer. Brother finds job with the Works Progress Administration and assumes some responsibility for support of the family. Wright ranks first in postal service examination in Chicago, but turns down offer in May of permanent position at approximately $2,000 a year in order to move to New York City to pursue career as a writer. Stays briefly with artist acquaintances in Greenwich Village, then moves to Harlem; by mid-June he has a furnished room in the Douglass Hotel at 809 St. Nicholas Avenue. Attends Second American Writers' Congress as a delegate and serves as a session president; stresses the need for writers to think of themselves as writers first and not as laborers. Becomes Harlem editor of the Communist newspaper *Daily Worker* and writes over 200 articles for it during the year, including pieces on blues singer Leadbelly and the continuing Scottsboro Boys controversy. With Dorothy West and Marian Minus, helps launch magazine *New Challenge*, designed to present black life "in relationship to the struggle against war and Fascism." Wright publishes "The Ethics of Living Jim Crow—An Autobiographical Sketch" in *American Stuff: WPA Writers' Anthology* (essay is later included in the second edition of *Uncle Tom's Children* and incorporated into *Black Boy*). In November, publishes influential essay "Blueprint for Negro Writing" in *New Challenge*, criticizing past black literature and urging a Marxist-influenced approach that would transcend nationalism. Lacking party support, *New Challenge* fails after one number. Befriends 23-year-old Ralph Ellison. Wright's second novel, *Tarbaby's Dawn,* about a black adolescent in the South, is rejected by publishers (it remains unpublished). Learns that story "Fire and Cloud" has won first prize ($500) among 600 entries in *Story Magazine* contest. Wright joins the New York Federal Writers' Project (will write the Harlem section for *New York Panorama* and work on "The Harlems" in *The New York City Guide*).

1938

Rents furnished room at 139 West 143rd Street. Engages Paul Reynolds, Jr., as literary agent. Reynolds makes arrangements to place *Uncle Tom's Children: Four Novellas* ("Big Boy Leaves Home," "Down by the Riverside," "Long Black Song," and "Fire and Cloud") with editor Edward Aswell at Harper and Brothers, beginning Wright's long association with Aswell and Harper; book is published in March and is widely praised. Sends Aswell outline of novel about a black youth in Chicago. Announces plans to marry daughter of his Harlem landlady in May, but then cancels wedding, telling friends that a medical examination had revealed that the young woman has congenital syphilis. Moves into home of friends from Chicago, Jane and Herbert Newton, at 175 Carleton Avenue in Brooklyn. Story "Bright and Morning Star" appears in May *New Masses*. Writes about the second Joe Louis–Max Schmeling fight in the June *Daily Worker* and July *New Masses*. In June, replaces Horace Gregory on the editorial board of the literature section of *New Masses*. Works steadily on new novel; often writes in Fort Greene Park in the mornings, and discusses his progress with Jane Newton. Asks Margaret Walker to send him newspaper accounts of the case of Robert Nixon, a young Chicago black man accused of murder (executed in August 1939). Moves in the fall with the Newtons to 522 Gates Avenue. Congressman Martin Dies, chairman of the House Special Committee on Un-American Activities, denounces "The Ethics of ▶

A Chronology of Richard Wright *(continued)*

Living Jim Crow" during an investigation of the
Federal Writers' Project. Finishes first draft of novel,
now titled *Native Son*, in October and receives $400
advance from Harper in November. "Fire and Cloud"
wins the O. Henry Memorial Award ($200). Travels to
Chicago in November to research settings and events
used in *Native Son*. Moves with Newtons to 87
Lefferts Place.

1939

Meets Ellen Poplar (b. 1912), daughter of Polish
Jewish immigrants and a Communist party organizer
in Brooklyn. Completes revised version of novel
in February and shows it to Reynolds. Awarded
Guggenheim Fellowship ($2,500) in March and
resigns from the Federal Writers' Project in May.
Discusses black American writing with Langston
Hughes, Alain Locke, Countee Cullen, and Warren
Cochrane during meeting of Harlem Cultural
Congress. After Newtons' landlord evicts them,
Wright moves to Douglass Hotel at 809 St. Nicholas
Avenue in May, renting room next to Theodore Ward,
a friend from Chicago. Becomes close to Ellen Poplar
and considers marrying her, but also sees Dhima Rose
Meadman, a modern-dance teacher of Russian Jewish
ancestry. Plays active role at Third American Writers'
Congress. Finishes *Native Son* on June 10. Ward
dramatizes "Bright and Morning Star." The story is
included in Edward O'Brien's *Best American Short
Stories, 1939* and *Fifty Best American Short Stories
(1914–1939)*. Begins work on new novel, *Little
Sister*. Marries Dhima Rose Meadman in August in
Episcopal church on Convent Avenue, with Ralph
Ellison serving as best man. Lives with his wife, her
two-year-old son by an earlier marriage, and his
mother-in-law in large apartment on fashionable
Hamilton Terrace in Harlem. Attends Festival of
Negro Culture held in Chicago in September. Moves
to Crompond, New York, to work on *Little Sister*
(it is never completed).

1940

Visits Chicago in February and buys house for his
family on Vincennes Avenue. Has lunch in Chicago
with W. E. B. Du Bois, Langston Hughes, and Arna
Bontemps. *Native Son* published by Harper and
Brothers March 1 and is offered by the Book-of-the-
Month Club as one of its two main selections. In
three weeks it sells 215,000 copies. Wright delivers

talk "How 'Bigger' Was Born" at Columbia University on March 12 (later published as a pamphlet by Harper, then added to future printings of *Native Son*). *Native Son* is banned in Birmingham, Alabama, libraries. Takes his first airplane flight when he accompanies *Life* magazine photographers to Chicago for an article on the South Side; tours the area with sociologist Horace Cayton, beginning long friendship (article is later canceled). Sails in April for Veracruz, Mexico, with wife, her son, mother-in-law, and wife's pianist. Rents ten-room villa in the Miraval Colony in Cuernevaca. Takes lessons in Spanish and studies the guitar. Reunited with Herbert Kline, friend from the Chicago John Reed Club, who is filming documentary *The Forgotten Village* with John Steinbeck; Wright travels with them through the countryside and takes an interest in the filming. Signs contract with John Houseman and Orson Welles for stage production of *Native Son*. Marriage becomes strained. Wright leaves Mexico in June and travels through the South alone. Visits his father, a poor and broken farm laborer, in Natchez, but is unable to make anything other than a token reconciliation with him. Goes to Chapel Hill, North Carolina, to begin collaboration with Paul Green on stage adaptation of *Native Son*. Meets producer John Houseman and drives to New York with him. Travels to Chicago to do research for book on black American life featuring photographs selected by Edwin Rosskam. Wright and Langston Hughes are guests of honor at reception given by Jack Conroy and Nelson Algren to launch magazine *New Anvil*. Returns to Chapel Hill in July to continue work with Paul Green. Elected vice-president of the League of American Writers. Harper reissues story collection as *Uncle Tom's Children: Five Long Stories* with "Bright and Morning Star" added and "The Ethics of Living Jim Crow" as an introduction. Starts divorce proceedings. Moves in with the Newtons, now at 343 Grand Avenue in Brooklyn; in the autumn Ellen Poplar moves into the Newton house. In September Wright is elected a vice-president of American Peace Mobilization, a Communist-sponsored group opposed to American involvement in World War II. Works with Houseman on revising stage version of *Native Son* (both Wright and Houseman think that Green has diverged too much from the novel); Houseman agrees that Orson Welles, who is finishing *Citizen Kane*, should direct. Story ▶

A Chronology of Richard Wright *(continued)*

"Almos' a Man" appears in *O. Henry Award Prize Stories of 1940.*

1941

In January the National Association for the Advancement of Colored People awards Wright the Spingarn Medal, given annually to the black American judged to have made the most notable achievement in the preceding year. Rehearsals for *Native Son* begin in February. Marries Ellen Poplar in Coytesville, New Jersey, on March 12. They move to 473 West 140th Street. *Native Son*, starring Canada Lee, opens at St. James Theatre on March 24 after a benefit performance for the NAACP. Reviews are generally favorable, though the play is attacked in the Hearst papers, which are hostile to Welles following *Citizen Kane.* Production runs in New York until June 15. Welles's striking but costly staging causes production to lose some money, but it recovers during successful tour of Pittsburgh, Boston, Chicago, Milwaukee, Detroit, St. Louis, and Baltimore. Wright asks the governor of New Jersey to parole Clinton Brewer, a black man imprisoned since 1923 for murdering a young woman, arguing that Brewer, who had taught himself music composition, has rehabilitated himself (Brewer is released July 8; Wright had previously sent one of his pieces to his friend, record producer and talent scout John Hammond, who arranged for Count Basie to record it). Begins novel *Black Hope* (never completed). Introduces Ellen to his family in Chicago during visit in April. Signs appeal of forty members of the League of American Writers against American intervention in the war that appears in *New Masses* May 27, and publishes "Not My People's War" in *New Masses* June 17. After Germany invades the Soviet Union, June 22, American Peace Mobilization changes its name to American People's Mobilization. Wright travels to Houston with Horace Cayton and John Hammond to accept Spingarn award from NAACP convention on June 27. Delivers enthusiastically received speech, in which his criticism of Roosevelt administration racial policies is muted in response to Communist party pressure. Lectures at Writers' Schools sponsored by the League of American Writers. Wrights move to 11 Revere Place, Brooklyn, in July. At John Hammond's request, Wright writes "Note on Jim Crow Blues" as a preface to the blues singer Josh

White's *Southern Exposure*, an album of three recordings attacking segregation. Hammond then produces recording of Paul Robeson singing Wright's blues song "King Joe," accompanied by the Count Basie orchestra. *12 Million Black Voices: A Folk History of the Negro in the United States*, with photographs selected by Edwin Rosskam (one taken by Wright), published by Viking Press in October to enthusiastic reviews. Wright reads *Dark Legend*, a psychoanalytic study of matricide by psychiatrist Fredric Wertham, then writes to Wertham about Clinton Brewer, who had murdered another young woman within months of his release. Wertham intervenes in the case and helps save Brewer from execution. (Wright and Wertham begin close friendship, and Wright becomes increasingly interested in psychoanalysis). Finishes draft of novel *The Man Who Lived Underground*. Signs petition "Communication to All American Writers" in December 16 *New Masses*, supporting America's entry into the war after the December 7 Japanese attack on Pearl Harbor.

1942
Mother and Aunt Maggie rejoin Addie in Jackson, Mississippi (brother remains in Chicago, though house on Vincennes Avenue is sold two years later). Daughter Julia, Wright's first child, born April 15. Wrights move in summer to 7 Middagh Street, a 19th-century house near the Brooklyn Bridge shared by George Davis, Carson McCullers, and other writers and artists. Excerpts from *The Man Who Lived Underground* appear in *Accent*. As the sole support of his family, Wright is classified 3-A and not drafted. Unsuccessfully tries to secure a special commission in the psychological warfare or propaganda services of the army. *Native Son* returns to Broadway in October (runs until January 1943). Publishes "What You Don't Know Won't Hurt You," article describing some of his experiences as a hospital janitor in Chicago, in December *Harper's Magazine*. Breaks quietly with the Communist party over its unwillingness to confront wartime racial discrimination and its continuing attempts to control his writing.

1943
Accompanied by Horace Cayton, Wright goes to Fisk University, Nashville, in April to deliver talk on his experiences with racism. Strong reaction from the audience leads Wright to begin autobiography ▶

A Chronology of Richard Wright *(continued)*

American Hunger. Neighbors and associates are interviewed by the Federal Bureau of Investigation. (Files obtained under the Freedom of Information Act in the 1970s show that the FBI began an investigation in December 1942 to determine if *12 Million Black Voices* was prosecutable under the sedition statutes. Although the sedition investigation is concluded in 1943, the FBI will continue to monitor Wright's activities, chiefly through the use of informers, for the remainder of his life.) Wrights move in August to 89 Lefferts Place in Brooklyn Heights. Helps organize the Citizens' Emergency Conference for Interracial Unity in response to widespread riots in Harlem following the wounding of a black soldier by white police in August. Finishes *American Hunger* in December.

1944

Writes film scenario "Melody Limited," about group of black singers during Reconstruction (scenario is never produced). Becomes friends with C. L. R. James, a Trinidad-born historian and Trotskyist, with whom he plans a book, *The Negro Speaks,* and a journal, *American Pages* (neither of these projects appear), and James's wife, Constance Webb. Writes series of radio programs on the life of a black family for producer Leston Huntley and is frustrated when Huntley is unable to place the series, in part because of criticism by middle-class blacks. Attends party held in honor of Theodore Dreiser on June 2, where Wright and Dreiser discuss the influence of life in Chicago on their attitudes. Deepens friendship with Dorothy Norman, New York *Post* editorial writer and editor of *Twice a Year,* who introduces him to existentialist philosophy and literature. Book-of-the-Month Club tells Harper that it will accept only the first section of *American Hunger,* describing Wright's experiences in the South; Wright agrees to this arrangement. Changes title to *Black Boy.* (Second section, telling of Wright's life in Chicago, is published as *American Hunger* by Harper & Row in 1977.) Wrights vacation in August outside Ottawa and in the nearby Gatineau country in Quebec. Excerpts from second section of autobiography appear as "I Tried to Be a Communist" in *Atlantic Monthly,* August–September, making public Wright's break with the Communist party. He is denounced by various party organs, including *New Masses* and the

Daily Worker. Helps the Chicago poet Gwendolyn Brooks to place her first book, *A Street in Bronzeville.* Expanded version of *The Man Who Lived Underground* is published as a novella in *Cross Section.*

1945

To circumvent racial discrimination, Wrights form the "Richelieu Realty Co." and use their lawyer as an intermediary in buying a house at 13 Charles Street in Greenwich Village. (Residence is delayed by their waiting for a Communist tenant hostile to Wright to leave and by redecorating.) Reviews books for *P.M.* newspaper; his highly favorable review of Gertrude Stein's *Wars I Have Seen* leads to correspondence with her. *Black Boy: A Record of Childhood and Youth* published by Harper and Brothers in March to enthusiastic reviews. The book is number one on the bestseller list from April 29 to June 6 and stirs controversy when it is denounced as obscene in the U.S. Senate by Democrat Theodore Bilbo of Mississippi. Takes part in several radio programs, including the nationally influential *Town Meeting,* where he argues the negative on the question "Are We Solving America's Race Problem?" In the summer, Wrights vacation on island off Quebec City, and Wright lectures at the Bread Loaf writers' school in Middlebury, Vermont. Writes long introduction to *Black Metropolis,* a sociological study of black Chicago by Horace Cayton and St. Clair Drake. Befriending a number of younger writers, white and black, Wright helps the 20-year-old James Baldwin win a Eugene F. Saxton Foundation Fellowship. Publishes a favorable review of Chester Himes's first novel, *If He Hollers Let Him Go,* and lends Himes $1,000. In the fall, Wrights move to an apartment at 82 Washington Place in Greenwich Village to be closer to a school for Julia. Wright undertakes four-month lecture tour but stops after six weeks because of exhaustion.

1946

Serves as honorary pallbearer at funeral on January 12 of poet Countee Cullen, attending service at Salem Methodist Church in Harlem and burial at Woodlawn Cemetery in the Bronx. By January 19, *Black Boy* has sold 195,000 copies in the Harper trade edition and 351,000 through the Book-of-the-Month Club, making it the fourth best-selling nonfiction ▶

title of 1945. Wright, his psychiatrist friend Dr. Fredric Wertham, and others found the Lafargue Clinic, a free psychiatric clinic in Harlem. Meets Jean-Paul Sartre in New York. Receives invitation to visit France, but requests for a passport meet with opposition. Wright goes to Washington for an interview and enlists the aid of Dorothy Norman (who appoints him coeditor of *Twice a Year*), Gertrude Stein, and French cultural attaché, anthropologist Claude Lévi-Strauss, who sends him an official invitation from the French government to visit Paris for a month. Wright leaves New York on May 1. In Paris, welcomed by Gertrude Stein and by almost all the important French literary societies and circles. (Stein dies on July 27 after operation for cancer.) Meets Simone de Beauvoir and André Gide, whose *Travels in the Congo* has impressed Wright, as well as Léopold Sédar Senghor of Senegal, Aimé Césaire of Martinique, and others in the *Négritude* movement. Assists Senghor, Césaire, and Alioune Diop of Senegal in founding the magazine *Présence Africaine* and attends its first board meeting at the Brasserie Lipp. Donates a manuscript to an auction for benefit of experimental dramatist Antonin Artaud. "The Man Who Killed a Shadow" published in French in *Les Lettres Françaises* (first appears in English in 1949 in magazine *Zero*). Leaves Paris in late December and travels to London.

1947

Meets the Trinidad-born intellectual George Padmore and dines with members of the Coloured Writers' Association, including its president, Cedric Dover, author of *Half Caste*, and the colored South African journalist and novelist Peter Abrahams. Returns to New York in January. Moves with family into their Charles Street house in Greenwich Village. Helps to welcome Simone de Beauvoir to New York in the spring. Refuses offer from Hollywood producer to film *Native Son* with character Bigger Thomas changed to a white man. Wright's works are being translated into French, Italian, German, Dutch, and Czech. Decides to return to Europe permanently with his family, partially in response to the racial hostility they are encountering in New York. Sells Greenwich Village house in June. Vacations at a cottage at Wading River, Long Island, owned by a friend. Buys an Oldsmobile sedan to take to Europe. Wright, his wife, and daughter reach Paris in August. They rent rooms from a friend, Odette Lieutier, in her apartment on the rue de Lille, then move into an apartment at 166 avenue de Neuilly. Albin Michel publishes French translation of *Native Son* in autumn.

1948

Begins to read more deeply in existentialism, including Heidegger and Husserl. Sees much of Sartre and Simone de Beauvoir. Wright is particularly impressed by Camus's *The Stranger*, and begins work on an existentialist novel, eventually titled *The Outsider*. Gallimard translation of *Black Boy* wins French Critics' Award. Wright establishes friendships with the Reverend Clayton Williams, pastor of the American Church, and with Harry Goldberg of the American Library. Becomes unofficial spokesman for African-American colony in Paris, which includes James Baldwin. Visits Italy for the publication there of *Native Son*. Meets with Carlo Levi and Ignazio Silone, who later introduces him to Arthur Koestler in Paris. Interviewed by his Italian translator, Fernanda Pivano, Wright says he likes to read *Metamorphosis*, *Moby-Dick*, *Ulysses*, and *The Sound and the Fury*. Travels through Belgium to London, where he sees a performance of *Native Son* and renews friendship with George Padmore, who stirs Wright's interest in the question of colonialism in Africa. Moves with family to 14 rue Monsieur le Prince in the Latin Quarter in May. Ellen returns to New York in June to select furniture and other possessions for their new life in France. Wright is beset by recurring sinus problems and influenza. His tonsils are removed. Aids Sartre and Camus in the leadership of the Rassemblement Démocratique Révolutionnaire (RDR), an organization of intellectuals critical of both the Soviet Union and the United States. Wright plays prominent role in its writers' congress, held in Paris on December 13, delivering lengthy speech (translated by Simone de Beauvoir). Spends $6,000 to buy Paul Green's share of film rights to *Native Son* in hopes of making screen version with French director Pierre Chenal.

1949

Daughter Rachel born January 17 at the American Hospital. Wright travels again to Rome and to Switzerland, for the publication of *Black Boy*. In ▶

A Chronology of Richard Wright *(continued)*

April, James T. Farrell and Nelson Algren visit him in Paris. Suspects socialist David Rousset of trying to shift the RDR toward a more pro-American, anti-Soviet stance. Refuses to attend large RDR rally held on April 30 (organization soon splits and dissolves). In May, visits London to consult with Richard Crossman, who is including "I Tried to Be a Communist" with similar essays by Koestler, Gide, Silone, Stephen Spender, and Louis Fischer in collection *The God That Failed* (published later in year, book is widely reviewed). Continues work on his existentialist novel. Assists George Plimpton and others in launching *Paris Review*. James Baldwin's essay "Everybody's Protest Novel," attacking Stowe's *Uncle Tom's Cabin* but including criticism of *Native Son*, sours relationship between Wright and Baldwin. Wright writes screenplay for *Native Son*, adding several dream sequences to the story, then revises it with Chenal. After Canada Lee withdraws from project because of new commitments and worsening health, Wright undertakes to play the main role of Bigger Thomas. Sails for the United States in August, briefly visiting New York before going to Chicago for filming of exteriors for *Native Son*. Sees old friends Horace Cayton, St. Clair Drake, and others. Leaves New York in September for Argentina, where film is being made (Chenal had worked there during World War II, and political pressure had blocked access to French studios). Makes brief stops in Trinidad, Brazil, and Uruguay before arriving in Buenos Aires in October. Loses 35 pounds in preparation for the role by following strict diet and exercise program. Continues working on screenplay with Chenal.

1950

Production is delayed by financial problems. Wright finds atmosphere of Argentine life under the Perón dictatorship oppressive. Filming ends in June. Wright leaves Buenos Aires in July. Stops briefly in Brazil and Trinidad, spends two weeks in Haiti, then returns to Paris by way of New York, where he visits Fredric Wertham and the Lafargue Clinic. In Paris, begins work on screenplay about Toussaint L'Ouverture of Haiti. Works with Aime Césaire on "Revelation of Negro Art," an exhibition that includes works from the Musée de l'Homme and song and dance performances at the Cité Universitaire. Vacations in the fall in the Swiss and French Alps, visiting Basel,

Zurich, and the Aoste Valley, where he is a jury member with Paul Eluard, Louis Bromfield, and others for international San Vicente literary prize. Founds and becomes president of the Franco-American Fellowship, intended to protest official American policies and oppose racial discrimination by American companies and organizations active in France. Fellowship members take precautions when meeting in anticipation of surveillance by the American government (files released in the 1970s show that the Fellowship was monitored by informers employed by the Central Intelligence Agency and the FBI).

1951

Lectures in Turin, Genoa, and Rome in January. *Sangre Negra* (the film version of *Native Son*) opens to acclaim in Buenos Aires on March 30. American distributor cuts almost 30 minutes from film under pressure from New York state censors (original length was approximately 105 minutes); shortened version opens in New York on June 16 to unfavorable reviews. (Several states ban the film, but it is shown in Beverly Hills and, in spring 1952, in Mississippi, where members of Wright's family see it.) A partially restored print is warmly received at the Venice Film Festival in August. The Milan press praises Wright's acting; in general, his performance is deemed sincere but awkward, especially by American critics who compare it with Canada Lee's stage version. Wright visits the sociologist Gunnar Myrdal in Geneva, beginning a long friendship. With Jean Cocteau, inaugurates the Cercle International du Théâtre et du Cinéma. *New Story Magazine* accepts excerpts from Jean Genet's *Our Lady of the Flowers* on Wright's recommendation. Baldwin's essay "Many Thousands Gone," an explicit attack on Wright in *Partisan Review* (November–December), leads to painful break between the writers. Submits screenplay about refugees forced to choose between sides in the Cold War to the French Association of Film Writers.

1952

Travels to England in February. Spends several months in London and Catford, Surrey, completing the first full version of *The Outsider*. Vacations with his family in Corrèze at the end of August and continues to revise and cut novel. Refuses suggestion by John Fischer, his new Harper editor, ▶

A Chronology of Richard Wright *(continued)*

that he come to the United States for the publication of his book, citing the risk that he would be subpoenaed by an anti-Communist congressional investigating committee. Begins work in December on a novel about a white psychopathic murderer, based in part on his experience with Clinton Brewer.

1953

Begins correspondence with Frantz Fanon. *The Outsider* published by Harper and Brothers in March. Reviews are mixed; sales are initially brisk but eventually disappointing in comparison to *Native Son* and *Black Boy*. Wright composes an introduction to *In the Castle of My Skin*, first novel by the young Barbados writer George Lamming. Friendship with Sartre cools as Sartre moves closer to Communism. Wright's circle of friends remains wide, including Americans such as Chester Himes and William Gardner Smith, but he begins to withdraw from official organizations and to avoid formal gatherings. He is a regular at favorite cafés such as the Monaco and Tournon, where he entertains a steady stream of visitors from America, including Elmer Carter, Dorothy Norman, Nelson Algren, E. Franklin Frazier, and Louis Wirth. Discusses treatment of Algerians in France with Ben Burns, editor of *Ebony* magazine, during his visit. Wright tells Burns that he avoids criticizing French policies for fear of being deported. Ellen Wright begins work as a literary agent with Hélène Bokanowski, a prolific translator of Wright's work. From June to August, Wright travels in the Gold Coast (then a British colony with limited self-government, after 1957 the independent country of Ghana) to collect material for a book on Africa. Boat stops briefly in Freetown, Sierra Leone, en route to Takoradi; from there travels by road 170 miles to Accra, his main stop. Meets Prime Minister Kwame Nkrumah and other members of the pro-independence Convention People's Party, as well as Osei Agyeman Prempeh II, king of the Ashanti, and other traditional leaders. Excursions take him from Accra to Cape Coast, Christianborg, and Prampram; visits slave-trading fortresses and dungeons. Travels almost 3,000 miles in a chauffeur-driven car, touring the interior through Koforidua to Mampong, and the Secondi-Takoradi to Kumasi regions. In general, Wright is fascinated by Africans but is reinforced in his sense of self as a Western intellectual. Visits England to discuss his impressions with George and Dorothy Padmore before returning to Paris in September to begin work on book about his trip. Undergoes surgery for hernia.

1954

Revises book on Africa. Decides to write an account of Spanish life and culture. Drives his Citroen almost 4,000 miles between August 15 and September 9 on a route that includes Barcelona, Valencia, Saragossa, Guadalajara, Madrid, Córdoba, Seville, Granada, and Málaga. On September 16 State Department and FBI officials interview Wright in Paris about his relationship to the Communist party when he goes to renew his passport. *Black Power: A Record of Reactions in a Land of Pathos,* about his African trip, published by Harper and Brothers September 22. Receives mixed reviews in America, but is widely praised in France. *Savage Holiday*, novel about psychopathic murderer, is published as a paperback original by Avon after having been rejected by Harper. Book attracts little attention in the United States but is well received as *Le Dieu de Mascarade* in France. Visits Geneva with Gunnar Myrdal for further research on Spain at the United Nations library. Lectures on Africa in Amsterdam in October, where he meets Margrit de Sablonière, his Dutch translator, and begins an important friendship with her. Returns to Spain on November 8. Hires a driver and travels through Irun and on to Madrid, where he stays before returning to Paris in mid-December.

1955

An old Chicago friend, the cartoonist Ollie "Bootsie" Harrington, arrives to live in France. Wright secures funding for his attendance at forthcoming conference of non-aligned nations in Bandung, Indonesia, from the Paris office of the Congress for Cultural Freedom, an international alliance of anti-Communist intellectuals. Returns to Spain February 20, and spends several weeks there, including Holy Week in Granada and Seville. Leaves Spain on April 10 for Indonesia. At Bandung, Wright shares room with missionary Winburn T. Thomas. Leaders attending conference include Nehru (with whom Wright speaks), Sukarno, Sihanouk, Nasser, and Zhou Enlai. Remains in Indonesia at home of Thomas until May 5, working on notes of his impressions, then ▶

A Chronology of Richard Wright *(continued)*

returns to Europe via Ceylon and Kenya. Begins writing an account of the conference. Spends July to October with family at their new country home, a small farm in village of Ailly in eastern Normandy. Plans series of novels dealing with the conflicts between individuals and society (including one set in Aztec Mexico), but abandons the project on the advice of Reynolds and Aswell (now with McGraw-Hill). Returns to Paris when daughter Rachel falls ill with scarlet fever, then goes back to Ailly when her continued quarantine makes work at home difficult. *Bandoeng: 1.500.000.000 hommes.* French translation of book on nonaligned conference, published in December.

1956

Prepares manuscript of book on Spain in February and March, often living alone at Ailly, where he enjoys hours of gardening. Fearing deportation, remains silent on Algerian war of independence while in France (will offer guarded criticism of war when in other European countries). *The Color Curtain: A Report on the Bandung Conference*, with an introduction by Gunnar Myrdal, published March 19 by World Publishers in America and receives favorable reviews. Revises and cuts book on Spain. Adapts Louis Sapin's play *Papa Bon Dieu* as *Daddy Goodness* but is unable to have it produced. First Congress of Negro Artists and Writers, sponsored by *Présence Africaine* and which Wright had helped plan, meets in Paris in September, attended by delegates from Africa, the United States, and the Caribbean. Wright speaks on "Tradition and Industrialization: The Tragic Plight of the African Elites" and participates in several sessions. Suspects that *Présence Africaine* is being secretly taken over by the French government through anti-nationalist Africans and considers withdrawing from its activities. Lectures in Hamburg on "The Psychological Reactions of Oppressed Peoples" and tours the city with Ellen. Attends a meeting in London of the Congress for Cultural Freedom, organized by Arthur Koestler. Travels alone to Stockholm in late November for the Swedish publication of *The Outsider*; it sells 35,000 copies in four days (*Native Son* had sold 75,000 copies and *Black Boy* 65,000). Lectures in Sweden, Norway, and Denmark before returning to Paris in early December. Agrees to help found the American Society for African Culture, inspired by the French Société Africaine de Culture. Returning to native material, Wright begins work on novel set in Mississippi.

1957

Aunt Maggie dies January 20 in Jackson, Mississippi, where she had been taking care of Wright's mother (Wright has continued to help support them through the years). Mother moves in with a niece, then goes to Chicago at the end of June to live with Leon Alan. *Pagan Spain* published by Harper in February to good reviews but weak sales. Works at Ailly on new novel. Travels throughout Italy with Ellen during the spring. Visits West Germany in July to interview black American servicemen stationed there. *White Man, Listen!*, a collection of essays drawn from Wright's lectures, published October 15 by Doubleday (where Edward Aswell is now an editor). The book is especially well-received by the black press in the United States.

1958

Finishes *The Long Dream*, Mississippi novel, and begins *Island of Hallucinations,* sequel set in France. Seeking to renew his passport, he is again compelled to report to the American embassy in February and sign a statement admitting his past membership in the Communist party. Becomes increasingly alienated from the black community in Paris, which is torn by suspicion and dissension; finds himself the object of resentment, including rumors that he is an agent of the FBI or the CIA. Depressed and isolated from other blacks, Wright suspects that he is being persecuted by agents of the U.S. government. Takes part in a session of the Congress for Cultural Freedom, and in seminars on American literature sponsored by the American Cultural Center in Paris. Supports Sartre and Simone de Beauvoir in their opposition to the new regime of General de Gaulle. Works on new novel at Ailly during summer. *The Long Dream* published by Doubleday in October to often hostile reviews and flat sales. When Leon Alan telegraphs that their mother is seriously ill, Wright is forced to borrow extra money from Reynolds to send to his brother. Edward Aswell, his long-time editor, dies November 5. Considers moving to England and enlists aid of Labour member of Parliament John Strachey, who obtains assurances from the Home Secretary that Wright's application for residence will be fairly considered. Wright ▶

distances himself from various organizations he had
previously supported, including *Présence Africaine*
and the Société Africaine de Culture.

1959

Mother dies January 14. Wright sends the manuscript
of *Island of Hallucinations* to Reynolds in February.
Later in the month, he spends a day with Martin
Luther King, Jr., who is passing through Paris en
route to India. Timothy Seldes (Aswell's successor
at Doubleday) asks for major revisions in *Island of
Hallucinations*; Wright puts book aside (it is never
completed). Discouraged by financial worries, weak
reviews, poor health, and frustrating state of his
novel, Wright continues to curtail his public activities.
Declines to attend the second Congress of Black
Writers and Artists in Rome. Plans a study of French
Africa. After Doubleday promises a $2,500 advance,
Wright asks the American Society for African Culture
for an additional $7,500, but is turned down; believes
CIA infiltration of the organization is responsible
for his rejection. Tired of what he considers to be
growing American political and cultural influence
in French life and in the wake of increased attacks
by other expatriate black writers, Wright prepares to
leave France and live in England. Sells farm at Ailly.
His play *Daddy Goodness* is produced in Paris in the
spring. Wright falls ill in June with attack of amoebic
dysentery, probably picked up in Africa. Illness
persists despite treatment at American Hospital.
Vacations at the Moulin d'Andé near Saint-Pierre
du Vauvray in Normandy. With daughter Julia now
at the University of Cambridge, his wife Ellen and
daughter Rachel establish themselves in London.
Ellen works there as a literary agent and looks for
a permanent home for the family. Wright begins
writing haiku (eventually completes some 4,000
pieces). Harassed by British passport officials during
visit to England in September. Sees George Padmore,
who dies not long after Wright's visit. Wright returns
to England for the funeral. Tries to obtain resident
visa from the Home Office, but is denied one without
explanation. Alone in Paris, he sells home on rue
Monsieur le Prince and moves to a two-room
apartment on rue Régis. Recovers from dysentery
but continues to have intestinal problems. Among
his close friends at this time are Michel and Hélène
Bokanowski, Colette and Rémi Dreyfus, Simone de

Beauvoir, Ollie Harrington, and the Reverend Clayton Williams. "Big Black Good Man" is included in *Best American Stories of 1958*.

1960

The Long Dream, adapted by Ketti Frings, opens on Broadway February 17 to poor reviews and closes within a week. Translation of *The Long Dream* well-received in France, but earnings are not enough to quell Wright's deepening anxiety about money. In April, driving his own Peugeot, Wright accompanies his gastroenterologist, Victor Schwartzmann, and Dr. Schwartzmann's father to medical conference in Leiden, Holland, where he visits Margrit de Sablonière. Selects and arranges 811 haiku for possible publication. Declines offers from Congress for Cultural Freedom to attend conferences on Tolstoy in Venice and New Delhi, believing that the organization is controlled by the American government (the Congress is later shown to have received substantial covert funding from the CIA). Records series of interviews concerning his work in June for French radio. Spends much of summer at Moulin d'Andé, where he begins new novel, *A Father's Law*. Falls ill on return to Paris in September. Julia Wright decides to study at the Sorbonne and visits her father before returning to England to pack her belongings. In September, Dorothy Padmore comes to visit. Later, old Chicago friend Arna Bontemps makes his first visit to Paris. Wright delivers lecture on November 8 at the American Church on the situation of black artists and intellectuals. Accuses the American government of creating and manipulating dissension among them through spies and provocateurs. Continues to suffer from intestinal difficulties and dizzy spells. Finishes complete proofreading of collection of stories, *Eight Men* (published by World Publishers in 1961). Welcomes Langston Hughes to his home for a brief but enjoyable visit on the morning of November 26, then enters the Eugene Gibez Clinic for diagnostic examinations and convalescence. Dies there of a heart attack shortly before 11:00 P.M., November 28. Cremated, along with a copy of *Black Boy*, at the Père Lachaise cemetery December 3, where his ashes are interred. ∿

About the book

> He saw the dim image of the traffic cop make a right-face turn and fling out a white-gloved arm, signaling that the flow of cars from the east should stop and that those toward the south now had the right of way, and, at the same instant he heard the cop's shrill whistle:
>
> Wrrrriiiiiicee ...
>
> Yes, that was a good rooky. He had made change-over in traffic smartly, the exact manner in which the Metropolitan Handbook for Traffic Policemen had directed. The footwork had been perfect and that impersonal look on his face certainly inspired confidence and respect. That's the way a policeman should work. Well done, Officer, he mumbled in his sleep as the officer now did a left-face turn, again flinging out his flashing white-gloved hand and sounding his whistle:
>
> Whreeeeeiiiiiee ...
>
> "Ruddy!"
>
> "Hunh!"
>
> "Ruddy! Wake up!"
>
> Wrrrriiiiiiieeeeee ...
>
> "Hunh? Hunh?"
>
> "Ruddy, it's the telephone, darling!"
>
> Wreeeiiiieeeeee ...
>
> "Oh!"
>
> "It's the telephone, Ruddy!"
>
> "I'll get it, I'll get it," he mumbled, blinking his sleep-drugged eyes in the dark and fumbling with the bedcovers. He sat half up and sleep rushed over him in a wave, seeking to reclaim him.

A typescript draft of A Father's Law

[At right:]
Manuscript notes made by Julia Wright, daughter of Richard Wright, shortly after the author's death. Ms. Wright (b. 1942) edited her father's manuscript and saw it through to publication.

guilt

Father cop	punishing racism
~~Antit~~ Son / rebellion against father's law	a racist.

the new generation knows something
which makes the father's law
meaningless.
the cop, the father, the negro.

father
- guilt about being a cop + how on
earth could anybody ask him
to help men and protect that would p 28

- guilt because he misunderstands his
son. and yet he is a father.

- guilt towards his race.

(- write. I am a writer but
cannot write)

beneath his look as a cop
a father
a negro
(and a writer).

Naturally, the boy would have
a life of his own, be preoccupied
with ideas of another world and
another generation - p 11.

But what if Tommy's kind of
problem could not be resolved like
he had resolved his own
p 28.

Then there had been times when he
had been a boy when he had
hated the authority of that world,
had thought several times of
violating its laws -

[Notes by
Julia Wright]
n.d.

Have You Read?
More from Richard Wright

Other classic works by Richard Wright available from Harper Perennial:

BLACK BOY

Black Boy is a classic of American autobiography, a subtly crafted narrative of Richard Wright's journey from innocence to experience in the Jim Crow South that remains a seminal work in our history about what it means to be a man, black, and Southern in America.

"Richard Wright uses vigorous and straightforward English; often there is real beauty in his words even when they are mingled with sadism."
—W. E. B. DuBois, *New York Herald Tribune*

"A major event in American literary history."
—*The New Republic*

NATIVE SON

Right from the start, Bigger Thomas had been headed for jail. It could have been for assault or petty larceny; by chance, it was for murder and rape. *Native Son* tells the story of this young black man caught in a downward spiral after he kills a young white woman in a brief moment of panic. Set in Chicago in the 1930s, Wright's powerful novel is an unsparing reflection on the poverty and feelings of hopelessness experienced by people in inner cities across the country and of what it means to be black in America.

"Certainly, *Native Son* declares Richard Wright's importance . . . as an American author as distinctive as any of those now writing."
—*New York Times Book Review*

THE OUTSIDER

The Outsider, a complex tale of crime and politics, shows the influence of French existentialist philosophical theory as filtered through Wright's unmistakable prose.

"It is in the description of action, especially violent action, that Mr. Wright excels, not merely because he can make the reader see but because he compels him to participate. There is not a murder in the book that the reader, at the moment of reading about it, does not feel that he would have committed under the same circumstances."

—Granville Hicks, *New York Times*

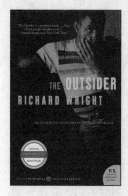

UNCLE TOM'S CHILDREN

Set in the deep South, each of the powerful novellas collected in Wright's first book shines an unflinching light on the lives of black people in the postslavery era, exploring their resistance to white racism and oppression.

"I found these stories both heartening, as evidence of a vigorous new talent, and terrifying as the expression of a racial hatred that has never ceased to grow and gets no chance to die."

—Malcolm Cowley, *The New Republic*

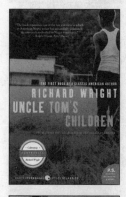

EIGHT MEN

Each of the eight stories in *Eight Men* focuses on a black man at violent odds with a white world, reflecting Wright's views about racism in our society and his fascination with what he called "the struggle of the individual in America." These poignant, gripping stories will captivate all those who love Wright's better known novels.

"There is not a touch of phoniness or fakery in the book. All eight men and all eight stories stand as beautifully, pitifully, terribly true. . . . All the way through this is fine, sound, good, honorable writing, rich with insight and understanding, even when occasionally twisted by sorrow."

—*New York Times Book Review*

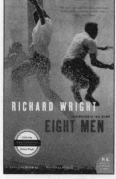

PAGAN SPAIN

Richard Wright chronicles his trip to Spain in 1954, capturing the beauty and tragedy of the country under the rigid rule of Francisco Franco.

"*Pagan Spain* is a book which required courage to write—and even greater courage to publish. For it is a volume which seems certain to call down upon another author and publisher a tempest of bitter, resentful, and frightened criticism."
—Joseph G. Harrison, *Christian Science Monitor*

BLACK POWER: THREE BOOKS FROM EXILE: BLACK POWER; THE COLOR CURTAIN; AND WHITE MAN, LISTEN!

Three late books by Richard Wright—*The Color Curtain; Black Power; White Man, Listen!*—are here gathered in one volume for the first time, with a new introduction by Cornel West. The title book is one of Wright's most persuasive works of nonfiction. First published in 1954, it is his impassioned chronicle of the conditions he found on his trip to Africa's Gold Coast, then in the process of becoming the free nation of Ghana.

"The reader of *Black Power* will be grateful . . . for many fascinating and even illuminating glimpses of primitive tribal life in a country marked out for precocious political development." —*New York Times*

Don't miss the next book by your favorite author. Sign up now for AuthorTracker by visiting www.AuthorTracker.com.